Chris Twigger was born in 1966 in Coventry and is still waiting for the England football team to revisit the heady heights of that illustrious year. Since graduating in English & European Literature from the University of Essex he has spent all his working life in public relations and advertising.

His formative years were very much the 80's and he cites The Cult and The The (along with a guilty pleasure of Kajagoogoo) amongst his musical influences. He now lives in Market Bosworth with his wife Jacqui, spending much of his leisure time drumming in covers bands.

'Good Morning Chamonix' is the sequel to his debut novel 'Thank you Leamington & Goodnight'.

*Also by Chris Twigger*
THANK YOU LEAMINGTON & GOODNIGHT

# Good Morning Chamonix

# Chris Twigger

Peter,
Happy Christmas!
Hope you enjoy the sequel.
All the best
Chris

First published in Great Britain in 2021

Copyright © Chris Twigger, 2021

The moral right of the author has been asserted.

*All characters and events in this publication, other than those clearly in the public domain, are fictitious and any resemblance to real persons, living or dead, is purely coincidental.*

All rights reserved.

No part of this publication may be reproduced, stored in a retrieval system, or transmitted, in any form or by any means, without the prior permission in writing of the author, nor be otherwise circulated in any form of binding or cover other than that in which it is published and without a similar condition including this condition being imposed on the subsequent purchaser.

ISBN 979-8-767-85916-0

For Jessie & Erin x

## Chapter 1

Pudding rolled over and felt a warm bare arse next to his. He had been dozing for about 10 minutes but this was the first time he'd shifted position. The sudden realisation that he was not alone produced a surge of adrenalin that almost had him sit bolt upright. However, he realised that even in this sorry state, he needed to act carefully. He tried to get his brain into gear, focusing on the cornice. Cornice? What cornice? Oh shit!

He started peeling away the layers of the onion that was last night, with the outer skin being his first recollection of being at Marcie's 50$^{th}$ birthday party. Next was the euphoria he had felt at the end of the night, thrashing at his guitar strings like a man possessed as Old School finished their encore.

A slight snuffling noise from his bed companion and Pudding stiffened, trying valiantly to fast forward to the end of the evening. But the fog wasn't clearing, certainly not fast enough to tell him just who was now starting to stir next to him. He risked a quick glance and saw some wisps of long grey locks disappearing below the duvet. As his bedfellow stretched out her own leg, it brushed Pudding's foot and he felt a tickle from the hairs. Oh my god. His regular friend with benefits Claire had been known to go more than a few days without the Immac but this was a whole new ball game. What had he done, or perhaps more aptly, who had he done?

A rip-roaring fart, the blast from which he swore had parted the hair on his own legs and Pudding leapt from the bed, all semblance of a careful extrication jettisoned as he wondered just who or what he had slept with last night. He collided with the wall, sliding down with a thud, as a head poked from beneath the covers.

'What the fuck! Pudding, what the hell are you doing man?'

The gruff voice and the appearance of bedraggled grey hair accompanied by salt and pepper mutton chop whiskers opened the sluice gate and the memories of last night came flooding through, surfing in on a wave of relief.

'Pipes, thank god it's you.'

'Who the hell did you think it was, Debbie bloody Harry?'

Thirty minutes and an argument over the shower later saw Pipes and Pudding seated at the breakfast table. Pipes' threadbare dressing gown hung open to reveal a gut that could really do without refuelling with the full English that lay before them.

'What a night eh?' mumbled Pipes through a mouthful of fried egg and beans.

'You could say that' replied Pudding, prodding a blackened sausage as he contemplated if he could actually face ingesting any of Pipes' culinary offerings.

'I bet Mark got a right old jump last night from Marjorie. She was almost drooling at the front of the stage.'

The mention of Marjorie had Pudding visualising the sea of faces, bouncing in time to the music, as he, Harsy, Pipes and Mark strutted their stuff on stage. It had been a fantastic evening and one that none of them had wanted to end, which perhaps explained why they'd done their damndest to ensure that it didn't.

After leaving the stage and circulating the impressive room at Cranby Hall, lapping up the plaudits for the band's first real performance, they had a celebratory beer, toasting the birthday girl for the umpteenth time before jumping into taxis to travel back to Harsy and Marcie's house to continue the celebrations. Pudding recalled being the wrong side of half a bottle of Jack Daniels before Marjorie had called a couple of cabs in the early hours, one to take her and Mark back to her boudoir to make the most of what was left of the night, while he, Pipes and Pipes' partner Kelly had poured themselves into the other.

Pudding had initially struggled to recall why he had ended up in a double bed with Pipes when he had expected to be sleeping on the settee. Surely it was Kelly that would take that dubious honour? With a concerted effort to focus, a second sluice gate had opened, a little like Pipes' oesophagus as Pudding recalled with a shudder his recent bed partner revisiting several pints, along with numerous vodka and oranges, all over the lap of his girlfriend. The Essex banshee shrieks of Kelly as she jumped up in the back of the cab had been supported by backing vocals from the squeal of the brakes as the cabbie came to a swift halt to see what was going on in the back of his Toyota Prius.

After a few minutes of remonstrating and gesticulating, Pipes pulled three crumpled twenty-pound notes from his pocket. Although the Queen was 'smiling, beguiling', Ivan the driver certainly was not and was only convinced to continue their journey by Pipes delving into his pocket for another twenty. They dropped off a decidedly aggrieved Kelly at her friend Becky's house as she refused to contemplate remaining in her vomiting partner's company any longer than she had to.

Her parting barrage had been 'you'll fackin regret this. That eighty quid you've given to laughing boy 'ere is nuffink compared to what it's gonna cost ya in a new outfit for me, ya drunken animal.'

This prompted the illumination of a couple of bedroom lights as the residents of Chestnut Avenue scrabbled to get to their curtains for a dose of real-life EastEnders. Ivan had then delivered them to the door of Pipes' flat, with little further incident but a decidedly frosty look as he surveyed the back seat of his car before shaking his head and driving off into the Warwickshire night.

Pipes' downcast demeanour at the thought of what lay in store for him when Kelly finally decided to return was short-lived as he cracked open a bottle of champagne left over from his New Year's Eve cache. He and Pudding had then relived the highlights of the night. Pudding's last recollection was listening to London Calling at a volume that was perhaps not wise at four in the morning. He didn't remember climbing into bed with Pipes but realised that the evidence was irrefutable.

A loud burp from Pipes as he demolished the last of his breakfast brought Pudding back into focus, or at least as focused as he was likely to get in his current state.

## Chapter 2

Pete's head was thumping. He'd had hangovers before but this one brought with it the realisation that the older he got, the worse they got and the longer it took him to recover. He shuffled to the fridge, wondering if he could contemplate the ultimate pub-talk cure of the raw egg. When merely the thought of it almost had him retching, he quickly concluded that the reality was never going to be an option. Instead he perused the contents – a block of cheddar, two decidedly limp spring onions encircled with an equally limp blue elastic band that was performing no useful function whatsoever, a jar of Branston pickle, half a tin of baked beans…. When the sight of the congealing mass of orange beans almost had the same effect as the raw egg scenario, he cut short his fridge audit and just plumped for the carton of orange juice. He took a big glug, reflexively turning to see if Marcie might be about to admonish him for not using a glass before realising that she was still upstairs and unlikely to reappear for some time.

He felt no better for the injection of Vitamin C but at least he was fairly confident that he was not about to regurgitate it over the kitchen floor. So, surely this contribution to the rehydration process would have a benefit at some point? But what about now? He felt like his head had been invaded by a gang of student squatters who had the dial turned to 11 on the latest contribution from Death Metal exponents Cattle Decapitation. Said students also appeared to be re-enacting the scene through which the band had acquired its name, complete with rampaging chainsaws. He glanced at his watch. Just the 36 minutes since he'd taken a couple of Co-codamol so no opportunity yet for a top-up.

Pete sank into the kitchen chair, realising that in the Odger Ikea had yet again gone for style rather than comfort. He wondered if the previous evening had been worth the misery that he was currently experiencing and concluded a resounding yes. Marcie's 50th party had undoubtedly been one of the best nights of his life. Despite the phrase 'it's not all about you' rattling around his head, adding to what was already a cacophony going on in there with the bellowing moos of the beleaguered cows now drowning out the chainsaws, Pete couldn't help but focus on himself. Although it was a celebration of his wife's milestone birthday, it was the inaugural performance of Old School that was his over-riding memory. He realised that the term inaugural was not strictly accurate. The band had actually played in front of an audience once before but the dramatic nature in which this had been cut short meant that Pete had reasons to forget. Yes, he decided that in his own head at least, Marcie's 50th would forever be the official debut of Old School.

Clicking back into the present he realised that he shouldn't let himself get caught with his tea-making trousers down and pushed himself gingerly from the table surface to fill up the kettle. His befuddled mind was now faced with a dilemma: would Marcie welcome being woken with a cup of tea or would he be better leaving her to sleep it off? The last thing he remembered was her trying to extricate herself from her tights and 'control pants' and not being particularly successful with either, staggering around the bedroom like a new-born calf with vertigo. If he was feeling decidedly delicate, then how was she faring?

The whistle from the retro kettle sounded like the home-time blast which signalled an exodus of grime-faced, flat-capped blokes from a 1940's factory in a documentary about the steel mills that he'd watched earlier in the week. Wincing at the assault on his senses, he plodded across the tiled floor, stopping momentarily to savour the single hot tile on his bare feet where the central heating water pipes crept perilously, but deliciously, close to the surface.

He dropped in a teabag and filled the World's Best Mum mug that Charlie had bought for Mother's Day. Despite it being chipped and faded, with a permanent tannin stain that would ordinarily have seen Marcie assigning it to the bin, the sentimental value of it being one of the first items that a ten-year-old Charlie had bought with her own pocket money meant that it had outlived most of its compatriots in the mug cupboard by a significant margin. A splash of milk and a heaped teaspoon of sugar that Pete hoped would help stimulate Marcie's senses into some sort of conscious state and he headed upstairs.

## Chapter 3

Mark was seated in Marjorie's compact living room, his head buried in a large book, as he tapped away on his laptop. Marjorie appeared in the doorway in a baby blue negligee and in her best Mariella Frostrup voice whimpered 'aren't you coming back to bed Pumpkin?'

Mark raised his head and with an apologetic shrug replied 'sorry Snuggles, I've got to get this done. The exam is tomorrow morning and I don't feel as if I'm anywhere near being ready for it.'

Mark was taking his ACA Advanced Diploma in Accounting (Level 3) in less than 24 hours and was beginning to realise that last night had hardly been the best of preparations. While he had managed to keep the drinking to a sensible level, the effects of taking Marjorie's prescription Prozac to calm his jangling nerves had now completely worn off and he was even more anxious than normal. He wondered if 100mg had been a little excessive and that he was now in the throws of cold turkey.

Despite his attempts to focus on the Principles of Taxation, a tough ask at the best of times, his mind wandered to last night. Although his recollections were a little clouded by the drugs, he'd actually loved playing the bass with Old School. Though there had been several stumbles by him and indeed by all his bandmates, the party-goers had lapped it up. The only one Mark had noticed who didn't appear to be enjoying himself had been a surly guy at the back who Pete had dismissed with 'don't worry about him. He's Marcie's brother-in-law and a total arse.'

Marjorie placed a large mug of tea next to his laptop and sat down. 'You were brilliant last night Pumpkin. Much better than I thought you'd be. You're my rock god.'

As she gave his thigh a playful squeeze, Mark mused if there were many rock god bassists with the pet name Pumpkin. He certainly couldn't see Mrs Lemmy calling in Pumpkin for his tea.

Marjorie continued 'but who was 'Harsy' that I heard your drummer referring to?'

Mark explained that Harsy was the nickname used for Pete by Graham and Charlton, or Pipes and Pudding as they were also known. His head already hurt from coming down off the Prozac buzz and trying to explain the Old School naming system only made matters worse.

'So why do you call them Pete, Graham and Charlton then?' said a clearly confused Marjorie.

Mark explained that the three of them had been friends for many years and that he, as a late addition to the holy trinity, felt uncomfortable in referring to them by their nicknames. Given his fragile state, he elected not to go into how Charlton's actual name was Brian, deciding to leave that particular revelation for another time.

Marjorie's playful pinch of his thigh had now progressed further up and he could feel the stirrings of mini-Mark. Though he knew what he should be doing, the lure of a morning carnal coupling surprisingly outweighed the musings of Adam Smith on systemising rules to govern a rational system of taxation.

## Chapter 4

It was Wednesday night and The Swan was bustling, a group of pensioners enjoying a Groupon deal at the nearby hotel swelling the buzz from the usual regulars. The members of Old School were settled in the snug. Pete glanced across at the OAPs who en-masse appeared to be drinking half a shandy and realised that it wouldn't be too long before he could join them.

He was well aware that setting up Old School at the age of 53 had, in part, been an attempt to stave off old age with the thought that he could still rock with the best of them. With Pudding being the same age and Pipes just a year younger, he was sure this Peter Pan yearning that seemed to be prevalent in many of his friends had also been a factor in their decisions to join him in his middle-age odyssey. Though there was the occasional incident which highlighted the discrepancy in age with 22-year-old Mark, his old head on young shoulders persona (plus his penchant for ladies of maturing years) meant that he fitted in with the dysfunctional Old School family pretty well.

It was half-term, so Pudding was present having travelled up from Watford on the way to meeting his on/off girlfriend Claire for a few days of R&R in the Lake District. His lecturing in Media Studies at a sixth form college never seemed to be too restricting in terms of his time commitments to the band, with Pete suspecting that he probably played hooky more often than his students. But it was unusual to see him mid-week just for a few beers and a catch-up rather than for a full-blown band rehearsal.

Pipes was animatedly gesticulating and now leapt from his chair to assume a power stance, drawing startled and somewhat disapproving looks from the shandy-supping senior citizens. 'Harsy, Harsy, this was you when we were playing I Predict a Riot. It was like watching Slash.'

'Yes, alright Pipes, I think we all got a bit carried away at times. What about you thrashing around the kit like Keith Moon on Ketamine at the end of You Really Got Me. I thought you might be about to start kicking the crap out of your cymbals.'

Pete pointed at Pudding. 'As for old matchstick here, I thought his beard was going to spontaneously combust he was that red in the face. And, who can forget our young Frank Zappa, off his face on prescription drugs?'

Mark blushed, taking a quick sip of his pint, hoping to divert attention away from himself.

'Anyway, you haven't seen this yet.' Pete took his phone from his pocket and proceeded to stand it on the table, supported by a pint glass. He pressed the 'photos' icon, selected 'videos' and in a few seconds, a cacophony of tinny sound burst from the small speaker. 'Marcie's cousin Seamus took some footage on his phone of us playing. The sound's obviously not great but at least it is living proof that we did play and didn't just dream it all.'

An 'OK, same again?' from Pudding as he pushed his chair away from the table signalled that it was time for more liquid refreshment. '3 Theakstons and a pint of lager dash for you Mark?'

Pipes immediately chipped in, 'can you get a couple of bags of pork scratchings as well?'

Pudding shook his head. 'Christ Pipes, you've already demolished two bags of chilli peanuts and a family bag of Quavers. Anybody would think you've got a sodding tapeworm if it wasn't for the fact that you look like you've swallowed a fucking wok.'

A two-fingered salute from Pipes brought a wry smile from Pete as he once again considered just how well these two actually got on despite most of the time appearing to be locked in a battle to see who could out-abuse the other. Pete's son Jack seemed to be under the illusion that his generation had invented the term 'banter' and visibly squirmed every time Pete used it. So, naturally he used it all the time, occasionally substituting it with 'bants', just to revel in the effect it had on Jack.

Pudding returned from the bar with the drinks perched rather precariously on a tray. 'Harsy, just how old is that barman? He looks like he actually died several months ago and the speed of him backs that up. I was tempted to have a whiskey chaser while I was waiting.'

Pete immediately jumped to the defence of Chas, The Swan's ancient barman. 'He may not be the quickest but I'd prefer him any day of the week to the surly kid they have serving at The Carpenters Arms who looks about 12. The place wouldn't be the same without Chas.'

The rest of the evening passed quickly, with more pints downed and the conversation never straying too far from Old School. The focus was primarily on the band's encouraging performance at Marcie's party but they also discussed plans going forward.

'OK, so practice at the church hall on Saturday 29th then' said Pete as they all rose from the table.

He and Mark were sharing a cab and the frost had obviously thawed somewhat since the throwing up incident as Kelly had agreed to pick up Pipes and Pudding. While Pipes would be heading home with Kelly, Pudding was making the most of a heavily reduced room rate that Pipes had managed to secure from the hotel in Warwick where he worked as General Manager. After a night's solo accommodation, which would inevitably include a check of the quality of the hotel's Adult Channel, Pudding would be upgrading to a more salubrious double room the following evening when he met up with Claire in Kendal to put the lessons from the screen into practical use.

## Chapter 5

'Marcie, have you seen my ski gloves?' Pete was turning his wardrobe upside down and was surrounded by jumpers, trousers, shirts and shoes, most of which he hadn't worn in years. His wife appeared at the bedroom door, hair straighteners in hand.

Marcie was three years younger than Pete and had retained her youthful looks without resorting to the surgeon's scalpel. She had broached the subject of a brow lift as she approached her $50^{th}$ birthday, giving Pete the opportunity to climb onto one of his many soapboxes.

'You are joking. Have you seen the state of some of these z-list celebrities on the tele these days? Most of them look like their lips have been stuck in a vacuum cleaner nozzle for a couple of days. And, as for Botox, what on earth possesses anybody to inject poison into their foreheads so that they haven't got a cat in hell's chance of expressing an emotion ever again. Did you see that woman on the news the other day? She was suing a surgeon because her left arse cheek exploded on a flight to Torremolinos. Do you really want to spend your life worrying about melting if you stand too close to a gas fire?'

With a wry smile that somewhat ironically she wouldn't have been able to achieve had she gone down the Botox route, Marcie replied 'so I take it that's a no then?'

'Too bloody right it's a no. A brow lift? You'd look permanently as if somebody had just flashed at you from behind a bush. You look great as you are Hon.'

'Thanks, but just to point out that don't think I didn't spot your eyes out on stalks the other day when we saw Sammy and Terry in The Swan.'

Any mention of Sammy Fletcher and her dramatically enhanced cleavage always brought back bad memories of her husband Terry's birthday party that had ended with Pete being clinically dead for almost a full minute.

Marcie put down the straighteners on the dressing table and sauntered over to the wardrobe. She reached in and within 30 seconds had produced Pete's gloves. 'I give up Pete. Bloody unbelievable. You can't see things when they're staring you in the face.'

Pete knew that finding errant items was not his particular forte. In Marcie's world, the adage 'a place for everything and everything in its place' was an unspoken mantra. While Pete appreciated it was an approach to life that inevitably had its advantages, it only worked when you knew where that damn place happened to be. He had often wondered if it was an age thing, recognising that his memory was not what it was, but then concluded that he'd never known where the tape measure, the emergency wind-up torch, the rabbit-shaped jelly mould…. should be. Or, if he did, he was sure that this had not been the official repository last time he'd looked. They had been married now for almost 30 years and the pantomime of Pete hunting for things only to then call-in bloodhound Marcie had been repeated time and time again.

'Thanks love' Pete said sheepishly, deciding to go for a conciliatory tone rather than the 'but what the hell are they doing there' which he'd employed in equal measure over the years.

The reason for hunting down the gloves was the looming of the Harriman family ski holiday. Sunday afternoon had been designated by Marcie as the scheduled slot for packing so the bedroom floor was currently strewn with salopettes, goggles, helmets, boots and thermals that only saw the light of day once a year. Pete had yet to try on the salopettes, putting off the annual test to see if the passing of another year had caught up with him and it was time to get a bigger size.

Marcie was currently slipping into her Spider jacket and thankfully it still fitted, avoiding not only the expense of a new purchase but the angst that inevitably accompanied any proof that she had put on weight.

'Looking good Mrs H' Pete said, meaning it but also still in slightly mollifying mode following his inability to find something yet again. His thoughts turned to his son Jack who had inherited his father's 'Where is it?' gene, although Pete was not prepared to take any responsibility for passing on a capacity for untidiness that was truly spectacular. He surveyed the bedroom floor and realised that it currently had more than a passing resemblance to Jack's bedroom on any given day.

The strains of the intro to Superstition had Pete reaching for his phone, Stevie Wonder's classic track being the latest in Pete's ever-changing ringtone of choice. In this case, the track selection proved particularly apt. It was Jack.

## Chapter 6

'I'm going to kill him.'

'Pete, calm down. Ranting about it is not going to help. Call him again.'

Pete and Marcie were standing in Departures at Birmingham Airport. It was Pete's second visit in less than a month, his previous trip having been to collect his sister and her sons on their visit from Australia. He pressed 'Jack' and heard the dial tone ringing out for what must have been the tenth time in as many minutes. He glanced up at the Departures screen and its Gate Closing message that he was convinced had doubled in font size since he'd last looked. He half-expected to see 'that means you Harriman' appear accusingly below the message that now appeared to be growing as he stared intently at it.

Charlie pushed her way through the toilet door and strode over to her parents. 'No sign of Jack then? Let's leave him.'

'As tempting as that is, I'm going to give him another couple of minutes before I trek back and drag him over here myself.' Just as Pete finished the sentence, Jack sauntered into view. 'Jack, get your arse over here now!'

Marcie scowled at Pete, clearly not enamoured with him bellowing across the Departures Hall and making them no better than the woman in the pink velour tracksuit that they'd seen earlier screaming 'Chantelle, put that back on the fucking shelf. You aint 'avin it' as a rather rotund child grabbed the huge Toblerone that only ever seemed to be available at airports.

With an infinitesimal increase in speed and a scowl that could kill, even at the 100 or so paces that separated him from his clearly irate father, Jack continued towards them.

'Jack!' shouted Pete, repeatedly pointing at the monitor.

'Pete, calm down' hissed Marcie, glancing around to check just how many of the surrounding travellers were enjoying this temporary interlude to their boredom that this family fracas was providing.

'Well, just look at him. I told him 10 minutes in the arcade and here we are, nearly half an hour later, and about to miss our plane.'

Jack had now joined his family, in physical presence though not necessarily in spirit. Marcie jumped in before Pete had an opportunity to launch another verbal barrage. 'Jack, we need to get to the gate now. Last call was a good five minutes ago.'

His 'alright, chill out, they always build in loads of time' brought a look from Marcie that he knew better than to ignore and, with a grunt, went quiet.

Pete made a theatrical grab of Jack's backpack that he'd dropped to the floor and set off at a rate of knots.

They jogged through the terminal, Jack a good 10 yards behind to make a point but still keeping up the pace.

'31, 30, 29, 28 – Geneva, here we are' said Pete, breathing heavily and hoisting his own carry-on bag back up onto his shoulder. He joined the queue of just two people who he imagined were of a similar mindset to Jack, deciding that airport scheduling didn't apply to them. Showing his passport to an attendant whose smile was clearly painted on was a businessman whose world-weary face suggested that he'd spent far too much of his life in airports. Behind him was an elderly lady who just looked bemused by the whole experience. The ever-resourceful Marcie was already handing round the passports. As Pete presented his to the attendant her smile increased even further, which, with the over-applied make-up, reminded Pete of Jack Nicholson as The Joker. An overly cheery 'just about made it then Sir' almost had Pete turning around to grimace at his son.

Just about keeping himself in check he said 'yes, sorry.'

'Not to worry Sir. We're boarding passengers now but we've been advised that there'll be about an hour's delay on the tarmac.' Pete could almost feel his son's eyes burning into the back of his head. This was going to be a long flight.

## Chapter 7

'Is this it?'

As the transfer coach pulled up in a snow-covered car park, Jack's less than encouraging response spoke for them all. Despite over an hour on the runway, a 2 hour flight, 40 minutes waiting at the baggage carousel and an hour and a half transfer, Pete was still not quite over his son's laissez-faire approach to air travel.

'Can we at least wait until we get inside' said Pete testily, getting up stiffly from his seat and retrieving their bags from the overhead storage.

The chalet was certainly not how it had appeared online. As an ex-advertising man, Pete was only too aware of the gilding the lily potential of Photoshop and the hyperbole often employed in marketing copy. However, he still had trouble reconciling what stood before them with the 'picturesque traditional Alpine style chalet nestled in the heart of Chamonix, offering the perfect base from which to hit the slopes.'

The photo on the website compared to what he was now looking at had Pete thinking of dating websites. He knew it was not uncommon for an expectant suitor to be anticipating a George Clooney look-a-like only to be faced with his dad who seemed to have won several pie-eating competitions since the taking of his profile picture.

The presence of snow always added a certain chocolate box quality to most buildings but this was one where the chocolate appeared to be melting. Pete wondered what a multitude of sins the snow might be hiding. The shuttered windows were undoubtedly typically Alpine in style but the fact that two shutters were hanging at 45 degrees somewhat lessened the aesthetic effect.

The front door was painted a rather unattractive hue, which set Pete musing if Farrow & Ball had Piss Yellow slotted neatly between Citron and Babouche on their colour chart. Above the door a sign welcomed them to 'Chalet Le Lapin Blanc', though the missing 't' and 'i' made it more of a challenging read. With his O level Grade C French, Pete wondered if they were all about to disappear into something that was anything but a Wonderland.

The path leading to the entrance had been cleared of snow up to a point when whoever had been tasked with the job appeared to have just got bored and stopped. The sense of general decay was hardly helped by an off-white rusty minibus, parked to the left of a tumble-down log pile, with the peeling vinyl lettering announcing that it belonged to 'C alet Le La in Bla c'.

As Pete turned at the sound of the coach's engine starting up to carry away the other transfer passengers to the splendour of their chalets, he spotted a middle-aged man with an all too obvious look of relief that this hadn't been his allotted stop.

Pete had booked this year's skiing holiday and, having been acutely aware of his position as a retired gentleman, had been conscious of adopting a value for money approach. But he had to accept that this appeared to be budget with a capital B. Normally holiday bookings were very much the domain of Marcie but with Pete having more time on his hands and Marcie working long hours with her publishing business, this year the task had fallen to him. When he had considered early retirement at 52, holidays had been part of the Excel spreadsheet that he and Marcie had poured over. However, somewhat inevitably, their estimates on living costs had fallen short in certain areas. Hence, he now found himself standing in front of a chalet that could be described as shabby chic, probably without the chic.

A mangy dog, that immediately had Pete desperately trying to recall if Rabies was still alive and kicking in France, cocked its leg against the side of the dilapidated minibus. The resulting colour of the snow was an almost perfect match to the front door. Trying to muster a spirit of positivity despite Jack already glaring at him, Pete hefted the suitcase onto its wheels and started the precarious journey across the potholed car park.

'Ding'. The third ring on the reception bell still appeared to be having no desired effect. Just as Pete was about to redouble his efforts, a cough preceded the appearance of someone. The first thing that Pete spotted was the leg of a crutch, followed, albeit somewhat slowly, by a swinging leg in a thigh-to-toe cast. A young girl of about twenty then appeared, attached to the leg, and made her way gingerly to the desk. Pete's growing irritation at not being attended to was now swamped by guilt at his impatience.

As Marcie hurriedly moved the suitcases to clear a pathway for the girl, Pete blurted 'Bonjour – pardon moi. I didn't realise that you errrr, had mal votre jambe. Pardon. Un accident de ski?'

'No' said the girl in a heavy Glaswegian accent rather than the French that Pete had anticipated, 'I'd had one too many Jägerbombs and tripped over Claude.'

In a weak attempt to lessen his embarrassment Pete resorted to what he thought was friendly banter. 'Oh, I hope Claude was OK?'

'Him, he's fine. You might have seen him outside, probably licking his balls.'

As Pete's mind conjured up an unwanted image of a Frenchman doubled over licking his own genitals, it was thankfully short-lived.

'He's the chalet's unofficial mutt: a stray that we took pity on, fed and he's been here ever since.'

## Chapter 8

Pete was staring surreptitiously at his plate, trying to work out what he was, or was not, about to eat. The Harriman clan had unpacked, Pete wondering if Jack had simply tipped his suitcase out onto his bedroom floor, and were now in the dining room, along with around 30 other guests of Le Lapin Blanc. In choosing their accommodation Pete had decided on a catered chalet, always a popular option for skiing and an opportunity to let somebody else do the cooking for you. Now he was wondering at the wisdom of his selection.

He used his fork to lift what he thought were potatoes to reveal a grey meat of some description, hopefully not Le Lapin Blanc. The green beans were easy to identify but the beige coloured mush at the side of his plate presented more of a challenge. He glanced across at Jack who, as a vegetarian, at least did not have any of the grey meat to contend with. But his huge pile of green beans, the same beige mush and what appeared to be something vaguely related to the mushroom family was certainly no more appetising.

Pete was acutely aware of the four other people who had joined the Harriman table and did not want to appear as the English family of fussy eaters turning up their noses at this 'foreign muck'. He therefore plunged in, deciding to give the beige offering a go. While it would certainly not get you through to the next round of MasterChef, it was just about edible. The meat, though, whatever its origin, was as tough as old boots.

He looked up from his plate and saw a gleaming red face staring at him, complete with bald pate and glasses, not unlike the ruddy-faced, long-lost brother of shouty MasterChef judge Greg Wallace.

'William Tissington, pleased to meet you' was delivered at a volume of which Mr Wallace would be proud, accompanied by a meaty hand thrust across the table.

'Hi William, I'm Pete, Pete Harriman and this is my wife Marcie, my son Jack and my daughter Charlie.'

'Hello all, this is the wife, Bunty. Kids at public school, so thankfully they've gone off for a few days snow-boarding in St Anton. Bit of 'us' time for me and the wife, eh Bunty?' This was said with a theatrical wink at a lady that looked like she'd just stepped off the pages of a WI calendar, though her ample frame was thankfully clothed. 'Banking. You?'

Pete realised that the shorthand, no nonsense approach of W. Tissington Esq was asking him what he did for a living. 'Oh, I used to be in advertising but I retired last year. Marcie here is the bread winner; she runs her own publishing business.'

Pete's attempt to introduce Marcie into the conversation seemed to have no effect whatsoever, drawing a response of 'Lucky dog. Hear that Bunty? This chap here has already put his feet up and is leaving his good lady to do all the work. Good job I haven't done that with you eh? We'd have to sell the bloody Porsche?'

The question directed to Bunty was clearly rhetorical and not one for which William expected, or indeed wanted, a response.

Pete was aware of his above average tendency to form an initial opinion of somebody based simply on their appearance or just the briefest of conversations. He blamed it on his creative mind needing to fill in the blanks. But he at least attempted to give anybody he met for the first time the benefit of the doubt, trying not to make snap judgements. In this case, though, he realised it was going to prove difficult.

The term 'gammon' had become one of the buzzwords appearing regularly in the media in the last year, used to describe middle-aged men on the political right who were particularly vocal in their support of Brexit. Pete suspected that here he was engaged with a fully-fledged Gammon, complete with the florid complexion that had led to the similar French-attributed nickname of Rosbif to their cousins across The Channel.

Right on cue, William launched in. 'What about this bloody Brexit debacle eh? Bloody Frogs – should leave them and the Krauts to it I reckon. Can't get out quick enough, eh?'

Pete elected not to bite, seeing the irony in a man who was sitting in a French Alpine chalet while seeming to argue for a ten-foot barb wire fence around the UK coast. He consoled himself with the thought that the back-to-basics approach of Le Lapin Blanc was unlikely to see William and he repairing to the drawing room with cigars and brandies to leave the ladies to talk about their latest crocheting projects.

## Chapter 9

Pete was gazing at the brown-jacketed ski lift attendant who was diligently shovelling snow at the entrance to his station, patting it down quickly in between the procession of skiers using the chairlift. He wondered who had decreed that such a non-descript colour was a suitable uniform for the army of personnel who worked tirelessly to keep the mechanics of the slopes operating smoothly. They were the unsung heroes of the skiing world's infrastructure and perhaps there was his answer? Maybe the choice of attire was to ensure they did not get ideas above their station? The bright 'look at me' red of the ESF ski instructors was certainly in keeping with their flamboyant image so perhaps the dirty brown get-up of the lowly 'Liftie' was understandable: quiet, unassuming and indicating an ability to get the job done without being noticed.

Pete thought if only the same could be said of the infamous Coventry City 'chocolate kit'. He thought back to the 1978 season when a designer at City's kit manufacturer Admiral had the mental aberration that resulted in what became roundly acknowledged as the greatest fashion crime in the history of British football. The look had not been helped by the choice of poster boy. Ian Wallace, the diminutive Scottish striker, had a shock of bright ginger hair and a pasty complexion that looked like he'd been brought up in a cave on two hours sleep a night and a diet of Irn Bru. As if his God-given colouring was not enough, his tightly-curled locks looked as if they had been permed at the local poodle parlour and were never going to add anything to a kit that not even the most ardent of Sky Blues fans was prepared to defend.

Pete's mate Parky had made the error of asking for a replica kit for his birthday, complete with 'Parks' picked out in white on the back of the shirt. He had then compounded said error into a decidedly schoolboy one in donning the kit for a school PE session. The resulting derision had meant the kit was only seen once. As Pete considered if the addition of the iconic Admiral tramlines would enhance the sartorial elegance of the Liftie, he was woken from his reverie by the giggling voice of his daughter.

'Jack, stop it. He'll hear you.' Charlie was trying to make Jack's mirth less obvious when she was clearly also struggling to contain her own. Pete, Marcie, Jack and Charlie were all standing at the bottom of the chairlift, awaiting the arrival of the chalet's chef who today would be doubling up as their ski guide. Pete just hoped his skiing was better than his cooking.

The object of Jack and Charlie's hilarity was the arrival of Mr & Mrs Tissington. They were waddling awkwardly along in their ski boots, Bunty clearly struggling with the technique of carrying her skis. William was decked out in a garish iridescent yellow ski jacket and red salopettes that screamed attention-seeker. He put Pete in mind of Nigel Wallace, the self-acclaimed Lord of the Manor back in Leamington Spa, as this was just the sort of get-up he would be sporting if he took to the slopes. Trailing several yards behind William, Bunty was in a one-piece purple and green ski suit that had clearly been purchased in her younger, more svelte days. It gave her the appearance of a burst sofa. William shot an exaggerated wave at Pete and, with a loud 'bugger it', dropped his own skis in the process. Jack gave a snort, his shoulders shaking, while Charlie held her ski-gloved hand over her mouth to try and cover up her own amusement.

A whoop of 'Morning Mr T' and a tap on the back with a ski pole heralded the arrival of Joey, the young Aussie chef/ski guide, as he sped past the Emperor penguin-like Tissingtons, coming to an impressive stop and spraying snow at Jack and Charlie.

Pete realised that he was evidently spending more time on the slopes than in the kitchen, which figured.

With a gleaming smile that clearly impressed Charlie more than Jack, Joey greeted them with a cheery 'G'day to the Harrimans. You ready to shred the gnar in Chamonix?'

A coy smile from Charlie had Pete not only wondering what the hell Joey was talking about but also if her boyfriend Stig might have been better getting over his concerns at holding them back as a complete beginner and coming on the Harriman annual winter break anyway. A thumbs up and a wink at Charlie, followed by a flick of his head before Joey encased his flowing locks in his racing helmet, did little to allay Pete's misgivings.

The sound of heavy breathing announced the arrival of William. In between gasps, he wheezed 'be gentle with us will you Joey, my boy. It's been a while since me and Bunty skied and, with the pounding she got last night, she might be struggling with a bit of pain in her pelvic region if you know what I mean.'

A grimace from Marcie, with her face averted from William, clearly showed her feelings about the man.

'No worries, Mr T. We'll be taking it relatively easy this morning to give us all a chance to get our ski legs.'

Pete glided to a halt, pleased that this year's first experience of the chairlift had been successfully negotiated without incident. As he tightened the clasps on his boot, he glanced up to see Jack and Charlie once again in fits of giggles. He redirected his gaze to the direction of that of his children and immediately saw a chair bouncing rather precariously as William tried to lift the safety bar with little success. Mrs T still had her skis planted firmly on the lower bar of the chairlift which was clearly hampering William's attempts to provide an exit route as they travelled inexorably towards the station. The chairlift attendant, brown ski-suited like his lower station compatriot, scampered out of his hut and started gesticulating wildly, accompanied with an 'Up! Up!' as the Tissingtons bounced ever closer.

A man with an impressive handlebar moustache sitting atop a buff pulled up to protect his lower face against the cold wind was now joining in with the attempt to lift the bar. His cries of 'Schnell, Schnell' confirmed what his well-oiled facial hair had suggested, prompting the already startled Bunty Tissington to reply with a high pitched 'What? What?'

In now what seemed like slow motion, the chair passed the point of no return and the backs of the Tissingtons, along with that of a very irate German, started their downward journey.

As William's cries of 'Bloody hell Bunty old girl, what the hell do you think you are playing at?' were carried off on the wind, Pete joined in with his children's by now uncontrollable laughter as Marcie just added under her breath 'Serves him bloody right, the obnoxious twat.'

## Chapter 10

'Pete, can you pass the mustard please?' Pete pushed a ceramic pot containing the sachets of mustard, ketchup and mayonnaise across the table to Marcie. He could hear William loudly holding court but, thankfully, at a nearby table rather than at their own.

Pete took the opportunity to take in his surroundings. It was a quaint mountain restaurant, busy with its lunchtime trade. Waiters flitted from table to table delivering what appeared to be mainly hot dog and chips, interspersed with the odd local favourite of Tartiflette or Raclette. With all of the Harrimans hungry, having picked at the previous night's offerings sparingly, they had decided to play safe and go down the hot dog route. Only Jack had gone native, asking the waiter if they could do a vegetarian Tartiflette. Pete pictured a French sous-chef complaining about the fussy English and picking out bacon lardons to create the vegetarian option but decided to keep his thoughts to himself.

Directly above Pete was a pair of crossed wooden skis that looked like they had been carved with a penknife by a 19th century gnarled French mountain guide. He wondered if there was a French equivalent to the warehouse that sold imitation antique junk to the pub trade in the UK. His mind conjured up an image of The Flagon of Ale in which he'd met Pipes when Old School was still just a seed of an idea. The pub's decor had sported rusty old bikes, numerous fake enamel signs and a wooden cartwheel from which dangled pots, pans and kitchen utensils. The ancient skis prompted the same response in Pete as the cartwheel had: rather than be impressed by the contribution it made to the restaurant's rustic authenticity, Pete just hoped that the screws fixing them to the wall were sound.

As he munched his way through his Le Hot Dog et Frites, Pete's mind wandered, a character trait he had never grown out of from his days as Creative Director at the Howchin, Hewson and Hanson advertising agency. Then, and indeed throughout his working career in advertising, it had been a useful technique that he adopted when suffering from creative block, averting his attention from the task in hand to let his mind run free in the hope that this would invite in the muse. Now it often manifested itself through him focusing on somebody in a crowd and creating an imaginary full-blown character for them, just from observation.

His gaze alighted on a lad in his early twenties. He was tall, slim, effortlessly good-looking and the height of cool in red racing salopettes and matching jacket. Pete's imagination went into overdrive. He was, Giuseppe, the son of a famous Italian racing driver who had died in a tragic accident at his home circuit of Monza, leaving the fruit of his loins with a small fortune and a castle on the Amalfi coast. Giuseppe lived there with his mother Sophia, an eccentric aristocrat who shared her time between the castle and a chateau in Cannes. He was staying in a penthouse apartment in Chamonix with his man-servant Stanley who made himself scarce each evening when young Master Giuseppe returned with his latest conquest. As the young Latin playboy got up from the table, flicking his dark brown Italian locks, there was a shout from the doorway of 'Dave – you coming then mate?' and a distinctly un-Italian response of 'Be there in a minute, just going for a piss.'

Pete was woken from his reveries by Marcie with 'Pete, are you listening to me?'

He wondered momentarily if 'of course I am' was the right line to take and risk being exposed but instead went for the much safer 'Sorry love, I was just wondering what route Joey will be taking us on this afternoon.'

'I said, do you think Joey will be upping the ante and having us do any Red runs this afternoon? I'm not sure I'm up to that yet.'

With Pete thankful that his response suggested that he had, at least in part been listening, he answered 'Not if the Tissingtons are staying with us. It would kill them.'

Five minutes later and Joey stood up from the third table that had been allocated to Le Lapin Blanc and shouted 'Right, my little rabbits, time to hit the slopes and work off all those calories.'

Pete could not help glancing at Bunty and thinking there were not enough runs in the whole of France.

## Chapter 11

Pipes was on the phone to Pudding. 'Do you think we should tell Harsy then?'

'Not a chance. I know he was fond of the old boy but there's no point in spoiling his holiday.'

'That's what I was thinking but I said I'd give him a call tonight about that Fender Strat he's watching on eBay. Apparently, he's on a budget so has switched off his data and he reckons that the wi-fi in the chalet they are staying in is crap. As I was due to give him an update, I just wondered if it was worth mentioning it in passing?'

'I wouldn't but it's your call.'

The subject of the discussion was the ancient barman at The Swan. Pipes had made a midweek visit for a swift pint and had been chatting to Stan, the Landlord, who'd told him that unfortunately Chas had passed away. Pipes had only met Chas on a few occasions and while recognising that his passing was sad, this was tempered with the thought that he was amazed that he'd lasted as long as he had.

Stan had reported that Chas was 84 – Pipes had assumed he was even older – and that he had worked at The Swan for more than 30 years. Stan knew that he was not the most sprightly of employees but out of a sense of loyalty, coupled with his popularity with the locals, despite them often having to repeat their order several times and then wait a good couple of minutes to get their drink, he had never had the heart to pension him off. Stan had told Pipes that Chas' wife had died almost 20 years ago and that without the pub, he would probably have had little interaction with anybody as all his family were back in his native County Clare.

Pipes picked up his iPad, checked on the bids on the Fender guitar that Pete was coveting and decided that the news on Chas' demise was best left for another day.

## Chapter 12

'This is nice Pete. It seems ages since just the two of us have had a drink on our own.' Marcie raised her glass of Pinot and clinked it against Pete's 'vase' of Hoegaarden witbeer. They were seated at a table in La Porte Rouge, a small but lively bar in the heart of Chamonix town. It was Wednesday, the day when the staff at Le Lapin Blanc had their night off, requiring the guests to fend for themselves in finding an evening meal. Pete and Marcie, probably along with most of the guests based on the hushed comments at the dinner table, had seen this as a welcome relief given that Joey's culinary skills displayed on the opening night of their stay had been consistent in their mediocrity. He really was a good skier.

They had finished their meal about an hour ago, an excellent fondue that the whole family had enjoyed. Jack had been given an impressive array of vegetables to dip into the melted cheese, tipping a quantity into his own bowl to prevent contamination from the slavering jaws of his carnivorous sister and parents. The waitress had even given him his own réchaud with its two flickering candles to ensure that his Emmenthal did not reconstitute itself into a solid block.

It had been a fun meal with tales of the slopes and a lot of general mick-taking which was so characteristic of many a Harriman family get-together. Pete being no longer able to keep up with the pace of his two children was a frequent topic, with Charlie offering to take it easy the following day to avoid him having a heart attack.

Jack, always one to push the vegetarian cause, added 'with the amount of red meat you lot have put away tonight, I reckon you'll all be lucky to make it to the end of the week.'

Despite the witty repartee and convivial company, staying with their parents when a club was beckoning from just a couple of streets away had proved too much for Charlie and Jack. They had departed with Charlie ribbing Jack that 'if you're turned away for being underage, then don't think I'm coming back here. You'll be on your own mate.'

Pete looked at the two of them and, not for the first time, realised that the gap between 20-year-old Charlie and 17-year-old Jack seemed much greater than three years.

So, Pete and Marcie were left to their own devices. Just as they had been about to seek out another bar to try, a trio had started to set up in the corner of the bar.

Marcie looked at Pete and knowing his love of live music said, 'I guess, we'll be staying here then?'

Pete grinned, recognising once again that Marcie knew him better than he knew himself and set off for the bar for another large Pinot and a bucket of Hoegaarden.

'Tweest & Shout. Shake eet it up your babeee now.' Despite the slightly weird inflections and the strangling of the Beatles lyrics, 'Les Trois Coeurs' were not too bad musically. A drummer, a lead guitarist and a very flamboyant bassist, they had started with a few French pop songs that Pete had never heard before. They had then moved onto their English set which consisted of a couple of Beatles numbers, a passable version of Fleetwood Mac's Go Your Own Way and an ill-advised attempt at the Tom Jones' classic Delilah, before reverting to their mother tongue.

The bass player was the stand-out of the three but not really for the right reasons. Pete guessed he was just a few years younger than himself but was sporting a white shirt open to the navel, from which sprouted a forest of chest hair that at least looked like he might be able to do a passing imitation of Tom Jones. He couldn't.

The main vocalist and his lead guitar had moved aside for the bass player to step up to the mic, almost bursting out of his leather trousers in his eagerness to take centre stage. From the opening line of 'I see the light, for the night that I pissed by her widow' Pete realised that they were in for a treat. It was like Officer Crabtree, the hapless policeman from 80's TV sitcom All Allo, had decided to ditch his truncheon for a mic stand. Pete was briefly tempted to shout out 'Good Moaning' but thought better of it.

A particular highlight was the forced 'Ho, Ho, Ho, Ho' after the line 'I feel the k-nife in my 'and but she did not laugh anymore.'

Pete was impressed that he still somehow managed to shoehorn his interpretation of the words into something that resembled the meter of the song. But that is where being impressed ended. Completing it with a strangled attempt to hit the final famous Tom Jones high note, Monsieur Bass had taken a dramatic bow, obviously delighted with his performance. When Pete thought of the shy and retiring wallflower that was Mark in Old School, you really could not have two more conflicting approaches to playing the bass.

After several more wines and beers, though Pete had sensibly switched to the local lager rather than continuing his Hoegaarden consumption, they had wandered back to Le Lapin Blanc. As Pete made his third attempt to insert the key into the chalet's front door, he heard the now familiar sound of running water and turned to see Claude making another deposit in a car park that was rapidly taking on the appearance of an incontinent pensioner's duvet.

## Chapter 13

Pete, Marcie, Charlie and Jack were on a chairlift, faces inclined to catch the warmth of the early morning sun. The birdsong from the pine trees was the only sound to break the silence. An empty piste glistened invitingly below, with just a couple of tracks from skiers that had somehow managed to beat the first official lift of the day to break the crisp uniform ridges created by the overnight efforts of the piste-bashers.

Pete loved his skiing but realised that it was not just the activity itself. He relished the opportunity to race down a mountain, on the edge of being out of control. Though he had slowed down a little in recent years, more conscious of the consequences of a fall, he still liked to push himself. It was his annual injection of adrenalin in a life that was otherwise fairly sedentary. Creating the band had been an attempt to have another source of adventure and the feeling he'd had fronting Old School at Marcie's party had been a huge rush.

Skiing gave him a similar feeling of being alive, of being 'in the moment' – a version of the world's current preoccupation with mindfulness that was far removed from the adult colouring books that he had eschewed when Marcie had suggested them as a possible option when he retired. But it was more than just the skiing. The adrenalin surge from the act itself was made all the more intense by starkly contrasting moments such as this. At home, quiet was never truly quiet. Even in the relative peace of his back garden, there was always an underlying thrum of traffic, a bark from his neighbour's dog, an angry blast from a car horn as a commuter was cut up on his daily crawl into the office. Here, quiet really was quiet. With no cars, plus the sound-deadening properties of the snow, it really was other-worldly.

Charlie sneezed.

'That'll be you catching Joey's cold' sniggered Jack.

Marcie, with the sixth- sense of a mother sensing potential danger for a child, said 'Why would Charlie be any more susceptible to Joey's cold than the rest of us Jack?'

'I'll let Charlie answer that one' said Jack, adjusting the goggles on his helmet.

'Jack, you little shit. And after I'd convinced that barman to let you have a drink when he asked to see your ID.'

'Charlie?' prompted Marcie.

'It was nothing mum. Just a bit of harmless flirting.'

A 'yeah, right' from Jack had Marcie querying further.

The colour of Charlie's cheeks was now distinctly redder than could reasonably be attributed to the combined effects of the cold and the morning sun. 'Mum, it was really nothing, just a dance and an affectionate peck, that's all. He's a nice guy. He was there with a couple of the girls from the chalet. They often go there on their night off. We got on well.'

Clearly wanting to divert the topic of the conversation without just pulling an obvious handbrake turn, Charlie added 'and anyway, his name's not even Joey. It's Mike. When he came over to London he worked in a pub with Karl, another Aussie. Karl was really tall and, as you've seen, Mike is pretty small, so the bar manager christened Karl, Kanga, and Mike, Joey. It obviously stuck.'

Pete realised that the penchant for blokes to give their mates nicknames was evidently not confined to British shores. In his experience it was predominantly just a shortening of surnames, hence his being Harsy at school and indeed still now at the ripe old age of 54 to some of his friends. He thought back to a stand-up routine he and Marcie had seen by comedian Greg Davies at Leamington's Assembly Rooms. In it Greg had talked about school nicknames and how they often stuck for life. He recounted a couple of purlers. There was Baghdad – a lad who had been re-christened simply because one day he arrived in the classroom with a new bag that had been bought for him by his dad. This had been trumped by a member of Greg's audience who had revealed that his schoolboy nickname had been Mumbo. When quizzed by the giant comedian as to the origins of said Mumbo, he said that it was apparently due to his friends deciding that his mum had BO.

Pete thought that Greg would have taken his hat off, on this occasion brimming with corks, to the relative creativity of Joey. It put him in mind of the christening of Pudding, though in this instance he would be doffing a flat cap. Brian Davies, who Pete had met in his first job at a Midlands advertising agency, was from Yorkshire and being a big lad had received his moniker from their boss. The fact that Pudding was now about 10 stone ringing wet was a great example of how difficult it often is to shift a nickname.

The chairlift station being only 15 metres away interrupted any opportunity for the further interrogation of Charlie, though Pete knew that the subject would inevitably be revisited at some point, potentially by Jack in earshot of Charlie's official boyfriend Stig if he was feeling particularly spiteful towards his sister.

## Chapter 14

'So, you're back then?'

Pipes' question to Pete was met with 'Yes, got back yesterday. A three-hour delay in Geneva so we didn't get home until the early hours, so in fact it was not yesterday, it was today. I'm knackered.'

'I'm guessing you haven't really had much of an opportunity to chat to anybody local then?'

'No, why?'

'Well, I didn't want to tell you while you were on holiday but Chas died while you were away.'

Pete's stomach did that weird flip that often happens when we get bad news.

Though Chas was hardly a close mate, Pete had seen him on a regular basis for about 11 years, even more regularly since Pete's retirement when an afternoon trip to The Swan had become part of a routine, if not quite daily then certainly at least a couple of times a week. Chas had seemed part of the very fabric of The Swan and, although Pete was well aware of his age, somehow he'd never really thought of his mortality. He was like a good malt, improving with age, although like all of the pub's regulars, Pete knew that in the last few years, Chas would not have been in the frame for Employee of the Month based purely on the ability to do what you were paid to do. But it hadn't mattered. Despite all his failings, Chas was always a welcoming face, a constant in a world of ever-increasing change. He would be sorely missed, by Pete and by many others.

'No. How did you hear?'

Pipes went on to outline his conversation with Stan, saying that this was all he had heard and was not aware of any of the funeral arrangements.

'OK, mate, thanks for letting me know. Sad but to coin the old phrase, he'd had a good innings. See you next week at band practice.'

Pete sat down, not sure what to do. He contemplated giving Marcie a call to let her know, but it being her first day back at work, with a book launch only a couple of weeks away, he knew she would be operating at full tilt. He looked at his Breitling Chronomat 44, a 50$^{th}$ birthday present from his parents. 11.15 so a bit early for a trip to The Swan, even in his new retirement regime. Having decided that he wouldn't go to the pub, at least not for a couple of hours, Pete still felt that he should mark the occasion by raising a glass to Chas. He reached for the Bushmills and poured himself a generous measure.

## Chapter 15

'To Chas.'

'To Da' came the reply to Pete's toast.

It was Tuesday afternoon and Pete was in The Swan with Fergyl who had flown in from Ireland to make arrangements for his dad's funeral. Pete had been introduced to Chas' son by Stan and in a matter of minutes felt like he'd known him for years. The gift of the blarney had certainly been bestowed on the rotund Irishman and Pete already knew more about Chas in less than half an hour than he'd managed to glean in more than 11 years across the bar. While always welcoming, Chas had been a man of few words, clearly not a trait that had been passed onto his son.

'He was a grand man. I hadn't seen that much of him since Ma passed away but I talked to him most days on the phone. The last time I saw him was about three years ago when he came back to Kildare for my daughter Colleen's wedding. What a blast that day was.'

Pete just let Fergyl talk, enjoying learning about Chas but also recognising that it seemed to be therapeutic for him to reminisce about his old man. Though there was no obvious similarity in character - his high-speed delivery being almost a direct antithesis to the laconic approach of his father - visually Pete could see a resemblance. He guessed Fergyl was a similar age to himself. He was significantly larger than Chas but the sparkle in the blue eyes, a pronounced dimple in the chin and the pudgy, almost boxer-like nose he had inherited from his dad. He was dressed in a smart open neck shirt, black waistcoat and matching trousers which seemed a little formal for a trip to the pub but, Pete thought, was perhaps reflective of the sombre reason for his visit.

He was a very engaging man, helped by the mellifluous strains of his west Ireland brogue, and Pete was really enjoying his company. Half an hour became a couple of hours, which became nearly four hours, with several whiskeys taken and various locals coming over to pass on their condolences to their bereaved guest.

Pete rose to go to the gents and felt decidedly unsteady on his feet. He returned to see a beaming Fergyl who had been joined by Sammy Fletcher. The reason for the Irishman's buoyant mood was clearly not just the effects of the alcohol. Sammy was bending towards him to reveal a cleavage that would not have been out of place in a Carry On film.

'Oh, hi Pete' said Sammy, fluttering her false eyelashes, 'I was just saying to Fergy here how sorry I was to hear of his dad's recent passing. Chas will be really missed, won't he?'

Fergyl, choosing either to ignore the mispronunciation of his name or perhaps delighted that he'd already been given a pet name by an attractive woman, jumped in with 'That's so kind of you to say so Sammy. Did you know my Da well?'

Pete thought that, by all accounts, Chas was probably one of the few local blokes that had not 'known' Sammy well and wondered if he should warn Fergyl that he could be in her laser-targeted sights. He decided against it, concluding that he was a grown man and was clearly enjoying the attention.

Sammy turned her gaze back to Fergyl. 'I did. He was a lovely man. Did Pete tell you that he has a band? They played at a party for me.'

Pete noted that she had not mentioned it was her husband Terry's party and the potential ambushing of Fergyl appeared to take a step closer. They then went into the story of how Pete had been electrocuted when the water from a marquee roof had been prodded to cascade onto Pete's guitar amp. With Fergyl offering the appropriate concern at Pete hopefully having no lasting ill effects, this soon turned into laughter when Pete reassured him that he hadn't.

'Jesus, Pete, that was a lucky escape, eh? I've not met many people that have come back from the dead. My Da would have loved that – he was a staunch Catholic you know. It hasn't put you off playing I hope?'

'No, we played at my wife's $50^{th}$ birthday a couple of months ago and we practice at least once a month.'

'That's it, then. Decision made – you'll play at my Da's wake!'

## Chapter 16

Pete and Marcie were having dinner, a vegetable lasagne that he had prepared earlier in the day. One consequence of Pete's retirement was that he was now doing the lion's share of the cooking. Initially it was simply a redistribution of chores, with Pete having a lot more time on his hands and Marcie working long hours in her publishing business which was becoming increasingly pressured as her stable of authors writing for the teen-girl market expanded.

As Pete's confidence in cooking grew, so his attitude changed from it being simply a necessary daily task to one that he positively enjoyed. He had invested in a number of cookbooks, including a couple of vegetarian ones to cater for Jack, and his increased confidence had seen a significant expansion of his repertoire. He'd learnt to reign in his natural inclination to add spice to everything, with the family not always appreciating his addiction to hot food. And, though he had the occasional stumble – the melted chocolate on a cheese pizza that he'd picked up from an internet recipe had proved a gastronomic step too far for everyone – he was turning into quite an accomplished cook.

'So, was it the drink talking or was he serious?' asked Marcie, adding some dressing to the green salad that accompanied the lasagne.

'We'd both had a fair few, but I think he was serious' replied Pete. 'I assumed they would be having the funeral back in Ireland but Fergyl said that Chas had made England very much his home, so the family has discussed having him buried in Leamington Spa cemetery. He said that Chas had spent so much of his life in The Swan and that was where most of his friends were, so he thought the pub was the best place to hold the wake. I think the drink might have been talking when he said the timing would also give the family a chance to come over for the Cheltenham Festival.'

'And he wants Old School to play?'

'Yes, he's asked me to check with the others and give him a call tomorrow to let him know if the date is OK for everybody.'

'Pete, isn't it a bit weird having a band playing at a funeral?'

'Well initially I thought the same thing but he told me that in Ireland, and in his family in particular, it is a tradition to really celebrate the life of a passing family member with the wake and music is central to that. He said Chas would love the idea that we'd be providing the soundtrack to his send-off.'

Pete checked with Pipes and Mark, with both confirming that they were available for Old School to play. He now turned to the final piece of the jigsaw. 'Pudding, it's Harsy......Yes, great holiday thanks but some bad news when I got back. You know Chas, the old barman at The Swan, well he's passed away.'

'Yes, I spoke to Pipes while you were away and he told me, though he didn't have any details at the time' replied Pudding.

Pete went on to explain that Chas had passed peacefully in his sleep before moving onto the main reason for the call. 'I know you didn't know him too well so that's not really why I phoned. I haven't turned into my dad just yet, reporting on the deaths of people that I've never heard of or that I last met when I was in short trousers, but his son has asked if we'd consider playing at the wake.'

'What, at the bloody funeral you mean?'

'Well, not in the church itself but at the gathering afterwards.'

'You mean we're all going to travel to Ireland to play at the old guy's farewell bash?'

'No, not to Ireland. He's being buried over here, just down the road from us actually.'

'OK, still a bit weird but if that's what his family wants. And, let's be honest, we don't appear to have hordes clamouring for our services.'

'It's next Friday, so short notice I know. Pipes and Mark are both OK. Can you make it?'

'Well, I'm supposed to be lecturing on the importance of diversity in the current advertising landscape to my bunch of half-wits on the media course. But it's been a few weeks since I've thrown a sickie so, yes, count me in.'

They had discussed logistics, with Pudding deciding that his stomach bug would be a two-day affair, enabling him to travel up on the Wednesday night so they could have a band practice the day before the main event. Pete confirmed that Pudding could stay with them and would have his own room as Charlie was currently up at Durham University until the Easter break.

'Hey, Harsy, have you had any requests for specific songs for us to play?'

'No, and given that it's only a few days away, there's no chance we'll be able to learn anything new.'

'I was just thinking of a few potentials given the event. How about Come on Baby Light my Fire?'

'Bloody hell Pudding, I'm guessing that's what you call gallows humour? And anyway, it's a burial, not a cremation.'

'That's No Diggity out then. OK, how about Going Underground or what's that old one by Bernard Cribbins – There I was Digging a Hole?'

## Chapter 17

Old School were assembled in the church hall for the pre-wake practice. Pete had spoken to the church warden, Mr Somersby, as soon as Pudding had confirmed his availability. When Pete had explained the reason for the practice, he had been surprised at the response from the waspish custodian of the hall's keys.

'Most Christian of you Mr Harriman. I'm sure we'll be able to waive the normal hire charge given the circumstances. I know Mr O'Sullivan made his living by selling alcoholic beverages, but I understand he was a God-fearing gentleman nonetheless, even if he was of a slightly different persuasion to that of my own church. After all, we are all God's children Mr Harriman, are we not?'

Pete was now setting up his amp, plugging in his faithful Fender Telecaster, having been outbid in his attempt to purchase the second-hand Fender Stratocaster on eBay. Pipes was attaching the second cymbal on his hi-hat, while Pudding stood impatiently watching Mark as he tuned his bass for the third time.

'OK, then' Pete said, as he passed around hand-written set-lists 'same set as Marcie's party but I've just changed the order around a little and I've dropped the Scouting for Girls number Elvis Ain't Dead as I didn't think it was particularly appropriate.' Nods of approval and a smirk from Pudding prompted Pete to add 'And, before, you say it Pudding, no we're not doing Going Underground instead.'

They played through the set, starting with the Beatles classic She Loves You and finishing with Call Me by Blondie. They then went back to those songs that had not gone so well, paying particular attention to Sweet Home Alabama as Pudding was struggling with the rhythm guitar part and to The

Killers' Mr Brightside as Pete had forgotten the lyrics to the second verse. Mark asked if they could have another run through The Smiths' What Difference Does it Make which they did several times as Mark's nerves and the thought that he wasn't going to get the bass part right proved to be self-fulfilling. They finally finished with a raucous rendition of I Predict a Riot at Pipes' request, just because he loved playing it.

They packed up their kit and drove to The Swan for a post-practice beer. Stan had already cleared a few of the tables in front of the bay window that was the designated area in which Old School would be playing the following day.

'It's going to be a bit tight' said Pipes, surveying a space that would normally have held four round tables and chairs.

'I know but I suspect there won't be masses of people here so we might be able to spread out a bit. I'm sure most of The Swan's hardcore of regulars will come along to pay their respects but I expect it will only be close family travelling over from Ireland' replied Pete.

'What are we going to wear?' said Mark, breaking his silence that the others knew better than to question as he was undoubtedly replaying What Difference Does it Make over and over in his head.

'Good point Mark' said Pete, putting down his pint. 'I was thinking the same thing. I don't feel we should play in the dark suits that I presume we'll all be wearing to the funeral but I wasn't sure what we should wear to strike the right tone for the evening. However, it's actually been taken out of my hands because Fergyl asked me for all of our sizes as he says he is arranging something for us.'

Raised eyebrows from Pudding displayed the nervousness that had just settled over all of them.

## Chapter 18

Pete and Marcie walked hand in hand into Leamington's St Patrick's Catholic Church to be met with a crowd that Pete was sure had not been seen there for many a year. He couldn't quite believe it. The last funeral he had attended had been that of his Great Uncle Jimmy. He and Marcie had been amongst about 25 mourners, which he thought was probably fairly typical for a 92-year-old, most of whose contemporaries had preceded him in shuffling off this mortal coil.

This was like a scene from Ben Hur. All of the pews were taken and it was standing room only. He knew some of the congregation as regulars at The Swan but there were many more that he did not recognise and assumed the majority must be family who had made the trip from Ireland. Pete wondered if they had chartered their own Aer Lingus jet.

He spotted Pudding and Pipes standing together at the back and sidled over. He was not surprised that neither Kelly nor Claire had joined them as they had not known Chas. Pudding and Pipes were unlikely to have attended had they not been playing as they were really only on nodding terms. Not that knowing the deceased seemed to be a pre-requisite for Pete's mum and dad these days. A couple of weeks ago they had attended 'a lovely service' for a bloke who was a friend of their local newsagent.

In the hushed tone that is the default setting for church and for funerals in particular, Pete leant into Pudding. 'Where's Mark, is he here yet?'

'Yes, he's in the pews on the right-hand side, about halfway up, with Marjorie. I reckon he'll be having a word with the priest after the service to see if he can reserve a plot for her.'

The discrepancy in age between Mark and his lady friend had caused a bit of tongue-wagging at the New Year's Eve party but they still seemed to be going strong. The fact that Marjorie was only a couple of years older than the three of them had not stopped Pudding referring to her as Methuselah on several occasions when Mark was out of earshot.

A resounding chord from the church organ signified that the service was about to begin. A few minutes in and Pete realised they were in for a full-blown Requiem Mass, wondering just how long it would take for the assembled throng to take Holy Communion. He found out almost an hour later as Fergyl and another man, a shorter version of Fergyl and presumably his brother, took the bread and wine to the altar. What then followed was like a scene from Lourdes, with a good 70 percent of the mourners lining up to receive Holy Communion.

After what felt like the feeding of the five thousand, Fergyl took to the podium to deliver what was both a moving and a humorous eulogy to his father. Pete was impressed, recalling his own difficulties in getting the tone right for one of the advertising clients he'd had back in his Howchin, Hewson and Hanson days.

He and Pudding had worked as the creative team on the Frederick Chester & Sons Funeral Directors account. When Chester Jr took over the business from his father, he was evidently looking to bring a new approach to the world of death. He came in all bright and breezy for a meeting with the H,H&H creative team, wearing a Paul Smith suit and Gucci loafers, not really the attire that Pete had been expecting from the new MD of a funeral home.

He had obviously been to a few marketing seminars and was full of all the latest buzz phrases, clearly determined to bring death into the 21$^{st}$ Century. When he started talking about taking a helicopter view of his target demographic Pete wondered if he had opted for the vantage point of his clientele. Pete had also thought the target demographic was pretty straightforward and not one which really warranted too much input from the agency's market research team: families of dead people. For Chester Jr, though, this was far too simplistic an approach.

In order to deliver his KPIs and achieve an optimum ROI for the business, he had taken them through a full presentation in which he outlined the brand values that underpinned his vision of this brave new world. Central to his brief was that while death was very sad, that did not mean that the advertising for his Funeral Home could not have a sense of humour. Despite the Account Director couching caution with such a sensitive subject, it was clear that Chester Jr had run his ideas up the flagpole and expected a full salute from his creative team.

So, adopting the old advertising mantra of 'tell the client once, tell them twice and then just take their money' Pete and Pudding had been instructed to come up with a light-hearted approach to caring for your loved ones once they had 'joined the choir invisible' as George Eliot, one of Pete's favourite authors, had so eloquently put it. Neither Pete nor Pudding had been able to conjure anything which bridged the chasm of humour and the sanctity of death. With only a matter of hours until their presentation and the copywriting muse clearly not visiting, one of the ideas that they had actually worked up was Pete's strapline of 'Frederick Chester & Sons – To Infinity & Beyond', applying the purple and green colours associated with Buzz Lightyear to the visuals. They were therefore not surprised when it somewhat aptly joined the agency's list of dead accounts. If only Fergyl had been around 15 years ago to lend his expertise, thought Pete as Fergyl made his way back to his seat.

## Chapter 19

The Swan was packed to the rafters. Pete was with Fergyl who was busily introducing him to sons, daughters, grandsons, granddaughters, nephews, nieces, cousins, aunts, uncles and even a couple of great grandsons as the man who was '…going to do a bit of a turn.'

The O' Sullivan clan was certainly extensive and had turned out en-masse to give Chas a good send-off. Pete wondered if there was anybody left in County Clare. He spied Pipes and Pudding at the bar, hoping that they were not going too early on the drink front and appreciating that they were there to do a job. Mark was nowhere to be seen, but based on past performances and his nervous disposition, Pete could hazard a pretty good guess as to his whereabouts.

'Right' said Fergyl decisively, 'gather the lads together and bring them behind the bar. Stan has agreed that you can get changed in his upstairs flat.'

The members of Old School were now standing with an air of trepidation that they hoped was not being picked up by Fergyl as he dragged a cardboard box from behind the sofa. 'Well, what do you think?' he said, pulling a t-shirt from the box with a flourish that would have made Paul Daniels proud. The catchphrase of 'not a lot' would have been a fair summation as Pete looked at his compatriots.

Front and centre of an emerald green t-shirt was the taciturn face of the recently deceased staring back at them. He looked like Victor Meldrew's dad. With no response from any of the others Pete felt it was up to him to respond but before he had the chance to say anything, Fergyl added 'I know, I know, it would have been great to get one of him smiling but he wasn't really one for a grin now, was he?'

Pete realised that he could delay no longer 'Er, it's great Fergyl. It will be a pleasure to wear them won't it lads?' glancing round quickly for support.

Pudding was the quickest off the mark, instantly reminding Pete of the times they had backed each other up in client pitches when they knew the creative campaigns they had come up with were, at best, average. 'Oh aye, they look fantastic. Chas will be close to our hearts in every sense of the word.'

'I know, I know' cried Fergyl enthusiastically, turning the t-shirt around to reveal in bold white lettering 'Charles 'Chas' O' Sullivan, 1935-2019' beneath an unmistakable gold harp. 'Right then lads, I'll leave you to get changed. See you downstairs and we can get the craic started eh?'

With that he turned on his heel to leave three slightly stunned band members staring at Pete who was now holding his t-shirt.

'Well at least the lettering is a pretty close match to the Guinness font – Agenda URW if I'm not mistaken?' said Pudding.

'You what?' retorted Pipes 'We're being asked to wear shirts with a dead bloke's face on the front and all you can think about is what sodding typeface it is? Doesn't anybody else think this is bloody macabre and not in the best taste? Is it just me?'

Pudding, unable to resist prodding Pipes a little further, replied 'Well, you've got that t-shirt with Keith Moon grinning maniacally at you. He's dead, isn't he?'

'Yes, but I haven't just watched Keith Moon being lowered into the fucking ground, have I?'

Pete realised that this had the potential to escalate and put a complete dampener on the positivity required for a decent performance from Old School. 'Look chaps, I know it's perhaps not what we'd choose to wear but it's not about us, it's about celebrating Chas's life and if his family wants us to do that with a photo of him on our chests, then that's what we'll do.'

## Chapter 20

The members of Old School walked into the bar to rapturous applause. The story of the t-shirts had evidently been circulated, building the expectation of the mourners. Pete caught Pipes muttering under his breath 'It's alright for them buggers – they don't have to wear the bloody things.'

His indignation had risen a couple of notches when he'd pulled his shirt on. 'Snug' was one way of describing it, consequently stretching Chas' face across his substantial belly so that he looked like he'd been inflated with a bike pump. The childish guffawing this had brought from Pete and Pudding had not improved Pipes' mood.

They took their positions in a space that had become even more cramped than when they'd seen it previously. All of the tables and chairs had been stacked in the pub's rear car park to accommodate the mourners, but the sheer number meant that it really was cheek to jowl. This was easily the biggest crowd The Swan had ever held and Pete wondered if the pub's Fire Certificate had been updated recently, though it would be a hard-hearted fire officer to raise the issue at a wake. Pete took the microphone from the stand, his mind racing at what was the right tone to take. He decided just to plunge right in.

'Hello everybody. We're here to celebrate the life of Chas, a man that was so many things to so many people. I knew him for about 11 years as the friendly face across the bar and, from looking around the room, I can see many of the regulars have come to pay their respects to a man that was always happy to lend an ear to your problems when you dropped in for a beer at the end of the day.'

A cry from the back of 'You'd have had to bloody speak up then' and laughter from around the room showed

Pete that the sombre mood of the church had already been replaced with a much more jocular air, a process that had been started with Fergyl's superbly judged eulogy.

Pete continued. 'From the family that I've met, and I can't believe how many of you have travelled over from Ireland….'

An interruption from the same voice with 'It's Cheltenham next week, why wouldn't we be here?' was this time met with a more muted response.

Pete didn't know if that was down to people wanting the heckler to pipe down or more a sense of guilt in the truth of the statement. 'As I said, from the family members that I've met, Chas was a dad, a grandad, a great-grandad, an uncle, a brother and, most of all a friend. From talking to Fergyl, he very much wants today to be a celebration of his father's life so before we kick off with some music, can I ask you all to raise your glasses. To Chas!'

A hearty and resounding response of 'To Chas' was followed swiftly by a '1,2,3,4' from Pipes and his crash on the cymbal was accompanied by chords from the three guitars and they were off with She Loves You.

They played the agreed five song first set, Chas's face taking on some quite alarming expressions as Pudding thrashed around his kit. Pete thanked what was proving already to be a boisterous but encouraging crowd and advised they'd be back later. Before he'd even had a chance to put down his guitar, Fergyl grasped him warmly by the hand. 'Pete that was grand. You boys are doing Da proud. He'll be up there having a bit of a jig himself.'

The thought of Chas doing anything other than at just about walking pace, let alone a jig, was a bit of an anathema to Pete given that in all the time had had known him, speed was not one of his standout attributes. But now was not the time to be a pedant. 'He will that' said Pete, tapping the image of Chas on his chest.

'Pete, get yourself and the lads a drink – just tell Stan that it's on me. I've got a tab running for certain people though I've decided not to go for a free bar beyond the first round that Stan kindly paid for. With some of the family we have over, let's just say that could turn a bit scary. That gobshite Michael who was shouting out when you were doing your bit of a speech there is already three-sheets to the wind. He'll be singing Kevin Barry before the night's out.'

## Chapter 21

Pete was outside with Marcie, taking an opportunity to escape from the fug in the pub created by what must have been close to 200 people. 'I have to say, not too bad given that you've not been together that long' said Marcie before taking a swig from the brandy that she had brought outside with her.

'Damning with faint praise' was the phrase that came to Pete's mind, though he knew that this was still praise indeed from Marcie who had always adopted the 'call a spade a spade' philosophy to life. One of the few times she took on a more circumspect approach was in dealing with the often fragile egos of her fledgling authors. Pete was constantly impressed at her ability to say just the right thing to keep them onside, somehow giving them a boost of encouragement while also steering them in the direction she felt they needed to go.

'What about that bum note in the chorus of You Really Got Me?' said Pete, self-analysing his own guitar-playing.

'Pete, do you really think that people watch Old School with such rapt attention that they'd spot a dodgy note? Get real.'

'OK, OK, I know we're not The Rolling Stones, but I like to think that we are as professional as we can be' said Pete, slightly bristling at the implied nonchalance of their audience.

'I see you've chosen one of the few bands that actually have a few years on you lot Pete. Don't beat yourself up and be too precious about it. You're an amateur band that plays songs that people love to hear and you're having a great time doing it. Isn't that enough?'

'Yes, I suppose so. I guess it's just that I've wanted to be in a band for so long that I need reassurance that we're not absolutely crap. I'd hate to be the old guy up there with people thinking what the hell does he think he's doing.'

Any further philosophical introspective navel-gazing was stopped by the door swinging open to reveal Pipes, already in the act of lighting up his e-cigarette. As the whiff of candy floss floated from a cloud of smoke, Pete wondered just what flavours the marketing whizz kids would dream up next.

'You two escaping the madness then? You've just missed two of Fergyl's sisters doing the Can-Can.'

With a roll of the eyes that clearly indicated that Marcie would not be losing any sleep over missing out on that particular spectacle, she said 'I'm impressed that you lasted nearly an hour Pipes without resorting to dashing out here for a crafty blast on your smoking stick.'

'It will only be a quick one' he replied, inhaling great lungfuls of sickly smelling smoke, 'they're about to start on the buffet.'

Coughing as they headed back to The Swan's main door, Pete said 'smells like you've started on dessert already Pipes.'

## Chapter 22

Pete was back at the mic for Old School's second set. 'OK everybody, we're back. Fergyl has just asked me to say a big thank you to Stan who not only arranged the buffet but also paid for it.'

A cacophony of clapping and cheering echoed around the pub, with Stan raising his hand self-consciously to acknowledge the thanks.

'So, we're going to play another couple of numbers before Fergyl comes up here to say a few words about his dad.' A count on the sticks from Pipes and they were into What Difference Does it Make. Michael, apparently now four-sheets to the wind, grabbed a daffodil from the vase of freshly cut flowers on the bar, stuck it into the back pocket of his trousers and started to strut about like a constipated peacock. Several of the guests joined him on the make-shift dancefloor, a tiny area in front of the band that the crowd were valiantly trying to keep clear for those revellers who had decided to strut their stuff. One benefit to the tightness of the space was that it tended to curtail Michael's stuff.

Pete took a surreptitious glance across at Mark whose grim features, complete with tongue peeking from between tightly compressed lips, showed just how much he was concentrating on the bassline. Though it wasn't perfect, Pete thought so far so good.

Michael clearly did not have the surname Flatley. His Morrissey impression involved simply walking up and down in front of the band, bumping into those trying to dance, interspersed with him tunelessly joining in with the What Difference Does it Make line whenever Old School reached the chorus. Conversely, a lady who looked like she was well into her seventh decade was swaying from side to side, eyes closed and mouthing pretty much all the words, surprising Pete that The Smiths' classic had such appeal with this particular demographic. But then Jack had taken to playing Meat is Murder, originally to vocalise his newly found vegetarianism and it was still very much a staple emanating from his bedroom lair. This was more than 30 years after the album's release. Apparently, the kings of introspective indie teenage angst had an audience that extended well beyond 80s teenagers.

Next up it was Pete's turn to concentrate hard as he tried to replicate the iconic intro riff to Lynyrd Skynyrd's classic Sweet Home Alabama. He thought he'd got away with until he played a jarring G# instead of a G, casting a glance at Marcie who mouthed 'yes, heard that one.'

The mourners were now really getting into celebratory mode, with one of Fergyl's brothers leading the charge in an alternative chorus of Sweet Home County Clare. Rather than go up against the newly appropriated Irish version with his own vocal, Pete decided to go with it. Pipes' dismissal of the song as 'Southern Hippy Shit' when they had originally discussed what songs Old School would play had surely not been a reference to Southern Ireland?

Pete's thanks to the assembled throng were difficult to hear over the cheering that came at the end of a reinterpretation which relocated Alabama some 4,000 miles across the Atlantic. He waited for the noise to subside. 'Thanks, you're all very kind. And now I'd like to welcome Fergyl up here.'

The whoops and clapping resumed as Fergyl waved and made his way to the front. It reminded Pete of a Best Supporting Actor's celebratory walk to the stage at the BAFTAs, with people slapping him on the back and grinning encouragingly as he squeezed his way through the crowd.

'Right, is this thing on?' A squeal of feedback as Fergyl yanked the mic from the stand confirmed that it was indeed on. 'Right, settle down, settle down and let's have a few words to remind us of why we're here. My Da. What a man!' Fergyl pointed to Pete's t-shirt, inciting a fresh round of cheering and rapturous applause. He lowered his hands repeatedly to quell the tumult. 'We obviously can't all get up to speak as we'd be here all night so I'd just like to pay a tribute to my Da on behalf of my sisters and brothers. So that would be Bridget, Keira, Aileen, Sinead, Regan, Sean, Conor, Ryan and Darragh.'

Fergyl pointedly counted the names off on his fingers, bringing more laughter from his audience. This went up a notch when he looked quizzically at a single remaining finger before adding 'Oh, sorry Declan, I didn't see you over there. I thought there was one more.'

It was like watching a stand-up comedian, one who had honed his craft and was as well-versed in the physical comedy trigger points as he was the vocal.

He continued in a similar vein, at times eliciting real belly laughs. The crescendo had been reached when he told the tale of a young and newly married Chas arriving home dripping wet when there had not been a cloud in a cobalt blue west Ireland sky. He delivered the tale in a dead-pan fashion, adopting the demeanour of his father in explaining his state to his wife. Chas' talented eldest could also add 'mimic' to his list of talents as he captured the essence of his dear-departed dad to a tee, even dropping his voice an octave to imitate his raspy tone.

'I was cycling down through the lanes of Ballyvaughan, down by O'Shaughnessy's Farm, just past the far field. I'd picked up that pheasant that young Patrick had promised me and was carrying it over me handlebars. The feckin thing's head only went and lodged itself in the spokes of me front wheel. Next thing I know I'm lying in a workman's hole they'd been digging up on Apple Pie Lane, bloody soaked to the skin. I said to Ma it's not feckin funny woman. You could have been a widow and then you'd be laughing on the other side of your face.'

Pete, along with many others, had tears streaming down his face. With a shaking hand he raised his pint of Theakstons as Fergyl toasted the memory of his father with a hearty 'Sláinte!'

## Chapter 23

Pete was seated at the kitchen table, scrolling through his e-mails. Since retiring he had managed to get out of the work habit of constantly checking to see what was required of him, interrupting yet again his planned workload for the day. With workload no longer being part of his regular vocabulary, he had settled into a routine of perusing them just once a day.

He deleted several spam e-mails, including one which invited him to rate some online purchase that he couldn't even remember having made. There was one from the garage reminding him that the service was due on his Audi A6 Avant and another from his mum. He speed-read the latter which detailed the latest saga about the woman next door who had been trimming the dividing privet hedge again without any reference to them. Apparently, Pete's dad Malcolm was to be sent round to have a word.

Pete still struggled with the concept of his parents using e-mail and always read them, even if he often glazed over, as he knew just how long it would have taken them to type it. Watching his mum's index finger search her iPad for a 'g' compared to the warp factor speed of both Charlie and Jack when texting was like pitting a Sinclair C5 against a Porsche 911.

Not recognising the name of the sender, he was just about to delete another e-mail as spam when the subject line made him stop just before the click of the mouse assigned it to cyber oblivion. 'A chance to put your band on the map!' He opened it, wondering how they knew he had a band but quickly presumed it was yet another example of the digital footprint that he left through his internet browsing history.

He took a long draught from his Nespresso Roma and let his mind drift back to a recent call from Kathy, one of his old work colleagues. She had been bemoaning the new GDPR regulations and how the agency now had to jump through hoops in making sure that their digital marketing campaigns for clients did not infringe the new rules. From what Pete had read, the objective of GDPR had been to reduce the number of unsolicited e-mails clogging up everybody's in-boxes. As far as he could tell, it wasn't working. He still received invitations to see what people he couldn't even recall were up to on LinkedIn, opportunities to invest in a sure-fire property development in southern China and the chance to give himself the erection of an 18-year-old with the help of a virtual doctor.

Given that he spent a good 50 percent of his online life drooling over guitars, watching bands and seeing what gigs were upcoming, he concluded that it was not unreasonable to suspect that somebody, somewhere had given his details to almpromotions.com, probably making a few pence in the process.

He read through the e-mail, the essence of which was that they were launching a Battle of the Bands, a national competition to find 'the UK's best amateur band'. This had Pete recollecting a series he'd watched and thoroughly enjoyed on the BBC. It had seen host Rhod Gilbert, one of his favourite comedians, travelling the length and breadth of the country on a road-trip to discover 'The UK's Best Part-Time Band'. It had aired before the chance meeting with his old friend Pipes had set in motion the formation of Old School. If he'd been watching it now, he felt he would have a more informed critique to add to those of Rhod's guest judges Midge Ure, Peter Hook and Jazzie B.

This new competition appeared to be a complete rip-off of the BBC's idea, presumably ALM Promotions seeing an opportunity when the Beeb decided against recommissioning Rhod and his cohorts for another series. Pete mused that surely this had not been down to Peter Hook's over-committed diary.

Having worked for so long in advertising, he knew that truly original ideas were few and far between. He and Pudding had been guilty on several occasions of 'borrowing' from other campaigns that they admired, though it had only once resulted in a copyright claim against H,H&H. Pete had thought of it more as an homage to a creative concept that he admired rather than downright plagiarism. And anyway, in the case of ALM Promotions, who was he to worry if it was treading on the BBC's toes? The idea of a battle of the bands had been around for years so the Beeb could hardly lay claim to being great innovators themselves.

The e-mail invited any amateur band resident in the UK to fill in an online form and send it through to an e-mail address to have the chance to be selected. There was not even the requirement of an mp3 of the band playing; just a few basic details, including brief background info on the members. He had nothing planned until the afternoon when he had allotted a couple of hours to tackle the blackberry bushes that were threatening to take over the garden. So, nothing ventured, nothing gained.

## Chapter 24

Pete, Mark, Pudding and Pipes were huddled around a table in The King George, a rather non-descript pub in Watford. Pete had driven Mark and Pipes down for a get-together with Pudding who, unusually, had not been able to make the journey north due to a work commitment. He was in the middle of an exhibition of his College students' work and had been unable to pull one of his regular sickies that allowed him to get up to Leamington for an Old School evening out and/or practice during term time. Pete had therefore said that if the mountain could not come to Muhammad...

Pudding was currently holding court about the state of education and of his own students in particular. 'You wouldn't believe the shit they've come up with. I gave them a really interesting brief to design a page advertisement that latched onto the revival in vinyl records. A few of the truly useless ones didn't even know what vinyl was so I sent them off to do a bit of research. It will do them good to realise there is life beyond downloads and streaming. Of those that did know what I was talking about, I reckon a good half of them came up with a round page design when there's no fucking way a magazine will be able to accommodate that format. And I'm then having to exhibit this crap at the town hall.'

Not for the first time Pete wondered if Pudding was really cut-out to be a college lecturer. His antipathy towards children was legendary and, having never had any of his own, he was one of the most intolerant people Pete had ever met when it came to the nation's future generation. A health scare and his need to reduce the stress levels of a career at the coalface of advertising had led him to take up the position as a lecturer in media studies at a sixth form college. It might have been reasonable to assume that more than five years of exposure to teenagers could have softened his attitude and brought out a desire to nurture the advertising moguls of tomorrow. In fact, if anything, he had become even more entrenched with his nihilistic views and a belief that the world of advertising had effectively ended when he decided to hang up his digital paintbrush.

Pete did wonder at indulging in a bit of banter, challenging Pudding with the fact that surely it was up to him as their lecturer to make sure that they didn't make simple mistakes. Pudding had been an excellent creative force and if he could pass on some of his experience and wisdom to his students, then surely that would be more rewarding than just haranguing them. But he decided against poking the hornet's nest, not because he would not have enjoyed the inevitable resulting tirade but rather because he had an agenda of his own.

'So, gentlemen, what are you all doing on 7$^{th}$ July?' he asked.

Pudding, clearly worked up into combative mode by his state of the nation address was the first to respond. 'Harsy, don't tell me that you've actually got something in your calendar?'

Pete's retired status and having plenty of time on his hands with nothing to fill it was a regular topic of ridicule from his friends. 'Well, I have as it happens, and so have you if you're man enough to take up the gauntlet.' Pete now had the table's undivided attention. He decided to eek it out a little. 'A few weeks ago, I was sitting at my kitchen table, having a cup of coffee. A Roma I think it was as we'd run out of my favourite, Livanto. It was Tuesday, might have been a Wednesday. Actually, it must have been a Wednesday as Jack came back and he has a free period after his morning lecture on sociology.'

A roll of the eyes from Pudding showed he knew exactly what he was up to.

'OK, I'll put you out of your misery. Cutting to the chase, I completed an application form for a Battle of the Bands competition and really thought nothing more about it. Last week I had an e-mail inviting us to compete in the Midlands' heat.'

'You what?' said Pipes, putting down a bag of pickled onion flavoured Monster Munch and sucking his fingers to make sure there was no wastage.

'Yep, Old School have been invited to take part in a national competition to find the UK's best amateur band.'

It had taken less than 30 seconds for Mark to take on the pallor of a ghost that had itself seen a ghost.

## Chapter 25

Pete was driving up the M6. Seated to his left was Pudding and in the bench seat behind were Pipes and Mark. He was doing a good 80mph, unusual at any time on one of Europe's busiest stretches of motorway but even more impressive given that he was at the wheel of a rather battered looking Ford Transit.

The destination was the Birmingham Arena where the Midlands heat of ALM's Battle of the Bands was being held. Pete had been contacted by Tash, one of the competition's researchers, to outline what was expected of them. He had anticipated having to bring just their guitars and Pipes' breakables - drum sticks, cymbals and snare - with a backline of amps and the rest of a drum-kit provided by ALM. However, Tash had explained that in order to get all the bands auditioned, there would be simultaneous sessions held throughout the day so each band needed to bring all of their own gear and set it up themselves. Hence the Transit.

They could have managed with three cars, particularly since Pete's swapping of his Mercedes Coupe for a '64 plate Audi estate. This had been partly an economy drive but also because it was eminently more practical for transporting the increasing amount of kit they seemed to be accumulating. However, by borrowing the van from his mate Tim who ran a window installation company, Pete also realised that they could all travel together and have a bit of band-bonding time. So, as a Wigston's Windows liveried van whizzed past Fort Dunlop, the silence was deafening.

It had all started fairly positively, with them all chipping in with loading the gear into the back of the van. But the spirit of positivity and comradery had proved somewhat short-lived. The normal edgy banter between Pudding and Pipes had been expected, and indeed welcomed, but when Pudding had irritably told Pipes to 'fuck off' when instructed that he needed to make sure he tightened up his rhythm guitar playing on Mr Brightside, the air had turned a little frosty. Pete realised that they were all nervous as the impending audition drew ever closer and Pipes should have been a little more aware of that in his choice of words and subject matter. But then he had not really inherited the consideration gene.

Pipes had retreated into a family bag of cheese and onion crisps. This had prompted a polite request, but a request nonetheless, from Mark, a man for whom the term shy and retiring had been invented. He asked Pipes if he minded putting his crisps to one side for a few minutes as he was feeling a little queasy. Mark's nerves were clearly already getting the better of him and the aroma from Pipes' crisp of choice on this particular occasion was evidently not helping.

With a 'Jesus, it's just a bag of crisps Mark', Pipes stuffed the half-eaten packet down the side of his seat.

This prompted Pete to say 'Bloody hell Pipes, this is a mate's van I've borrowed. Can you try not to treat it like your own dustbin on wheels.'

This had further elevated an already tense mood. So, when Pudding's navigation skills in following Google Maps given that the van had no sat nav resulted in them heading south on the M6 rather than North, the atmosphere had moved to Defcon 1. Not a word had been spoken for some 15 minutes now.

'Pete, Pete, can we stop please?' The content of the comment from Mark didn't really register with Pete as he was just delighted that the uncomfortable silence had been broken.

'Sorry, Mark, what was that?'

'Can we pull over – now!'

Pete heard the sense of urgency in his voice and Mark, being the furthest from a drama queen of anybody that Pete knew, he immediately slowed down and moved into the inside lane. 'Sorry Mark but unless it's a full-blown emergency, I can't. The Smart Motorway System is active so there is no hard shoulder. Any chance you can wait a minute?'

The sound of the window being wrenched open suggested not. Mark stuck his head out and proceeded to empty the contents of his stomach in a technicolour yawn all down the side of the van. Pete glanced in his rear-view mirror to see a man swerve and angrily gesticulate from the window of his BMW M3 Convertible, the windscreen of which he was hastily trying to clear. The effect of his wipers was largely to just smear Mark's semi-digested cooked breakfast in greasy streaks. Pete couldn't help but think that the angry driver should be thanking his lucky stars that he didn't have the top down.

Pudding asked Mark if he was OK but Pipes was already doubled up with laughter.

'Yes, sorry everybody but I'm feeling a lot better for that. Does anybody have a Wet Wipe?'

Hilarity erupted around the van and the atmosphere switched back to a decidedly more relaxed Defcon 5.

## Chapter 26

Gary Barlow's dulcet Northern tones rang out with 'Today, this could be, the greatest day of our lives.' Though Pete was no fan of Take That, he felt changing his ringtone for the day might raise a smile. Glancing at the screen he saw 'Tash – BoB'. 'Pudding, can you get that for me? I couldn't work out how to pair my phone with the van's Bluetooth.'

'Hello, this is Mr Harriman's PA' said Pudding, smirking as he did so. 'Ah, hello Tash. This is Charlton, sorry but Pete is driving…Yes Pete mentioned you…According to Google Maps we should be with you in about 20 minutes.'

After a brief conversation, Pudding ended the call and then relayed the basics of the conversation to everybody. Tash had been calling to see how far away they were as the auditions were running behind schedule. She had reckoned Old School's audition would now be about 2.30pm rather than the originally scheduled slot of 1.00pm. There then followed a discussion between the four of them as to what to do with the time.

Pudding had been up for a beer but Pipes had interjected. 'You know I like a pint as much as the next man and while I would love one to perhaps wash down a nice pub lunch, I reckon we should put the time to good use. We'd built in an hour to set up all the kit but if we now have an extra hour and a half, I reckon we should use that to make sure our sound is as good as it can be.'

They had all agreed, this time Pipes having unusually taken a decidedly more conciliatory tone and Pudding electing to bow to his greater experience of playing in bands. Harmony reigned.

Despite Pudding's declaration that a trail of puke down the side of the van would make them look edgy, Pete had found a garage with a hand car wash. Mark insisted on washing the van himself, saying that the fresh air and the spray from the lance would do him good. Pipes appointed himself as official lunch monitor and headed for the forecourt shop to see what delights he could find. Five minutes later and courtesy of Pipes each member of Old School was furnished with a Ginsters' pasty, a jumbo sausage roll, a family bag of crisps, a bottle of Coke and a caramel flapjack. Mark had accepted them graciously but said he'd be leaving his till later.

With only a minor wrong turn which saw them heading for a Bus Lane on Broad Street, they soon rectified the situation, with no recriminations this time for Pudding's lack of Google map-reading skills. Pete wondered just how much it was hurting Pipes to reign in his natural inclination to bait his sparring partner at every opportunity.

They arrived in the designated bands' car park, clearly sign-posted with a huge map of the UK and the strapline 'A chance to put your band on the map!' which Pete immediately recognised from the original e-mail. There were several cars, mainly estates, along with numerous vans, including a gleaming black one professionally sign-written with The Scarlet Charlottes in striking red lettering.

'Jesus, the fucking A Team are here. Harsy, you did say this competition was for amateur bands, didn't you?'

'Come on Pudding, remember that Marketing Manager from the mobile phone company we did some work for? Looked like he'd just finished chatting with Don Draper on the set of Mad Men. Also seemed to have all the patter but was booted out after only six months. Just because you look the part, it doesn't mean you are any good. You know the old saying 'All the gear, no idea'.'

As they stepped out of the van, Pudding replied 'Fine, I'll give you that one. But you'd better change that frigging ringtone before we go in. If it goes off in front of anybody, then the little street-cred we might have had will be straight out the window. We don't want people thinking we are Take That's fucking dads.'

## Chapter 27

'Old School, Old School?' A lad who looked about 14, identified as Barney from the ALM lanyard hanging from his neck, was checking his list and was onto the third page. For an awful moment Pete wondered if he had been hallucinating and they had never been invited to audition. Despite the conversations with Tash ringing in his head, it didn't stop a feeling of paranoia creep up his spine and into the back of his neck, the famous Bobby Ewing shower scene in Dallas bubbling to the surface.

Just as Pete was about to grab the list from the sweaty hands of Barney, he said 'OK. Yeah – here it is Old School. Sick name.'

Pete elected not to mention the aptness of Barney's comment given Mark's exploits on the M6.

Old School were then delivered into the hands of Tamzin, an effervescent South African with pink and purple hair and a quantity of piercings that Pete thought must prove a challenge at airport security. The tattoo of a scorpion on her neck seemed to be crawling towards her ear. Good luck with that mused Pete, with the amount of metal presenting a heavily fortified entrance. They walked past several rooms, with varying degrees of noise spilling from them, until they reached '17 A'.

'OK, this is us' said Tamzin, glancing at her iPad and coming to a halt. 'If you want to go and fetch your gear and I'll meet you back here.'

Three trips later and Old School were reassembled in the room, surrounded by their amps, mic stands, guitar cases, the constituent parts of the drum kit and Pipes' latest pride and joy, a shiny 16-input Behringer mixing desk. 45 minutes later and they were set up and ready for a sound check. Another hour and they were about ready to rock. The intervening hour had been spent with Pipes adjusting the mixer's faders, Pipes and Pudding squabbling about the volume of Pudding's guitar and Mark making several trips to the Gents.

Just as Pudding was advising Pipes that he was 'a condescending twat', the door opened and in walked three people.

'So, Old School, I'm hoping?' said a 20-something girl looking down at her iPad. She had apparently not heard the drummer/rhythm guitarist spat or, if she had, then she had the good grace to gloss over it. 'Which one of you guys is Pete?'

'That would be me' said Pete, putting down his guitar and extending his hand.

'Hi Pete, great to meet you. Tash – we spoke on the phone. And this is Will and Jeff.'

Introductions were made to everybody and then Will took control of proceedings. He was very tall and gaunt, with a receding hairline and the slight stoop that is a common trait in those who tower above the vast majority of the people they meet. Pete felt his day-dreaming gene kick in, thinking 'a tall Steve Lamacq with a beard', before forcing himself to focus.

'Right guys, sorry that this is a bit later than your original slot but if we can crack on. If you're ready, then if you give us what you consider to be your two best songs. The floor is, as they say, yours.'

Will's colleague Jeff looked like an accountant. He was dressed in a smart suit, with large horn-rimmed glasses and what looked like plastic shoes. Appearing to not want to be left out of the equation, he added 'just imagine we're not here.'

Pete thought 'Uncle Edmund 10 years ago', despite his sub-conscious yelling at him to focus. The look that Will shot Jeff suggested that he wished he was not here.

'Right you are' said Pete, wondering why he was suddenly talking like his dad and smashing any semblance of rock n roll cool that he might have otherwise projected. 'Pipes?'

A four count on the sticks and they started up Mr Brightside. This had been the topic that had resulted in the 'condescending twat' outburst. The band had been debating which two songs to play, with the three contenders being Block Buster by The Sweet, The Kinks' You Really Got Me and Mr Brightside from The Killers. The effort of Pipes to maintain relative harmony had just proved too great and when he'd voted for Mr Brightside, almost like a man with Tourette's he had blurted out 'as long as Pudding can sort out his guitar on the lead break.'

Despite the inauspicious murmurings, or perhaps because he was fuelled by a determination to silence Pipes, Pudding had played well throughout and they had done a decent job of delivering an Old School version of The Killers' anthem. As the resounding final chords echoed around the room, Pete was not sure what to expect from their sparse audience. With Tash tapping away on her screen, Will just said 'Nice. And the next one please.'

This time Pete started with the iconic riff intro to You Really Got Me. Halfway through Pete glanced across at Mark who had beads of sweat breaking out on his forehead. Hoping to God that this was not the pre-cursor to him revisiting his jumbo sausage roll, the only item that he'd managed to eat from Pipes' extensive catering foraging, Pete looked back at their audience. There was an encouraging smile from Tash but completely blank expressions from both Jeff and Will. Pete did not know what to think: were they just being deliberately inscrutable, were they punch-drunk from sitting through so many auditions or were Old School just crap?

Four cymbal crashes from Pipes brought their second offering to a close. Still looking completely indifferent and as if it was a physical effort to even talk, Will said 'well thank you so much gentlemen. We'll now be having a conflab with the other judges for the day and we'll be getting back to you. I'll leave Tash here to explain what happens next.'

Tash thanked Will and Jeff as they turned and left the room before excusing herself for a quick trip to the loo before she filled them in.

'Well that's fucking that' said Pipes, throwing his sticks to the floor like a petulant toddler.

'Shut the fuck up' retorted Pudding in an angry whisper 'they might be outside the door.'

Lowering his voice slightly, Pipes said 'Does it really fucking matter? There's no way they are going to put us through. Did you see the look on that Will's face? He couldn't have a less apt name if he tried – he looked like he'd lost the fucking will to live.'

Pete did not want this to descend into another Pipes/Pudding verbal barrage so cut it short with 'Let's just wait and see, shall we?'

## Chapter 28

Tash had returned from her comfort break to explain that the numerous judges who had been viewing the various bands' efforts throughout the day would now be getting together to produce a shortlist. The shortlisted bands would be asked to play again on stage in the Arena's main performance area. The judges would then have another round of deliberations to decide the winner of the Midlands' heat who would go through to the national Grand Final at Wembley Arena to compete for the title UK's Best Amateur Band.

She had advised that they should hear within the hour if they had made the cut. In the meantime, if they wanted to put their gear away, then there was a bar at the end of the corridor in which a drink for all the members of the competing bands was available with the compliments of ALM Promotions. Having handed Pete four printed drinks tokens, with a cheery wave, Tash was gone.

'That's the last we'll be seeing of her' said a morose Pipes.

'Will you just shut the fuck up, you miserable fucking fucker' exploded Pudding. 'How the hell do you know that we haven't made it through?'

'Well, the fact that she's asked us to pack up our gear for one.'

Pudding was stumped by that one and, very unusually, was lost for a response.

Pete decided to intercede. 'Look, even if we haven't made it through, it's been an opportunity to play and an experience that I, for one, wouldn't have missed.'

Mark meekly added 'me too.'

'Mark, you reckon being sick with nerves all day, throwing up over a BMW and trembling like a leaf throughout the performance is your idea of a good time. Jesus, I wouldn't like to be with you when you're having a bad day.'

As Mark looked like he was about to burst into tears Pete said 'Pipes, that's enough. It's not helping. We are all disappointed but let's just go to the bar and have a beer.'

'That's a great idea Harsy, let's all just get bladdered.'

'Well, perhaps not all of us. Remember one of us, i.e. me, is driving the van back.'

Having packed away all their gear in the van, Old School were now standing dispiritedly at the bar. Around 200 people were in there which, assuming an average of four in a band, meant around 50 bands had auditioned. Pete ordered three pints of Stella and a Carlsberg shandy, all of them turning up their noses at the bitter on offer. They were all in plastic glasses, an indicator that the bar was used to serving drinks to crowds that were not averse to filling them with recycled beer and hurling them in the direction of the stage.

Pete raised his 'glass' and said, with a cheeriness that he hoped wasn't too false, 'Cheers gents.'

They all raised their pints, Pipes and Pudding somewhat reluctantly, not bothering to try and chink as the plastic was never going to make that satisfying sound and anyway, just gripping them without squashing the flimsy receptacle and spilling the contents was proving a challenge in itself.

'For what it's worth, I thought we played well' said Pete, leading the way to a table in the corner and taking a seat.

There then followed a good 20 minutes of navel-gazing as they discussed the highs and lows of their performance, with Pipes focusing very much on the lows. Despite his obvious irritation at the miserable drummer's comments, Pudding managed to keep himself largely in check, conscious that airing the band's dirty washing in public was not the best course of action.

Pipes was halfway through his fourth beer when a guy with hair almost down to his waist asked 'Anybody sittin' 'ere mate?'

'No, help yourself' said Pipes, making room for the not inconsiderable frame of Hairy Guy to pull up a chair.

'Nails, over 'ere mate' shouted Hairy Guy, waving to a similarly hirsute individual who was trying his best not to crush two pints of beer between massive hands. As Nails took a seat, Hairy Guy introduced himself. 'Colin, but me friends call me Spanner.'

'Alright, err, Spanner' said Pipes not sure if he had already been welcomed into the inner circle.

'This 'ere is Nails, aka Simon.'

Over the next 10 minutes, Old School learned that Nails and Spanner were a duo called Smash It Up, a nihilistic post-punk thrash metal band from the Black Country.

'So, how do you reckon you got on?' said Pipes, now well into his fifth pint.

'We'm don't think ALM Promotions am quite ready for post-punk thrash' said Spanner in a thick Yam Yam accent, ruefully stroking his ZZ-Top beard.

Any further deliberations on the inability of people to appreciate the somewhat niche talents of Smash It Up were halted by a loud 'Can I have your attention please everybody. The judges have made their decision so if you could all just listen out for your names.'

## Chapter 29

Tash had read out two lists of bands and asked those from list A to make their way into Conference Room 1 and those on list B to head to Conference Room 2. There had been a few stand-out names, including The Screaming AbDabs and Chunky Funky Monkey. Old School were in List B along with, Pete noted, The Scarlet Charlottes.

Pipes had also made the same mental note and, as he downed the last of his pint, said 'Looks like you were right Harsy – all the gear and no idea.' Pudding stood up, giving Pipes daggers. They all trudged rather dejectedly out of the bar and along the corridor.

Standing at the front of the room were several people in ALM lanyards who Pete presumed were the judges. Will stepped forward and started to speak, prompting a muttered 'that's all we need' from Pipes.

'Ladies and Gentlemen, first of all can I thank every one of you for taking the time and effort to enter the competition. It's been a long day for many of you, and for us, but we have all enjoyed listening to you play. We know it's not easy to put yourselves out there to be judged and it's been a tough decision for all of us.' He pointedly looked around his fellow judges, many of whom nodded in silent agreement. 'However, the nature of competitions is that there are, inevitably, winners and losers. That's not to say those that aren't going through are not good musicians in their own right. It's just that perhaps they weren't quite what we were looking for this time around.'

'Come on mate, just tell it like it is rather than sugar-coating it you patronising bastard' whispered Pipes, drawing a glare from Pudding.

'So', continued Will 'to the results. As I said, my fellow judges and I have deliberated long and hard. The standard was very high and we have had some interesting discussions about what we've seen today.'

'For fucks sake' hissed Pipes.

'After a lot of argument and counter-argument, I'm delighted to tell you that you are the bands that have made it onto our shortlist.'

Shouts, screams and general mayhem engulfed the room. A pixie-like girl with bright red dreadlocks ran up and hugged a clearly uncomfortable Will as she squealed at an impressive volume. After an initial look of incredulity, Pipes had grabbed Pete, Pudding and Mark around the neck and they bounced madly around the room like some eight-armed, eight-legged kangaroo on ecstasy.

'Yeeessss. Yeeessss' cried Pipes, 'You fucking beauty.'

As a degree of calm started to slowly return to the room, Will said, extricating himself from the embrace, 'OK, OK everybody. Settle down please. Congratulations again but we now need to go to the next stage of our process. As I'm sure Tash here and her colleagues explained to you, we need to see you all play again. If you can make your way through to the main arena, you'll see we have a full stage set-up. You'll all be asked to perform just one of your songs this time, one band at a time. So, to help us keep things moving as quickly as possible, if you could all get your instruments; no amps or mics required and drummers, you'll need only your snare and cymbals as we have a full kit already set up for you.'

Pudding raised his eyebrows at Pipes, now having the answer to his question as to why they had been asked to return their gear to the van.

The bands all filed out of the conference room, the noise levels rising again as the euphoria kicked back in. As Pete opened the double doors leading out into the car park, he spotted Spanner leaving Conference Room A, flicking the v's at the judges as he left and in his strong Black Country accent giving them some useful advice. 'Fuck yous. Yam all fucking idiots and wouldn't know a decent band if you fell over 'un. You ain't 'eard the last of Smash It Up. We'm the future.'

## Chapter 30

Old School trouped back into the building and headed for a set of double doors that led off the corridor. They entered what was a truly staggering space. 'Jesus' said Pudding, almost dropping his guitar case, 'you've got to be fucking kidding.'

They all scanned around an arena with steeply raked seats disappearing into apparent infinity, incredulous that they were soon to be playing, admittedly not to a capacity crowd of 15,000 but nonetheless…

A young runner with the requisite ALM lanyard scampered enthusiastically up to them. 'Old School, isn't it?'

'Err, yes said Pete', still trying to take in the sheer scale of their surroundings.

There was a slight squeak from Mark before he headed at a rate of knots for the doors through which they'd just come.

'Is he OK?' said the runner, watching Mark as he barged open the doors.

'Oh yes, he'll be fine. He's feeling the after-effects of a dodgy kebab that he had last night' said Pete, keen to hide the fact that Mark was clearly scared shitless. He then realised that the alternate image he'd created was the polar opposite of shitless, with the runner presumably now trying to dispel a mental picture of Mark with his trollies around his ankles recreating the Trumpet Voluntary into the bowl of one of the Arena's many toilets.

'Oh, OK' said the runner self-consciously, 'we are running to a tight schedule so if you can make your way over to the stage, then I'll wait here until your friend is err…...' He was clearly struggling to find the right word, settling with 'finished' and blushing when he realised that he could perhaps have plumped for something better.

As they walked across what Pete presumed would ordinarily be the standing area, complete with mosh-pit for the more raucous of gigs, he could feel the sense of trepidation in all of them. It had rendered both Pipes and Pudding speechless, not a condition he was used to experiencing with either of them.

The stage was set up as if for a full gig. There were twin towering speaker stacks either side of the stage, with a series of monitors at the front and a full lighting rig bathing the stage in a pale green glow. Bright white spotlights picked out the points where the band members would be positioned.

Yet another lanyard-clad member of the ALM team came over to them. 'Hi, I'm Kiki and I'm the Stage Manager. Great to meet you.' Clearly recognising the collective rabbits caught in the headlights look of Pete, Pudding and Pipes, she quickly added 'don't worry, we won't be using the full set-up. Those speaker stacks were installed yesterday for Iron Maiden who will be playing tomorrow night. We'll just be using the much smaller speakers that you can see at the side of the stage.'

Pete experienced a mix of relief, tinged with a sense of regret that he would not be able to say that they had played through Iron Maiden's rig. It was, though, mostly relief.

Directly in front of the stage were about 10 chairs, with another 100 or so set up behind. 'We did a draw' said Kiki, re-focusing their attention briefly from the setup, 'and you'll be on second, after…' she glanced down at her iPad '…The Scarlet Charlottes.' Pete spotted Pudding's Adam's Apple bob like a Granny Smith at a Halloween dunking competition as he silently gulped. Kiki continued 'If you'd like to take a seat over there while we sort out a few things,' pointing to the three rows of seats set up in consecutive semi-circles behind the prime slots directly in front of the stage.

The area being used was a fraction of the arena's cavernous space but ALM Promotions had tried their best to make it feel as cosy as possible, setting up screens behind the temporary seats to bring the focus onto the area immediately in front of the stage. The fact that you could obviously see the great expanse of seats over the top of the screens meant that it had effectively been an impossible task.

As Pete took a seat halfway down the second set of chairs, he realised that he was breathing heavily, not quite hyper-ventilating but not far from it. Pudding took a chair next to him, whispering 'Harsy, for fucks sake, what have you got us into?'

Plonking himself down heavily next to Pudding, Pipes leaned over and with beer laden breath soothed 'don't worry lads, we'll be fine.'

Pete knew that Pipes was by far the most confident of performers in the Old School quartet, but this was brave even for him. The five pints of lager was clearly having a calming effect. Pete wondered if there was time for him to rush to the bar for a quick stiffener.

Pete glanced across the floor to see Mark making his way unsteadily towards them. Pete waved with a false sense of cheeriness, but it did nothing to dispel the ghostly apparition that was Mark. Even under the dimly-lit area reserved for spectating he looked like Marcel Marceau. Pete wondered what he was going to look like under the spotlights, what effect they might have on his delicate constitution and how the hell they were going to make it through this.

## Chapter 31

The members of Old School were standing in the wings, watching The Scarlet Charlottes and awaiting their own turn to take to the hallowed stage. Despite his terror, Pete's natural inclination for his mind to wander was intact and he was wondering just who of his musical heroes he would now be following in the footsteps of. The Arena was one of the few venues in Birmingham where Pete had never attended a gig, so he had no direct experience to draw from. But he knew from his friend Dave that The Killers had performed here only last year and now he was about to do his own version of Brandon Flowers' vocal. Oh god, that particular thought brought him very much back to the reality of the here and now. He gripped even tighter on the neck of his Telecaster, wondering just what had he been thinking of all those weeks ago when he had filled in the entry form?

Standing to his left, Pudding was just silently staring at The Charlotte's rhythm guitarist, hoping by some form of musical osmosis that the confidence of his playing would somehow seep into his own body. Mark was standing a few feet back, almost in a catatonic state, the rise and fall of his chest being the only indication that he was still in the land of the living. Pete thought that had Las Ramblas in Barcelona been searching for an addition to its famous living statue performers, if they required a shit-scared bass player then they need look no further.

Pipes was the only one amongst them who seemed to be embracing the moment. 'Harsy, this is fucking brilliant. Who'd have thought 18 months ago that we'd be about to step onto a stage that Iron Maiden will be performing on in 24 hours' time? This is mad.' Though he was not slurring his words, his eyes had a slightly glazed look about them. Turning his attention to The Charlottes, Pipes said 'I know it's hard to tell from here as we don't get the full effect of their performance out front, but I don't reckon they are that good. Style over substance, eh? - all the gear no idea, all the gear no idea.' Pipes had started to get into a slow rhythmical chant, prompting a sharp look from Pete that had the desired effect.

A resounding high note that even from the side of the stage was impressive signalled that The Charlottes had finished their self-penned song. Pete caught Will's distant voice saying 'Thanks lads. Great performance.'

As they left the stage, in normal circumstances Pete would have been quick to congratulate The Charlottes. But these were hardly normal circumstances. All he could manage was a nod at the lead singer, his mouth dry and his lips seemingly stuck together as if he'd been silenced like the poor bastard who'd had his lips sewn shut in Saw IV. At the moment, Pete thought taking on the role of one of Jigsaw's victims was probably preferable to what he was about to face.

Before he knew it Pete was standing in the spotlight at the front of the stage. He could not really remember how he got there but there he was. A technician was busily plugging in his guitar while a friendly face had appeared from nowhere. Tash handed him a bottle of water, gave him a wink and reassuringly said 'you'll be great.'

While Pete was not sure of its factual accuracy, he appreciated the sentiment of Tash's comment and it somehow shook him from his stupor. He took a big slug of water as his inner voice said 'Come on Pete, get your arse into gear. You may never have an opportunity like this again? Man the fuck up!'

From the centre of the row of seats in front of the stage Will looked left and right at his fellow judges and, satisfied that they were suitably focused, said 'OK, Old School, ready when you are.'

## Chapter 32

A count on the sticks and Old School were into yet another Mr Brightside. All was going well and Pete was actually starting to get lost in the performance and enjoy himself. He stole a glance at Pudding whose sweat-soaked face had little to do with the spotlight that was shining down on his bald pate. Mark was standing stock still, playing what sounded like the right notes on his bass but staring out into space, still in an almost catatonic state.

Pete was reminded of Ron Mael who, with his brother Russell, had formed 70's synth-pop duo Sparks. Ron, with his Hitler toothbrush moustache, had cornered the market in scowling intently from behind his synthesiser, looking like he was planning to murder everybody who had come to see them. Mark's look was more blank than menace but there was a certain similarity in performance values.

Pete was just reaching for the high notes of '…it's killing me' when there was a clatter and the drums just stopped. He heard a 'fuck it' from Pipes and then, a couple of seconds later, the snap of the snare announced that he was back. But the damage had been done. Mark was now a couple of beats behind the pace, Pete was stuttering into 'Jealousy, turning saints into the sea' and the term rhythm had been wrenched from the description of Pudding's guitar playing. After a couple of bars, they got it back together and limped to a conclusion.

The applause from the judges and the other bands was muted and could best be described as polite. A 'Thanks gents' from Will was accompanied by a sympathetic smile and an extension of his open hand to indicate that they needed to vacate the stage for the next band.

Pete turned to see Pudding glowering at Pipes as he rose from behind his drum kit. Pete, in turn, glowered at Pudding, trying desperately to transmit silently the need not to make a scene on stage. Whether Pudding had spotted Pete or it was just that pragmatism had kicked in, he said nothing, just slinging his guitar onto his back and striding off the stage.

As they passed into the wings, the members of Chunky Funky Monkey, awaiting their own turn in the spotlight, stepped back to let them through. As Mark walked stupor-like past them, the lead singer grabbed him by the arm and said 'nice bass playing mate. You need to join a young band that is going places rather than wasting your time with The Grateful Dead here.'

It was at this point that a guitar arced over Mark's back and connected full on with the startled face of the would-be funk star who went down like the proverbial sack of potatoes.

## Chapter 33

Pete was sat on a plastic chair, nursing a cup of tepid tea. He glanced around the room for the umpteenth time but the scene had not changed in the hour that he had been there. Dim fluorescent lights cast grey shadows over grey walls and a grey plastic-tiled floor. Glancing between his legs at the hard grey plastic of his chair, Pete thought that at least there was consistency in the colour scheme and wondered if they had been going for fifty shades. Laurence Llewelyn-Bowen would be impressed. Across from him sat a shaven-headed, middle-aged man, with a neck that looked like it could bench-press 200 pounds.

Boredom kicked in, prompting Pete's natural inclination to construct a back-story for the man opposite. He was 'Spider', a veteran criminal who had spent all his adult life in and out of jail. As a young lad he had been orphaned and passed around various foster parents, desperately trying to fit in but somehow always messing up as his anger and frustration at the injustice of the death of his parents bubbled to the surface. At 16 he had received six months community service for stealing a Sega Mega Drive from his local Woolworths. He, along with seven other fluorescent-jacketed teenagers, had been set to work tidying up the gardens of a stately home. This had given him the opportunity to case the joint. Caught red-handed with a bag full of silverware from the drawing room had led to a year spent in Brinsford Young Offenders Institution near Wolverhampton.

Just as Pete was veering off into an alternative version of Cluedo, with Spider having committed murder in the drawing room with the candlestick, he was woken from his reveries by a gruff voice saying, 'is there somebody here for a Mr Graham Piper?'

Pete looked up to see a uniformed custody officer with an old-fashioned clipboard. 'Yes, that would be me officer. I'm Pete Harriman.'

Officer Galbraith looked him up and down, Pete feeling like he was automatically deciding if Pete was a wrong-un. 'OK, stay here please Mr Harriman, I'll go and fetch Mr Piper.'

Another 15 minutes passed, during which time Pete had got to the point in Spider's career when he had been involved in a bank robbery in which he had hit the bank manager over the head with the butt of a pistol. The arrival of the police, sirens wailing, and Spider screaming at Officer Galbraith 'you'll never take me alive copper' coincided with the opening of a door and the re-appearance of Officer Galbraith. He was followed by a clearly contrite Pipes, shuffling along with head bowed and looking even more dishevelled than usual.

Officer Galbraith led Pipes over to a counter manned by what appeared to be a lad of about 15. Pete knew he was indulging in stereotypes with the notion that coppers were getting younger and younger but this one had tried to grow a beard and simply ended up with some wispy bum-fluff on his lower chin.

Pipes scrawled his signature on a sheet before receiving his phone, wallet, belt and shoelaces. He slumped into the chair next to Pete to re-lace his battered trainers and hoick up his trousers before replacing his belt. He rose silently and headed for the door, with Pete following and throwing a last glance at Spider who returned it with a look that suggested had he not been in a police station, Pete might have been on the receiving end of a sharp right hook. As Pete hurried Pipes out of the door, he said 'right, we're up here mate, on the left.'

It was 20 minutes into the journey back to Pipes' flat and the silence had been deafening. It was finally broken by a whispered 'sorry.'

'That's OK' said Pete, turning down the climate control so that he could better hear Pipes. 'What got into you mate?'

'As we walked off the stage, I knew I'd let you all down. So, when the twat from that group of foetuses posing as a funk band had a dig, I just lost it. I'm sorry.'

'It's OK with me. It would have been better had you limited your beer intake a bit but let's be honest, we were never going to win. I reckon it's Pudding you really need to be apologising to. You've absolutely wrecked his guitar.'

'I know, I know. I'll get him another one. It was just the nearest thing to hand when that chippy fucker had a pop.'

'So, not wishing to pour more petrol on your last 24 hours but do you reckon he'll be pressing charges?'

'I honestly don't know. In the melee that followed he was just shouting 'you've bust me nose, you've bust me nose' over and over. Then those two security guards appeared from nowhere, got hold of me and dragged me into that room until the coppers arrived. Thanks for coming to get me by the way.'

'No problem. I'm guessing it might be the first time you've spent a night in a police cell and probably not an experience you'll be wanting to repeat?'

'Too bloody right Harsy. The catering was awful.'

## Chapter 34

The Leicester tones of Kasabian front man Tom Meighan invited Pete to 'Shoot the Runner, Shoot Shoot the Runner.' 'Hi Pudding' said Pete, picking up his mobile from the kitchen table.

'Alright Harsy, so we're on for Wednesday then?'

'Yes, but don't give Pipes too hard a time, will you? He still feels awful.'

'So he should. The stupid tosser gave us all that crap about us having no chance of winning and when we do get through then it's him that fucks everything up by dropping his sticks because he was pissed.'

'Yes, I know, I know. But raking over it again will not help the situation will it?'

'No, I suppose not. And he did give me more than my guitar was worth so the one I've got now is a step up from what I had.'

'There you go, silver linings and all that.'

It had been nearly two months since Old School had got together, Pete deciding that a bit of time for Pudding to calm down was a sensible option. There had been a few phone calls, Pete playing mediator on a couple of occasions when it looked like the band might be no more. They were now in 'a better place', as a professional counsellor might call it, and Pete had tentatively suggested a practice session at the church hall might be in order.

The cloud of a potential court case had been lifted with the lead singer of Chunky Funky Monkey electing not to press charges, accepting Pipes' written apology. This had been sweetened by ALM Promotions offering the band a place in the competition final, effectively a bye as they had been unable to take to the stage for their second performance due to their lead singer being somewhat incapacitated.

Pete had thought this a canny move on the part of ALM. Rather than try and quash any negative publicity for the competition that the Birmingham fracas might have created, he suspected they had positively encouraged it, albeit with a more positive spin. An article had appeared in the Birmingham Evening Mail under the headline 'Aging Rockers Hit More Than High Notes.' The article had all the hallmarks of a PR led story, with several comments attributed to 'an insider'. The final paragraph had focused on the fact that ALM had given Chunky Funky Monkey a place in the final, complete with a quote from Head Judge Will Craven.

'It was an unfortunate incident but was handled very efficiently by our trained security staff. Though I am in no way condoning the actions of Mr Piper, emotions obviously run high when you are under the scrutiny of the judges. These are not professional musicians so are not used to the pressures that come with such intense live performance. However, despite their amateur status, let me tell you that we have seen some serious talent. We decided that it was only right that Chunky Funky Monkey go straight through to our Grand Final. We are expecting a great atmosphere and a real treat for the audience on 27 July at Wembley Arena.'

Pete thought that the oxygen of publicity, a bit of rock n roll bad behaviour (albeit from a 53-year-old hotel manager), complete with a blatant plug for the final, would do no harm to ticket sales. It was hardly trashing a hotel room, driving a Rolls Royce into a swimming pool, or biting the head off a small mammal, but in an age where musicians seemed more likely to bring out a range of leisurewear, it would have to do.

## Chapter 35

Pete and Marcie were in the garden making the most of the Indian Summer. With chicken and salmon sizzling enticingly on the BBQ and a bottle of chilled Pinot Grigio on the go, they were sitting under the apple tree that was providing welcome shade on a glorious sunny September Saturday.

Pete was scrolling through his phone, alternating with cupping his right hand over the screen to shield it from the glare of the sun. 'Pipes is going to go ballistic. It says here that on the back of winning Battle of the Bands, Chunky Funky Monkey have now been awarded a record deal. It even has a photo of the lead singer, though it might please Pipes that his nose looks bent. Maybe they can rechristen themselves as Chunky Funky Wonky Monkey.'

'Can you make sure you tell Pipes when I'm around. I just have to see his face when he finds out. He was lucky that the guy didn't take it any further. I was surprised in this era of seeking compensation when you stub your toe on a paving stone that he didn't sue. Particularly given the publicity. You'd have thought the 'no win no fee' vultures would have been lining up. I'm not sure how the hotel would have responded to their General Manager having a criminal record for ABH.'

'By all accounts, he'd have been in good company. Pipes told me that the Head Chef did six months for drink driving and the guy responsible for looking after the grounds did 18 months for supplying cocaine. Apparently, he had about 20 kilos of the stuff in the hotel's outbuildings. Everybody thought it was fertiliser. Add to that the sexual shenanigans that appear to regularly go on in the rooms and it's a veritable den of iniquity.'

With a throaty laugh, Marcie said 'Pass the wine will you. Or you can top me up if you're feeling particularly energetic. Maybe we can get you a job at Pipes' hotel as Head Sommelier.'

Pete was swinging in a hammock, enjoying the dappled sunlight as it filtered through the leaves of the tree. He waved at Marcie whose face was morphing from her own to Clare Grogan and then into Kate Beckinsale. The strains of Bill Withers confirmed that, despite the tree, the sunlight was apparently hurting both of their eyes. Pete reached for his sunglasses to rectify the situation. Bill continued 'Then I look at you, And the world's alright with me', echoing Pete's feelings perfectly as Kate held his now Oakley-filtered gaze with a sultry smile. The volume was increasing slightly as Bill seemed to be getting a little agitated, despite it being a lovely day. Starting to come into focus was a ceiling rose, with a water stain to the left that looked a bit like a Gremlin.

Though still groggy, Pete realised that he was not in a hammock but in his own bed, confirmed by the Gremlin staring down at him as it had done for the last 18 months, despite Pete's regularly voiced promises to get it sorted.

He reached for the phone as Bill confirmed that '…it's gonna be, a lovely day,' squinting at the screen to register that it was 03.26. Silencing Bill with a press of the answer button and a croaky 'hello', Pete started to raise himself into a sitting position, trying not to disturb the slumbering Marcie.

The panicked shout of 'Peter, your dad' immediately shot a bolt of adrenalin through his system and his instincts told him that this was not going to be a lovely day and one that could well be impossible to face.

## Chapter 36

'I'm sorry Mrs Harriman. We did all we could but sadly your husband had suffered a massive heart attack and we weren't able to revive him. I really am very sorry.'

Joyce collapsed into her son's arms, with a wailing that sounded like a wounded animal.

Pete had arrived at the hospital half an hour after the call from his mum, only about 10 minutes behind the ambulance that had rushed her and his Dad to A&E.

He knew that nothing he said would make any sense right now, so he just held her tightly, as much for his own comfort as for his mum's. He felt numb, not able to comprehend that he would never speak to his dad again. The fluorescent strip lighting of the visitors' room highlighted a tableau that he knew was all too common for the doctor and nurse that looked on sympathetically. But this was his dad. This wasn't some scene from Holby City. This was real. Wasn't it?

He looked up, half expecting to see his Dad's goofy grin as he walked through the door, laughing that it had all been a mix-up and that he was simply in here to get his piles checked out.

But he didn't.

Marcie placed two cups of tea on the wood-effect table-top. She had arrived about an hour ago, unbidden by Pete but clearly knowing that he would need the support. Pete just wanted to regress to the little boy, letting his dad sort out the adult stuff as he had done so many times before. But he knew that he couldn't. Not this time. He had to try and stay strong for his mum.

She was quietly crying into her hankie, the one that she always carried tucked in her sleeve. Pete had a flashback to the hankie being licked and used to wipe ice-cream from his squirming face on the seafront at Bude. Again, the hankering to be that young boy, with none of the responsibilities that inevitably came with being a man, almost overwhelmed him.

A gentle pat on the back from Marcie and he looked up. Though she was clearly hurting herself, the innate born organiser was still there, the look on her face gently indicating that there were decisions to be made. 'Pete love. If you want to go and see him, then I think you should do it now.'

A whimper from Joyce had Marcie placing her other hand gently on the arm that wasn't holding the hankie.

Pete rose slowly from his chair. 'Mum?' A simple nod of her head and he helped her to her feet.

They walked slowly along a corridor, led by a nurse who regularly stopped to check that Joyce was OK. Pete was supporting her by the arm, grateful for the human touch and the physical proof that at least she hadn't abandoned him. They came to the door of a private room and he felt a wave of nausea as he wondered if he was actually going to able to do this. As his vision blurred, the result of a mix of fear and tears, he glanced up to see the outline of the nurse's face. 'Mrs Harriman, Mr Harriman, are you both OK? I know this is incredibly difficult but in my experience you'll be glad that you did.' A final 'OK?' and the nurse gently pushed open the door.

## Chapter 37

It was 10 days until Christmas and Pete was up a step ladder on his annual trip to the loft to get the Christmas decorations. He hauled himself through the hatch, flicked on the fluorescent tube and glanced around, mentally restating his annual promise to sort out the mess. As he crouch-walked like a modern-day Gollum, he spied the three big boxes. One had fallen over spilling an assortment of fairy lights, festive garlands and the inflatable snowman that in its current deflated state grimaced like something from a Stephen King film.

As he started to slide the nearest box along the part-boarded loft, careful not to snag the precarious stack of Panini football sticker books, he saw the albums that he had last perused when choosing photos to make up the montage for Marcie's $50^{th}$ birthday party. He sat down, ensuring he was perched on a joist, welcoming the relief this afforded his already aching back.

He opened the first album and flicked through, returning the grins of his five and eight-year-old children as they stared back at him. He lingered over one capturing Jack dressed as Woody and Charlie as Jessie the Cowgirl. He immediately relived the tense scenes in the Harriman household as Marcie tried to convince the two of them that Toy Story 2 was not a book and therefore unsuitable as an inspiration for World Book Day. This had elicited howls from Jack, coupled with an impressive and spirited defence from Charlie, citing the book she had received from Nanny and Grandpaps that Christmas. Marcie started to explain that merchandise based on the films didn't really qualify but her heart really wasn't in it and, with the two of them looking so cute and faced with a wailing toddler who was refusing to go to school unless he was Sheriff for the day, practicality had ultimately prevailed.

Pete picked up another brown faux-leather album. He brushed the dust from the cover. It gave a satisfying creak as he opened to the title page which was yellowing and curling at the edges. He carefully turned it to reveal a close-up of his dad. It was taken at Christmas. If the gold tinsel framing the gilt-edged mirror in the background had not been a give-away, then the bright red paper hat perched precariously on his dad's head certainly was. He read the scrawled handwriting beneath: 'Dad, Xmas 1989.' Pete realised that he was looking at his dad at roughly the same age that he was now. As he was enveloped by a longing to see him in the flesh rather than simply reproduced on paper via a chemical process, the floodgates opened and Pete wept uncontrollably.

Once the great sobbing heaves had been replaced by intermittent sniffs, with tears still trickling down his face, Pete took a 2D walk through his dad's life. The photos were not in any chronological order, a clear indicator that Pete had put the album together rather than Marcie. Here was one labelled 'Dad, Skirting Board Project, 1976' showing Malcolm attacking a piece of wood enthusiastically with a plane.

This had Pete recalling his dad's many DIY projects, always undertaken enthusiastically but invariably featuring some choice language as a particularly tricky 'bastard screw' or 'pissin' poxy saw' temporarily thwarted him. The young Pete always tried to hang around during such projects, not through any desire to learn skills that might prove useful in later life, but rather due to his fascination with the expletives which were countermanded at regular intervals by his mum's cries of 'Malcolm, the children, language!' This probably helped to explain Pete's complete ineptitude when it came to DIY, but his resulting grasp of Anglo Saxon had certainly seen his stock in the playground rise considerably.

Pete wiped away a fallen tear from his dad's crisp white shirt to ensure that his sartorial elegance in 'Mum & Dad,

Grimshaw's Office Party, 1983' remained unblemished. The gurning face of Grandpaps, with Charlie and Jack balanced on each knee, brought a smile amidst the tears from 'Dad & Kids, Marcie's Birthday, 2004.'

As the topsy-turvy 'This is Your Life' of Malcolm Peter Harriman veered from page to page, 'Mum & Dad, Clacton, 1958' had Pete realising that he had alighted on the Before Children era. He quickly calculated this was about three years BC, his sister Judith having been born in 1961.

Pete plucked out a grainy black and white photo which was tucked in behind Clacton. It was of an even earlier vintage, his dad front and centre in a group of smartly dressed young men. With no caption to pinpoint the date or event, Pete guessed that the lads would be in their late teens. They were all standing around a car, what Pete thought might be a Ford Anglia. Given his prominent position and the fact that Pete recalled tales of his dad's Anglia, he assumed this was his dad's car and possibly his first day of ownership.

The ability of photos, particularly printed ones, to stimulate seemingly long forgotten memories kicked in. Pete remembered with a sudden intense clarity a conversation that had hitherto been assigned to the furthest recesses of his mind. It had taken place in their Bromsgrove kitchen when he had been bemoaning yet another breakdown of his reliably unreliable Ford Capri – yellow with a black vinyl roof. His dad had chimed in with a diatribe against the motorists of today not knowing they were born. He had spoken of his Ford Anglia and the cheap vacuum system that powered the windscreen wipers, resulting in the wipers slowing down as the car sped up.

Pete looked again at the snapshot of a moment in time, an era that he had never experienced. He mused over the names of those pictured, wondering if the blokey nicknaming system had been flourishing back then. He also realised that it felt unnatural, even a little disconcerting, to have tangible evidence that his dad had ever had a life before Pete joined the world. He felt the sharp tang of realisation that the human condition was to be largely self-centred, anything existing outside our own orbits being difficult to grasp.

Pete thought his earliest actual memory was of a swing, aged around four, being pushed by his mum. While he had no recollection of the previous three years, he knew he had been around, ergo his mum and dad had been around too. Somehow, their lives prior to this point seemed such an alien world that it didn't really exist. And, as for their lives before they had met….

Pete carefully tucked the photo back into place, allowing Clacton to hide the secret world of his 18-year-old dad and his mates. Like Sheriff Woody and his companions in Toy Story, once screened from the prying eyes of Pete, perhaps they would spring to life to continue their playful jibes about dad's car and its shitty windscreen wipers.

The next photo showed Pete and his dad, arms around each other at a Birmingham City game. Pete was unable to read the caption as the floodgates opened once again, huge salt-laden tears falling onto and smudging the ink that held the secret as to who they had lost to on that particular occasion.

## Chapter 38

Boney M's 1978 Euro disco hit Ra Ra Rasputin had Pete reaching for his phone. He knew without looking at the screen who was calling as he'd assigned the tune as an homage to Mr Somersby when he'd added him to his contacts. With the church warden's appearance reminding Pete of a modern-day reincarnation of the infamous mad monk, it seemed an apt introduction, though Pete doubted that Mr Somersby had been anywhere near the Russian Queen and an unlikely candidate for anybody's lover.

'Mr Somersby, how nice to hear from you.'

'Mr Harriman. A pleasure to talk to you. I trust you are keeping well?'

Once Pete had responded in the affirmative, with characteristic efficiency Mr Somersby immediately moved onto the reason for his call. 'Well, Mr Harriman, I presume that your musical combo is thriving given that you continue to avail yourselves of the services of the church hall?' Despite the question, the caller didn't wait for an answer. 'That being the case, I was hoping that you would be able to help us out by playing at a fund-raiser we are organising. As you have undoubtedly witnessed from your recent practices, we have been experiencing problems with the ingress of water in the entrance vestibule. We have had some investigative work done by a Mr John Croxley, a reputable roofer who was introduced to me by one of our parishioners. He advised, having undertaken a thorough evaluation, that we need to replace the entire flat roof that spans the entrance. I'm sure you will appreciate that such remedial action comes at not inconsiderable expense, so we are looking to raise the money through a series of events. Mrs Prendergast has generously agreed to hold a coffee morning, Mr Carling is organising a sponsored walk and at our last meeting I suggested that we might consider an evening of musical light entertainment.'

As he stopped to draw breath, Pete took the opportunity to jump in. 'Mr Somersby, we'd be delighted to help out. That is if you think the type of music that we play is right for your audience?'

'Splendid. I was hoping that you would say that. There would be no remuneration of course, which I trust would be acceptable, particularly in light of us having provided the church hall free of charge to you in advance of the funeral of the recently dearly departed Mr O'Sullivan.'

Pete could not help but be impressed by Mr Somersby's negotiating technique, honed undoubtedly by his days in the Belgian monastery and handling the contracts for the monks' Trappist beer production. Pete refocused before his creative musings took complete hold and he had Mr Somersby operating as the right-hand man of Saint Benedict, barking orders to his monastic brethren through highly animated hand gestures as he sought to maintain his vow of silence.

Mr Somersby continued. 'As for the nature of your music Mr Harriman, though not to my taste, I'm sure there might be some of the younger members of the parish that might enjoy some songs from the hit parade.' The venomous tone in which 'hit parade' was delivered had Pete visualising the curl of the lip that he had witnessed at his first meeting with Mr Somersby. He clearly held a healthy disdain for the perverting and pernicious influence of rock n roll on the moral fibre of the country. He was evidently firmly in the camp of the NME columnist who had been quoted in an article that Pete had recently read about the birth of rock n roll. The columnist had railed '…His violent hip-swinging…was revolting – hardly the kind of performance any parent could wish their children to witness.' And who had been the artist that had incurred such wrath from the NME? Elvis the Pelvis, Jim Morrison? No – none other than the infamous hell-raiser Sir Cliff Richard, who had gone on to belt out such morally corrupting filth as Whenever God Shines His Light and Saviour's Day and who would surely be welcomed with open arms at Mrs Prendergast's coffee morning.

Pete wondered why Mr Somersby had so readily ushered in the devil's music to a church fundraising event but concluded that his pool of available musical talent was probably somewhat limited, even more so when it needed to be an outfit that felt somewhat dutybound to offer their services gratis.

## Chapter 39

Old School were midway through their second set at St Cuthbert's Church Hall Roof Restoration Fund-Raiser. The interval between their first and second sets had seen a game of bingo, with first prize of a Christian retreat weekend in Prestatyn going to a Mr & Mrs Smedley.

The prize-winning couple were now the only ones on the dancefloor, presumably keen to celebrate their unbelievable windfall by impressively waltzing to the strains of I Predict a Riot. Though a somewhat unusual choice of dance, Pete thought it was not as incongruous as it might ordinarily have been. The band were playing at what was about half their normal volume. With the event being staged in the church hall for which the funds were being raised, they were acutely aware of the hall's noise limiter. Mr Somersby staring somewhat disconcertingly at them throughout meant there was no opportunity for Pipes to resort to placing his sock over the limiter's microphone: the standard approach for all of their practices. Instead, Pipes had set the PA level at three and had resorted to using brushes rather than drumsticks to ensure they didn't reach the maximum level of the limiter and shut down the electricity supply. The result was an atmosphere which more closely resembled a tea-dance and therefore far more in keeping with the assembled throng.

That throng numbered 19. Pete had counted. Had it not been for the attendance of the WI Keep Fit Club, then Pete thought that the band members might have outnumbered the guests. He was also grateful for the presence of the voluminous Mrs Jenkins, leader of said Club, whose physical presence at least took up a distinctly larger percentage of the available floorspace than your average punter, making the hall seem that little bit fuller. She was amongst the 17 who had elected not to join the waltzers, instead deciding to sit on the chairs placed around the edge of the room like some extended judging panel at a geriatric special of the X Factor. There was a guy in the corner who would beat Simon Cowell hands down in a 'guess the height of the waistband' competition.

As they came to the end of what had been the most sedate interpretation of I Predict a Riot in the history of music, Pete nodded at the smattering of applause. He wasn't sure if it was for them or for the efforts of the Smedleys. Pete concluded that the only way there would be a riot tonight was if the TV in the corner had suddenly burst to life with a newsflash announcing a government decision to halve the state pension and double the TV Licence fee for the over 65s. Pete glanced across at Pudding. He had the same 'bored with a hint of serial killer' expression that he'd adopted since they'd taken to the stage. Though Pudding's mood was the most apparent, no member of Old School had particularly relished the evening's performance when they arrived to see party goers that looked like the cast of 'Cocoon'. Even Mark, normally hyper with nerves whenever they performed, seemed positively serene.

'Rock n Roll man' hissed Pipes from behind his drum kit. 'Right, the least we can do is have a laugh. Pudding?'

'Oh yes, said Pudding, let's give it a go and hopefully wake the living dead.'

Pete placed his hand over the microphone and whispered 'Pudding, watch what you're saying, they might hear you.'

'Oh right, Harsy, that bloke over in the corner going to be getting out his ear-trumpet is he?' pointing to Simon Cowell Senior.

Conscious that he was responsible for agreeing to this evening's booking and feeling guilty, Pete acquiesced, knowing what was coming.

They launched into The Size of a Cow. This had been Pipes' suggestion when Pete had reported that the WI Keep Fit Club would be attending. Mrs Jenkins was undoubtedly the lady for whom the club seemed to have had the least benefit but, as its leader, several of her cohorts certainly seemed to have taken her as a role model. Pudding had threatened to replace the 'i' of 'Fit' with an 'a' when they had come across the club's banner during a practice, but Pete had managed to catch him before he applied the magic marker. They had, though, had several run throughs of The Wonder Stuff's signature song. Though it was far from match-fit and ordinarily would never have made it onto the set list in its current questionable state, given the fact that most of the people there were paying little, if any, attention, Pete opted for the line of least resistance.

The same muted applause that greeted the end of the song suggested that had Old School gone for the Sex Pistols' Friggin' in the Riggin', it probably wouldn't have made the slightest difference.

## Chapter 40

The slam of the front door woke Pete from a crafty afternoon nap. He quickly grabbed the washing basket from the side of the sofa and started folding clothes. 'Alright love? A good day at work?'

'No not really. I'm going to have a shower.'

Pete had learned that Marcie after a bad day was best left alone for the lava to cool. He was sure somebody else might have witnessed the eruption but as molten matter flowed downhill, he was always conscious to stay well out of the way to ensure he was not burned as collateral damage.

He carried on folding, reaching for the remote and switching on the late afternoon news. He lasted 30 seconds into the latest offerings from the supposed expert political commentators on the current state of Brexit before switching off to prevent his blood pressure reaching a point which might see an eruption of its own.

Pete sauntered into the kitchen and added a generous glug of red wine to the boeuf bourguignon simmering on the range. He then poured two glasses and added them to the place settings at the table. Sinking into a chair he grabbed The Times, flicking straight to the sports pages to see what Henry Winter had to say about the latest boardroom shenanigans at his beloved Birmingham City.

The sound of another slammed door, this time the bedroom, suggested that the shower had perhaps not had the desired effect. This was confirmed by the stomping feet coming down the stairs and Pete prepared himself for a flow of fresh magma as the kitchen door opened.

'Absolutely sodding unbelievable.'

'What's that love?'

'Kitty Stimpson. She's sodding unbelievable.'

Pushing her glass of wine towards Marcie as she sat at the table, Pete settled himself in for a good listening. 'Isn't she the one you had a few issues with last year when she wanted you to sack your editor?'

'Yes, that's the one but this time she's gone too fucking far. She thinks she's Queen Bee, but she is going to get a rude awakening. I took the latest set of designs for her book cover to her today – the fourth lot I've commissioned. She said they were all rubbish, like the last lot. So, she then produces a design that her mate Felicity has done that looks like something from a five-year-old, not a particularly talented one at that, and says that's the cover she wants. Over my fucking dead body.'

Pete made soothing noises, conscious that this time Marcie appeared even more wound up than usual. He then served up the fruits of his cooking labours and for a few minutes Marcie's ire seemed to be somewhat soothed by an excellent cut of beef from Stan, their local butcher. The lull was, however, only temporary.

As she banged her now empty wine glass back on the table, she re-ignited the after-burners. 'She's the worst but at times I could throttle the lot of them. With Fran I feel like I'm a cut-price psychotherapist. I don't know why she doesn't just dump that dead-beat of a boyfriend and move on. There she is giving advice to teenagers to take control of their own lives and not to stand for any shit from their boyfriends and she is living with a bloke who thinks putting his empty beer bottles in the recycling bin is his contribution to the household chores. And, as for Chelsea, she has fallen off the wagon so many times that I'm surprised she hasn't broken her fucking neck.'

Pete shivered at the recollection of the night of Chelsea Carmel-Smythe's book launch and the part he'd played in the whole thing almost coming completely off the rails but for a star performance from Marcie. As he refilled his wife's wine glass, Pete sensed that this might be some sort of watershed moment. As Marcie's stable of authors for the Teen-Lit market had grown, so had the pressures on her. While there had always been the occasional outburst as she had gone through difficult and frustrating patches that are pretty much par for the course for most self-employed entrepreneurs, it had largely been just blowing off steam. Pete had been happy to be the safety valve. Recently, though, he had noticed that things had changed. The rants had become ever more frequent, and, particularly in the last couple of months, ever more vitriolic.

They were now halfway through their second bottle of Zinfandel and while the effects of the delicious full-bodied red had taken the edge off Marcie's venom, the flow still continued. 'I sometimes feel more like a baby-sitter than a publisher. Pete don't you ever think that we should give it all up and try something completely different. Oh, you already have.' Marcie reached for the bottle and drained the last dregs into her glass.

Pete concluded that this was now officially a three-bottle conversation and went over to the wine rack to see what was left. 'Be careful what you wish for love. When I first finished work it was great, a real sense of liberation at being out of the rat race, off the hamster wheel, outside the daily grind. But I have to say that recently I've been missing some of the hustle and bustle. I know what you mean though about doing something different. There's no way I'd go back to H,H&H and probably not even to advertising.'

'So, are you saying that you want to go back to work?'

'I'm not sure but I do know that I want a bit more direction and something that challenges me. As tempting as an afternoon beer at The Swan might sound, even that pales after a while. Having nothing to do and all day to do it in might sound idyllic. And I guess it is when you're 8 and you have the whole 6 weeks of the summer holiday stretching out in front of you. But when you're 55 and it's pissing down with rain, not so much.'

'OK. So, what are we going to do then?'

'Well, I have that money that my dad left me and while it's not exactly burning a whole in my pocket, we could look at investing that in some sort of new venture.'

After another couple of glasses of Cabernet Sauvignon – not up to the quality of the Zinfandel but at this point neither Pete's nor Marcie's palettes were particularly discerning – Pete put the heel of his hand to his forehead (on the second attempt, having missed first time round.) 'I've got it love, we should run our own ski chalet.'

## Chapter 41

Pete passed the salt cellar to his mum. 'So, what do you think mum?'

It was a couple of weeks since Pete and Marcie's drunken foray into planning for their future and Pete was at Graces Garden Centre in Bromsgrove. The café was his mum's go-to-choice for lunch and while Pete was not a fan of the beige coloured cuisine, he had found a lasagne which just about passed muster once he liberally applied hot pepper sauce to its surface of nuked crispy cheese. This was the sixth time they'd been in three months, alternating with the local Toby for their weekly lunch out, and Pete realised that he would need to try and expand his mum's culinary horizons at some point. While they had been the haunts of his parents when his dad had been alive and Pete had been conscious not to introduce change straight away, he thought it would be helpful for his mum not to dwell too much in the past. And anyway, the food was bloody awful.

Pete's largely throw-away suggestion of becoming a hotelier, albeit on a small scale with a ski chalet, had subsequently morphed into something worthy of consideration. He had assumed the 'ffnatstic idea Pete' from Marcie would not be remembered in the cold light of morning but a couple of days later Marcie had broached the topic over dinner. 'Pete, you know your suggestion of the ski chalet, do you reckon it's something we could actually do?'

'I don't know. I was the wrong side of several red wines when I suggested it.'

'Yes, I know, so was I. But I've been thinking about it more and more. I'm not sure I can carry on much longer dealing with the tortured artistic souls of my authors so if we could find something else to keep the wolf from the door. And, as you said, you are getting a little bored at being a man of leisure and want a new challenge?'

'True. And don't think I've forgotten how supportive you were when I decided that the world of advertising was no longer for me. If you've had enough of publishing, then maybe it is time for a fresh start. Let's be honest, surely we couldn't do any worse than the shower that ran Le Lapin Blanc. The one big sticking point is that I wouldn't want to leave my mum on her own so soon after Dad passing away. Jude is on the other side of the world so if we upped sticks, then I'm not sure what she'd do. I suppose we could look at the UK, but Aviemore clearly doesn't have the same appeal and anyway, if we were in Scotland, then we might as well be in another country.'

'Yes. I agree. I was thinking we could take her with us.'

That comment was why Pete was now asking 'So, what do you think mum?'

'I don't know love. It's all a bit much to take in.'

'I know mum, I know. Please don't think you've got to make any immediate decisions. I just wanted to put it out there. It's something that me and Marcie are only considering at the moment and we would only take it to the next step if you thought it might be an option.'

'France eh? Me and your dad went to Normandy once but that's the only place I've been. Is it nice?'

Pete went on to give her his take on France, assuring her that it wasn't cold and snowy all year round; no, you didn't have to drink wine if you didn't want to; it wasn't true that they were always on strike and no, the French didn't hate the English. They had left it that she'd 'have a think' as they got up from the table to head off for the hour or so perusing comfortable shoes in the centre's Leisurewear section which always had Pete vowing never to purchase Velcro-fastening slip-ons, whatever ripe old age he hopefully reached.

## Chapter 42

Pete was on his MacBook investigating flights to France. Things had moved on apace since the conflab with his mum. While she had not committed to anything, she had spoken to her doctor about the potential benefits of Alpine air to her worsening asthma and had not ruled out a new life in La République. Pete and Marcie had therefore had further exploratory discussions. Jack had already said he was planning to take a gap year at the end of his A Levels and Charlie indicated that her outline plans were to rent a flat with Stig and search for a job up in the North-East.

The potential for free ski accommodation had also been a contributing factor in a very definite thumbs-up from the younger element of the Harriman family.

In terms of his own drive, Pete realised that his dad's death had been a not inconsiderable motivator: a 'grab life by the balls before it's too late' moment. This was heightened by the fact that both he and Marcie had suffered with empty nest syndrome when Charlie had gone off to university. The thought of the impact on homelife with neither she nor Jack being there was already giving Pete the odd palpitation. So, all things considered, the timing seemed as good as it was ever likely to get.

Marcie had suggested the second week in January as the best time for her to take a break. Ever practical, she had pointed out that this was still very much a tentative investigation and that she could not jeopardise her publishing business, their only source of income, if buying a ski chalet proved to be a completely unrealistic prospect. She had therefore committed to four days, with the hope that they could combine viewings of potential chalets with a spot of skiing.

Pete had done a little internet research and it was already clear that a chalet of any decent size that could accommodate guests was not going to be cheap. The original plan had been to see if they could raise the funds through a combination of their savings, recently bolstered by the inheritance from his dad, and a mortgage/business loan. They hoped not to have to sell their own house in Leamington, rather renting it out to cover the mortgage and retaining ownership to offer a bolthole in case everything went the proverbial tits-up. Though an important factor was to allow Marcie to give up her publishing business, the proceeds from the sale of which would certainly help in the purchase of a chalet, Marcie's practicality gene had suggested that she initially retain at least two of her authors and look to run a scaled down publishing business from France. Eggs in one basket and an untried basket at that, with plenty of potential holes in it, was not the sort of leap of faith that Marcie was prepared to take.

Keen to garner opinion from somebody who had made a new life for herself, Pete had FaceTimed his sister Jude in New Zealand. Though her emigration had been to the other side of the world and theirs would be just a short hop across La Manche, Pete suspected that the wise counsel of his big sister would be invaluable. While she had couched a little caution with the comment that she had found the first few months particularly difficult, her overall take on their plans was a positive one. Pete elected not to resurrect memories of the death of Jude's husband Ken less than a year into their new Antipodean life and the stoic resolve and determination that she had shown during what must have been the most difficult period of all.

She had addressed the issue of their mum. 'Pete, I know I have no right to ask really seeing as I have pretty much zero input with mum other than a couple of FaceTime sessions a week, but have you thought how she might feel with both of us being effectively out of her life?'

'Yes, that was one of the first thoughts I had when we began seriously considering this possibly hair-brained pursuit. We are planning for her to come with us. I've spoken to her and while she has yet to commit – and I don't blame her as she doesn't really know what she'd be committing to – reading between the lines I think she is tentatively looking forward to the possibility of a fresh start now dad has gone.'

Having got what he considered to be the green light from his sister, Pete felt that while there was still obviously much to do, the potential for it turn from pipedream into reality was inching slowly forward, with the gears crunching from first into second.

Pete had mentioned the outline plan at The Swan after an Old School practice. He had thought nothing further of it until a couple of days later he'd had a call from Pudding. 'Harsy, you know the other day you mentioned your plan to become France's Rocco Forte and how it was going to prove more expensive than you'd anticipated. Well, how do you fancy the idea of a sleeping partner?'

After a bit of ribbing from Pete about Pudding's performance as the sleeping partner of Pipes following Marcie's fiftieth party, Pete said 'Always interested in ways of lessening the financial load. Pray, continue.'

Pudding had gone on to explain to Pete that as part of his post heart attack fitness regime he had taken up walking. He had been on several overseas walking holidays and had considered investing in a property himself. A few years ago he had spent a couple of weeks viewing potential properties in the Italian Dolomites but it had ultimately come to nothing. Pete mentioning his plans for a ski chalet in the French Alps had rekindled his interest, particularly as Pudding had skied a few times and liked the idea of having another bash. He said he would consider part-funding the enterprise, as long as '…it doesn't involve me having to wash bodily fluids off sheets, cook, or deal with the obnoxious progeny of pretentious public-school wankers i.e. it will only be my cash that I'm offering. I don't have any kids to leave my money to so it might as well be doing something useful.'

This revelatory conversation had given Pete a bright idea that now saw him on skyscanner.net searching for potential flights. This would be for Marcie only; his mode of transport would be somewhat different.

## Chapter 43

Pete was bouncing along the M20 on his way to the Channel Tunnel. He was in an Enterprise van, having resorted to rental as his mate Tim Wigston had been unable to commit to a loan of 12 days from the Wigston Windows fleet of two. The constant rattling from Pipes' kick drum that Pete had evidently not strapped down as well as he'd thought had proved an irritation throughout the journey and he made a mental note to re-secure it during the tunnel crossing.

Pete thought back to how he had got to this point. Pudding's interest in becoming a sleeping partner in the ski chalet business had provided the foundation for him to hatch a plan, the first active leg of which he was now putting into action.

Marcie had tentatively agreed to the potential involvement of Pudding in the business, once Pete had confirmed that he had no intention of playing any part other than as a financial investor. That, along with the opportunity to use the chalet in the summer months for walking holidays and for the occasional ski trip if he got back into it. Marcie had agreed that the remuneration he would receive as an investor was a discussion best left for further down the track.

Pete had then mentioned to Marcie his feeling that they should draw on Pipes' expertise and years of experience in the hotel industry in ensuring that they minimised the potential pitfalls. While she had agreed with the logic, she'd added 'But don't think for one minute Pete that this is going to be Chalet Old School.'

Pete had anticipated the response and was ready for it. 'No, I wasn't ever thinking of Pipes being involved financially. From the state of his wardrobe, I don't think he's particularly flush and I think Kelly and her love of the finer things in life doesn't help.'

'So, what are you saying then?'

'Well, I was thinking of getting him out there to cast an expert eye over any potential chalets so that he can look at them from a hotelier's perspective.'

'So, you're planning to spend money on sending him out to France and putting him up just so he can tell us what he thinks. Pete, we need to keep a control on costs – we can't be spending money needlessly before we've even started earning any.'

This provided the perfect 'in' for Pete and he grasped it with both hands. 'Yes, I'd thought about that. I think I know a way we can get him out there without any cost to us and actually with no costs to us for Pudding either.'

'Go on, I'm listening.'

'Well, you know how I'm always complaining there is not enough live music in the bars when we go on our skiing holidays. I reckon I could get some gigs for Old School.'

## Chapter 44

Pete pulled up at the Eurotunnel's security checkpoint. A thick-set uniformed security officer, his breath clearly visible in the biting January early morning air, approached the van with a mirror on a stick and performed a perfunctory scan of the underside of the vehicle. Pete couldn't help but think that in age when you were supposedly never more than a few feet from a CCTV camera, was a mirror on a stick really the best they could do? His mate, sporting a particularly impressive afro, circled his gloved hand in a seemingly internationally accepted mime. Pete considered the anachronism of a gesture that mimicked an action not required for about 40 years. Unless you were in a 1987 Trabant, a simple push of a button should suffice to lower the window.

Windy-window man, with a bored expression, asked Pete if he would open the rear doors of the van. On seeing the assembly of instruments, he quipped 'a one-man band then, are we?' Tempted to come back with some equally witty observation of his own, Pete thought better of it and forced out a laugh. He recalled the time his mate Des had taken a similarly light-hearted approach going through security at a Turkish airport. On being pulled aside for his bag to be searched, he had thought it funny, apparently mistakenly, to tell the moustachioed security man to make sure he checked the concealed bottom as that is where he kept his heroin stash. While Pete did not anticipate a full inspection of his anal passage if he indulged in banter with windy-window man, he decided better safe than very very sorry.

Having been deemed no threat to the security of the French populous, Pete proceeded to the Eurotunnel entrance for 'Low Vans'. He marvelled at the optical illusion that made it seem impossible he would pass under the striped bar indicating the maximum height restriction. Having successfully negotiated this game of vehicle limbo, he joined the queue awaiting the green light to let vehicles carrying a 'D' ticket dangling from their rear-view mirror drive onto Le Shuttle. He reached down for a Werther's Original, realising that he had eaten almost the whole packet on his journey down.

As the barrier lifted, he put the van into gear and followed the snaking line of traffic. He gave an appreciative nod at the particularly energetic Eurotunnel employee who was theatrically waving him and his fellow passengers through to the filter road. Though it was probably an attempt to keep warm in the near zero temperatures, his flamboyant and smiling approach to his work Pete felt warranted acknowledgement.

He cautiously edged his way onto the train, hearing several squeals as he scrubbed the van's tyres driving into the carriage. Having done the crossing many times, though never before in a van, he half-opened the windows (with no winding involved in the process), switched off the engine and shifted the gear stick into first. This elicited a smile from Le Shuttle's hostess as she made her way through the carriage, turning her attention to Eurotunnel virgins and advising them of the appropriate procedure.

This thought of safety procedures put a thought into Pete's head that was a regular and unwelcome earworm whenever he crossed. During his days at H,H&H Pete had worked on several accounts in the fire and security industry. He had attended a conference with a client on Mass Transit Fire Safety. During the evening's liquid refreshment session that seemed to be a staple of pretty much every conference he'd ever been to, he'd got into conversation with a group of guys who spent their time installing fire detection systems in vehicle engine compartments. One particularly loud individual, the wrong side of several beers, was holding court about the 'acceptable loss' policy that he'd heard the owners of Eurotunnel were considering adopting.

The gist of it was that in the event of a fire during the crossing, the doors at the end of each carriage in which the fire broke out would be supplemented by the closure of additional steel fire shutters. The idea was that in this way the fire would be contained in one place, preventing it from spreading to the rest of the train. 'So', exclaimed shouty man, 'if you happen to be in that carriage, then you're fucking toast mate.' While Pete believed it to be pub-talk, an apocryphal story that was now being recounted by a bloke that would have fallen over if he'd not been propped up by the bar, as the shutters came down at the ends of his own carriage, a shiver still ran down his spine.

As he drove off the tunnel, thankful that he'd once again been spared the irony of being a flaming human kebab travelling at 90 mph in a sealed kettle BBQ when just 75 metres above sat trillions of gallons of water, Pete looked at the sat-nav as it recalibrated for Chamonix.

They had decided on this particular resort as the focus of their chalet search. They knew it well, had enjoyed their best skiing holidays there and recognised it as one of the most popular Alpine resorts with the British skiing fraternity. With his mind becalmed by the other drivers confirming that he was on the correct side of the road, Pete headed off towards Calais and the start of his 10-hour drive to the French Alps.

## Chapter 45

The van's sat-nav informed Pete that he had arrived at his destination. He parked up and went into what was, on outward appearances at least, a significant improvement on Chalet Le Lapin Blanc. With no mangy dog pissing in the snow and a warm welcome from a young French girl at reception, his first impressions since his last visit to Chamonix continued to be encouraging.

Having checked into what was a sparsely furnished but comfortable room, Pete went down to the hotel's reception to ask where he'd find The Igloo Bar. This was one of six out of the 15 or so bars that Pete had contacted by e-mail or phone who had agreed to some cost-effective evening entertainment from a UK band. He toyed with the idea of paying the bar owner a visit to let him know that at least one quarter of the band was here and to confirm the plans for their first night 'on tour'. However, glancing at his watch and realising that he had an early start in the morning, he decided just to have a swift beer in the hotel bar before calling it a day.

He sat down next to a young man with an impressive beard. An acknowledging nod of the head and within a couple of minutes, they were engaged in conversation over a couple of beers. Lucas was Dutch, with an excellent grasp of English that seems such a common trait to those from the Lowlands. Only a hint of an accent suggested that he was not English, reminding Pete of ex-England Manager Shteeve McClaren's hilarious attempts to conduct an interview with the Dutch media in English but with a strange Dutch twang following his appointment as Head Coach at FC Twente.

Despite Lucas being excellent company, Pete stuck to his one beer plan, made his excuses, and left. The tiredness from a full day's driving took hold and he was asleep almost before his head hit the pillow.

The following morning saw Pete pulling into the short stay car park at Geneva airport. The van was still full of Old School's kit but there would still be more than enough room to accommodate a suitcase. He had talked about hiring a car and leaving the van parked up for the duration of Marcie's stay, but she had balked at the suggestion with a 'Pete, we need to keep costs to a minimum.'

He walked into the terminal and headed for the arrivals board. An hour later and Pete and Marcie were in the van and heading to Chamonix.

'So, I'm hoping the accommodation is a step up from Le Lapin Blanc' said Marcie, admiring the spectacular view of Mont Blanc as they sped along the Autoroute Blanche.

'Yes, it's surprisingly well appointed and really cosy.'

'The sort of place that should be on our shopping list?'

'I'm not sure we can stretch to a hotel just yet love. Let's look at the chalets that are actually on our list and we know are for sale first, shall we?'

They relaxed into an easy silence, both revelling in views that had always been part of the allure that brought them back to skiing, and to this area in particular, time and time again.

Pete dropped Marcie's suitcase onto the floor of their room. 'OK, shall we go and get something to eat?'

'You go ahead. I had something on the plane so I'm not really hungry and I want to get unpacked. Plus, I've got a call scheduled with Kitty in half an hour. It looks like she's finally settled on a theme for her new book, but she wants to run through '… a few ideas'.' A roll of the eyes from Marcie made Pete realise that he would be better off out of the way so, planting a kiss on her cheek, he headed downstairs in search of a local pizzeria.

## Chapter 46

Pete pulled back the curtains to reveal a spectacular view of the Alps. He craned his neck to get a glimpse of Mont Blanc, the Roof of Europe, sitting imperiously above the Chamonix valley and looking down on its neighbouring peaks like a proud mother surveying her children. Sunlight streamed into the room and fell across the face of a recumbent Marcie causing her to squint at the sudden brightness.

'OK then Pete, we've got an hour until our first viewing.' Still squinting, she reached for her phone and opened her diary. 'Monsieur Prince is showing us around Chalet Angelique first. He's picking us up from reception so let's go down and get some breakfast, shall we? What was it like yesterday?'

'Really good. Fresh croissant, loads of pastries, warm baguettes, various local jams, fresh fruit and eggs any way you like.'

Pete and Marcie now stood in the hotel reception area, having feasted well to set themselves up for what would be a busy day of viewings. Marcie glanced impatiently at her Apple watch, tardiness being one of her pet hates when it came to business. Pete mused over the contradictions in Marcie's approach to timekeeping. While she always ensured she arrived by the designated slot in her business dealings, in her personal life she was quite happy to adopt a much more laissez-faire approach. He had raised the topic of how such an organised businesswoman could turn into a laggard when they were getting ready for a social occasion, often wondering aloud from the bottom of the stairs, car keys clutched increasingly tightly in hand.

'OK, so where is he then?'

'I don't know. It's only 9.40 so he's only ten minutes late.'

Looking back at her watch, Marcie said 'I've got his e-mail here which clearly says that he'd meet us in reception. He couldn't have meant anywhere other than here could he?'

Just as Marcie's gaze was starting to dart around to suss out any potential alternative meeting points, the door opened, bringing in a blast of icy Alpine air.

'Monsieur and Madame Harriman?' said a man that had Pete thinking 'blimey, it's Super Mario.'

While Monsieur Prince was sporting a smart suit rather than bright blue overalls and a peaked red hat emblazoned with a large 'M', his likeness to the short, pudgy Italian plumber was nonetheless uncanny. Pete, unable to repress his genetic predisposition for daydreaming, visualised M Prince leading the way in one of Mario Kart's several ice & snow courses, blasting Yoshi with a banana skin to send Nintendo's diminutive dinosaur spinning out of control.

'Pete, Pete?'

'Oh, sorry love, I was just trying to remember if I'd picked up the room key. Sorry Monsieur Prince, Pete, Pete Harriman.'

'It's a pleasure to meet you Mr Harriman. Shall we go?'

'Yes, of course, lead on.'

As they walked into the car park Pete half expected to see a bright red go-kart. Instead, M Prince led them to a shiny black Range Rover which had evidently been freshly cleaned that morning given there was not a hint of slush or snow on the 4x4s' gleaming paintwork nor the tell-tale streaks on the windscreen generated by the rock salt used to grit the Alps' winter roads. It was clear that M Prince, his slight tardiness notwithstanding, was a follower of the French equivalent of the 6Ps business philosophy – prior planning prevents piss poor performance – with the car's huge tyres encircled by sturdy snow-chains.

As M Prince deferentially opened the front passenger door, Pete said 'Go on Marcie, you take the front and I'll jump in the back.'

They set off, the chains making a satisfying crunch as they gripped the fresh snow that had fallen overnight. Pete looked at the reflection of M Prince in the rear-view mirror, his bulbous nose sitting atop an impressive full moustache seeming even more Mario-like. Pete hoped that he was not going to head for the nearest chevroned speed-up ramp, engaging the Thunderbolt power-up to zap any other motorists who might be travelling around Chamonix's roads.

A 15-minute drive and M Prince announced, in his impeccable English, 'OK, we are here.'

He opened the door to let Marcie out before striding purposefully towards the chalet's front door at a speed that was impressive given the length of his legs. He opened it in a matter of seconds, none of the fumbling of Mr Somersby when he'd first let Pete into the church hall which had subsequently become the de facto practice room for Old School. Pete and Marcie followed him into a small hallway. The first thing that Pete noticed was that it was almost as cold inside as it was out. Seeming to read his thoughts, M Prince said, 'The chalet has been empty for some months now so it is a little cold in here, no?' So much for the 6Ps, thought Pete, realising that with a bit of foresight M Prince would have turned on the heating, particularly given his plumbing background.

'You could say that' replied Marcie, stamping her feet on the tiled floor.

'Shall we begin with the kitchen as, in my experience, that is one of the most important rooms for a successful ski chalet business?' said M Prince, bowing slightly and extending his hand to let Marcie take the lead into the kitchen. It was a shame that Le Lapin Blanc hadn't focused on the kitchen and, more importantly the people who worked in it, thought Pete as he followed Marcie, stamping his own feet in the process.

## Chapter 47

Pete flopped onto the bed back at their hotel, exhaling loudly as he did so. 'Jeez, that was a long day.'

Marcie sank into the chair. 'I know. M Prince was very patient with us, but I think he could tell we were losing the will to live when we were looking around that last one.'

'I obviously couldn't say anything while he was with us but did he not remind you of Super Mario?'

'Ahhh, that's who it was' said Marcie, slapping her thigh. 'I knew he looked like somebody, but I couldn't for the life of me work out who it was. I haven't played as many video games as you but even I know Mario – he's the little fat plumber guy, right?'

'That's the one, although he now seems to have given up plumbing to try his hand at estate agency. If we do find somewhere, then at least we have a contact who might not only be able to secure the deal but also sort out any issues with the pipes.'

After an excellent meal, in which they had both confined themselves to a single glass of wine, Pete and Marcie were back in their bedroom. Spread across the bed were details of the seven chalets they had viewed during the day.

Pete said 'If I can suggest a Britain's Got Talent approach to this, love. Let's make a pile of those that we're discounting straight away and then discuss those that we think might be possibles for the 'Live Finals'.'

'Agreed. But pour me a glass of wine will you Hon.' I know we were sensible at dinner, but I think I'll need one to wade through this lot.'

The next couple of hours were spent sifting through the estate agents' take on what they had seen that day. It took Pete back to the hyperbole of his own copywriting days. A chalet that had been little more than a dilapidated shell directly opposite a seedy looking supermarket was described as having 'huge potential for development, with immediate access to the heart of Chamonix's retail sector.'

The veracity of the printed details was, though, largely immaterial now they had seen the chalets in the flesh. They were just an aide memoire, sparking recollections from both Pete and Marcie as they struggled to separate out the different features of the respective properties.

'Are you sure that Chalet Lily was the one with the spiral staircase? Wasn't that Chalet Classique?' said Marcie, squinting at a floor plan.

'Lily was the third one we looked at, wasn't it? If so, then that was the one with the spiral stairs. I wouldn't fancy carrying anything of any size up those'

This evaluation of the chalets, regularly punctuated with queries as they started to blur into one, eventually resulted in a short list of two: Chalet Angelique, the first one they had seen and Chalet Mardi Gras that they had both really liked, despite the ridiculous name.

'OK', said Marcie, glancing at her Notes on her phone. That's seven down, 12 to go!'

'Do you think we've bitten off more than we can chew?' said Pete before downing the last of his wine.

'Maybe' said Marcie thoughtfully. 'No viewings now until tomorrow afternoon though so let's make the most of the morning. I can't wait to get back on the slopes, particularly as this time I won't have to listen to that braying arse William Tissington.'

Pete couldn't have agreed more, though he smiled as he recalled the sight of him sailing off back down the chairlift, complete with a German who looked like he would have happily whacked either of the Tissingtons with his ski pole had it not been trapped below the safety bar by the hefty legs of Bunty.

## Chapter 48

'Marcie, Marcie, come and look at this.'

Pete was out on the balcony, wrapped in a blanket against the intense morning chill. Marcie groggily joined him after slipping her feet into her designer furry boots which she'd bought a couple of years ago at a swanky boutique in Courchevel. She had one-upped Pete, choosing the bed's duvet as her body-wrapping of choice.

'Look, look' cried Pete gesticulating wildly at a scene that was straight from a Christmas card.

'You really are a big kid aren't you Pete? But you're my big kid' she added, planting a big wet kiss on his trembling lips.

It had snowed overnight. Not the couple of inches that they had received on the night of Macie's arrival but a genuine dump. A good couple of feet had fallen, covering everything in a white carpet whose crystals shimmered in an early morning sun that was already burning off any residual cloud. Pete pointed to the van, which was just an amorphous blob, looking like a huge meringue had been created by a giant insomniac French pastry chef. The boughs of the fir trees were weighed down, the lower ones almost touching the ground which had risen up to meet them. The rumble of a snow plough was the only noise, its giant snow-chained wheels rattling but still muffled by the sound-deadening properties of the stuff it was now intent on clearing.

Pete stood behind Marcie, wrapping his arms and his blanket tightly around her. They both gazed up at Mont Blanc, its summit circled by wispy clouds. The last couple of piste bashers were preparing the slopes, making their way down Le Savoy green run that led into the town after what would have been a very busy night shifting the extensive overnight snowfall.

'Yeeeeesssss' shouted Pete, unable to contain his joy at the prospect of an epic powder day of skiing, drawing a startled look from an elderly lady with an armful of baguettes making her way gingerly along the pavement below.

Pete and Marcie stood with a small group of other skiers, outnumbered by a gaggle of snowboarders, all eager to catch the first lift of the day. As a skier Pete still held a healthy distrust of boarders and their antics on the snow, now wondering if a more apt collective noun might be 'a blockage' given their penchant for sitting/lying down in the middle of the piste. For Pete and Marcie, the clock seemed to be ticking at twice the normal speed with a one o'clock cut-off to meet Madame Martine for another session of hunt the chalet.

Pete was in his element, creating graceful arcs in the fresh snow with his carving skis. He glanced to his right to see Marcie flying past in a tuck position, the quality of the soft surface subverting her natural inclination to take it carefully. She whooped with delight, screaming 'Come on old man. You call that skiing?'

Pete assumed a similar tuck position, quickly catching her up, and they raced each other down the slope, giggling like excited children who'd overdosed on blue smarties. Marcie pulled an impressive stop in front of a quaint mountain restaurant. Pete stopped several yards further down, not anticipating Marcie's move, which meant he was now side-stepping back up the hill to get to her.

'Coffee?' said Marcie, lifting her goggles to reveal her piercing blue eyes that Pete had always loved.

'OK, but just a quick one, eh? We can't waste these conditions.'

Having finished his latte in double quick time, Pete now lay in the deep snow, vigorously sweeping his arms and legs to create a snow angel.

'Pete you are 55 not 5 you know' said Marcie, with a grin that was accentuated by a line of creamy foam on her top lip, a spiral of steam rising from her cappuccino.

'Young at heart love, young at heart. You nearly finished your drink? Let's try and get a few more runs in before we have to make our way back. You don't get many bluebird powder days like this and in just over an hour we'll be trudging around another load of chalets. We can't phone Madame Martine and cancel, can we?'

'No, we bloody well can't. Let's remember what this trip is all about shall we. It could be the start of a completely new life for us. I'm not particularly enamoured with the idea of being indoors on a day when the great outdoors is such a wonderful playground, but priorities, Pete, priorities.'

Marcie bent down and scooped up a handful of snow, expertly crafting a snowball. Hitting Pete right in the middle of his chest, her impressive aim suggested that her proficiency in 'ladle fencing' demonstrated at Chelsea Carmel Smythe's ill-fated book launch was not her only sporting ability. If snowballing ever became a Winter Olympic sport, perhaps she could become a double Olympian.

## Chapter 49

It was Marcie's final day before she had to head home. It was late-morning and they were with their third estate agent in as many days, viewing a property that had no chance of making it out of the heats, let alone taking a place in the Grand Finals. As Pete poked his head around the door of yet another non-descript bedroom, he caught Marcie's exasperated expression. Making sure that Stephan, the estate agent, wasn't looking, Pete made as if to yank a noose tightly round his neck, with an exaggerated accompanying facial twitch. This raised a smile from Marcie as she opened a wardrobe door to at least appear as if she was interested.

Back at the hotel and in the bar, Pete said 'right love, let's make this a quick one.'

'Why it's hours until dinner so we're not in any rush are we?'

'Well, I've got a little surprise for you.'

'Pete! You know me and surprises – not great bedfellows. All your furtive communications with my birthday party planning nearly killed me.'

'I know, I know. But you'll like this one. Come on, down the last of that vin chaud and we'll get going.'

Having walked hand in hand through a winter wonderland, Pete and Marcie arrived at a small wooden hut. Marcie had chipped away at Pete since he'd revealed the surprise in what proved to be a vain attempt for it not to be a surprise.

'Bonjour' said Pete loudly.

'Ah, Monsieur' replied a moustachioed face as it peered around the hut's door frame. 'Les chiens vont bientôt arrive.'

'Les chiens – the dogs? Pete what are we doing?'

Realising that it would not take a great leap of imagination for Marcie to now work out what was afoot Pete was about to reveal his surprise when the need was taken out of his hands. A cacophony of barking announced the arrival of a team of huskies, pulling a sled that came to a halt right in front of them.

'Pete are we going on a sleigh ride?' said Marcie, eyes wide like a child as Monsieur Moustache laid out bowls of food for the baying dogs.

'Yes. Nice surprise?'

Marcie threw her arms around his neck, suggesting that indeed it was.

Pete looked again at the team of dogs and was shocked at what appeared to be two interlopers. Amongst the team of achingly beautiful huskies were what could only be described as a couple of mutts. Though they appeared strong and powerfully built, their short-haired cream coats, mottled with brown splodges, made them look an incongruous sight amongst their hirsute grey and white cousins. Pete thought that it was good to see the French adopting an inclusive and non-discriminatory employment policy.

The dogs had wolfed down their brief repast in less than a minute and Monsieur Moustache was now gesticulating for Pete and Marcie to take up the wooden seat on the sled. His colleague who had been driving the sled placed some sheepskin throws on the seat and, once they'd taken their places, wrapped them around their legs and bodies. He grinned, revealing more gaps than teeth. Pete wondered if his dental issues were the result of constantly falling off sleds, a thought that he decided not to share with Marcie.

With a double thumbs up Monsieur Sans-Dents checked that Pete and Marcie were ready. Unable to return the gesture due to his arms being tightly wrapped in the sheepskins, Pete just smiled and nodded. A sharp snap of the reins, another explosion of barking and they were off.

For the first 30 seconds or so, Pete and Marcie said nothing, getting used to what was an impressive turn of speed that seemed even quicker given that their respective arses were a matter of centimetres from the ground. He turned to look at Marcie who beamed a smile back, snuggling her head in against his shoulder. Having started across an expanse of snow, what was probably a field in the summer, they were now rapidly approaching a wooded area. As the sound of the runners gliding through the snow sharpened in the shallower cover, they entered the trees and what truly felt like Santa's grotto. The light faded in the shade of the trees and the glistening snow took on an even more ethereal quality as they took a tight bend around an impressive log pile.

The snow nestled on the overhanging branches as they came to a small clearing. That was until their playful sled driver cracked his whip against a branch to releases a cascade onto the unsuspecting couple. Marcie squealed, bringing a deep, throaty laugh from Monsieur Sans-Dents, suggesting that this was not the first time he'd done this.

They continued to career through the narrow woodland path, the speed accentuated as the trees rushed past only a few feet away in a blur of green and white. As they slowed slightly to take a sharp left, Pete spied light at the end of the fir tree tunnel and they soon re-emerged onto open ground. They traversed a ridge, offering a spectacular view down into the Chamonix valley, the bell-tower of the pretty Église Saint-Michel clearly visible in the late afternoon sunshine.

Pete felt some mud splatter on his ski jacket. He was somewhat surprised given the depth of the snow as they now started on a downward slope towards a chairlift station. Seconds later and he saw a similar clump of mud hit Marcie's jacket. It was then that Marcie turned to him with eyes opened wide, her nose wrinkled in disgust. 'Pete, what the fuck!'

As the pungent aroma assailed Pete's nostrils, he realised that this was not mud at all but a consequence of the dog's earlier meal. As he struggled to free his arms from his sheepskin shroud, Marcie started to gag. After a few seconds he managed to free his right arm and raised it high into the air. Monsieur Sans-Dents gave him a hearty high five from behind, snapping the reins to encourage the dogs to go faster and increase the exhilaration that he assumed his happy punter was experiencing.

As another brown missile exploded from the rear of a husky and hit Pete on his outstretched arm, Marcie started shrieking. Monsieur Sans-Dents took this as the signal to go even faster, with the sled now seemingly at full tilt, the dogs loving the thrill of running in a pack and also encouraged by the prospect of another meal as the small wooden hut hove into view. Bringing the sled to a halt, Monsieur Sans-Dents jumped from his position on the sled's runners, grinning wildly to reveal even more gaps. His compatriot Monsieur Moustache appeared from the hut, handing a small pack of wet wipes to Marcie as if this was all part of the service.

## Chapter 50

'OK, so that gives us five possibles then.' Across the breakfast table Marcie handed Pete a sheaf of papers containing the details of the chalets that had made the final shortlist. 'So, make sure you get the most of Pipes and Pudding being out here and I don't mean in terms of your collective endeavours to drink the bar dry. Remember, the next few days are not just about a lads' trip. Pipes has a lot of experience in the hotel trade so he can give us some really useful insights and, if Pudding is going to invest, then he has to be happy with the choice.'

'I know, I know. I will. The last few days have gone so quickly – just think if we were out here permanently. What a blast.'

Ever the pragmatist, Marcie could not help but dampen Pete's natural enthusiasm and exuberance with a dose of reality. 'Yes, it's been great and I'm excited too. But we need to go into this project with our eyes open. It's going to be really hard work – when the chalet guests are out enjoying the slopes, you could be up to your armpits unblocking the toilet and smelling like we did yesterday.' She visibly shuddered at the recollection.

'Spoilsport' said Pete, throwing a napkin at her. 'And anyway, if that happens then I'll be calling Monsieur Prince.'

The van sped along the Autoroute Blanche, this time in the opposite direction as Pete drove Marcie back to Geneva Airport.

'What time do the Three Stooges arrive?' said Marcie.

'Their flight is due in at 4.30.'

'So, you're going to have quite a bit of time to kill. What are your plans?'

'I thought I might drive into Geneva and have a look around. All the times we've flown into there, but we've only ever really seen the airport.'

'Good idea but remember Pete, Switzerland is not cheap, and we are watching the pennies. Talking of which, I know you've got Euros, but do you have any Swiss Francs?'

'I stuck £50 worth on the Caxton card. I might just grab some lunch but I'm not planning to do very much. I'll probably take a look at the Jet d' Eaux on the lake as I've only ever seen it through a car window. Charlie also mentioned The Reformation Wall which is in the Parc des Bastions. She studied The Reformation as one of her modules at Uni and tells me that Geneva was central to the Calvinist movement. And, you'll be pleased to know, both are free.'

Pete was in Arrivals. He'd had a pleasant afternoon in Geneva and was now looking at the board to see that the flight from Birmingham had landed on time. He reckoned it would be about 20 minutes before Pipes, Pudding and Mark would come through, assuming that the baggage handlers weren't on a go slow. He thanked the lord that they were across the border in Switzerland. Despite his assurances to the contrary in his conversation with his mum, the bolshie French seemed to be perpetually protesting about something, often designed to have maximum impact on the poor air traveller. Conversely, his experience of Switzerland was a level of clinical efficiency and precision time-keeping that one would perhaps expect from a nation that gifted the world the cuckoo clock.

He decided to grab a coffee and take a seat which would give him a clear vantage point of the Airside exit. As he inhaled the aroma of his steaming latte, he indulged in a spot of people-watching and his gaze settled on a large man with a bleach-blonde ponytail leaning against a pillar, presumably waiting for somebody to arrive. Somewhat inevitably Pete's back-story-generating-gene kicked in.

This was 'Man Mountain', a WWE wrestler on a visit from the USA to promote the sport to the Swiss. He was waiting for two of his wrestling mates – the Typhoon Kid and The Slaminator – who were travelling together. All three would then be heading to a TV interview with Telebasel, the Swiss business, lifestyle news and sports channel. Unlike his grapple-fest colleagues who were both in their first year on the WWE circuit, Man Mountain was in the twilight of his career. His battles were no longer confined to the ring, with much of what had been impressive muscle now turning to fat. He was an elder statesman of the sport and had been chosen for his experience, partly to ensure that semi-coherent sentences would be strung together at the TV interview and partly to chaperone and keep in check the natural exuberance of his younger cohorts. Just as Pete was moving onto Man Mountain's internal turmoil at having to keep his gay life secret for the sake of his career, he spotted Pudding wheeling a trolley containing three large suitcases. He unfolded from his pocket the Old School sign that he had handwritten, rising from his seat and holding it in front of his chest.

Mark was the first to spot him, pointing in his direction and saying something to Pudding. In an exaggerated mouthing of what Pete clearly recognised as 'fucking arse', he turned the trolley in the direction of Pete but evidently too sharply as a case fell from the trolley onto the foot of Pipes. He dropped his sandwich and started to jump around like a scalded cat, holding his foot and gesticulating at Pudding whose predictable smirk was clearly not helping matters. Mark jumped out of the way as Pipes' trajectory veered in his direction. People behind were scattering quickly, evidently concerned by Pipes' antics and his Anglo-Saxon language. Pete started walking over, trying not to laugh too obviously at the pantomime performance that was unfolding before him. It was then that he spied two uniformed and heavily armed airport police officers also heading towards the fracas.

Pete speeded up his walk. 'Afternoon gentlemen. All well, are we?' nodding surreptitiously in the direction of Switzerland's answer to Bodie & Doyle.

'It's this arse, he's broken my fucking ankle and thinks it's hilarious' said Pipes, though the fact that he had reduced the volume considerably suggested that he'd spotted the approaching gendarmes.

Said police officers had now reached them. Officer Un said, in a thick French accent, 'iz everything OK 'ere messieurs?' while Office Deux watched on menacingly, his hand resting on his semi-automatic weapon.

Pete decided to step in just in case Pipes' anger management capabilities were still impaired. 'Oui, errr officers. Pardon mais mes amis et moi, errr leaving maintenant.'

Not waiting for an answer, Pete pointed to the exit and the reunited Old School headed for the doors, Pipes still scowling and limping theatrically.

On reaching the van, Pete, eager to pour oil on troubled waters, said 'Pipes, why don't you sit up front so you can stretch out your leg?'

'No, you'd better let Mark sit in the front. We don't want a repeat of the M6 with him spewing over some unsuspecting Frenchman and causing an international incident.'

## Chapter 51

The members of Old School were sitting in the dining room of Chalet Vin Rouge having breakfast.

'It's not exactly the Ritz is it?' said Pipes, almost swallowing a whole croissant in one go.

'Well, we're on a budget. We're only getting around 150 Euros a night for the gigs so in order for this trip not to cost you guys too much, I've kept the accommodation pretty basic.'

'You mean Marcie has told you to keep costs down' said Pudding, scowling at Pipes as a cascade of croissant flakes and a big blob of strawberry jam fell from his mouth onto the table.'

'Well yes, that was also admittedly a contributory factor' said Pete, realising that denying it would only make them rip into him all the more.

'So, what time is tonight's gig, did you say it's at 'The Igloo'?' said Mark, wiping butter from his knife with his paper napkin before placing it carefully on his plate.

'We are on at eight and then again at ten so I reckon we should be setting up at six to give us time for a decent soundcheck given that it's our first gig on foreign soil. It's in the next street along so I was thinking we might even carry the gear rather than driving round there in the van.'

'If you think I'm carrying my fucking bass drum up the street like I'm some Orangeman on a march, then you're off your bloody head Harsy' exclaimed Pipes, reaching for yet another croissant. 'You'll be giving me a friggin' bowler hat next.'

'OK, OK, keep your mutton chop whiskers on. I'll drive the van then.'

Having finished breakfast, the four of them were now in Sport 2000 getting sorted for their ski gear. While Pete was already equipped and eager to get on the slopes, there was no way he was going to miss Pipes' first experience in a ski shop.

'My weight? What the bloody hell has that got to do with anything?'

'It allows them to set your ski bindings at the correct tension so that your skis come off if you fall over' replied Pete.

'If? You mean when,' said Pudding. 'Though when he does fall, we better get out of the way as there'll be a fucking avalanche.'

It was difficult to detect the two fingered responding salute given Pipes' gloved hands, but the intent was pretty clear.

'Anyway' added Pudding 'where the hell did you get that white jacket from. You look like the Michelin Man.'

'Off eBay, second hand. I wasn't going to spend hundreds of pounds on ski get-up if this proves to be the one and only time I ever ski now was I? We're not all made of money you know.'

'Too right, looks like some of us are made of marshmallow. On reflection, you could be that giant fucker they had in Ghostbusters. Mr Stay Puft.'

As the banter continued, a young Frenchman came over and smiled courteously. 'Size of your feets sirs please.'

Pudding advised an eight, Pipes a ten and Mark deliberated – 'sometimes I'm a nine and sometimes I'm a ten. The last time I went skiing was with the school and I was only 14. I think I had an eight then but I'm sure my feet have grown since.'

'Jesus, Mark, why not just try a nine and if it's too tight then go for a ten. It's not bloody rocket science,' said an exasperated Pudding.

The young lad returned with three pairs of ski boots and passed them around.

After a couple of minutes of struggling trying to get them on, resulting in his face turning the colour of what would have been 'heart attack beetroot' on the pantone colour chart, Pipes looked up pleadingly at Pete. Supressing his natural inclination to fall about laughing, he said 'open the clasps at the front fully and on the foot part of the boot as well. Then really point your toes. Stand up as your weight will help you push your foot into the boot and pull on that strap at the back at the same time.'

Pipes stood and after another minute or so of puffing and panting he was in. 'Right, now tighten the clasps and see how they feel', said Pete, quite enjoying his role as ski equipment expert.

'Christ, you've got to be fucking joking. You're supposed to walk in these? I feel like a sodding stormtrooper in Star Wars.'

'More like Jabba the Hut mate' said Pudding, not even looking up from tightening his own boots.

Pete soothed 'I know, they're not the most comfortable but hopefully you won't be doing too much walking in them.

If they are not too tight or too loose, then you now need to take them off so that they can set your ski bindings.'

'Take them off, take them off? It's taken me ten sodding minutes to get them on.'

Mark was still deliberating between a pair of Salomon nines or Rossignol tens. 'Do you have the Salomons in a ten?' brought a snort from Pudding and he strode over to the desk to sort his skis. Pipes looked at Pete and he indicated that he should follow Pudding.

A stout, middle-aged lady stared at Pudding and barked 'What level skier: beginner, intermediate, advanced?'

'Advanced please,' said Pudding.

'We'll be the judge of that' said Pipes, looking to reclaim some of the ground he'd lost on the banter front with his primary adversary.

Unusually, this brought a look of indecision on Pudding's face. 'Actually, I've spent lots of hours on dry slopes but only skied on snow twice before. And, as it's been a while since I last skied, let's make it intermediate.'

A smug look on Pipes' face suggested that Pudding might be about to change his mind, balking at handing him such an easy victory. But, ever the pragmatist, he clearly decided that safety was more important than point scoring.

It was now Pipes' turn. 'Beginner, intermediate, advanced?' said the scary French woman, looking him up and down.

'Oh, definitely advanced' said Pudding with a grin.

'Sod off, will you Charlton' said Pipes with a narrowing of his eyes. 'I'm a complete beginner Madame, so whatever you think I need for that.'

'Stabilisers?' quipped Pudding.

20 minutes later and they were all sorted, including Mark who had tried three different lengths of pole.

As they stood outside the ski shop, waiting for the road to clear, Pipes dropped his skis with a clatter, bringing hearty laughs from both Pudding and Pete and a concerned expression from Mark.

## Chapter 52

'OK, so what now?' Pipes had managed to waddle awkwardly to the foot of the nursery slope, dropping his poles twice and his skis yet again. He was already blowing quite hard and Pete realised that he would have to take this carefully if they were not to be performing as a trio that evening.

'Well, I don't think you should try too much. You have the first of your lessons this afternoon so let's keep it simple this morning. The instructors are much better placed to get you up and running than I am. Pudding, Mark, if you want to go off and do some skiing, I'm quite happy to spend the morning here with Pipes.'

'What and miss the antics of Franz Klammer here. No way José. Mark, you can go if you want, but I wouldn't miss this for the world.'

'No, I'll stay as well. It's dangerous to ski on your own so I'll wait until the three of us can go together this afternoon while Graham has his lesson.' Mark was still uncomfortable with the Old School nicknames and continued to steadfastly use Pete, Graham and Charlton.

'All for one and one for all it is then' said Pete, placing his skis in the rack so that he could concentrate fully on the task in hand. 'Right then. Pipes, if you can make your way to that rope-pull over there, we'll see if we can at least get you partly up the hill.'

After ten minutes showing Pipes how to put his skis on, he was now equipped with all the requisite gear. With Pudding and Mark looking on intently, Pipes was standing just to the side of a rope that ran for about 150 metres – a so called 'drag lift' via which newbie skiers could make their way up the gentle incline.

'OK, first of all you need to get your skis in line.' Pete bent down to help Pipes manoeuvre his currently splayed skis into a side-by-side straight line. 'That's good. Let these kids go and then we'll try and get you onto the lift. Watch what they do.'

Four toddlers, the youngest of whom Pete guessed to be about two, grabbed the rope in turn, travelling up the slope like a quartet of Oompa Loompas on their way to Willy Wonka's celebrated Chocolate Room. Pudding obviously had a similar thought, launching into 'Oompa Loompa Doompety Doo, Careful as a fat bloke's right behind you.' Had Pipes not been concentrating so hard on staying upright, he would certainly have responded but, as it was, he simply grimaced.

'Right, there's nobody coming so take a couple of small steps forward, keeping your skis in line and, when you're ready, grasp the rope with both hands and let it pull you along. Ready?'

A quick nod of the head, a couple of tentative steps and Pipes lunged for the rope. He travelled about 10 metres before his right ski turned 90 degrees and he fell heavily onto his side. Pete started up the slope, digging the toes of his ski boots into the snow, as Pipes rolled like a stranded walrus trying to get upright.

'Stop, stop,' said Pete. 'You need to get your skis together and sideways to the hill before you try and get up.'

'Sideways, fucking sideways? Harsy, I can't move.'

Pudding was already crying with laughter, doubled up as his hapless friend flailed around, creating a cloud of snow as he thrashed his arms trying to get some purchase.

A queue was already forming at the foot of the lift, with the toddlers pointing and giggling.

As Pete reached Pipes he shouted down 'Pudding. Rather than just standing there peeing yourself (he had the presence of mind to moderate his language in the presence of the kids), make yourself useful and get up here.'

Still laughing uncontrollably but recognising that Pete was already struggling on his own to right Pipes, Pudding started up the hill. 'Mark, you should come too. I reckon this is a three-man job.'

Ten minutes later and Pipes was back at the foot of the nursery slope. 'Ready to try again?' said Pete.

'I suppose so. How come those bloody kids just grab it and off they go?'

Pudding chipped in 'they weigh about a fiftieth of what you do for a start.'

Pete shot an accusatory stare at Pudding, recognising that it wouldn't take much for Pipes just to take off his skis, give up on the whole exercise and repair to the bar. 'It's more that they have such a low centre of gravity Pipes. It's never going to be easy to take up skiing at 53 rather than 3 but you'll get it.'

This time, as Pipes grabbed the rope Pete walked quickly beside him, grabbing his arm for support when he had a wobble. 'OK, let go and come off here' said Pete, not wanting him to be faced with the whole of the slope for his first experience of actually skiing. With a bit of tugging from Pete, Pipes managed to slide across to the piste itself without falling. He came to a stop, his ski tips crossed but still upright.

'OK' said Pete, breathless and with his glasses steamed up from his own exertions. 'Let's get your skis straight but keep them pointing across the slope for now. No, lift the left one up and turn your foot. That's it mate, well done. Now you need to watch my lovely assistant'. He gestured to Mark who was about five metres away. 'OK, Mark, show us the way.'

Mark assumed a crouched position, his skis angled wide at the back, with the tips close together but not touching. He placed his hands on his thighs and began to move slowly down the slope. As he started to gather speed, he twisted his feet to create an even greater angle between the rear of his skis, slowing down again as he did so.

'Right' said Pete 'that's a snow plough. Did you see how, by widening his skis at the back, Mark slowed himself down. You need to keep your hands on your thighs, even on your knees, as that will keep your weight forward.' He cast a surreptitious glance at Pudding, warning him not to take the weight reference as a feed for a quip. 'OK, then, ready to give it a go? Don't worry, I'll walk down beside you and look, it's only about 30 metres until the slope flattens out so you'll be fine.'

Holding Pete's arm for balance, Pipes shuffled his feet around like a celebrity on their first week of training for 'Strictly' (or Ann Widdecombe for the whole series).

'OK, that's it. Push your heels out at the back to create the v shape – more, more. Better. Now, put your hands on your knees. Good. I'm going to let go of you now and you should start moving slowly down the hill. Remember, if you start to pick up speed just push your heels out further and that will slow you down. Ready?'

With a deep breath and a nod of his head, Pipes suggested that he was. Pete let go and his anxious friend started to slide. Pete quickened his own pace as Pipes started to gather speed. 'Push your heels out, push them out. Harder' said Pete, now breaking into a jog.

'Pipes, you're skiing mate, you're actually skiing. You're doing it' cried an exultant Pete, genuinely thrilled that his old mate was hopefully on the road to what he considered to be one of the most thrilling experiences you could ever have. It was then that Pipes' ski tips crossed and he gambolled over like some massive toddler in a Wacky Warehouse ball pit before Pete even had time to try and react. As he ran to the spot where Pipes had come to a juddering halt, fearing the worst Pete shouted, 'you OK mate?'

Grinning like a 90's clubber on ecstasy, with his helmet at a jaunty angle, Pipes replied 'OK, OK? That was bloody brilliant Harsy. Get me up. I'm going straight back up there.'

## Chapter 53

A round of applause rang around the bar of Chalet Vin Rouge. Its source was Pete, Pudding and Mark, who rose in unison as Pipes walked in.

'Come on Franz' said Pudding, 'it's my shout, what are you having?'

'A beer. The local one, whatever it's called.'

As Pudding shouted up a round of beers, they immediately launched into a bout of après-ski banter. Reliving the thrills and spills of the day was another feature of skiing that Pete had always loved. He, Pudding and Mark had taken it steady, sticking to blue and green runs all afternoon to allow both Pudding and Mark to find their snow legs. But the focus of attention was very much on Pipes and how he had got on in his first ever lesson.

'To be honest, big lad, I was just relieved to see you walk into the bar' said Pudding, raising his glass in salute.

'Thanks' said Pipes, raising his own glass in response.

'So how was it?'

'It was great. I fell over a fair bit but then so did everybody apart from some smug teenager who thought he was ready for the Italian Olympic squad. At the end of the lesson, he asked the instructor, very conspicuously, if he could move up a class, precocious twat.'

'So, cocky Italians aside, who else was in your group?' said Mark.

'Well, there was a quite fit looking sixty-year-old so I can put a word in for you tomorrow if you want me to mate?'

Mark blushed and took a quick sip from his pint to hide his embarrassment.

'And there was this German bloke called Hans who spent a lot more time on his arse than me. He was bloody hopeless. We'd all be lined up waiting for our instructor Pierre who would be halfway up the slope trying to get him to his feet yet again. I've already christened him 'Look-No-Hans'. There was a nice guy called Brian from Manchester with his wife Mandy and a bloke from Newcastle with a belly that could compete with mine. You know what Geordies are like, I half-expected him to rip off his shirt and ski down bare-chested shouting 'Come on the Toon'. I didn't really get a chance to talk to the others but there must have been about 15 of us in total.'

'So, you reckon you did OK then?' said Pete taking a slug of his beer.

'I think so. Though I was finding it much easier to turn right than left. Is that normal?'

'Not sure mate – it's so long since I started skiing that I can't really remember. We'll just have to find you a mountain where all the runs spiral down clockwise.'

'Also, my legs ache like fuck. You know you suggested possibly walking to The Igloo, well I'm not sure I can get myself there, let alone my drum kit.'

'No problem. I don't want to worry you but wait until tomorrow morning and see what your legs feel like then. I'd already decided that it will be easier to drive and we can all help out with your kit. Talking of which gents, get your drinks down you as we need to get going.'

## Chapter 54

After a journey lasting less than two minutes, Pete brought the van to a halt outside The Igloo. It seemed small from its frontage but with a large wooden door that had the look of an entrance to a baronial manor house.

'Right' said Pete 'let's go and find Christophe.'

Pushing open what turned out to be a surprisingly light door, Pete led them into a dimly lit bar. He quickly surveyed the scene. A series of tables and chairs occupied the main body, with a small bar running along the wall on the left-hand side. He peered into the gloom and made out an area at the back which had evidently been cleared of tables and chairs.

Pete walked over to the bar and said, 'bonjour monsieur, je cherche Christophe.'

'D'accord' said the young barman, placing the glass that he was cleaning onto the shelf behind him and disappearing through a door.

A minute or so later the door was opened by a great bear of a man, with a shock of unruly ginger hair that gave him the look of somebody who had just got out of bed. 'Pete Harriman?' queried the man.

'Oui' said Pete extending his hand.

'Right, let's dispense with all the French nonsense shall we' said the man in an accent that had more than a hint of South African. 'I'm Christophe, great to meet you. And I presume these guys are the rest of your band?'

'Sorry Christophe. I remember being impressed by your grasp of English in your e-mails, but never having spoken I assumed you'd be French, particularly with the name.'

'No problem mon amie. My mum is French and my dad South African. I grew up in Cape Town, in the shadow of Table Mountain. I've had the bar for about three years now, so my French is pretty good but English is still easier, I presume for you guys too?' He looked around at the other members of Old School who all nodded in agreement.

With introductions over, Christophe said 'Right lads. I presume you'll be wanting to bring in your gear. I'll get Marcelle to give you a hand.'

'Thanks Christophe. I know that will be particularly appreciated by our drummer Graham here. He's had his first ever ski lesson this afternoon and he's already suffering a bit from snow-plough legs.'

'Christ mate. You left it a bit late to take up skiing didn't you? And, no offence intended but as a man with a fuller figure myself, hats off to you. Good effort.'

40 minutes later and all the equipment was in and set up. Though the area they had been allotted was quite small, it was positively huge in comparison to what they'd had to work with at Chas' wake in The Swan. They had set up in their usual configuration: Pipes' drum kit in the centre, Pudding to his right, Mark to his left and Pete straight in front. They were all having a quick break, downing large glasses of coke, Pete having declined their host's generous offer of free beers saying that they might have a few later. As Christophe disappeared through the door at the back of the bar, Pipes had been particularly vocal at Pete's unilateral decision to order soft drinks. However, a swift 'can I just remind you of the Battle of the Bands' had him quickly back-tracking and returning to fiddling with the setting of his cymbals.

Pipes said 'Right, if everyone is ready?' the tone of his voice indicating that he was still a little abashed at Pete's rebuke and the reminder of his faux pas in Birmingham. 'Let's see if we can get the levels right. Pudding, if you can go out front please and me and Mark will just play bass & drums first. Mark, you choose which song.'

Mark, completely unaccustomed to having much of a say in band decisions given his natural reticence and the strong characters of those he played with, looked up from tuning his bass, completely non-plussed. 'Oh, err, OK, what about....no, there's not really very much bass in that one. Then there's..... oh no, I'm guessing that is a bit dull for you on the drums. Or... no, I struggle with the bass part on that.'

'Jesus Mark. Right, You Really Got Me it is' said Pipes, his patience clearly already exhausted by Mark's deliberations.

Pete smiled, secretly pleased that the kind and considerate alter-ego of Pipes had surfaced for a matter of seconds, only to be quickly beaten into submission by the cantankerous, crotchety, belligerent old sod that they all knew and loved.

## Chapter 55

Pete was standing at the bar, along with the rest of Old School, chatting to Christophe about what had been a colourful career path. Having completed his National Service in his native South Africa, amongst his many jobs he had been a security guard, a supermarket manager, a mobile phone salesman, a nightclub bouncer and a chef. It gave Pete pause to reflect on his own career which had been in advertising from start to finish. Christophe's nonchalance in speaking of his moving from job to job, usually in wildly different spheres, encouraged Pete that the leap of faith that he and Marcie were now potentially embarking on was slightly less daunting. Glancing at the clock above the bar, Pete said 'OK Christophe, do you want us to start playing?'

'Yes, why not. It won't start warming up in here for another half an hour or so but at least you might get old Clément over there to get his toes tapping.'

He pointed at on old guy in the corner, nursing his half litre of beer. Pete wistfully thought of Chas before the strains of Plastic Bertrand's 70's new wave anthem Ça Plane Pour Moi broke his reverie. He'd decided to embrace the spirit of Entente Cordiale in his choice of ringtone for the week, hoping that the literal translation of 'it is gliding for me' would prove prophetic, both on the skiing and the chalet planning fronts. A photo of Marcie that he had taken at her fiftieth birthday party, a beaming drunken grin on her face, flashed up on the screen.

'Hello love. Missing me?'

'Of course. Bed's too big without you.' Marcie's reference to one of the lesser-known tracks by The Police had become a standard opener whenever they were apart. 'How are you lot doing? Pipes still alive?'

'Just about. It was touch and go this morning but apparently, he's loved his ski lesson this afternoon so here's hoping he really takes to it. Anyway, how are the kids?'

'Fine. I spoke to Charlie about half an hour ago. She is planning to come back for a weekend at the end of the month, so you'll get to see her. She says Stig has got a second interview for that graduate trainee scheme with Aldi.'

'That's good news. Let's hope he gets it and we can find out all the secrets of the Aldi 'Specialbuys' aisle. Last time I was in there they were selling an inflatable canoe next to a garden gnome dressed in a Liverpool kit.'

'Jack's OK too. Though he's driving me crazy. I think that girl he's currently chasing is giving him the run around and it's making him even more surly than usual. Anyway, I just wanted to say hello and to wish you all the best for your first foreign gig.'

'Thanks love – we're just about to go on actually.'

'OK, I won't keep you. Bon Chance. Break a leg. Love you.'

'Love you too. I'll give you call when we finish if it's not too late but, if it is, then in the morning.'

Old School were now playing Sweet Home Alabama, the fourth song in their first set. Clément had been joined by another couple of old guys and it was beginning to feel a little like the French equivalent of the St Cuthbert's church hall fundraiser but on an even smaller scale. Just as Pipes got to the final crash and Pete was thanking 'the crowd', who actually appeared completely oblivious to the fact that they were playing at all, the front door opened and a group of six girls walked in.

Pete could feel a palpable change in the energy on stage. 'Right, next up we have an old Rolling Stones favourite, Jumping Jack Flash.' Only a couple of bars in and they were already getting more attention than they'd had all evening. One of the girls, a tall, striking redhead, was actually mouthing the lyrics. Then, halfway through the song two of the others came to the front and started dancing.

Pete heard the drums increase in volume as he glanced across at Pudding who had suddenly taken on a much more upright posture. They finished the song and all of the girls applauded. Still not a hint of recognition from Clément's posse but Pete thought you can't have everything. Buoyed by this and hoping to maintain the momentum, he quickly introduced Blondie's Call Me. He decided not to turn around to see if Pipes had adopted his traditional lascivious leer at the thought of Debbie Harry. That would be enough to send the girls scurrying from the dancefloor.

Rather than leaving, the girls who had strutted their stuff to The Stones were now joined by two of their friends. One took out her mobile and started videoing, resulting in an energetic flourish on the strings from Pudding, while Mark switched his gaze to the pub's ceiling. As the girl then started tapping away on her phone while still dancing, Pete tried to maintain his concentration on the lyrics, fighting his own mind as it tried to wander off on an internal diatribe against the inability of the youth of today to focus on any one thing at a time. The irony was not lost on Pete that he was currently struggling himself to stay in the moment, but he still felt he was positively steadfast in his concentration levels compared to the attention span of a gnat that he saw as the default setting of the stimuli-hungry younger generation.

Old School went straight into Elvis ain't Dead, drawing admiring nods from the girls, obviously impressed that they actually knew anything released in the new millennium. As they reached the chorus, the door opened and a group of young lads came in. The girl with the butterfly mind waved to them and pointed at Pete. He concluded that she'd probably sent the video clip to her friends to encourage them to come over and he felt his ego inflate at the thought. It was then that he heard a yell from behind, followed by a crash, as Pipes' hi-hat went tumbling to the floor.

## Chapter 56

Pipes lay flat on the floor. There was a hush in the bar. That was until cries of 'straighten it will you, bloody straighten it. Aaaargghhh' cut through loud and clear.

Pipes had his right leg raised as far as his flexibility would allow which, in truth, was not very far. Pudding had hold of his foot, trying to straighten it in an attempt to alleviate the cramp that had pole-axed Old School's drummer.

'No, No, Jesuuussss H Christ.' Pudding's attempts at physiotherapy were clearly not having the desired effect.

'Come here' said Christophe having made his way over from the bar. 'Let me have a go. I used to play rugby for the Cape Town Cardinals and we had one guy who suffered with cramp most games. Keep hold of his foot while I try a bit of massage. I bet you're glad you took up skiing now aren't you mate? With all that snow ploughing, I'm guessing the pain is in your thigh? Here?'

As Christophe pressed the centre of Pipes' thigh a 'Fucking Hell' suggested that he'd found the spot.

'Wow, that's an impressive knot' said Christophe as he kneaded Pipes like a giant sour dough loaf. After a good couple of minutes, regularly punctuated by moans from Pipes, Christophe said 'it feels as if the knot is loosening?'

'Mmmmm' said Pipes, still through gritted teeth but clearly no longer in the paroxysm of pain that he had been.

'Do you reckon you can stand?' said Christophe, offering his hand to help him up.

Pipes struggled to his feet, grimacing, before being helped over to a stool at the bar.

Pete decided to go to the mic to do a bit of explaining. 'Sorry ladies and gentlemen. You can see that our drummer is errr, somewhat incapacitated. We'll take a break here and hopefully be back for our second set shortly. Refill your glasses and don't go anywhere.'

Pete joined the others at the bar, with Christophe handing Pipes a litre glass full of water. 'You need to get yourself rehydrated mate. Just sit there, keep your leg stretched out and drink this.'

Fifteen minutes and two litres of water later and they were back at their instruments. Though Pipes was far from fully match-fit, in walking back to his drum kit he certainly seemed to be more mobile and was now perched on his drum stool, gingerly massaging his thigh.

Leaning into the mic Pete said 'OK, thanks for bearing with us. Let's get you back on the dancefloor with a favourite of ours and hopefully yours. Our interpretation of I Predict a Riot by the Kaiser Chiefs.'

The rest of the evening had gone relatively well. The numbers in the bar had gradually grown, not to the point where it was standing room only but certainly to what Pete hoped would be a respectable turn-out for Christophe on a Monday night. There had thankfully been no further interruptions from Pipes' ski-challenged limbs, although they had a short impromptu break in proceedings due to the quantity of water he'd consumed. His drumming had not had its normal gusto, particularly his kick drum, but better that than him once again being laid out like a Ronaldo who had very definitely gone to seed.

Pete had finished with 'Thank you Igloo and a big thanks to Christophe for having us over to play for you. We're at The Signal Bar tomorrow night and it would be great to see you all.'

Having dismantled their equipment, they were now at the bar enjoying a drink with Christophe. As he handed over a wad of Euros to Pete he said 'Thanks Pete. You went down well, though I could have done without you advertising my competition in my own bar.'

Pete winced at his schoolboy error. As a man who had spent all of his working life in marketing, he should have known better than to bite the hand that fed them. 'I'm really sorry Christophe. I should have engaged my brain rather than let my natural exuberance get the better of me. I just didn't think.'

A smile from Christophe and a pat on the back with a meaty hand showed that he was joking, or at least not too put-out by the faux pas. 'No worries. I know Jules who runs The Signal. He's a good bloke and there's more than enough business during the ski season for us all to make a decent living. And anyway, are you sure old Graham here is going to be in any fit state to play tomorrow?'

As Pipes carefully got to his feet and limped over to start carrying his kit to the car, Pete wondered if Old School's French tour had come to a halt after only one performance.

## Chapter 57

'Are you going to be OK mate?' Pete's question was directed at Pipes who was walking like John Wayne but at a pace reminiscent of Chas in The Swan.

'I think so. But bloody hell Harsy, you never said that skiing was going to hurt this much.'

'Would you have done it if I had?'

'No, probably not.'

'And then you'd have missed out. Block out the pain and tell me that you're not loving it.'

'Easy for you to say block out the pain. You're not the one who feels as if he's run a marathon chased by Mo Farah. But, you're right, I do kind of love it already. Remind me to tell you about the spectacular crash by Look-No-Hans today that had us pissing ourselves.'

Pete returned to tuning his guitar. They were due to go on in about half an hour, The Signal's owner Jules wanting to let the bar fill up before they started. By the look of it he had done a pretty good job of promotion with about 50 people already in, including four of the girls from the group who had been at The Igloo. Pete's delight at them being back for a second go was slightly tempered by a guilt that perhaps they had poached them from Christophe. Pudding was fiddling with his amp while Mark had disappeared, the increasing influx of people seeming to be in direct correlation to the frequency of his toilet trips.

Old School were now all on stage. This time it was an actual stage rather than just an area cleared in the bar, though at just a foot or so above the bar's floor, platform was probably a more accurate description. Even though they had played only a handful of actual gigs, Pete was already changing his attitude to staging. When he had first explored the idea of setting up a band, playing on a stage was very much an important goal to tick off his bucket list. Though he still relished the feeling of stepping up onto a dedicated performance area, they had played one gig on a particularly high stage, and he realised the potential this had to make you feel disengaged from the audience. Or, perhaps they had just been crap that night and he was looking for excuses? Either way, The Signal's stage seemed ideal, combining the feeling that you were indeed the appointed 'turn' while still feeling connected to those who had come along to watch.

Pete adjusted his mic. 'Good evening Signal. I hope you are all in the mood for dancing? I don't know how many of you are from the UK? A show of hands please.'

About half of the bar's patrons self-consciously raised their hands, while a group of teenage lads raised theirs with a hearty 'Yeeeessssss.'

'OK, then. That makes us feel a little more at home. But whatever your nationality and whatever your age, I'm sure you'll know this one. Pipes?'

A four count on his sticks and Pipes brought in She Loves You. While the Beatles' classic did not tempt anybody onto the dancefloor, there was an encouraging round of applause at the end, accompanied by some energetic whooping from the British teens.

'Thank you. You're very kind. We are Old School and, as I guess you've worked out already, we are over from England. We'll be playing a few songs now, taking a short break and then coming back to play until around 11.30. So, I hope you've all had a good day on the slopes and are now ready to indulge in a bit of The Signal's legendary apres ski.'

Another hearty cheer from the lads suggested that their day had perhaps not involved any ski, just the apres, and probably from about midday.

As Old School continued their first set, the numbers in the bar gradually increased. About halfway through their rendition of The Sweet's Blockbuster, an elderly lady in what appeared to be a very expensive full-length fur coat and matching hat walked in. Pete spotted Jules almost sprint from behind the bar to welcome her, making a space through the crowd so that she could take a seat at the table at the front which had clearly been reserved for her. She was accompanied by a huge guy, at least forty years her junior, who took up a seat opposite, casting an eye around the bar and sizing up the clientele.

Following the extended note to accompany the final elongated 'Blockbuster', Pete said 'thanks very much. One more song and then we'll be taking a short break.' They finished with Queen's Crazy Little Thing Called Love, with the tricky middle eight that they'd always struggled with going OK. Though nobody had yet taken to the dance floor, the atmosphere was warming up, helped by the quantities of booze that appeared to be passing across the bar.

'OK then, a short break for us now but we'll be back' said Pete, placing his Fender on a guitar stand. Pipes switched the PA to pick up the playlist from his phone, with the intro to Joe le Taxi kicking in. Pete wondered what other French delights Pipes might have decided on as a suitable interlude. They all made their way over to the bar where Pete ordered pints of diet Coke for him and Pudding, a mineral water for Mark and a full fat Coke for Pipes who reckoned he was allergic to any drink with the prefix 'diet'.

'So, Jules' said Pete 'who's the lady sitting at the front there?'

'That is Countess Agatha. She comes in here often. She is very, how you say, known. She lives in big chateau in west of town. Very rich lady.'

Pudding craned his neck to get a good look, saying 'well, I reckon she must be the most well-heeled audience member we've ever had.' He turned away quickly as the Countess' companion caught his eye. But evidently not quickly enough as the man rose from his chair to his full, very impressive height and started walking towards them.

'Shit' said Pudding, 'I'm off. If Arnie looks like he's going to follow me in, give me a quick ring on my mobile.' With that he shot off, heading round the back of the bar towards the neon Les Toilettes sign.

As Arnie made his way through the crowd, a middle-aged man who somehow hadn't spotted the man-mountain bumped into him and bounced back a couple of feet. As he focused on the brick wall he had just hit, he quickly raised his hand and garbled a profuse apology. There was a steely glare from Arnie before he re-engaged his tree-trunk legs and continued towards the bar.

'Bonjour Emile. Sava?' said Jules, having already placed a bottle of champagne in an ice bucket.

A grunt and a nod from Emile and he turned towards Mark. 'Hello, I am Emile. I work for Countess Agatha. She wants to talk to you. Come with me.' Without waiting for an answer, Emile picked up the champagne, turned with a speed that reminded Pete of the infamous oil tanker the Amoco Cadiz and started back towards his employer, with a clearly startled Mark in his wake.

## Chapter 58

Pete, Pipes and Pudding were all trying to observe the goings-on at the front table without being too obvious about it.

'What the hell is that all about?' whispered Pipes. 'She looks a bit like Cruella de Vil in that fur coat and, as for Emile, presumably he's one of her henchmen? What does she want with Mark?'

'Well, I'm not asking her and I'm certainly not asking Emile' replied Pudding. 'Harsy, aren't we due back on?'

'Well yes, but we can't start without our bass player. Hang on.'

Pete waved to get the attention of Jules who came down from the other end of the bar. 'Sorry Jules, we are supposed to be playing again but our bass player has been commandeered.'

'Com-and-er, sorry I not understand.'

'No, I'm sorry. I mean Mark, our guitar player, he's….' Pete pointed to the Countess.

'Ah, the Countess. She let him go when finished.'

'Right then' said Pete, turning to Pipes and Pudding 'I guess we'll wait then.'

Ten minutes later and Mark came walking over to the bar. Without the inevitable questions having passed any lips, he said 'I'll tell you later.'

'OK then' said Pete, 'let's get back to it.'

Old School had been playing for an hour, with the crowd getting increasingly boisterous as the drink flowed. The small area that had been cleared for dancing in front of the stage was currently full, with one of the drunk English lads precariously swaying on his mate's shoulders. Pete was impressed by how many of the bar's clientele seemed very familiar with the songs they were playing. It certainly highlighted the reach and popularity of UK and US music in Europe and, Pete felt, demonstrated that their set lists were pretty sound. While they had all wanted to play music that they liked, they were all, Pipes in particular, mindful of trying to ensure they would be popular choices. Talking of which, Pete said, 'Right, this is our last one for tonight.'

Pipes counted them into Mr Brightside and, within seconds, there was a flood of bodies squeezing into the already packed dance area. Pete spotted Emile rise to his feet and thought 'surely not'. Instead of throwing some shapes he simply took up a protective stance, effectively providing a brick wall for any reveller that might have the audacity to encroach on the personal enclave of the Countess. The writhing sea of bodies in front of them added an even greater intensity to the music, with Pipes finishing with a dramatic thrash around his drum kit.

Cries of 'more' from the crowd had Pete looking around at his colleagues before he spotted Emile staring straight at him and shaking his head. Pete could not decide if his look was any more menacing than usual, but the inference was clear. For whatever reason, he was suggesting that an encore was not an option.

For a fleeting moment Pete thought about pretending he hadn't seen him. However, the thought of the potential repercussions, with the underscore of the deference that Jules had shown to the Countess and the fact that he was their paymaster for the evening, made Pete think that on this occasion discretion was very much the better part of valour. 'Thank you, you're all very kind. Sorry, but, as you can see, three of us are old guys and it's way past our bedtime.' He just stopped short of mentioning they would be playing again the following evening at Le Renard bar, switching off the mic and nodding at Pipes to switch to his phone's playlist.

As Pudding placed his guitar on its stand he whispered 'Harsy, why are we stopping? They can't get enough of us. It's not like you to turn down an opportunity to carry on.'

'I know, but let's just say that Emile has made his feelings obvious and I don't think any of us are prepared to take him on.'

Pudding turned around, casting a surreptitious glance at Emile, just as he was nodding at Mark. Mark nodded in return and put down his bass. He came over to Pete and Pudding. 'Pete, Charlton, can I ask a favour?'

As he politely waited for a response rather than just ploughing on, Pete said 'Go on.'

'Is there any chance you can pack away my kit and take it back to the chalet for me? It's just that Agatha has asked me back to her place.' He was already blushing profusely and while ordinarily this would have been a golden opportunity for mick-taking that neither Pete nor Pudding would have been able to resist, they felt the beady eyes of Emile burning holes in the back of their necks. As it was, they both just stared open-mouthed at Mark, with Pete nodding to confirm that they would indeed sort out his stuff.

As Mark stepped down from the stage, Pipes interrupted the dismantling of his cymbals and came over to Pete and Pudding. 'So, what's the score then?'

Still speaking in hushed tones as the Countess, Emile and Mark made ready to depart, Pudding said 'Let's just say that Mark's penchant for old ladies is alive and kicking, though in this instance, I'm not sure he has too much say in the matter.'

## Chapter 59

'Do you reckon he's been kidnapped as a sex slave?' Pudding was taking up a bench seat next to Pete and Pipes. 'Shift your fat arse will you Pipes? I need to sit down.'

The three of them had met up for lunch in a mountain restaurant close to the meeting point for Pipes' ski lesson. Pudding and Pipes had decided to have a morning off skiing and Pete had only done an hour or so, having taken the opportunity for a lie-in. There had been no sign of Mark, nor any communication from him, prompting Pudding's question.

Pudding placed his bowl of soup next to Pipes' tray of soup, hot dog and chips, large coke and crème brûlée. 'I hope she took off her fur coat, otherwise it would be like shagging a polar bear with rickets.'

Picking up his phone, Pipes said 'shall I text him?'

'What, just the aubergine emoji?' said Pete. 'No, I'd leave him be. He's probably living the life of luxury in her chateau. And anyway, we need to go and look at those two chalets from the shortlist later today and I can't see him wanting to tag along to that. Let's leave him sampling the delights of the aristocracy.'

Putting on an accent approximating the Queen if she'd smoked forty woodbines since the age of ten, Pudding said 'Emile, pass the ribbed prophylactics would you, there's a good fellow.'

Pipes choked on his hot dog, spraying ketchup and mustard across the table.

Having finished their meals, they were now standing outside the restaurant. Pipes was taking the opportunity to indulge in an e-cigarette. As he disappeared in a cloud of smoke Pudding vigorously wafted it away from his face. The crowds for the afternoon ski lessons were starting to gather below the bright red signs indicating the class levels. As an ungainly man tried to use his poles to push himself along the flat terrain and navigate his way through the sea of bodies, he fell awkwardly to the floor, taking a small child with him. Pipes burst into laughter and said 'that's him. Look-No-Hans.'

'Blimey, I thought you were bad,' said Pudding. 'He can't even stand up when it's level.'

'I know it's hilarious. And I won't lie, it's great to have somebody as bad as him in the group as it makes us all feel a lot better. Pierre is actually taking us up on the chairlift today.'

'A word of advice. Make sure you're not next to Look-No-Hans, when you get on,' said Pudding.

'OK then Eddie the Eagle, off you go' said Pete, reaching for his own skis that he'd thrust into a pile of snow near the restaurant entrance. 'We'll see you back at the chalet. Take it easy. Remember, another gig tonight. Pudding, where do you fancy skiing this afternoon?'

As Pudding pulled his piste map from his jacket pocket, Pipes made his way to the ESF Ski School sign 'Level 1ER Ski'. While he would not win any awards for style, he was significantly better than Look-No-Hans. As he continued to move, rather gracelessly, to his assembling group, Pete, and he suspected also Pudding, felt a certain sense of pride in his old mate, though neither would ever dream of saying so.

## Chapter 60

Another round of applause rang around the bar of Chalet Vin Rouge. This time the recipient was not Pipes but Mark. 'Yayyy. The conqueror returns' said Pudding. 'Your Dukeness, will you be partaking of a beverage this evening?'

Mark was already scarlet. Pete thought he could feel the heat from a good ten feet away as he continued towards the bar. 'I'll have half a beer please Charlton. Thank you.'

'But of course, my liege.' Pudding pulled a stool away from the bar and gestured theatrically towards it. 'Please sire, be seated and rest thine weary bones.' He then made a great display of removing Mark's jacket, bowing low and tugging a non-existent forelock.

Mark was now beyond scarlet, a colour that Pete thought he'd never seen before on a human face, unless he counted that time when his RE teacher at school had been debagged in full view of all his pupils.

Recognising Mark's discomfort, Pete decided to intervene. 'Good to see you Mark. You can imagine that we are full of questions but if you'd rather leave it for another time?'

'Yes please Pete, if we could.'

They were all now back in the chalet bar following a gig that had not been as good as the previous night but had still gone okay. Both Pipes and Pudding had taken every opportunity to rib Mark throughout the evening. On arriving at the venue Pipes had reached for Mark's guitar from the back of the van, insisting that somebody of his standing should not be carrying their own equipment. When they met Oscar, Pudding had introduced Mark to the quizzical bar owner as The Count. And, when they had launched into Crazy Little

Thing Called Love, Pipes had quipped, 'hey Mark, here's one from your mum.'

As they had only been booked to play for an hour, when they finished the band mates had plonked themselves on seats at the bar and taken full advantage of Oscar's hospitality. They had quaffed several beers each. So many in fact that that Pete offered to knock 50 Euros off their fee which Oscar agreed to on the proviso that they have a Cognac on him to finish off the evening. They had left the van where it was, full of the equipment, agreeing to come and collect it in the morning. They meandered back to the chalet, with Mark taking a minor tumble which was not solely due to the snow underfoot.

The chalet bar had still been open, so they had decided to have a nightcap before retiring to bed. The drink of choice, at Pipes' suggestion, was Drambuie. 'Right, I presume you've all had a go at this' he said, reaching for his lighter. He set fire to the amber liquid in the four glasses lined up on the bar and passed three of them around. He lifted his, put his hand swiftly on top of the glass to quench the flames and downed it in one. The others followed suit, Pipes ordering another round before it had even reached their stomachs.

'I'm feeling a bit woozy,' groaned Mark.

'Me too' said Pete. Let's go and grab a seat over there.

As they sat in the comfy chairs in front of the blazing log burner, Pudding said 'this is the life.'

'Not bad eh', said Pete, 'and, just think, if we can sort out the right chalet, we'll be able to do this on a much more regular basis.'

'Oh, and there was me thinking we were setting up a business' retorted Pudding.

'You know what I mean.'

Pipes approached with a silver tray on which were perched eight glasses of flaming Drambuies.

'Christ Pipes, have you bought shares in a distillery?' said Pudding, still reaching for one of the glasses.

'Hold on, I want to show you a magic trick.' Pipes passed the tray to Pudding and took one of the flaming glasses. As before he placed his hand over the top of the glass but this time pressed it down hard on the rim. It extinguished the flame and stuck tight. Pipes then circled his arm wildly like a Mick Channon goal celebration showing just how effective the vacuum was in securing the glass to his hand.

Mark stumbled to his feet saying, 'that's great', grabbing one of the Drambuies. He decided to replicate Pipes' impressive performance, clamping his hand over the flaming liquid. A second later and his palm was on fire as he had clearly failed to create a seal. He jettisoned the glass, clapping his hands together to try and put out the flame succeeding only in alighting his other hand. The glass spilled its contents onto the tray, creating an impressive conflagration with the remaining glasses now alight among a sea of flames. Pudding dropped the tray, resulting in the burning liquid setting fire to the carpet. Pete leapt from his chair, jumping up and down trying to extinguish the flames by stamping on them. About 30 seconds later, though it seemed much longer, the members of Old School stood in a pall of rising smoke, with the acrid smell of burnt carpet assailing their nostrils.

## Chapter 61

'You mean she's invited us all to her chateau. What for? She's not hoping for a ménage à cinq is she?' Pudding put down his coffee.

They were in a mountain restaurant, having a rest on the first day that they had all managed to ski together. Though it had been confined to sedate green runs and hardly challenging for Pete, Pudding and Mark, the chance for them all to ski as a group had been too good an opportunity to miss. Pipes had fallen several times, clearly pushing himself to try and impress his friends, and, after a particularly spectacular incident in which he had almost taken out a line of children listening to their 'Flocon' ski instructor, Pete proposed stopping for a short break. Pipes' pride had prevented him from being the one to suggest a breather, but he was clearly delighted at the prospect.

Mark, already colouring at the question posed by Pudding, replied 'No. She just said it would be nice to meet you all.'

'So, what's it like this place she's got? Though I'm presuming you only saw the bedroom? She hasn't got a sex dungeon has she?' Pipes had joined Pudding in the interrogation.

Mark's discomfort was evident from his uncharacteristically robust response. 'Look you don't have to come. I thought it was a nice gesture.'

Smirking at having generated a modicum of irritation that would have been a positive tirade from most people, Pipes replied 'Yes. You're right Mark, I'm being churlish, particularly given that it's an invitation rather than a summons to the commoners. You two up for it?'

A nod from both Pudding and Pete and the decision was made. They would be accepting the invitation to Château Cheval Gris.

'OK,' said Pipes 'so we'll be needing to educate our palates to appreciate larks' tongues in aspic and beluga caviar so how about a swift le hot dog and chips to start the process?'

## Chapter 62

'Christ, I feel like I should be wearing a crucifix.' Pudding stamped his feet to warm them, theatrically making a sign of the cross as Pete reached for the heavy brass knocker on an imposing oak door.

Chateau Cheval Gris certainly did have an air of the Transylvanian about it. Two large turrets reached for the clouds scudding across the Chamonix sky, with a twilight backdrop of the Alps accentuating the feeling of Vlad's lofty eyrie.

Right on cue a suitably bone-chilling creak announced that the door was opening. Rather than Renfield, the insect-eating manservant of Bram Stoker's fevered imagination, a cheery 'Hello guys, I'm Brad, come on in' was delivered by a young man who looked like he'd come straight from a swanky US prep school.

Pete led the way across the threshold, shaking the snow from his boots.

They entered a large entrance hall that immediately transported Pete back to Cranby Hall, the venue for Marcie's 50$^{th}$ birthday party. Heraldic banners hung from ceiling to floor, with the stone flags softened by a huge red carpet, complete with a coat of arms proudly displayed at its centre.

'I'll take your coats. Grab a seat guys.' The effervescent Brad pointed to three old leather settees ranged around a gnarled low table, reaching to help Pudding remove his ski jacket.

As Brad bounced away like one of the Kids from Fame, they all sat down, bringing a comedy fart from the leather as Pipes settled his substantial frame. 'You can't be doing that when we sit down for dinner,' said Pudding. 'It might be acceptable in China but the Countess will have you sent to the tower for a flogging by Emile.'

'Look, before we go in, can I just say something. Agatha is a very nice lady and she has kindly invited us into her home. Can we try and tone it down a little please?' They all glanced at Mark, completely unaccustomed to a rebuke from him, however gentle.

'Of course Mark. Sorry, we're being childish' said Pete, with the sniggering from Pudding and Pipes illustrating his point only too clearly.

Brad positively leapt back into the hall with an 'OK, gents. This way please.' He ushered them along a corridor and opened a door, making a theatrical entrance and announcing, 'Mistress Aggie, your guests.'

Said Mistress was sitting on the floor in front of a raging open fire in a yoga pose that would have been impressive at any age, let alone for somebody who was certainly beyond her three score years and ten. 'Hello Gentlemen, welcome to my humble home.' She extricated herself expertly from what Pete thought he remembered as the Dhanurasana from Marcie's brief flirtation with yoga.

It was not only her pose that was striking. The Countess was wearing a shocking pink leotard, with leg warmers that would not have been out of place on Louis Spence. Her silver hair was tied up in a bun that sat on top of a regal head and angular face that positively oozed breeding.

Pete elected to take the lead. 'Hello m'lady.' He immediately realised that he sounded like Parker from Thunderbirds. There was a stifled snigger from Pudding and, in turn, a harsh stare from Mark as Pudding tried to cover up his hilarity with a wholly unconvincing cough. Pete kicked himself that he'd not considered in advance the appropriate etiquette in addressing a Countess but it was too late now and he decided that the best option was just to plough on. 'It is a pleasure to meet you. Thank you very much for your most generous invitation.'

As she jumped up, again belying her years, m'lady strode purposefully over, planting a hearty kiss on Mark's lips. Mark's face immediately tried to match the colour of her leotard, as the Countess said, 'please don't stand on formality – Aggie, please.' She gave a nod of acknowledgement to Pudding and Pipes and continued. 'Please excuse me gentlemen. I lost track of time. I get lost in my yoga. You should be glad it wasn't one of my tantric sex sessions.' As Pudding coughed again, she said, 'Brad, make sure these gents are made to feel at home while I pop upstairs to have a shower.'

## Chapter 63

'So, what's your poison then guys?' asked Brad.

'Do you have any gin?' said Pete.

'Aggie has everything. As for gins we have Tanqueray, Bombay Sapphire, Hendricks, a rather fine Monkey 47 Distiller's Cut and a particularly fruity one that Aggie has distilled in New York and shipped over. It has apples added to the juniper berries – really nice and my personal favourite. It hasn't really got a name so we just refer to it as the Grey Mule. A bit of a play on the name of the chateau and it does have a bit of a kick.'

'I'll have a Grey Mule and tonic then said Pete. Thanks.'

'Classic Indian Tonic, Slimline, Elderflower, Clementine, Watermelon or Sicilian Lemon?'

'A Slimline Indian please.'

'Make that two' said Pipes 'but full fat tonic, not that Slimline stuff.'

'What about rums?' said Pudding.

'Well, we don't have anything produced specifically for us but there's a rather nice Havana Club Máximo Extra that is particularly popular with guests.'

Pete recognised the brand from researching potential client Christmas gifts when he'd worked at H,H &H. It had been quickly discounted, coming in at around £1,000 for a 50cl bottle. Actually, 'bottle' was doing it a dis-service. It came in its own handmade crystal decanter.

'Sounds great, I'll have one of those, straight with ice please,' said Pudding.

'And for you Mark?'

'Can I have one of those cocktails that you mixed for me the other night. That was delicious.'

'A Brad Special coming right up.'

Brad pirouetted and left the room with a jauntiness that was starting to become irritating to the three Brits of a certain age who were accustomed to taciturn rather than jovial on speed.

Pipes was clearly keen to make the most of the opportunity of Brad's absence. 'Blimey Mark, the Countess is a game old bird isn't she? I bet you had a right old time the other night. Can she get her legs behind her head?' The accompanying lascivious grin was one that he normally reserved for whenever Blondie appeared on the set list.

'Look Graham, she is a very nice lady and we had a lovely time. Let's just leave it at that.'

'I'm just saying. I wasn't expecting that. There's not many 70-year-olds who could rock a leotard. Then there's the flexibility and she's also a bit of a looker for somebody who's old enough to be your grandmother. My Nan, god rest her soul, wouldn't have been able to get one of her legs into that outfit. Even if she had, it would have looked like a sausage about to burst free of its skin.'

Pete realised he needed to steer the conversation in a different direction. Mark was clearly uncomfortable, a state that would only encourage Pipes, and he wasn't sure of the room's acoustics. He knew that in old houses sound could carry and while he was fairly confident that the Countess wouldn't hear anything, particularly above the noise of her shower, he still didn't want any risk of her being exposed to Pipes' critique.

'Come on Pipes, let's leave it for a more appropriate time shall we. What a pad eh?'

They all took the opportunity to give their attention to the room. The most striking thing about it was the fact it completely turned expectation on its head. While the gothic grandeur of the exterior had been carried through into the entrance, the door to this living area was a gateway to another world. It was the door equivalent of the wardrobe to Narnia. This was modern with a capital 'M'. The entire room was painted a stark white, accentuated by the vibrant colours of a series of modern art pieces which dotted the walls. The only interruption to the expanse of marble floor was a single black rug, around which was placed a large sofa and three accompanying chairs. Their simple, angular lines screamed modernity.

The only element in the room that gave more than a nod to the building's heritage was the large open fireplace. But even that was short-lived as either side were two large expanses of glass. At present the gathering gloom allowed just the outline of the Alps to be made out, inciting Pete to wonder just what the view would be like during the day when they were revealed in their full majesty.

Pete was about to approach a large painting and inspect it more closely to see if he could see the artist's signature and perhaps get an idea of its value when Brad returned carrying a tray of drinks. He was accompanied by a man of similarly tender years dressed in chef's whites. In a timid voice, chef said 'gentlemen, dinner is served. Please follow me.'

## Chapter 64

With his free hand Brad opened a door and with a nod invited Pete to step through. Standing at the end of a huge dining table was Countess Agatha, resplendent in a shimmering red and gold kimono. 'Gentlemen. Come in and take a seat. Don't stand on ceremony, anywhere is fine.'

Despite the instruction, Pete wondered if there was an etiquette he should be following in being the first to select a seat. But, drawing another blank and wishing that he'd got a copy of Debrett's to hand, he simply pulled out the nearest chair and sat down. Pudding took a seat to his left, with Pipes and Mark opposite and the Countess finally assuming her position at the head of the table. Natural authority will out thought Pete, admiring the natural grace with which she took her place.

There was an intimacy to the table, despite its size, as the settings had been placed at one end. Pete looked down its length, realising that they had used less than a quarter of what would easily accommodate more than 20 guests.

Glancing up at chef, Aggie said 'OK, Louis, what delights do you have for us tonight?'

'Well Mistress Aggie, we have a starter of double-baked cheese soufflé or bouillabaisse. For the main we have leg of lamb with pumpkin gratin or salmon en croute with dauphinoise potatoes, followed by apple, pear and quince membrillo tarte tatin.'

'Wonderful. You know how much I love your lamb. That sound OK for you gentlemen? Mark said that none of you has that dreadful affliction, vegetarianism.'

Pete's 'sounds fantastic' was greeted with appreciative nods all round.

'OK, thanks Louis. If you could send in Curtis.'

A couple of minutes later and in came who Pete presumed to be Curtis. He was a similar age to Brad and Louis, tall, lithe and with a shock of long jet-black hair. Pete thought he detected a trend here and wondered about the interview process that Agatha adopted. So much for Mellors, the gardener in Lady Chatterley's Lover; it looked like Agatha had a male harem.

Curtis took their orders, not bothering to make a note but simply committing it to memory. Youth, thought Pete, reflecting on his own inability to remember even the shortest of lists and once again thanking the god Steve Jobs for the iPhone Notes function.

There followed as convivial a meal as Pete could remember. Countess Aggie was the perfect host, asking them about how they knew each other, how the band had come about and generally showing a real interest, as well as a wicked sense of humour. She ensured everybody was included, even occasionally managing to draw the naturally introverted Mark into the conversation.

She spoke openly of her own privileged upbringing, including attending one of Switzerland's top finishing schools. Much of her ongoing fascination with the male species she attributed to that fact that it was an all-girl school. She had then gone on to study fine art at Yale, remaining in the US for a number of years working as an interior designer. Pete now realised the foundations for both her impeccable English and the beautiful environment in which they sat. Aggie had never married, preferring to 'keep her options open and take her pleasure as and when required.' She'd added that this was pretty often, citing this as another reason for her single status as she'd never found 'a man or woman with sufficient stamina to keep up.'

The drink was flowing freely but even in his slightly hazy state, Pete recognised that it seemed to have positively gushed in Pudding's direction. He had stuck to the rum rather than joining in the rather splendid Premier Cru Pinot Noir from Aggie's extensive cellar and it was showing. From the half empty decanter, Pete realised that there must be around 500 Euros worth sloshing around inside him. He was slurring his words and his occasionally nodding head showed that the soporific effects of the Havana Club were starting to kick in.

Curtis cleared away the few remnants of the main course, replacing them with fresh dishes, and as he closed the door behind him it jolted Pudding to attention. 'What's this?' he mumbled, glancing down at the cherry red offering before him.

'That's a sorbet' replied Aggie, reaching for her spoon.

'What's it for?' said Pudding prodding the fruited ice with his index finger.

'It cleanses the palate. It's designed to remove the residue of the lamb from your tongue so that you can properly appreciate Louis' excellent tarte tartin.'

'S'okay' said Pudding, fumbling in his pocket. 'I don't need it. I've got my Wrigleys', producing a stick of America's finest.

The look of thunder from Mark had Pete about to apologise for Pudding's oafish behaviour but before he could get a word out, the Countess burst into laughter, throwing her head back and cackling uproariously. It was so infectious that it immediately cut through any awkwardness, with Pete, Pipes and even Mark joining in, bringing a quizzical look from Pudding whose synapses were clearly not fully firing.

An hour later and they were all sitting back at the roaring fire which had been restoked by Brad. All apart from Pudding were enjoying one of the best ports that Pete had ever tasted. As Brad refilled his glass, he couldn't help but think that he was probably about to quaff another hundred Euros.

'Just this one and then I think we'd better be going Aggie' said Pete, nodding towards Pudding. He was slumped in the chair, bearded chin on chest, softly snoring. The warmth of the fire had pushed him over the edge. 'I'll call a cab.'

'Nonsense. I won't hear of it. Brad will drive you back.' With a twinkle in her eye Aggie added 'Mark, I'd like to think you might want to stay over. I'd love to show you my grandfather's etchings again if you think you are up to it?'

Blushing profusely, Mark gave an almost imperceptible nod. Pete was thankful that Pudding was not in any position to cough inappropriately, though he now knew that Aggie would not have given a hoot if he had.

As she saw them to the door, Aggie said 'Pete, don't forget to get in touch when you've decided on your chalet. As I said, I know a few people who can help things run smoothly.'

'I bet you do' thought Pete, 'I bet you do.'

## Chapter 65

'Do you think you could eat those crisps a little less noisily?'

'Sorry – these French ones are crunchier than the ones I'm used to' replied Pipes, spraying a few bits onto the floor of the van in the process.

Pete and Pipes were about four hours into their journey to Calais. They had dropped Pudding and Mark at the airport for their return flight. Pipes had opted to make the return leg with Pete, citing as his motive the fact that he thought he'd appreciate a travelling companion. Pete suspected it was more of a cost-saving exercise. However, as Pete had encouraged him to come out to France in the first place and his hotel experience had actually proved invaluable when they'd viewed the prospective chalets, he felt it would be churlish to point this out. And anyway, he did relish the company rather than facing the long journey back on his own.

'Piss stop?' said Pete spotting a sign for a service area coming up in 5 kilometres.

'Yes please. I think we could also do with replenishing our snacks – we're getting a bit low.'

'I wonder why that is' said Pete, viewing the various empty packets sitting in the passenger footwell.

With a grin, which clearly showed the residue from his latest snack stuck in his teeth, Pipes said 'I don't know what you mean.'

They sat at a high counter, Pete with a latte and Pipes with a bottle of coke and a croissant.

'The boys should be landing in Birmingham in about half an hour,' said Pete.

'Lucky sods. Here's me taking one for the team just so that you're not Norman No-Mates travelling back on your own.'

Pete elected to let the comment pass.

Pipes continued. 'I bet Mark's guilt levels will go up a notch when he gets back on UK soil. Do you reckon he'll tell Marjorie about his holiday romance?'

'I don't know. It's up to him. It's not as if he's married and you've suggested more than once that at his age he should be sowing his wild oats.'

'Yes, I know, but I was thinking on more fertile soil rather than with somebody whose furrow has been ploughed over and over by multiple farmhands for half a century. What is it with him and old women? I mean the Countess was a real looker for her age, but she is genuinely old enough to be his grandma.'

'I know, but each to their own, eh Pipes?'

They were now back in the car, Pete feeling refreshed after their short stop and thinking he might now do the next six-hour stint without another, bladder permitting.

'So, do you reckon you are going to buy that Chalet Mardi Gras?' asked Pipes.

'I think we might. Obviously, I need to discuss it more with Marcie but it was certainly in our top two and your assessment of it was encouraging. It was also Pudding's favourite.'

'Yes, I think there's definitely an opportunity to charge a higher rate for that one than Chalet Angelique. It was only a couple of minutes' walk to the chairlift, the rooms were bigger and the décor was clearly more in keeping with a traditional ski chalet vibe which is what I think most people want. I know you can redecorate but given your legendary ability for DIY, I reckon the less you have to do the better.'

Pete had to acknowledge that the thought of having to put his non-existent DIY skills into action had certainly been a contributary factor in his own decision-making process. 'I'd obviously employ tradesmen. Marcie wouldn't let me near anything with a hammer, let alone with something as sophisticated as a drill. But I take your point. Countess Aggie also knew the chalet and had some positive things to say about it.'

While they had not gone into any detail during their visit to Chateau Cheval Gris, Pete had outlined his plans to become a French chalet owner. Aggie had listened attentively, saying that she knew the owners of some of the chalets that he'd mentioned. She had been encouraging when he had mentioned Chalet Mardi Gras, saying that the only reason that it was up for sale was that Monsieur Charpentier had died and his idiot son had inherited it. Apparently, he had ideas way above his station and was investing in some folly of a business venture involving some dodgy Arab sheik. He'd decided to cash in on the chalet to give him some additional capital. She had also added that the local gossip suggested he was pretty desperate to sell as the clock was ticking on this investment opportunity, so she thought there was a deal to be done. Pete realised that in addition to being a hugely enjoyable evening, the trip to the Chateau had proved potentially very fortuitous in terms of his new career prospects.

## Chapter 66

'OK, this is it' said Pete, coming to a halt outside a nondescript white building.

'Wow, cheap and not particularly cheerful by the look of it.'

'Look mate, it's free accommodation as far as you're concerned, and it helps keep Marcie happy on the budget front.'

The focus of their comments was an F1 hotel on the outskirts of Calais, their appointed stop-over before taking an early morning tunnel crossing. Though its name suggested the cream of motor racing technology, in reality it was more of a Ford Ka.

They both grabbed their overnight bags from the back of the van, checking that the instruments had not shifted during the journey. Pete said, 'Do you reckon we'll be OK to leave the kit in here overnight?'

'Unless you plan on taking it all out and trying to get it into a room that is likely to be the size of a cupboard then yes. I'm certainly not shifting my drum kit but if you want to take your guitar, then be my guest.'

'No, I'm sure it will be fine. Look there's a CCTV camera up there.'

Pete punched the access code into the keypad at the hotel's main entrance and, on the second attempt, they were in. Pete headed straight for the stairs, Pipes veering off to the left towards the lift. 'Pipes, it's two flights of stairs. Surely even you can manage that.'

'Look, you haven't spent a week bloody snow-ploughing. I'll see you up there.'

Pete took the keycard that he'd picked up from the automated system at the unmanned reception and opened the door to the room. Though not quite the cupboard that Pipes had suggested, it was not overly large but it had two beds and really that was all they needed,

Dropping his bag on the bed nearest the door, Pete said 'right, let's go and get something to eat before the restaurants close.'

'You're pushing at an open door there Harsy.'

Just across the road from the hotel, on a non-descript industrial and retail park, Pete spied a restaurant. It did not look particularly enticing but as the thought of getting back into the car after their 10-hour journey was not an appealing one, he looked at Pipes who gave a nod.

They sat in a small booth, with cracked vinyl seating and a plastic flower table arrangement that had evidently not been dusted in years. Pete's thoughts turned to Marcie and the realisation that by now she would have been back on her feet and out of the door. Pipes had already grabbed the menu, which Pete took to be tacit approval that it at least lived up to his requirements.

A surly looking young waiter with dirty fingernails took their order. 15 minutes later and they were both tucking into pizzas. Pete had gone for the simple small Margherita. His logic was the smaller the surface area and the fewer the ingredients, the less chance of botulism. There had evidently been no such qualms for Pipes who was devouring a large Meat Feast, accompanied by fries, onion rings and a large coke. His ability to put away vast quantities had originally been a source of amazement to Pete but now he was simply used to it.

The only other people in the restaurant were a middle-aged couple sitting quietly on the opposite side of the restaurant. Pete thought he recognised the man and said as much to Pipes.

'Where from? What are the chances of somebody you know being in a dodgy French restaurant on the outskirts of Calais at 10.30 on a Thursday night?'

'I know. That's what I was thinking but he is familiar, though I can't for the life of me think why.'

'That reminds me. Have I ever told you the story of my mate Jez who works at the hotel?'

'No, I don't think so.'

'Right then' said Pipes putting down his slice of pizza. This raised Pete's expectations immediately since it must be a half decent story if it had the power to interrupt Pipes eating.

'Well Jez was on holiday with his missus in Antigua. I think it was their silver wedding anniversary, so he'd pushed the boat out considerably as they normally go to the Norfolk Broads. Anyway, he's lounging by the hotel pool and spots this bloke who he recognises. But, a bit like you, he doesn't know where from. He spent a few minutes considering who he might before going back to his book.

'The following day they are on the beach and he sees this bloke again. His mind starts ticking over. Is it their old milkman, was it the bloke that used to run the newsagents, might he have seen him in the local Tesco? Still no joy in remembering.

'A couple of days later, he and his wife are enjoying a drink in the hotel bar and who should he spot. It's now really starting to bug him. He stares intently at the guy, really wracking his brain. Has he worked with him at some point, has he seen him in the local pub, has he been a guest at the hotel? Then a lightbulb moment: he reckons he might be the bloke who owned a second-hand car dealership in Warwick where he'd bought his knackered old Fiesta.

'He can't stand it any longer, so he goes up to him at the bar and says 'look mate. I'm sorry if you might have spotted me staring at you over the last few days but I know you from somewhere and I've been struggling to remember where from. I think I've got it though – didn't you used to run Mike's Motors at the end of Bishop Street in Warwick?'

'The bloke turns to him and says rather frostily 'No, I'm Eric Clapton'.'

It was Pete's turn to repeat an action that was more commonly associated with Pipes, bursting out laughing and spraying a mix of dough, cheese and tomato over the plastic flower arrangement.

## Chapter 67

Pete and Marcie were sitting in the kitchen waiting for the kettle to boil. 'So, what do you think?' said Marcie. 'I have to say I'm dubious.'

'Me too but it is his 18$^{th}$ and if that's what he wants then we need to at least consider it.'

The topic of conversation was Jack's birthday and his suggestion that he wanted a house party. When he had broached the subject, for one fleeting moment Pete harboured a forlorn hope he might mean somebody else's house. But no, he meant the family home. Pete knew that he'd been the target for Jack's opening foray as he had always been a softer touch than Marcie. However, even he would not contemplate a straight yes to a proposal with such potentially horrifying consequences. He had therefore gone with the standard 'I'll speak to your mum.' He detected a mixed reaction in Jack's features: disappointment that this would be going to a higher power and one that would most likely result in a no but tinged with a glimmer of hope that it hadn't yet been rejected out of hand.

Pete had tentatively offered an alternative, partly tongue-in-cheek he told himself (though he wasn't completely sure). 'So, you don't want us to hire a venue then and perhaps have Old School playing?' A snort followed by a 'yeah right' and that avenue very quickly transformed into a cul-de-sac.

The kettle started whistling and Pete went over to make a cup of tea. 'Marce, think back to when we were that age. Do you remember that party I had when my parents were away on that cruise around the fjords?'

'Yes, don't remind me. That's one of the reasons why I'm thinking it's not a good idea to subject our house to a gang of marauding drunk teenagers.'

'It wasn't that bad. A few spillages, a dead goldfish and that cigarette burn on the mantlepiece, but I managed to get away with it. Or, at least I thought I had. For weeks they didn't know I'd even had the party. That was until my dad cornered me and asked if I'd had anybody round while they were on holiday. Of course, I said no but then he asked me again. I still said no but my resolve was crumbling. It was when he produced a bottle of Woodpecker cider that he'd found in the toilet cistern that I had to 'fess up. I still don't know to this day who stashed that bottle away. Anyway, my point being that at least Jack has asked us rather than trying to organise something behind our backs.'

'I know, but sometimes ignorance is bliss. Now we actually have to make a decision. And what about social media? You hear nightmare stories of these events going viral and getting completely out of hand.'

'Come on Marce, It's only the electronic equivalent of the jungle telegraph we had back in the day. I made the mistake of inviting Michael 'Mouthy' Clarkson only because my mate Simon Parks – you remember Parky – fancied his sister. In no time at all the whole of the school knew about it. Mouthy's sister didn't turn up but about 10 of his mates who I didn't even know did.'

'OK Pete, but not even Mouthy had the ability to let the whole world know.'

'Don't get carried away love. I can't see the San Jose chapter of the Hells Angels turning up at a teenage get-together in Leamington.'

The conversation went on for another half an hour, with the pros and cons identified and debated. While neither of them could identify many, if any, pros from their side, the opportunity to give Jack something that he really wanted was a strong motivator.

'OK then. Let's say a tentative yes on the understanding that Jack agrees to us putting some definite rules in place.' Marcie's steely look in delivering her verdict made Pete realise that Jack was in for a negotiation session that would not be out of place at a NATO summit.

## Chapter 68

'Mum, you cannot be serious.'

Pete thought about lightening an increasingly tense atmosphere by asking Jack when he'd decided to start channelling the legendary John McEnroe. But he then recalled his reference to Miami Vice and Don Johnson - when Jack had questioned his father's sartorial elegance in an 80's photo - and decided that the withering response of 'who?' was likely to be repeated.

'That's a non-negotiable Jack. She's your sister so you should be inviting her anyway.'

During his many years in advertising Pete had picked up a few tips on reading body language from the H, H&H Behavioural Science department and Marcie's folded arms spoke volumes.

Jack thrust out his jaw in a classic 'chin jut' and Pete thought he would be better adopting a less aggressive posture if he was going to get anywhere with his redoubtable mother. 'But you're just making sure that somebody is there to keep an eye on me.'

'Yes, and your point is?'

This battle of wills had been going on for about an hour. Marcie had started with the classic 'Right Jack, this party. We are prepared to entertain the idea but it's on certain conditions.'

Pete had nodded sagely, realising that he needed to support Marcie, not only for marital harmony but also because that was the only way Jack was going to have any chance of getting this through. An image of Marcie with a black cloth draped over her head and delivering a thumbs down gesture jumped unbidden into Pete's head.

Pete had been impressed by Jack's initial conciliatory approach. There had been concessions on both sides. Pete's question as to how many would be invited had been answered by Jack with no more than 80. Marcie's opening gambit of 40 maximum had eventually ended up at a reasonable compromise of 60 – straight down the middle and no loss of position for either of the chief negotiators. A similar result had been achieved with what parts of the house would be off-limits. Marcie's initial ban on anybody being upstairs had been countered with a 'what about my bedroom?' Marcie had conceded on that and then also on Charlie's bedroom, providing Charlie was happy with that arrangement and was always one of the people in there. Pete & Marcie's bedroom had been non-negotiable, with a steel in the enforcement protocol that had Pete wondering if he might have to install barbed wire and sniper turrets on the landing.

Things had started to go downhill for Jack when he had snorted at Marcie's proposal of a midnight finish. While Pete thought this was too early, Jack's response was ill-advised. When he then went for a 4.00am, Pete realised that the strains of the negotiation, coupled with his natural teenage instinct for not agreeing with just about anything his parents said, were starting to bubble to the surface. Despite this bump in the road, there had been a slight shift to 1.00am achieved through Pete's intervention. He had suggested that there was no reason why they could not go onto a club, essentially treating the house party as part of the 'prinks' pre-drinking culture which now seemed entrenched in a night out for anybody under the age of 30. This was agreeable to both parties, but it was clear that Marcie was starting to gain the upper hand.

Jack had then made a schoolboy error, not too surprising given that he was one, albeit a college sixth-former. He had revisited a point that had already been agreed and ratified by the Chief Negotiator. Having accepted that his sister had to be at the party, he was now griping at the prospect, hence the impasse that they had now reached. In the classic teenage response at the frustration of not being able to vocalise his thoughts to win the argument, Jack turned on his heel, slammed the door and left the negotiating table.

An hour later, he had slinked downstairs, apologised to his mum, and acquiesced to 'the Charlie Clause.'

## Chapter 69

It was the night of Jack's party and Pete and Marcie were at the cinema. Pete had found an 11.00pm showing of The Exorcist at a small, independent place that they'd visited on a few occasions. They preferred it to the soulless multiscreen options, particularly its excellent and reasonably priced art deco bar which compared very favourably to the cost of a coke and a bag of pick n mix at the multiplex which equated to the GDP of a small African country.

They had left the house at eight, Marcie still issuing strict instructions to Jack as she put on her coat. They first port of call was a recently refurbished pub that had been on their radar for a couple of months. But, only a few minutes in and Pete realised that it was unlikely to be a memorable meal, however good the food.

'Pete, have we done the right thing? Do you think we can trust him? And it's not only Jack, what about his guests?'

'Look love, worrying about it is not going to make any difference. It's done now so let's just let them get on with it. If anything happens then I'm sure Charlie can handle it. I wouldn't want to take her on, would you? And, if worst comes to worst, then she can always pick up the phone.'

'OK, if you're sure.'

One sip of red wine later. 'You did put away that glass sculpture from Venice that my mum gave me, didn't you?'

'Yes, and the designer lamp, the expensive clock and the rug we bought in Marrakech.'

The meal had been interspersed at regular intervals with similar queries. Marcie had picked at her beef stroganoff, clearly her mind otherwise engaged with thoughts of cavorting, bacchanalian teenagers, surrounded by trashed objet d'art and her prized Laura Ashley curtains ablaze. Pete hoped that he would be able to ply her with enough drink to at least take the edge off. But, when he'd asked if she wanted a refill of her half-drunk small red wine, it had been met with a 'Pete! I think we both need to keep our wits about us, just in case, don't you?'

After the meal they had headed on to the cinema. Pete knew that it was largely just an attempt to keep their minds occupied and to give them something to do until they were allowed to return to the house. As they had driven away, Marcie had even suggested that they might just park up around the corner and listen out, but Pete had managed to dissuade her from what was effectively a stake-out of her own son.

The fact that the film was The Exorcist was very much a plus to Pete. Not only were they both keen fans of the horror genre, but this William Friedkin classic was amongst their favourites. It had been one of the first films they had seen together, admittedly with a large group of friends who had jumped at the chance to see a pirate video copy of a film that had gained such notoriety when nuns had demonstrated outside cinemas in attempts to stop people going in.

The film being banned meant that video copies were in high demand and like catnip to teenagers in the late 70's and early 80's bred on a diet of video nasties such as I Spit on Your Grave and Driller Killer. This certainly had moral crusader Mary Whitehouse's voluminous nickers in a twist for a while, as she and her National Viewers and Listeners Association cohorts became the damp squibs to teenage fun.

However, this time around, Pete and Marcie were not teenagers and it wasn't fun. One of the first things Pete normally did on entering a cinema was to turn off his phone, long before being instructed by the on-screen reminder.

However, on this occasion he would have to swallow one of his pet-hates and perhaps himself be the irritating twat.

Mike Oldfield's instantly recognisable Tubular Bells emanated ethereally from the sound system creating the Pavlovian response in Pete of the hairs on the back of his neck standing immediately to attention. He glanced at Marcie to see she was delving into her handbag to take out her phone, presumably just in case it had rung and she'd missed it. Marcie's fidgeting continued throughout the film. Though she was clearly not giving it much attention, she did turn to Pete at one point. In the iconic scene in which the young Regan MacNeil spews vivid green projectile vomit all over the long-suffering Father Karras, the look on Marcie's face suggested that it had triggered the thought that a similar scene was currently being re-enacted all over her beloved Lexington sofa.

Five minutes later and Pete jumped out of his skin. It was nothing to do with the on-screen action. James Brown screaming 'I feel good' told him that he had a call.

## Chapter 70

Pete and Marcie were back in the car within 5 minutes of Pete receiving the call. 'So, what did Trevor actually say?' squeaked Marcie. Pete considered a white lie to make the drive home less fraught but decided that honesty was the best policy.

'He just said 'Pete, sorry to bother you but I think you should come home, the police are at your house'.'

'That's it, that's all he said?'

'Yes, I was already self-conscious at my phone going off in the middle of the film, so I thought brevity was the best approach.'

'Brevity, Pete, fucking brevity. Sod the film. The police are at our house!'

'I know. Let's just try and remain calm shall we and wait until we get home before making any snap judgements?'

It was normally Marcie that was much better in a crisis but Pete was actually feeling a little guilty at not having tried to get more information from his neighbour Trevor before signing off. He knew he was therefore over-compensating.

'Call him back and ask him what's going on?'

'Look, we're only five minutes away so let's not interrupt his night any more than I suspect it already has been.'

As they turned the corner into Oakland Road the flashing blue lights were clear to see. As they drew closer Pete exclaimed 'Oh shit'. It was not just two police cars with their blues and twos. There was also an ambulance.

Marcie had her seatbelt off in a flash and was out of the car before Pete had even engaged the handbrake. She ran up the drive to be met by a stout police officer standing in front of the door. 'Madam, can I help you?'

'Yes, this is my house what is going on?'

'Well, there has been an incident and the paramedics are in there now.'

Pete had joined Marcie and just as she was about to further question the policeman, a stretcher attended by the paramedics came through the door.

'Oh my god' said Marcie straining to see who was under the blankets. But an oxygen mask, an intravenous drip and blankets pulled up to chin level made it difficult. 'Stand back please madam' said the police officer, 'we need to let the ambulance crew do their work.'

'But my kids' whimpered Marcie.

'Mum.' An ashen-faced Jack appeared in the doorway. 'I'm sorry.'

Marcie just grabbed Jack and held him close with a 'thank God. Where's Charlie?'

'She's inside somewhere' managed Jack, before bursting into tears.

Pete ran into the house. There were kids everywhere. He shouted 'Charlie, Charlie.'

Receiving no answer, he stepped over two lads who were sitting in the hall, bottles of Corona grasped protectively to their chests. 'Charlie?' As he entered the living room it was noticeable that the majority of the guests were gathered at the top end. Pete made his way over and saw glass everywhere and a substantial pool of blood in the centre of the carpet. The patio door leading out to the garden was shattered. He turned to a gangly teenager with lank, greasy hair protruding from a beanie hat. 'What happened here son?'

'Dunno, nothing to do with me. I was in the kitchen.'

Pete realised that the lad's self-preservation gene had kicked in at the sight of a fully grown adult. His answer was a combination of blame deflection and a commitment to not incriminate anybody else by giving any information away. He realised that this line of questioning was unlikely to get him anywhere with this particular individual. Just as he turned to continue his search in the kitchen, there was a loud cry of 'Dad!'

Charlie stepped through the empty doorframe and hugged her dad tightly.

'Are you OK' said Pete, involuntarily stroking his daughter's hair and regressing to the time when he'd consoled her on a much more regular basis in her younger years.

'Yes, I'm OK. Dad, it was awful.'

'OK, love. We're here now. Let's sit down and you can tell us what happened.'

As Pete made to go through to the kitchen, he was intercepted by the police officer who had been stationed at the door. 'Sir, I believe you are Mr Harriman. I am now going to ask everybody to leave. Once that's done, if we could speak to yourself, your wife and your children as we need to understand what happened here.'

## Chapter 71

'I'm PC Shipman and this is PC Matthews. Please understand that we're not here to apportion any blame to either of you but we need to know what happened this evening. Just take it from the start and please take your time.' PC Shipman had removed his hat to reveal thinning hair and greying temples, suggesting many years on the force and the probability that he had seen just about every situation in his time.

'Can I get my children a glass of water' said Marcie, now calm and back to her usual practical self. 'Would you like one yourself or perhaps a cup of tea?'

'Yes please Mrs Harriman. A tea would be most welcome. Milk with two sugars for me please and black for PC Matthews.'

Jack and Charlie glanced at each other, looking like a pair of baby rabbits caught in the headlights and clearly unsure how to proceed.

PC Matthews leant forward. She was small, with elfin features and Pete guessed that she was not much older than Charlie. Despite her tender years, she said in a quiet but authoritative voice 'I know it's difficult for you both. We have all been at parties which have got a little out of hand. We just need to establish how…' she glanced down at her notes '…Mr Carlisle was injured.'

'Is Billy going to be alright' said Jack, his lip trembling.

'Let's hope so' said PC Shipman. 'Whoever called the ambulance did the right thing. They got here quickly and, though there was clearly a lot of blood, the paramedics didn't think that a major artery had been severed.'

Pete winced at the reference to blood and arteries, seeing Jack also gulp reflexively. He patted Jack's shoulder and nodded encouragingly for him to speak.

'OK' said Jack. 'I'll tell you what I saw.' He took a deep breath and a sip from his water with a hand that was still trembling. 'Sparky, one of my college mates, is a weekend DJ so he brought his decks.' He glanced at PC Shipman – 'you know, record decks, for playing vinyl?' PC Shipman, looked up from his notetaking and nodded for him to continue. 'He decided to go a bit retro which was fine for a while, but then he played Pretty Vacant by the Sex Pistols and everybody stared po-going.'

Pete thought he detected an appreciative nod from PC Shipman and he wondered if the authoritative figure that now sat before him had once been a punk anarchist intent on overthrowing the establishment. Despite the seriousness of the situation, Pete's imagination genie kicked in and he visualised the slightly balding pate replaced with a pink Mohican.

'It got a bit raucous, with some of the lads starting to fight dance.' Pete saw Jack's eyes widen at the thought that this might incriminate somebody. 'Nothing violent of course, you know just play fight-dancing.'

A nod from PC Shipman indicated that indeed he did know.

'Anyway, next thing there was a massive crash and somebody had gone through the patio door. I pushed my way through and saw Billy lying on the patio. He wasn't moving.'

Jack's lip started to tremble and, spotting her brother's distress, Charlie stepped in. 'I was in the kitchen when I heard the crash and I came running into the living room. I saw this lad lying on the patio and it was obvious that he'd gone through the door. There was glass everywhere. I did a first aid course in my first year at university, so I suppose instinct took over. I asked somebody to fetch me a clean tea towel while I checked for a pulse. That was strong which I took to be a good sign. Most of the blood seemed to be coming from his arm so I made a tourniquet out of the tea towel and tied it above the wound. One of Jack's friends held his arm up in the air to slow the bleeding. He was also bleeding from his stomach so Jack fetched some towels from the airing cupboard and I applied pressure to them on his abdomen.'

PC Matthews gave an encouraging nod to Charlie and smiled at Jack to indicate that he'd done the right thing.

Having recovered his composure, Jack, eager to press home the fact that he'd helped, added 'then I rang 999 to get an ambulance.'

Another ten minutes of questioning and notetaking and PC Shipman seemed satisfied with what he had heard. 'Well, it looks like this was just a very unfortunate accident. I'll leave your parents to discuss this further with you but try not to worry too much about your friend Billy. We'll head over to the hospital now. Mr Harriman, if I can take your mobile number, then I'll give you a call as soon as I know anything."

## Chapter 72

'Here you go mum. Just as you like it.' Pete placed a cup of steaming cappuccino on the table and sat down. He was pleased that she had agreed to try a new venue for their weekly mother and son lunch. Though her opening shot on entering the cosy country pub on the outskirts of Leamington had been 'it's not as spacious as the Toby', she had warmed to it over what had proved an excellent meal. This had undoubtedly been helped by an elderly waitress who had complimented her on her new cream cardigan. In the ensuing conversation, with Pete just an onlooker, he learned that it was from the M&S Per Una collection and had been reduced to less than half price in the sale. With his mum conspiratorially writing down the price on a napkin like she was about to share the Colonel's secret recipe, she handed it to 'Florence' and they seemed to be well on the road to becoming BFFs.

Joyce blew on her cappuccino, widening the point of the heart that had been traced into its surface which resulted in it looking more like an arse. Pete's thoughts turned wistfully to his dad and his much-discussed haemorrhoids. He elected not to mention this to his mum as she took a sip. Placing the cup back on the table she asked 'So how is that young lad that hurt himself at the party?'

'He's OK. They kept him in hospital for three days but I spoke to his dad last night and he's doing well. He's still not back at sixth form yet but they expect him to return next week.'

'I hope you weren't too harsh with Jack. He's a good boy.'

'We had words, obviously, but we both know that it was not his fault. And, we were impressed with how both he and

Charlie handled the situation. They must take after their mother.'

A wry smile from Joyce revealed that she knew that her son had never been great in a crisis.

'Talking of Marcie, I still think the chances of him ever having a house party again are pretty much non-existent, even if he wanted to.'

Florence came bustling over, giving Joyce a beaming smile and a wink. 'If you fancy a refill of that cappuccino, just let me know. The boss isn't in on Tuesdays so it's easier to get away with a few things.'

As Pete wondered if Florence might be the wife of one of the old boys who had masterminded the Hatton Garden heist, he smiled at the bond that had developed between his mum and Florence in the space of a couple of hours. He was confident that he would now be pushing at an open door in suggesting that the Coach & Horses become a regular haunt for their weekly get-togethers. Though he realised this would all be changing, and soon he could well be having lunch with his mum on a daily basis.

'So then mum, are you all set?'

'Yes, I think so. I can't believe that in a couple of months' time, I'll be living in France after spending nearly 80 years here. I wonder what your dad would have to say.'

Pete spotted a tear in the corner of her eye and patted her hand. 'He'd have been very proud of you mum, taking on such an adventure at your time of life. It's going to be a new start for us all and he'll be looking down on us, rolling his eyes if I even try and pick up a hammer to hang a picture in the chalet.'

## Chapter 73

'Your turn at the bar Marky boy. I'll have one of these bad boys again.' Pudding handed his huge empty plastic beer glass to Mark. The four of them had decided on the two-pint reusable behemoths in a bid to keep trips to the bar to a minimum.

Old School were at The Institute in Birmingham's Digbeth for a gig by The Specials. Pete had bought them all tickets to have what was effectively a last hurrah before he, Marcie and his mum left for France the following week. Although he was hardly travelling to the other side of the world – in fact about a 90-minute flight from Birmingham to Geneva – Pete knew that his new life inevitably marked a watershed for the band. They had all got used to the regular get togethers for practice and, while the commitment was still there to not let the band fold, they all knew that it was going to prove a lot more difficult with The Channel separating Pete from the rest of his band mates.

'So, what do you reckon to this lot?' said Pete, gesturing towards the stage where a young ska band were playing what he assumed to be one of their own compositions as he'd never heard it before.

Pudding said, raising his voice as the brass section kicked in, 'It's hard for a support act isn't it? They know that nobody is there to see them so the best they can expect really is for people to give them a listen. I remember going to see The Lightening Seeds a few years back. They had a support, the name of which I can't even remember, but what I do remember is the lead singer having a bit of a meltdown. People were inevitably arriving halfway through their set and you could see it was pissing him right off. Eventually he just lost it and started ranting that the latecomers were missing 'the best fucking band you're ever going to see'. After five minutes of watching them I didn't agree but I could see his point.'

As if reading Pudding's mind, from the stage came the words 'thanks for listening. We've been Ska Attak. This is our last one of the night before we hand over to the legends that are The Specials.'

The mere mention of the headliners brought the loudest cheer of the evening, prompting an 'I told you so' nod from Pudding.

Pipes turned away saying 'Right, I'll go and give Mark a hand. He'll never carry four of those monsters on his own', before starting to make his way through the crowd.

A few minutes later and Ska Attak left the stage to polite applause, apart from some very enthusiastic whistling and cheering from a small group gathered to Pete's right. Probably the band's friends and family thought Pete. The roadies started to reset the stage. The young drum-tech enjoyed his 30 seconds of fame with an impressive roll around the kit. He then sauntered off, his jeans halfway down his backside revealing what, even from a distance, was a decidedly grubby pair of boxers. Pete wondered if roadies came from the same secret town as the so called 'Carnies' of his youth who jumped on and off the waltzers with consummate ease and clung to the back of the dodgems as sparks showered them from the electrified roof.

Pete took a look around the venue which was now starting to fill up quickly. He put the average age of the audience at mid-fifty, not surprising given that The Specials were at their height in the 80s. There was the inevitable odd pork-pie hat and many blokes that were sporting the skinhead look, with the obligatory Doc Martins, stone-washed jeans and Fred Perry t-shirts. Some had even manged to get hold of two-tone check braces. A few had gone for the tonic trousers that changed colour depending on the light and Pete wondered if there was some huge warehouse in Milton Keynes knocking out clobber for the discerning but overweight aging rude boy.

He also realised that back in the day the skinhead haircut had been a fashion choice – for most there was now no choice involved. It also looked as if some brave souls had tried to squeeze into their original Fred Perry's, with the bloke next to him clearly struggling as it rode up a substantial pot belly.

The expectant air was cut through by a huge cheer as the lights dimmed and silhouettes of the band made their way onto the stage. The haunting strains of the brass section were followed by Terry Hall's laconic delivery of 'Is this the in place to be?' Back to the trumpet and trombone and then 'What Am I doing here?' Brass section again before 'Watching the girls go by, Spending money on…'. A blinding flash of lights and the whole band exploded into Nite Klub.

The result of the cry of 'BEER!' on the crowd was electric. It was as if the guy in charge of London's millennium firework display had lit the touchpaper, with rockets in the form of middle-aged men and a few brave rude girls/mums/grans exploding in a chain reaction. It was many years since Pete had been in a mosh pit and he realised why. Back in the day it had been a case of taking your life into your hands but with the collective poundage of 50-year-old skinheads now looking to relive their youth, the buffeting was on a whole new level. As Terry spat out 'And the beer takes just like piss' Pete raised his now half empty beer to Pipes as they joined in with the iconic line which reverberated around the room.

The fourth song of the set saw the band take on Monkey Man. As the 'dancing' in the mosh pit moved up another notch, Pete turned to Pudding, Pipes and Mark. A raise of his eyebrows and flick of his head towards the bar was enough to signal his intent, with nods from all three, a particularly vigorous one from Mark. They squeezed their way through the crowd, still bouncing up and down whether they wanted to or not. As they reached an area where the crowd was a little sparser and a lot less rowdy, Pete shouted 'blimey, was it that crazy back in the day?'

Pipes replied 'probably – we're just getting old. How about we watch the rest from the balcony?' He gazed at his empty plastic glass. 'I reckon I drank about a quarter of that. The rest is on the fucking floor.'

## Chapter 74

'Pete, where did you put that box with all the plates in it?'

Marcie, flushed and with an expression that suggested Pete had about two seconds to respond with the correct information, put down the large linen basket she was carrying.

'It's in the kitchen, where it should be' said Pete, hoping to god that he'd remembered correctly.

They were finally moving into Chalet Mardi Gras, though that was already a misnomer. A shiny new sign displaying Chalet Le Nid was one of the many changes that had been made during the 12-week refurbishment programme that Pete had project-managed from his study in Oakland Road. Rather than subject his schoolboy French to a test for which it was ill prepared, he had employed an English builder. This process had been assisted by Countess Aggie who seemed to know just about everybody in Chamonix, recommending Bill as a man that had done a great job in renovating one of her many outbuildings.

Though born in Pinner, Bill had lived in France for over twenty years so was well versed in overcoming the natural reticence of the locals to employ anybody not born and bred in their own fair country. He had an excellent team of French brickies, carpenters, sparks and labourers, with a real knack for getting the most out of them through a combination of coercion and downright bribery. This had, however, contributed to the project going significantly over budget, with sweeteners a regular requirement in getting the job done on time. But, on time it was and, at least to Pete's untutored eye, to an impressive standard.

Pete picked up a box of the brochures that he'd had produced and took one out. Pudding had done the design and

Pete had pulled a favour from a printer he'd given lots of business to during his time at H, H&H to get them run-off at cost. Proudly front and centre on the cover was a stylised nest. Chalet Le Nid had been the choice from a shortlist of names that he'd discussed with Marcie, having first had a brainstorming session with Pudding to come up with potentials. The French translation of The Nest had conjured up the cosy image that they'd wanted to portray: a place where people would feel warm and safe. And, as Pete explained, one from where newbie skiers and boarders could spread their metaphorical under-developed wings to become fully-fledged eagles, swooping down the gleaming pistes offered by Chamonix to return tired and happy at the end of the day to hearty nourishment at Le Nid. Marcie had responded with 'bloody hell Pete, I'm not one of your clients that you have to impress with your flamboyant marketing bullshit' but she had nonetheless agreed that the proposed name did indeed fit the bill. Pete elected not to mention Pudding's comment that baby birds ultimately 'sod off, never to return' as Le Nid had been Pete's suggestion and one that he was determined would not be sullied by such trivia.

Pete put down a box and sat at the large table that would soon be surrounded by guests buoyed by what he hoped would be excited chatter about the day's exploits on the slopes. It was now only three weeks until Le Nid would host its first paying guests and while there was still much to do, Pete was feeling quietly confident. Yesterday had seen another significant step forward with Suzy agreeing to take on the role of chalet girl. She had been working at Le Lapin Blanc when the Harrimans had taken their ski holiday and had seemed the only one of the staff who had any real sense of a work ethic. Pete had made a tentative call to potentially poach her once the contract had been signed for the purchase of what was to become Le Nid. She had not been particularly happy with her lot at the time but had said she was going to stay for personal reasons.

A tearful call only a couple of days ago had revealed that those personal reasons had been a relationship with Joey, the chef. While she had seen it as a monogamous coupling, her finding Joey in bed with a leggy Swedish blonde guest had suggested he felt otherwise. She was therefore looking for somewhere new to live, as well as work. Pete proposed that while the live-in position was hers if she wanted it, she should take a couple of days to think it over and then get back to him. She did and was duly appointed Chalet Host.

This had made Pete even more relieved at an earlier decision. What had proved a particularly tricky conversation was when Joey heard of the change of ownership at the newly christened Le Nid and had approached Pete for a job as head chef. While Pete knew that his ski-guiding abilities would be useful, this was far outweighed by the recollection of his grey meat offering, the origins of which Pete was still dubious about to this day. The potential of an Aussie chalet lothario, though not specified on his CV, had also been an unwanted attribute. Pete had therefore let Joey down gently, truthfully saying that initially he would be taking on the chef role himself to keep costs down but (perhaps less truthfully) with the promise that he would be in touch if that changed. He now recognised that he had dodged an even curvier ball than he previously realised. The thought of a teenage on-off romance between two of his staff was the stuff of nightmares.

A shout of 'Mum' saw Joyce poke her head around the door. It was adorned with a floral headscarf that made her look like a land girl from the war. 'Have you managed to find my MacBook?'

'Your map book?'

'My laptop computer. I'm pretty sure I packed it in with the sheets and blankets to make sure it travelled safely.'

'No love. Not yet but there's still some boxes I haven't looked in.'

'No problem – no rush but if you can let me know when it turns up.'

Pete was eager to check that the internet router was working and even more eager to see the latest incarnation of the chalet's new website. Pudding had taken responsibility for it, working with one of his students who he'd described as 'absolutely crap at design but he's a nerd of the highest order and knows his way around the techy stuff.' They had done a great job, Pudding's accomplished design skills clearly evident in what was a clean look but one that still managed to capture the cosy and traditional feel that was at the heart of Pete's marketing strategy. Having given Pudding his feedback a few days ago Pete hoped that the tweaks had been made: another piece of the jigsaw in place as the opening date for Le Nid loomed ever closer.

## Chapter 75

'I now declare Chalet Le Nid open.' Countess Aggie cut the red ribbon with a flourish and a beaming smile. 'Now, over to your new hosts, Mr & Mrs Pete and Marcie Harriman, to say a few words. I wish you both all the luck in the world.'

Pete went to shake hands with Aggie but she waved his hand away and gave him a warm embrace, then turning to Marcie to do the same. She applied three kisses on their respective cheeks, causing a comical hesitation from Pete as he wondered if it was to be her home nation's two or the three adopted in her formative years at her finishing school. Kissing etiquette aside, Pete realised that his invitation to the Countess to officially open the Chalet had been a masterstroke. The lounge area was filled with the great and the good of Chamonix. Pete had estimated there would be around 50 people attending but in fact it was closer to 70. Even the mayor was here. Ever the pragmatist and with her experience in book launches, Marcie had ensured the planning had not only run like clockwork, but that they had over-catered. It had clearly been a wise decision. She had also employed the local bakery to do the catering and a local vineyard to supply the wine, another shrewd move as they looked to try and integrate themselves with the locals.

Pete stood in front of the newly installed bar. He had suggested setting up his mic and amp, but Marcie had overruled him. 'Pete, you'll not be belting out Brown Sugar this time. Let's keep it informal and intimate, shall we? We'll only be speaking to a relatively small room.'

So, without amplification, Pete addressed the assembled guests. 'Bonjour tout le monde. I was going to try out my French but as it is truly appalling, I hope that you'll forgive me if I stick with my mother tongue. You're all very welcome and it is great to see so many of you here. Some I have already met and some of you I look forward to meeting properly. One thing I would like to say to you all is a huge thank you for making 'Les Rosbifs' feel so welcome.'

A smattering of laughter from the assembled throng suggested that Pete had gauged the self-deprecating humour about right. And, even more importantly, it also showed that they understood what he was saying.

'This is a new and exciting venture for us and we are very much looking forward to hopefully becoming part of your Chamonix community. We are inexperienced so if any of you have any tips or suggestions, they would be very welcome. With our small team here, we are all excited for our new challenge. My wife, Marcie, you'll hear from in a second. Suzy is our chalet host, who joins us from Chalet Le Lapin Blanc where she spent last season. Francoise is also a chalet host and will be our ski guide. Many of you will know him as he's lived in Chamonix all his life and has spent the last eight years as an instructor with ESF. And, last, but by no means least, we have Joyce Harriman – my wonderful mum – who will make sure that we are all kept in line. Say hello everybody.'

Joyce, Suzy and Francoise stood and waved from the back of the room.

Pete looked across at Marcie who now took her cue. 'Again, a warm hello everybody. I'd just like to echo my husband's thanks to you all for extending us such a warm welcome. It's been a little daunting leaving our old home to try and make it not only in a new country but in a business venture in which neither of us has any experience. I'm sure we'll make lots of mistakes but hopefully we'll get there and have some fun along the way. I'd like to say a special thank you to Countess Agatha for all her kind support and for agreeing to officially open Chalet Le Nid for us. She has been nothing short of magnificent – generous with her time, her contacts and her considerable wisdom. I don't know what we would have done without her.'

'Here, here' cried Pete starting a round of applause that was quickly picked up by everybody around the room, clearly illustrating the regard in which the Countess was held by the Chamonix community.

'So, if you'd like to raise your glasses' continued Marcie. 'To Chalet Le Nid and all who sail in her.'

'Chalet Le Nid' echoed round the room, with Pete thinking 'so, here we go.'

Three hours later and the last of the guests had gone. The mayor had been the last to leave, poured into a taxi murdering Charles Aznavour's 'She'. Pete and Marcie stood on the balcony, with a glass of champagne. 'Here's to us' said Pete, planting a big kiss on his wife's lips.'

'To us' said Marcie, taking a big glug of her bubbly.

Pete gazed out across the Chamonix valley. He contentedly mused that though not quite the vista of Countess Aggie's chateaux, it certainly beat looking out at Trevor's clapped-out Ford Transit back at Oakland Road.

## Chapter 76

Pete pulled into Geneva Airport. As he climbed out of the gleaming silver Mercedes minibus, he took an admiring look at the Chalet Le Nid logo applied in the black and gold Baskerville Old Face font that Pudding had selected. Marcie had questioned the cost of a brand-new Mercedes as the chalet's mode of transport but Pete argued strongly for the importance of that first impression, reminding her of 'C alet Le La in Bla c', and had won the day. He had parked a little further away than was ideal but was happier in the knowledge that there were no vehicles either side to potentially ding the shiny new paint work.

He pressed the key fob three times to make sure that it was locked, went back and checked anyway, before walking towards the airport terminal. Despite the significance of the day and the one thousand and one things on his mind, his day-dream genie jostled his way to the fore and Pete wondered at the sense of calling it a terminal. Though not a nervous flyer himself, he realised that the name was perhaps not the best for those of a nervous disposition who really didn't want to be reminded that this flight might be their last.

This was the first ever transfer of Chalet Le Nid. Pete had chatted to Gabriel, the owner of a nearby chalet, at the opening of Le Nid. He had spoken at length of the airport transfer being the worst day of the week, fraught with potential issues and a lot of hanging around. Maybe it was because it was Pete's first experience of it, and everything was still shiny and new, but he was loving it. The trip to the airport had combined the pleasure of driving the smooth and well-appointed Mercedes with some of the most spectacular scenery in the world. There had been little traffic on the roads, no queues at the tolls and he had quickly found a parking space. So far so good. He now entered the terminal, determined to make this the smoothest ever transfer experience for his guests.

He looked up at the arrivals board. First, he spotted flight EZS8464 from London Gatwick – on time and due to land in just over an hour. Then there was the BA726 from Heathrow due in some 10 minutes later and also on time. Finally, there it was, the afternoon Manchester flight which was currently showing as per the schedule. Things were looking good.

He checked his iPad for the list of guests – there were two parties coming from Gatwick, three from Heathrow and four from Manchester: a total of 32 so just four short of full capacity for the inaugural week of their new venture. Half of them he'd be able to get in the Mercedes and then the Manchester contingent would be travelling in the minibus of a local taxi company that Countess Aggie had recommended. She had actually offered the services of Emile, but Pete had politely declined, saying that she'd already done quite enough for them and they had to start working things out for themselves. The real reason had been that Pete did not want his granite features and nightclub bouncer physique to be the first encounter that guests had with Chalet Le Nid. First impressions counted and while he was sure that Emile had many impressive attributes, a welcoming demeanour wasn't one of them.

Pete had toyed with the idea of making two trips as he could probably just about make it back for the Manchester flight. But Marcie had been the voice of reason. Though she understood Pete's desire to make a good first impression, she had said it was too much. More than six hours of driving for Pete, additional miles on the Mercedes and there would also be plenty for him to do back at the chalet. He knew she was right so called the taxi company. Suzy would be travelling over with the second minibus to make sure a friendly face was there to greet the guests. He had even managed to ensure a bit of branding, producing some magnetic signs with the chalet's logo which would be temporarily applied by the minibus driver.

Pete realised he had time for a coffee so headed towards the Montreux Jazz Café, his preferred option from the airport's several watering holes. Although jazz was not his favourite genre, he still lapped up the opportunity to see performances on the café's screens of some of the biggest names to grace Switzerland's world-renowned event.

He ordered an Americano with a croissant and settled into a seat that allowed him a clear view of the arrival's board. As he took his first tentative sip from the piping hot coffee his thoughts turned to base camp. Back at the chalet he envisaged a scene of military precision, with Marcie marshalling her troops to get everything ready for their guests. Suzy's experience as a chalet host had already proved invaluable in the run up to today. She had shown a willingness not only for hard work but also a lack of reticence in offering suggestions. Pete knew that Marcie would have to feel that she was in control but having a willing ally who was happy to follow instruction, as well as draw from her own familiarity of the workings of a chalet, would be welcome support as Marcie sought to navigate her way through unchartered waters.

Pete had a vision of his mum, complete with land girl headscarf, trundling around with the vacuum. Pete and Marcie had discussed long and hard how to approach her role. He knew that it was vital that she felt part of the adventure though he was also mindful that she was nearly 80. She was very sprightly and active for her age. When Pete had been working, at the agency he would sometimes arrive home to find her cleaning his windows or weeding the lawn. This had led to the tongue-in-cheek remark from Trevor his neighbour that he'd be reporting Pete to Help-the-Aged for exploitation of the elderly.

Though he was keen to encourage her to continue this can-do approach in this new life in France, Pete also needed her to do what she wanted. They had therefore agreed she would contribute as much or as little to the day-to-day running of the chalet as she felt comfortable with. This had been with the proviso from Joyce that she be responsible for the daily task of folding and laying out the napkins, along with setting the tables for evening meals. Pete readily agreed, recognising this would give her a bit of ownership and focus to her day, allowing her to take as long as she needed to complete the task while the guests were out enjoying the Chamonix slopes.

Pete realised that in his musings almost an hour had flown by. He glanced up at the arrivals board to see that flight EZS8464 had landed ten minutes early. Surely this was a good omen?

He picked up his iPad and flicked to the Power Point he'd created with the words 'Welcome' and the Chalet Le Nid Logo, followed by the names of the guests scrolling through. He thought back to the scrawled piece of paper he'd held up for Old School's arrival. This was no time for playing the fool: it was showtime.

## Chapter 77

Just 15 minutes later and the Gatwick travellers were all assembled. One party consisted of Harry and Penny Golding and their children Max and Olivia; the second comprised four friends - Hilda, Gwyneth, Carol and Margaret - who Pete guessed were all in their early sixties.

'Right folks, the next party of guests should be landing in about 10 minutes so if you want to take a comfort break or have a quick look around the shops, if you can all be back here by half-past?'

As the guests headed off in different directions, Pete turned his attention back to his iPad and the next list of would-be 'Nids'. As he found the new file with their names, he looked up at the arrivals board. Next to the Heathrow flight read 'Expected: 11.50'.

'Bugger' muttered Pete under his breath.

The flight was now running almost an hour behind. With the words of Gabriel ringing in his ears, Pete quickly dispelled them, determined to not let this first hiccup ruin his maiden voyage.

With the Gatwick posse now re-assembled Pete put on his best agency pitch smile. 'Thanks for all being back on time folks. Unfortunately, the Heathrow flight has been delayed by about an hour. Sorry. It looks like you made the right call with EasyJet rather than BA. If it's OK with you all, we'll make our way to the café over there and I'll buy you all a coffee and a pastry. I have to say for airport food, the pastries are pretty good.'

'No problem' said Harry on behalf of his family, though the glare from his teenage son suggested differently.

'Do they have Chelsea Buns?' said one of the pensioner party (Pete thought it might be Gwyneth, though he hadn't committed names and faces fully to memory yet).

'Not sure, but I reckon we'll be able to find something that you like. Thanks for your understanding folks.'

The café conversation had been very good natured. Pete had already learnt that this was the Golding's second ski trip of the season, having spent a week in January in Zermatt. Harry ran his own business supplying spare parts for Bentleys which evidently paid well as when Pete asked what Penny did, she'd replied 'lunch mainly'.

It turned out that the four ladies were all old school friends who had decided that Chamonix was a perfect venue for a long overdue school reunion. When Carol excused herself to go to the ladies, Hilda immediately dropped into a conspiratorial whisper. 'We have all kept in regular touch over the years, but this is the first time we've all been on holiday together. Both myself and Gwyneth are widowed, and Margaret here is single. It's been a bastard of a year though for poor old Carol. Her husband upped and left her after 30 years of marriage so we all decided a trip away would do her the world of good.'

Pete nodded sympathetically, slightly taken aback at the potty mouth of a sixty-something lady who he'd only met less than an hour ago.

Hilda leaned in closer. 'He went off with her hairdresser you know. The shit. Wouldn't have been quite so bad if he hadn't been called Derek.' Her face creased into an infectious grin and Pete thought that he must introduce her to Aggie – she'd love her.

Pete had kept a watch on the arrivals board without appearing to be rude to his guests. He took another look and couldn't quite believe what he saw – 'Expected 14.15'.

'If you'll all excuse me for a moment folks, I just need to go and check something.'

Pete made his way quickly over to the information desk. 'Excuse me, but is that right, the Heathrow flight is now not expected to be here until quarter past two?'

A lady with the appearance of an anorexic Barbie pumped up on coke put down the stapler that she was manically tapping and looked up from her computer terminal with a scary smile and dilated pupils. 'That's right sir, 14.15' she replied rather pedantically. 'Apparently they are having pilot staffing issues at Heathrow.'

Pete thought back to the time he'd picked up Charlie and her boyfriend from Warwick station when the train was delayed by several hours due to a driver being unavailable. It appeared that the British railway network was not the only mode of transport with incompetency issues. Having somebody to bloody drive it - whether a train or a plane - was a pretty basic requirement.

With a terse 'thank you' Pete left the grinning skull and headed back towards the café.

He stopped by a pillar that put him out of the eyeline and also out of earshot of his guests. On the third ring Marcie answered. 'Hi Pete, how's it going?'

'Well, it was all going fine. The first party landed ahead of schedule, but the bloody BA flight hasn't even taken off yet. I can't expect the Gatwick guests to hang around the airport with me for another couple of hours. I've already had them in the coffee shop for the best part of an hour.'

'OK Pete. I agree. Let's think this through. What time is the Manchester flight due in?'

'14.35.'

'And is that showing as on schedule?'

'At the moment, yes.'

'And the revised arrival time for the Heathrow flight?'

'14.15.'

'OK, well the minibus from the taxi company is booked to be at the airport by 14.15 to pick up the Manchester guests. So, that will be just about right for the delayed Heathrow flight – might be worth seeing if they can be there at about two, on the off-chance that it could be early.'

'Yes, but there's now going to be 24 people needing to get to the chalet, so they won't all fit in.'

'I know. I'm thinking another mini-bus or, even better, I'll see if they have a small coach instead. Leave it with me. You just concentrate on the ones who have already landed and I'll sort the rest from here. And yes, I can read your mind. Don't worry about Suzy. She's more than capable and has much more experience of airport transfers than either of us.'

Grateful for his wife's no-nonsense practicality Pete put away his phone, put on a smile and headed back to the café. 'Right folks, I'm sorry but the Heathrow flight has been delayed even further. So, we'll make separate arrangements for them to be picked up later which means we can now head off to the chalet. If you can make sure you have all your luggage, then please follow me.'

## Chapter 78

A dusting of icing-sugar snow had been visible on the sides of the road as they entered the Haute Savoie region. Pete threaded his way through the twists and turns of the mountain road. As they climbed, the depth of the snow increased and with it the buzz of anticipation in the minibus. Pete recognised the feeling. Weeks in advance of any skiing holiday he was making daily visits to the webcams and weather reports to check on the snow conditions. But there was nothing like actually seeing it on the ground. This time, though, the thrill of expectation was different. For Pete it was not the promise of a great week of skiing but the hope that their first ever guests would like what they had to offer.

'Welcome to Chalet Le Nid' said Pete, bringing the Mercedes to a smooth stop right outside the front door.

Right on cue, even before the guests had climbed out, Marcie, Francoise, Suzy and Joyce appeared at the door like a crack Formula One pit crew. Francoise immediately headed for the back of the minibus. Pete lifted the automated rear access door with a satisfying press of a little button in the driver's door panel and Francoise started removing the luggage. Pete jumped out and opened the side door. 'Come on in everybody. Let's get you all settled.'

As Marcie booked in the guests and handed them their keys, Francoise and Suzy introduced themselves. Joyce hung back, a little reticent, until Hilda held out her hand with 'I'm Hilda. And who might you be?'

'Pleased to meet you Hilda. My name's Joyce and I'm Pete's mum. I'm nearly 80 you know.'

'Never. I hope I look as good as you when I'm 70, let alone 80.'

Pete, watching on, thought 'fucking bless you Hilda' as Joyce broke into a wide grin.

With everybody now clutching their keys, Marcie addressed the group. 'So, if you want to drop your bags in your rooms and get yourselves sorted, in 20 minutes or so we'd like to invite you join us for a welcome drink at the bar over there to our right. I don't know if Pete mentioned it, but you are our first official guests here at Chalet Le Nid and we'd like to mark the occasion. Francoise will then be doing a run to Sport 2000 for you to select your skis.'

With all the guests heading off to their rooms, Pete made his way to the kitchen. He had his first dinner for 32 people to prepare!

He opened the fridge to an array of vegetables that he'd chopped at 5.00am to get some of the prep out of the way and get ahead of the game. He was also delighted to see that the chickens had been butchered and made a mental note to thank Suzy later.

He'd thought long and hard about this first meal. He'd wanted something that was typically French. As his first official dish, he had also wanted it to be special and something that the guests would remember. And, remembered for the right reasons rather than Joey's 'grey meat and mush' that brought bile to the back of Pete's throat whenever he recalled that night at Le Lapin Blanc. But it also had to be within budget and not set the bar too high leaving the potential for disappointment on subsequent nights. Managing expectations was a skill he'd learned early on in his advertising agency days. He also knew that in catering for a large number he could not be too flamboyant in his choices. It was quite a balancing act.

So, after much deliberation, his inaugural offering would be Chicken Fricassee with Lyonnaise potatoes, baby carrots and green beans. He decided to go with the classic French onion soup as the starter, with another stalwart choice of tarte tatin for dessert. Louis had given him his recipe for the wonderful apple, pear and quince membrillo tarte tatin, but Pete had decided to err on the side of caution, going for the more traditional apple only option. He told himself that this was more likely to appeal to more of the guests, though cost and doubts in his own culinary abilities were undoubtedly contributary factors.

Pete heard the voice of Hilda talking to Marcie at the bar and decided it was time for him to show his face. He would get on with the cooking, helped by Suzy once she got back, when Francoise left for the ski shop.

Marcie was offering Hilda a complimentary drink. 'Have you got any Aperol? I was introduced to Aperol Spritz on a skiing holiday last year in the Italian Dolomites and I got quite a taste for it.'

'One Aperol Spritz coming right up' said Pete as he pushed his way through the kitchen's swing doors and into the bar.

'Oh, that sounds lovely' said Penny 'me and the girls sometimes have those at our First Friday get-togethers.'

'Not for me' said Harry, 'have you got a nice whisky?'

'Scotch or Irish' asked Pete.

'Irish please.'

'Bushmills Black Bush OK?'

'That'll do very nicely.'

As Pete poured a generous measure into a tumbler he said, 'and for you Max and Olivia?'

Both had gone for Cokes, Olivia for a Zero, and with all the guests now with a glass in hand Pete said 'As Marcie mentioned earlier – you are our first guests in the chalet and you're all very welcome. The others should be along later this afternoon and we'll get a chance for everybody to meet this evening over dinner. But in the meantime, if I can propose a toast – here's to an excellent week.'

'To an excellent week' rang around the bar with Harry adding 'and the best of luck to you with the chalet. Salut.'

## Chapter 79

It was now 20 minutes until dinner was due to be served. There was an air of quiet panic bubbling under the surface of the kitchen, a little like the onions in the soup, and it was all emanating from Pete. Marcie had tried her best to stay out and leave him and Suzy to it, but the door now swung open. 'All OK?'

'Yes thanks Love. If you can attend to 'front of house' as we agreed.'

A raise of the eyebrows from Marcie but she turned on her heel and retreated.

Raymond Blanc perched on Pete's right shoulder kept reassuringly whispering in his soothing Gallic tones that he was a decent cook. But he was currently being drowned out by Gordon Ramsay on his left with 'you've never fucking cooked for 32 people in your fucking life, let alone for paying fucking guests. What on earth possessed you, you absolute fucking useless fucking cretin.' Thankfully Suzy appeared to be devoid of visitations from either Raymond or Gordon and was quietly and diligently getting on with the preparation of the pastry for the tarte tatin.

'Suzy, come over and have a taste of this sauce for me will you. I think it might need a touch more garlic?'

Suzy took a big spoonful and, clearly recognising that Pete just needed a bit of reassurance, replied 'Pete, that really is lovely. I wouldn't add anything.'

15 minutes later and Pete was in the walk-in freezer. 'Pete, sorry but can you smell burning?' His head shot up and he burst back into the kitchen. A quick sniff of the air immediately revealed the unmistakable smell of burnt onions.

'Shit, shit, shit' he said, rushing over to the range. He lifted the lid on the large saucepan, his glasses immediately steaming up but not sufficiently to mask the apparition of the ruined soup. It had boiled down to about a third of what he needed to serve the guests and the acrid smell told him that even what was left was not salvageable. 'Shiiiiittttttt!!!'

Suzy was now behind him, peering into the remains of the spoiled dish. 'Not to worry, what else have we got that's quick?'

Pete was tempted to fetch Marcie to draw on her measured and practical counsel but didn't want to admit defeat on his first outing as the chalet's chef. His mind careered back to the time he'd sought her out in the kitchen at the infamous Chelsea Carmel-Smythe book launch. That had not gone well. He was going to sort this one out himself.

'OK, OK, let's think' he said, slapping the top of his head in some sort of attempt to get his brain into gear. 'Right, we've got the brie that Victor delivered this morning which we were going to serve tomorrow. Let's do some melba toast with that and see if we can't knock up a quick garnish.'

Ten minutes later, and only five minutes beyond the appointed start of service, saw Suzy taking the first starters through the swing doors. Marcie now came in to help with the waitressing. Picking up the brie, she looked at Pete her eyebrows raised quizzically.

'Later' said Pete, rushing to the oven to stop the baby carrots boiling over.

The rest of service went by in what felt like the blink of an eye. As Marcie took the last of the deserts to the waiting guests, Pete walked over to Suzy and gave her a big hug. He wasn't sure if this was at all appropriate in the modern workplace but his relief and gratitude trumped the potential for a sexual harassment case.

'We did it Suzy. I couldn't have done it without you. Same time tomorrow?'

With a big grin in a red and sweating face, she said 'You bet. Loved it.'

It was now just after midnight and the last of the guests had retired for the evening. Pete had anticipated an earlier finish. He thought the weariness from the journey, coupled with the thought of the first full day on the slopes, would have been sufficient inducement for them to be scurrying to their beds. But he took real pleasure in the fact that it had not been the case. Everybody had stayed up. Actually, that was not strictly accurate. Carol had left shortly after dinner, seemingly a little upset, with Gwyneth accompanying her back to her room. But everybody else had been keen to stay, chat and get to know their fellow Nids.

The complimentary wine served with dinner seemed to go down well and Pete made a mental note to include a question about it on the feedback form he was preparing for guests to complete before they left. There had been some very encouraging comments about the food. Carl, a thirty-something builder from Essex, had said that it was much better than the stuff he got at home, drawing a withering stare from his hairdresser wife Dawn.

Most had then moved from the wine to drinks from the bar, with Carl knocking back an impressive quantity of lager, almost matched by Dawn's assault on the Disaronno and cokes. Eventually, though, a 'that's me done' from Hilda had prompted a slow exodus, leaving just the chalet's staff now at the bar.

'Well, that's the first day over and I think a pretty successful one at that. Thanks to you all for working so hard. Now, you all get off to bed – another big day tomorrow. Me and Pete will set up for breakfast.'

'Thank you Marcie. It has been very enjoyable' said Francoise, with a nod of the head to each of his colleagues.

'Too right' added Suzy, giving her kitchen companion a theatrical wink – 'we pulled it out of the fire didn't we Pete?'

'We did that. Thanks Suzy for a calm head when it was needed. Mum, when was the last time you stayed up till after midnight?' said Pete, giving her a warm hug.

'I know. I'll have to tell the ladies at the bingo. Night night everyone.'

## Chapter 80

It was 7.00am and Pete had been beavering away in the kitchen for over an hour. Suzy popped her head through the door with a cheery 'Good Morning'.

Without requiring any instruction, she immediately went to the fridge and started filling the glass jugs with a variety of fruit juices. Pete and Marcie had already put out a selection of cold meats, French bread, cheeses, cereals and yogurts. Pete had contemplated offering a full English breakfast but had been cautioned against it by Gabriele. As he had over twenty years' experience of running a chalet compared to his own twenty hours, Pete elected to heed his advice. He was, however, determined to offer something hot for his guests so had decided on eggs. Their versatility allowed different options each morning and today saw Pete working up a sweat beating a bowl of them to produce the scrambled variety. There was also the option of porridge for those who wanted the slow-release energy for the morning's exertions and although he was sure the French would be horrified at the thought of par-baked croissants, the sweet aroma from the oven would welcome the guests into the dining room.

The enticing smell took Pete back to his days in advertising when, as a junior account executive, he had been placed on a newly won project for a supermarket. As part of his introduction to the retail client he had been taken around their flagship store in Birmingham. He had spotted some tubing coming from the back of the in-store bakery ovens and, eager to appear interested in all the nooks and crannies of the operation, had asked what it was for. 'Oh, that takes the smell of the baking out to the store entrance to entice customers in – they can't get enough of it' said the supermarket manager.

Breakfast had passed without incident. The only potential hiccup had actually turned into a positive and had won Pete some brownie points. Penny Golding had, very apologetically, asked him if there was any chance of some Coco Pops as that was the only thing that Max would eat for breakfast. In his head Pete wondered at the wisdom of allowing a teenager to dictate his diet quite so narrowly but hoped that his face did not betray his inner musings and instead had the smile of 'the customer is always right'. In fact, Coco Pops were one of Pete's own guilty pleasures. He had therefore taken the precaution of bringing over a stash from the UK in case the food of champions had not yet made it into the culinary landscape of the French. He produced a fresh box with the assurance that there were plenty more where that came from and Max could have them every day.

As Pete went to pour milk over the chocolate balls, Penny said 'No, sorry, not milk. He doesn't drink milk. He likes them dry.' Her guilty look spoke volumes regarding her concerns about failing as a mother as she thanked Pete profusely. Determined to demonstrate that she still had some parental control over her surly son, a glare and a vigorous nod prompted a grunted 'thanks' from Max himself.

The chalet was now a hive of activity. Marcie was running Dawn back to the ski shop as she had decided that her boots weren't right, even though they had not yet been anywhere near snow. Francoise was helping in the boot room as the guests went through the torture of the first morning's preparations. Some were picking up various pairs of skis trying to locate their own, others repeatedly clasped and unclasped their boots in a vain bid to make them tolerably comfortable while a couple checked and re-checked their pockets for the golden ticket that was the lift pass. Carol had tripped over a set of skis, thankfully not resulting in her bursting into tears, but it undoubtedly added to the sense of chaos, confusion and general faffing.

Pete was floating, helping where necessary as guests remembered various things that were essential to sort before they set off for the slopes. Francoise would be ski-guiding a party of 22, with the guests eager to tap into his knowledge of the mountains to orientate them around Chamonix's extensive ski area. Pete had always loved following a guide on his own skiing holidays, relishing the opportunity not to have to constantly refer to the piste map, as well as enjoying the camaraderie of skiing in a group. This had been the spur for him to ensure that free ski-guiding was an essential part of the Chalet le Nid experience.

Hilda's party had elected to do their own thing, wanting to take their time with, as Gwyneth put it, 'more hot chocolate stops than skiing'. Another six guests had decided not to take up the ski-guiding, which Pete realised was probably a good thing as Francoise would have his work cut out with 22 as it was. 'Herding cats' was the phrase that sprang to mind. He made a mental note to remind Francoise to state clearly to the guests that he was a guide only and that it was the responsibility of everybody to look out for each other. Pete did not fancy a lawsuit on the first full day of business.

Pete took a wistful glance through the window which provided natural light to the reception area. He saw a powder blue sky. He had printed out the forecast for the week and pinned it on the noticeboard in the dining room. Apart from around 30cm of snow set to freshen up the pistes on Wednesday, it was promising to be a bluebird spell. Pete contented himself with the thought that he and Marcie hoped to get out for a couple of hours towards the end of the week if everything went to plan.

As Pete waved off the last of Francoise's group from the boot room, he knew that he now needed to kick into gear for the rest of the day's jobs. First call was the kitchen to make the cakes to greet the guests on their return.

An hour and a half later and Pete was surveying his chocolate and orange cake. Though it would not have won him a handshake from Paul Hollywood, it was OK. Next to it were two beautiful Victoria jam and cream sponges. Suzy had made a small version earlier in the week for Pete to try and it had more than passed muster. Pete now placed Suzy's two freshly baked creations along with his own in the fridge, realising that he would have to up his baking game.

'Cup of tea?' said Pete.

'Yes please, lovely' replied Suzy, 'I'll have one while I'm prepping these onions.'

Pete made the tea and fetched a box of fresh carrots from the pantry.

'Pete, do you mind if I ask you something?'

'No, fire away.'

'What made you buy a chalet at errr…. at your time of life?

'It's fine – you mean what is an old git like me doing making such a drastic career change?'

'Well, I wouldn't put it quite like that, but yes.'

Pete then spent the next half hour telling of his career in advertising, his relatively brief flirtation with retirement and how he now came to be chopping carrots for 32 guests. 'Anyway, enough about me. What are you looking for from life?'

Suzy explained how she'd been brought up by her mum in Luton, her dad having left when she was just six. 'I can't understand when kids grow up and have this burning desire to 'reconnect'. He made no effort to stay in touch once he'd decided he wanted a different life so why should I help salve his conscience by wanting him to be my dad now. It's been me and my mum for as long as I can remember and that's fine. We did OK.'

Pete was surprised at the nonchalant, matter-of-fact way in which Suzy had written her dad out of her life. He realised from his brief experience of her so far that she had the same 'get on with it', no-nonsense approach to her work. He liked her.

'Anyway, I reckon all blokes are shits, no offence. Look at Joey.' She looked up at Pete for a response, clearly still hurt and raw at the recent break-up.

'Well, I only really knew him from the week we spent with you at Le Lapin Blanc. But, and I hope you won't mind me saying this, he did seem a bit of a player.'

'He was. He is. My mate Penny told me to have nothing to do with him but that sexy Aussie accent made him seem so exotic.'

'Suzy. You're young and I know it's a cliché that you'd expect to hear from an old bloke, but there's plenty more fish in the sea. Take it from somebody looking down the other end of the telescope – there's no rush to sort your life out. And, even when you do, remember that it's not necessarily set in stone even then. I spent far too long thinking 'what if' rather than just doing but look at me now. Only a couple of years ago I was writing copy for the brochure for a new range of plumbers' merchants and here I am now in this pinnie chopping carrots for 30 people. Again, another old cliché but life is not a rehearsal.'

'Thanks Pete. That helps. Can you pass me that other chopping knife please? I think this one could do with a good sharpen.'

## Chapter 81

The rest of the inaugural week at the chalet went well. There were a couple of cock-ups in the kitchen but nothing that Pete and Suzy couldn't put right. Francoise had swelled the number in his ski-guiding group to 26 on the last day and had counted them all out and counted them back in again. A torn calf muscle for Carl was the only injury of the week and that had happened on the Thursday, so he'd only missed a day's skiing. Pete and Marcie had not managed to get out on the slopes themselves but had agreed that there was plenty of time for that once they'd got a bit more used to the routines of running the chalet. At the end of the week the guests were fulsome in their praise, many saying that they'd be back the following year. It was music to their ears as repeat business was central to the success of Pete and Marcie's business plan

It was now seven weeks into the winter season and Pete was sitting at his Mac checking on the reservations. He spotted an e-mail from a w.tissington@farley-sheldon.com. With a sense of trepidation, he double-clicked.

'Greetings Peter dear boy. I hear on the old grapevine that you and the good lady have bought a ski chalet – you sly old dog. I've had a handsome bonus from the bank this year (thoroughly deserved I might add) so I thought I'd spend some of my spondulix with you rather than giving it to some French chappie. Me, Bunty and the Tissington Juniors will be with you in a couple of weeks. If you've got a nice large room with a springy double bed, that'll do nicely if you know what I mean! Not too worried about the one for the offspring as they're not paying. Get some decent cognac in would you, old fellow. Best. William.'

Pete didn't think it was possible to carry the full pomposity of a spoken voice through to the written word, but William Tissington Esq had managed it. He visualised him dictating it to one of his secretaries, smoking a cigar and staring down her cleavage as he did so. Though any booking for the fledgling business was welcome, he wondered what Marcie would make of this one.

He went back to the booking system and there it was, a reservation for four under the name of William Tissington. It was one of three that had come through in the last few days, meaning that they had strong bookings right through to the end of the winter season. Pete did a quick mental calculation, switching to his online banking app to see what that meant for cash flow. Though they had made only a modest profit so far, it was encouraging and established a good foundation going forward. Marcie had continued with two of her authors, supplementing the income from the chalet, which meant that they were doing OK. By no means setting the world alight but OK. Pete leant back in his chair reflecting on the last few weeks. It had certainly been hard work and a steep learning curve, but he felt more alive than he had in years.

After his mum having a bit of a dip in January when she seemed a little homesick, she had rallied and was now fully engaged in French life. She had joined a local embroidery group which she went to three times a week and was even picking up the odd smattering of French. Pete had been particularly impressed with a sharp 'merde' when she pricked her finger with a needle, suggesting that the group was not averse to the odd colourful phrase.

Francoise had proved a great choice. The guests loved him and though his English had already been pretty good, he was now picking up more of the vernacular. If Pete had a criticism it was that he needed a good prod to do anything around the chalet but his excellent skiing, local knowledge and increasing rapport with the guests more than compensated.

Suzy had proved an absolute godsend. Unlike Francoise, the problem with her was that Pete occasionally had to stop her doing too much. She threw herself with gusto into any task, often working under her own initiative and always with a smile on her face. The only real fly in the ointment was that she was taking three months off in the summer to travel around South America with her BFF Penny, and Pete knew that they would miss her.

The following week he'd lined up interviews for her temporary replacement and she had agreed to sit in to give Pete her take on the candidates.

He went back to the emails and decided that a response was in order to William. After several iterations which he was not happy with, he settled on simplicity. 'Hi William. It's great to hear from you. I trust that you and Bunty are on good form? Marcie and myself look forward to welcoming you both and your boys to Chalet Le Nid where there will also be another familiar face – I hope you will remember Suzy who has joined us from Le Lapin Blanc? Till then, all the best. Pete.'

He knew that Marcie would be far from looking forward to welcoming William but would be professional enough to grin and bear it. As he glanced through the other bookings he saw a name that he was really relishing joining them. 'Charlton Davies – single room, 22-29 June'. Pudding had booked a week's walking holiday with them and Pete realised just how much he was looking forward to seeing at least one quarter of Old School.

## Chapter 82

Pete pulled up at Le Nid after what seemed like the longest transfer he'd ever done.

'This it then old boy? Bit smaller than I was expecting. If ever you fancy building an extension, then yours truly is your man. I have a lot of clout at the bank you know so could arrange for the shekels pretty damn sharpish.'

'Thanks William' said Pete, trying desperately to ensure that the boredom in his voice after nearly three hours in the minibus with the Tissingtons was not obvious. Of all the times for heavy traffic, Pete had begged for this to not be one of them. But it had. And that meant he'd been trapped, with no prospect of escape, for over an hour longer than it normally took. What had been even worse was the fact that it was only the Tissingtons on board, with no other guests to provide welcome relief. They were arriving on an evening flight so Pete would be returning to the airport later. At least that would provide some respite from William.

Suzy was on dinner duty, supported by Chloe who Pete brought in on an ad-hoc basis whenever he was unable to cook. That meant entertaining of the Tissingtons would fall to Marcie. Pete just prayed she could hold it together.

'Come on Percy, look lively will you. You don't expect your mother to lug those bags on her own do you?' This was directed at William's eldest son who was so slight that Pete wondered if he'd be able to carry Bunty's handbag, let alone a suitcase.

An almost whispered 'Yes father' had a retort almost before he'd finished speaking - 'I've told you lad. Speak up will you, you're a man not a mouse.'

'Father, father, have you heard Percy's new nickname at school? It's Micky. Jennings, the new Head Boy who started last term - the one whose father has a helicopter - he chose it and Percy's best friend Samuel is Minnie. Rather good I thought.'

Pete had assumed the term 'harrumph' was confined to Jeeves & Wooster but that was the best way of describing the response from William to the comment by his younger son Toby.

'Is that so, Tobes?' said William. 'If you can help your mother too, there's a good lad.'

If the conversations during the journey had not been sufficient to indicate where the battle lines were drawn, then this brief exchange certainly did. Although to describe them as battle lines was hardly apt. The Colonel in this family was clearly William, ably supported by his First Lieutenant Toby. The rank-and-file infantry, who showed no sign of standing up to the top brass, were Bunty and her elder son. Though he was the complete antithesis to his mother's more than ample frame, they had the same quiet disposition that Pete suspected had been cowed into subservient submission over years of haranguing from the Colonel.

Francoise appeared at the door. He was normally nowhere to be seen on a Saturday, it being his day off from ski-guiding. But Pete suspected the hand of Marcie had been at play to coerce him into helping out. 'Good afternoon, Mr & Mrs Tissington. And you must be Tuby and Percy, let me help you with that.'

'It's Toby, not Tuby' said Tissington Junior in a tone that clearly implied 'you stupid Frenchman.'

'No, let him carry it. The lad needs to grow some backbone, as well as toughen up. A strong wind and he'd be over' said William dismissively. In what was presumably his version of a whisper, though Pete thought it was probably still loud enough for everybody present to hear, he added – 'Peter, old man. You've employed a Frog? I thought better of you. He'll be taking over before you know it, mark my words. I bet he's a lazy sod, isn't he? They can't help themselves; it's in the genes.'

Pete wondered if now might be the best time to nip this in the bud but seeing no reaction from Francoise he wasn't sure if he had actually heard. He decided the easier option was to believe not. He salved his conscience with the knowledge that William was his guest and Pete's role was to ensure that he and his family had the best holiday experience, not to be his moral compass. But it didn't stop him feeling like the cowardly lion as he followed a very large Dorothy in the shape of Bunty through the front door.

Seated in reception, looking like she was engrossed in admin, was Marcie.

'Ah hah, the lovely Mrs Harriman. Stand up, let's have a look at you.'

Pete could see that Marcie was already biting her bottom lip at being treated like a prize heifer but, to her credit, responded with 'William, and Bunty. How lovely to see you both!'

As William made a lunge for a kiss, Marcie deftly turned her head and said 'Francoise, can you take the luggage down to rooms 6 and 7 please while I check-in the Tissingtons.'

William tried to style it out, pretending that he'd been leaning in to see the framed photograph of the staff pictured in front of the chalet. Pete looked for a tell-tale sign of recognition from Bunty, but she was apparently so used to it that it didn't even register. Or, if it had, she knew better than to draw attention to it.

With the formalities over, Marcie said. 'Pete, I presume you're OK to show William and Bunty to their room?' Handing over the key to Bunty she said 'You're in room 7 Bunty and I've put the boys in room 6. There's an adjoining door between the two which I thought you might like. I'll see you all for drinks with the other guests later.'

Pete said, 'We're just down that flight of stairs on the left.' He brought up the rear, casting a quick glance back at Marcie who had an expression that he last recalled seeing in the infamous showdown with the chef at the fateful Chelsea Carmel-Smythe book launch.

## Chapter 83

'So, if you can all make up your teams. Don't worry too much about having completely equal numbers as it's just a bit of fun but it would probably be in your interests to have a mix of ages.'

It was Tuesday evening and, with all the dinner plates cleared away, it was Pete's quiz night. Marcie had been unsure about the idea but he'd convinced her to give it a go. It had proved popular and a good way to get the guests mingling so was therefore now a regular fixture on the chalet's weekly calendar. The beauty of it was that Pete could use the same questions again and again given the fresh audience. As people shuffled around to establish their teams, Pete noted that nobody was making any move towards the Tissingtons. William, obviously used to taking charge, shouted across the room to Jason and Wendy, a nice couple from Wigan. 'Hey, you two, if you want to win this thing, come and join Team Tissington.'

With a rabbit caught in the headlights look and a quick glance at his wife, Jason got up with a 'Thanks, love to' and they made their way over.

'OK then, Round 1 is geography, with a bit of a French focus given that is the delightful country in which we find ourselves' said Pete.

'That'll be over to you then' said William loudly, pointing at Jason. 'I know nothing about the Frogs unless it's regarding the Banque de France or their dismal performance in the war – bloody cheese eating surrender monkeys.'

Looking around the room for general hilarity at his sardonic wit, William was instead greeted with largely silence and a couple of embarrassed coughs.

'OK, then. Question 1. What is the name of the high-speed French railway – the first high-speed rail service in Europe? I'll take the abbreviation by which it is commonly known but I'll be impressed by anybody that can give me its full name. Impressed, but no extra point.'

Whispered discussions ensued around the room, apart from Team Tissington where William just appeared to write down the answer without any consultation. Pete mused that there might be no 'i' in team but there were two in William (as well as another two in Tissington).

Round 2 had prompted an unusual response in that William had apparently deferred to his eldest son. 'Come on Percy. Make yourself useful. How many moons has Saturn?'

Turning bright red at being put on the spot, Percy whimpered 'sorry father, I don't know.'

'It's all right love, neither do I' said Bunty, putting a protective arm around his shoulders.

'You don't know, you don't know' hissed William. 'What the hell am I paying out all this money for a private education for? £8,000 a term and you don't even know how many moons Saturn has. Bloody useless. I bet even those Neanderthals at Carstall Comprehensive know that and it's not costing their parents a bean. I'm putting five unless you have a better idea?' He looked at Jason, not even bothering with Wendy, who gave a meek shake of his head.

After a round on general knowledge Pete said 'right, it's time for the 'interlude' round where I'll need a bit of audience participation. If you'd like to choose a team member and if they could come and join me.'

Again, this prompted much discussion, this time louder, with people suggesting who they thought should go, counter arguments and, eventually, a trail of people to the front, some more reluctantly than others. They joined Pete, along with William, who had elected himself from the off by simply striding purposefully forward.

'Right then' said Pete, reaching behind the bar. 'Your challenge involves these 15 silver cups. You need to stack them in a pyramid and then return them to this state – one inside the other. I'll be timing you and fastest wins 10 points, second 8 and so on. Let's get our reigning champion to give you a demonstration'

Francoise put down the glass he was cleaning and took a bow. He knelt on the floor, the cups in a stack to his right.

'3,2,1, Go' said Pete, starting the timer on his phone.

Almost in a blur, Francoise deftly stacked the cups into five rows and then, with a flick of his wrist, they were all back in their original stack formation.

'4.23 seconds Francoise – a personal best' cried Pete.

As vigorous applause, whoops and cheering erupted from the guests, Francoise took another theatrical bow before returning to his station behind the bar.

William, pointedly not clapping, leaned into Pete. 'Peter old man, Frenchie is obviously spending all his time practicing this bloody stupid game when he should be working. You'll come to rue the day my boy, mark my words.'

Nodding at William and hoping that nobody had heard, Pete ploughed on with 'Right, who's up first?'

Five team members had completed the task with varying degrees of success. Ewan, a scrawny teenager with a mop of black hair and round glasses that gave him an air of Harry Potter in his 'Deathly Hallows' incarnation, was currently leading. He'd finished in an impressive 8.4 seconds, admitting gallantly to the cheering throng that he'd done it several times a few months previously during Freshers.

Last up was William. If Ewan had been Harry Potter, then here was Vernon Dursley.

He gingerly lowered his substantial frame to the floor, emitting a light groan as he rested on his knees.

'Ready William?' said Pete, holding up his phone.

What then followed was what could best be described as carnage. The first row of five cups he placed rather well but on starting to stack the next, his meaty hands were evidently not made for dexterity. On the seventh cup the original lot went flying, scattering across the floor. Titters were already turning into barely supressed laughter from the onlookers as William scrambled on his knees to get them, looking like a grizzly bear foraging for food (albeit that this particular grizzly had his arse cheeks poking from a pair of burnt orange chords).

With the first row now back in place, William started on the second. This time it was the eighth cup that proved his downfall, getting wedged inside the ninth. A furious shaking and it shot out, not only knocking over those he had already placed but also flinging the remaining cups across the dining room with a loud clatter.

By now, the other guests were unable to contain themselves, laughing uproariously as a red-faced William stared incredulously at the spot where his pyramid should be.

He got to his feet, with a loud grunt of effort, turned on his heel and marched from the room.

Pete caught Marcie's eye and, with the telepathy that comes from 30 years of marriage, no words were necessary to convey – 'serves the obnoxious prick right. There's one for Bunty and Percy to remember next time he's bullying them.'

## Chapter 84

'Harsy. Blimey, you must have been working hard these last few months by the look of you. That hairline has gone back a good inch.'

'Pudding – great to see you too.'

The two of them embraced at the entrance to the chalet.

'Nice motor' said Pete looking admiringly at a shiny red BMW coupe.

'Yes, I decided to push the boat out a bit. I wouldn't have even contemplated a rental BMW had I been here in the winter. With their rear wheel drive it'd be like having a blast around a skid pan. But once you'd said that the snow had melted, even up here, I thought why not.'

'As I said, I would have picked you up from the airport you know.'

'What and lose precious hours of you working to protect my investment? No chance.'

Pete showed Pudding the car park at the rear of the chalet and was now checking him in.

'Pudding, it's lovely to see you' said Marcie coming up the stairs carrying armfuls of sheets. She dropped them and gave him a big hug. 'I'll let Pete give you the grand tour as I need to get all this lot over for a service wash. We'll have a drink later on, yes?'

'More than one, I hope. I'm on holiday.'

'OK, don't rub it in.'

As Marcie regathered the laundry, Pete said 'Right, we'll start with your room.'

Pudding followed Pete up two flights of stairs constantly looking around to take in his surroundings. 'OK, this is it' said Pete opening the door to room 12. They walked into a bright and airy room with a king size bed.

'This is impressive Harsy. I don't think I saw this room when we viewed the property. It's great. I was expecting a single room'

'Well, we're not full this week. It is our best and one we reserve for VIPs, or those who have a financial investment in us.'

Pudding strode over to the double French doors which opened out onto a large balcony. Stepping through into the warm late Spring sunshine he said 'Wow, what a view. I hope you make the people who have this room pay extra.'

'I'll show you the books when we've finished looking around. We're hoping to be able to pay you a dividend on your investment a little earlier than planned.'

'Now that's what I like to hear – earning money without lifting a finger. The exact opposite of the crap I have to go through at College to earn a measly crust. Talking of crusts, what delights have you got planned for dinner?'

'Well, in honour of you gracing us with your presence, I thought I'd go for paté and melba toast to start, followed by duck in orange sauce with dauphinoise potatoes and seasonal vegetables. Suzy is a bit of wizard with a crème brulee so we're having that for dessert.'

'Sounds great. If you're not full, how many guests have you got in this week?'

'Sixteen, including you, which is down on the numbers for the winter, but we had allowed for that in our business plan. The summer season was always going to be quieter but forward bookings are looking encouraging.'

'Good to hear, but let's save all the business talk for later, finish the tour and go and have a beer eh?'

'That sounds great. Come on, I'll show you the kitchen – you won't recognise it from the one you saw before.'

## Chapter 85

Work was finished for the day and all the guests had gone to bed. That was apart from Pudding who was reclining in a chair looking out from the dining room at the majestic moonlit outline of the Alps.

Pete sat down, placing a glass of Glenfiddich in front of Pudding who looked up a little startled from his reverie.

'So, how are Pipes and Mark. Have you seen much of them?'

Taking a big slug of whisky before replying Pudding said 'Not so much given that you upped and left and effectively disbanded Old School. But I do see them occasionally. Actually, I saw Pipes only last week. Him & Kelly are looking decidedly dodgy. He reckons she's having an affair and the silly old sod is even considering hiring a private detective.'

'I do miss you lot you know, said Pete', taking a sip from his own Glenfiddich.

'How much of that have you had?' said Pudding, with a mock shake of his head.

'Well, when I say you lot, it's the playing rather than any of you, obviously' Pete said, quickly recovering himself with the realisation that he'd been too long out of the cut and thrust of his mates.

'So is that why you've organised this 'welcome back tour' for the two of us?'

'Well. I'd hardly call two gigs a tour but I thought it would be a laugh. Though I do feel a bit guilty about it being us and not involving Pipes and Mark. It feels a bit like a betrayal.'

'Come on Harsy, you're hardly Rod Stewart deffing out the Faces.'

'True, but you know what I mean. You've not mentioned it to them have you?'

'No, you precious little flower. It'll be our dirty little secret.'

'I'll show you why I feel like it's a particular betrayal of Pipes. I'll be back shortly.'

A couple of minutes later and Pete returned carrying a small box.

'What the hell's that Harsy?'

As Pete slid a black console out of the box he replied 'it's a drum machine.'

Pudding shook his head, chuckling out loud. 'Well, it will be a lot more reliable, will keep better time, won't constantly whinge and will take up considerably less space than Pipes. But I thought you said we were going for unplugged. Back to the old days playing in the flat. I've only brought my guitar and small practice amp. That cost me a fortune in excess baggage as it is.'

'I did and we are. That'll be fine. But we don't need to be completely retro. It won't hurt to have a bit of support from modern technology. I've been playing around with this and I think it will just give us a steady rhythm to follow. I only intend to have the volume set to low.'

'Talking of low' said Pudding, tapping his glass.

Pete got up and brought the bottle of whisky over from the bar, refilling both of their glasses with a generous measure.

'So, what are the places like that you've got us booked into?'

'Well you know one. It's The Signal. Jules is still running it and he said he'd love to have us back, even if it is a considerably paired back Old School.'

'So, we're sticking with the name Old School then for these extra-curricular activities?'

'No, I thought maybe P&H, you know, Pudding & Harsy.'

'It makes us sound like a packet of fags. But I'm too tired to argue, particularly as you've had the good sense to put the talent up front and at least avoid us sounding like a bottle of sauce. P&H, it is. Let's drink to that.'

They spent another pleasant hour reminiscing and talking about music before Pete glanced at his watch. 'Right, that's it for me. Some of us have work in the morning. Feel free to stay and polish off the bottle if you want.'

'No, I'll call it a day too Harsy. I want to be up relatively early to do that Grand Balcon Sud hike. One of the lecturers at the College said it was spectacular. It won't be too difficult will it?'

'No, if you'd had Pipes with you, I'd have said no chance, but you'll be fine. It's one of the most popular walks: woods, meadows, rocky outcrops and you end up right in front of Mont Blanc. Don't forget to look out for the sign to 'Via des Evettes'. If it's a clear day - and according to the forecast it will be - if you look up you'll see some brave souls crossing the Via Ferrata high wire bridge. Me and Marcie walked across it a few weeks back – it took some convincing, but she did it. Anyway, you'll love the hike. It really is breath-taking and you'll probably see a few paragliders as there's a spot towards the end which they use as a launch area. It gets busy but you'll be able to do it in well under three hours so you can have a bit of a rest before we head off to The Signal.'

## Chapter 86

'Harsy, do you know what you're doing with that thing?' Pudding looked up from tuning his guitar as Pete's amp spewed a loud burst of electronic drums. 'Christ, I thought you said the plan was to have a quiet backbeat. It sounds like Pete Tong is in the house.'

'I know, I know, don't worry. I just need to get the settings right and make sure I've got the different rhythms lined up to match the set list. Just focus on what you're doing.'

Pete was pleased that they had decided to get there early. The bar was closed for a couple of hours, the last walkers having left after a quick post-walk bracer and the evening session was yet to start. They had not played together for several months and never as just a duo. Well, they had back in the day in the flat but then there had not been an audience to boo them off stage. He knew it had been a bit of a gamble but his yearning to play had overcome his reticence and now it was too late to back out. All the same, having some time to iron out any kinks suddenly seemed like a wise move.

'OK, chuck us the set list' said Pudding, placing his guitar on the stand.

'You'll see it's all stuff we've played before. It was too much of a stretch to add anything new.'

'Yes, I've been practicing them since you sent it over to me. The only one that I've really struggled with is I Predict a Riot. I think it might sound a bit empty without the bass and drums. It'll make the version we did at the church hall fundraiser sound like a Prodigy cover.'

'I agree, so I've played around a bit and I think if we increase the volume on the drum machine for that one, we should get away with it.'

Jules came over with two beers, handing them both to Pete and shaking Pudding warmly by the hand. 'Mr Pudding, it is delightful to see you again. Thank you for playing in my bar.'

'No, thank you Jules. It's great to see you again too. You've decorated since I was last here.'

Jules swelled with pride. 'Yes, we are always much quiet at end of ski season so we close for 10 days and give us what I think you call 'a makeover'? I chose colours.'

'A makeover indeed. It looks great. Will we be seeing the Countess tonight?'

'Oh yes, she hear that Pete is playing and she says she come later on. If you excuse me, I need to prepare bar for tonight. I think we have big numbers as a local holiday.'

As Jules made his way back to the bar, Pudding said 'well, it's probably a good job that Mark isn't here. That comment would be the cue for him to head straight for the toilets. Actually, I have to admit that the old nerves are kicking in for me a bit.'

Even though Pete felt the same, he saw no benefit in increasing the tension. 'We'll be fine. We've got an hour or so to run through anything that you think needs some work. I'd like to try Losing my Religion as a starter if that's OK?'

An hour and a half later and The Signal was packed. From his position on the small stage Pete looked over at Jules who gave him a big grin and a double thumbs up.

'Harsy, there are more in here already than at the end of the night last time. Are we going to be OK?'

'Come on Pudding, where's your joie de vivre – this is great. Don't forget that we've both played the Birmingham Arena.'

'Oh, yes. Thanks for that timely reminder. That has clearly reduced my palpitations.'

As Pete grinned and reached over to the drum machine he said, 'right, first up She Loves You – 158 bpm and the key of C Major. Ready?'

Having concluded their first set, Pete and Pudding were standing at the bar having a beer and chatting to an American who introduced himself as Chuck. 'You guys are great. This is the wife, Pearl. We're over from Connecticut. I play a little guitar myself but strictly Country and Western. You haven't got any Country in your second set have you?' The reference to his love of Country was pretty superfluous given his tasselled shirt, waistcoat and cowboy boots.

Pete put down his beer. 'Well, the closest we've got is Sweet Home Alabama, I don't know if that qualifies?'

'Well, strictly speaking it's Southern Rock, along with stuff by The Alman Brothers and Ozark Mountain Devils. But there is definitely an element of crossover with Country. More recently, for example, there was Kid Rock. From his name, you'd guess that he was associated with Rock, although some said he was Country. He couldn't really be classified as Southern Rock as he was from Michigan.'

Pete noticed Pudding squirming, clearly looking for a way out of a conversation that was quickly heading for an encyclopaedic history of Country and its sub-genres. Right on cue, the door of the bar swung open and in walked Countess Aggie and Emile. She immediately spotted Pete and waved.

'Oh, I'm sorry Chuck, but you'll have to excuse us for a moment. A friend of ours has just arrived and is calling us over. I hope you enjoy the second set and we'll promise to learn a few country songs for next time.'

'Great fellas. I'll come and find you when you've finished and perhaps I can make some suggestions.'

'That would be great. See you later' said Pete as he waved back at the Countess and started heading over, with Pudding in hot pursuit.

'Jeez, that was good timing' said Pudding. 'I never thought Emile would be a preferable option to anyone, but he certainly beats a yawn-in with Johnny Cash.'

## Chapter 87

It was almost 11.30 and though the crowd was smaller than earlier in the evening, there was still a good 80 or so guests.

'OK everybody. Thanks for listening and being such an appreciative crowd. We've been P&H and this is our last one of the evening which we'd like to dedicate to a dear friend of ours. Countess Agatha, this one is for you.'

Pete and Pudding launched into the iconic intro of You Really Got Me, drawing a smile and an acknowledging nod from Aggie.

As they played the last four chords, an appreciative round of applause started up around the bar. It wasn't the whoops, hollers and cries for more that they'd had at their last outing at The Signal but it seemed genuine nonetheless. Pete hoped that the more muted response was down to the fact that it had been an altogether more mellow sound compared to the full band and also an older and less raucous clientele. It could, of course, have been that they'd not been as good but he quickly tried to banish negative thoughts from his mind, not wanting to sully the thrill at playing again.

They packed up their gear in less than 10 minutes. Sliding the drum machine back into its box was a damn site quicker than dismantling Pipes' kit but Pete knew that, given the choice, it would be Pipes every time. He also knew that the French adventure had proved the right decision for him and Marcie but that didn't stop him missing elements of his old life and Old School was very definitely one of them. He made a mental note to book a trip back to England at the end of the summer season, to catch up with his old mates and hopefully to get a few gigs in.

Pudding caught his eye and whispered 'quick, let's head over to Countess Aggie's table. Old Johnny Cash is eyeing us up for Round 2.'

'Countess Agatha.' said Pete approaching the table.

'Pete, I've told you, it's Aggie. I can't be doing with all these airs and graces. Take a seat. And Pudding, what a delight. I hope you're enjoying your stay. Do you fancy a rum?'

The twinkle in her eye made Pudding realise that she bore him no ill will for his slumbers at her soiree at Château Cheval Gris. 'No thanks Aggie. You'll perhaps not be surprised to hear I haven't drunk it since.'

They spent the next hour chatting animatedly, with Emile regularly visiting the bar to keep them topped up with drinks. They had been the only people left in the bar for the last half an hour or so but Jules showed no signs of wanting them to leave. Pete realised that there were definite advantages to being friends with a Countess. Aggie said how much she had enjoyed their performance. Pete hoped it was genuine and not just an indicator of her impeccable manners. She was also eager to catch up with how the chalet business was doing. 'I'm hearing great things Pete. And even from the locals. You know us French are not generally the most hospitable to outsiders, let alone a Brit, so you must be doing something right.'

Pete gave her a brief outline of how they had done over the winter months, saying that, as expected, they were now a little quieter but still ticking over nicely. He talked of their plans to do a bit of refurbishment work over the Autumn. She'd responded with 'I'd be happy to make some suggestions, if you felt they would be useful. As you know, I've dabbled a bit in interior design so feel free to make use of my talents. Everybody thinks being a lady of leisure is the perfect life but it's not all it's cracked up to be. Sometimes I do struggle with not having enough purpose, so you'd actually be doing me a favour.'

After their first meeting Pete had done a bit of inquisitive googling of the Countess. Her 'dabbling' in interior design was, it turned out, an illustrious career that had drawn plaudits from the great and the good. She was a two-time winner of the IDA Design Awards and had numerous celebrity clients, all eager to indulge in a bit of one-upmanship by boasting about employing her skills in their often palatial residences. There was also a lot of internet gossip about her escapades and liaisons with several A-listers, both male and female, all of which pointed to a life well spent and one that, from his own experience, she seemed intent on continuing in the same vein. A friend of Pete's had often said he planned to enter his coffin skidding and sliding at 100 miles an hour rather than sleepwalking into the docility of his dotage. The Countess seemed to want to up the ante to 200 miles an hour.

'I know what you mean about too much time on your hands Aggie. My retirement lasted less than two years. As for your kind offer, that would be wonderful but I'm not sure we have the sort of budgets you are used to.'

'Oh Pete. Don't be fooled by the hype. I can make, what is it you Brits say, – 'a silk purse out of a sow's ear?' Just because I'm a wealthy woman, it doesn't mean I can't appreciate frugal. Good design doesn't have to cost the earth. I'm sure your financial investor here will back me up. Try me.'

With the Countess throwing a challenging stare at Pudding, he blurted 'How can you say no to a proposition like that? Harsy, we could have done with Aggie when we pitched for that trendy furniture account. You remember, the one when that foetus of a Marketing Manager said you reminded her of her Dad!'

## Chapter 88

Pete and Marcie were saying bye to Pudding as he climbed into the BMW for his trip back to the airport. 'Don't forget Harsy, you promised to come back to Blighty for a gig once the summer season is over.'

Casting a quick glance at Marcie, Pete replied 'yes, I'm sure we can sort something. I know Marcie wants to see her mum & dad so perhaps we can combine the two.'

With that, Pudding put the car into gear and edged forward, waving from the window as he turned the corner and picked up speed.

'Well, it was nice to see him. I guess particularly so for you' said Marcie, turning to head back into the chalet.

'Yes. I do miss him. I'm so glad we got back in touch but this move has inevitably put some distance between us again. It's been great for you and me and I wouldn't change it for the world, but I sometimes wish it was easier to see my friends.'

'I know you do love. You've always needed your friends more than I have. The only one I really miss is Carrie, but our regular FaceTime calls keep me up to speed with what is going on. Anyway, no time for sentimentality, those new skirting boards are not going to fit themselves.'

Pete grimaced, remembering that he'd promised to replace two skirting boards in one of the bedrooms. There were large gouges out of both of them. Pete was still not sure how it had happened but was pretty confident it had been when they'd had a stag party from Hunstanton to stay. While they had been a pretty nice bunch of lads, there had been a few issues, including Pete finding one of the lads trussed, naked and asleep behind the bar when he went down to set up for breakfast.

Ordinarily Pete outsourced all refurbishment work: the smaller jobs to local handyman Pierre and anything bigger to Bill who had done all the renovation work before they'd taken over at Le Nid. But the skirting board job had somehow tugged at his heartstrings, rekindling the memory of his dad replacing them all at their Bromsgrove home. He had decided to pay homage to his dad and hoped that he wouldn't now live to regret it.

The rest of the summer season had passed with little incident, including the skirting board replacement being a success, only a few expletives escaping as Pete wrestled to wrench the existing boards from the walls. He even used the term 'bastard screw', which brought a wry smile as he realised that at least he'd remembered something from watching his dad at work.

Jack and Charlie had come over for 10 days in early September and they'd had a great time, slipping seamlessly back into the Harriman family mick-taking almost as soon as they'd arrived. Charlie was still with Stig and suggested that they were thinking of buying a house together. Jack had returned from his travels and was living with two of his mates in a flat in Warwick. He had sent a couple of tentative enquiries about jobs in social care and was currently working in a local garden centre. He was 'between girlfriends' and had surprised Pete with the announcement that he and some mates had joined a five-a-side football league. Pete had a flashback to the incident of the man-mountain Jack had elected not to face in his earlier football career and was glad that, almost a decade later, he seemed to have overcome his demons.

It was now 4am on a chilly October morning and Pete and Marcie were closing down the chalet for a couple of months. The last booking had been a week ago so they had made the decision to go back to Leamington for a while, with the plan to return to France in late November to prepare for the new ski season. At Marcie's insistence Pete had delegated the refurbishment programme to Bill. Countess Aggie would be on hand to give some design advice and had promised to keep in touch with Pete and Marcie for any necessary decision-making. Pete had offered to pay her for her time but a response of 'Pete please, do I look like I need the money?' had quickly quashed any further discussion.

As Pete tuned the key in the lock they went through the middle-aged mental checklist ritual to ensure that everything had been turned off. Satisfied that it had, they jumped into the fully laden Audi Estate. Joyce poked her head from under a duvet stuffed into the backseat, her spectacle-magnified eyes giving her the appearance of a dormouse waking from hibernation. 'How long will it take us to get to Calais love? It's just that I'll need a few loo breaks along the way, you know.'

'It'll be fine mum. I've got our first stop planned for a quick breakfast about 3 hours into the journey but if you need to stop before then, just shout.'

With Marcie asking one more time if Pete had double-locked the backdoor, they set off back to what they all still thought of as home.

## Chapter 89

Marcie turned the key and pushed the door. There was not too much resistance. Only a small pile of mail confirmed that their neighbour Trevor had been doing a good job, popping in every few days to check and let them know if there was anything that looked important.

'It smells musty, let's get these windows open' said Marcie, heading for the living room. Pete made way for his mum before trundling in one of the suitcases which wobbled on its loose wheel. Joyce had been asleep for quite a portion of the journey and, suitably refreshed, offered to put the kettle on. 'Hang on mum' said Pete 'we won't have any teabags.'

'Yes we have' replied Marcie who had wandered through to the kitchen. 'Trevor must have bought them and, hang on a minute, yes, the darling, there's also some milk in the fridge.'

They all sat down to mark their return with the English ritual of a cup of tea before tackling the emptying of the car.

'The house somehow seems smaller than when we left it' observed Marcie.

'I guess it's because we've got used to being surrounded by space in the chalet. Still, nice to be home' replied Pete.

He shuffled through the mail: a new menu from the local Chinese, a bank statement, a catalogue for the latest offerings from Johnnie Boden and a glossy brochure extolling the benefits of a new retirement village that had opened in Warwick. Despite being all too aware that he would be 56 next birthday, it still pulled him up sharply when he realised that he was now categorised as 'old' by the direct marketers. He'd read an article recently that queried the wisdom of advertisers treating the over-50s as one homogenous greying group. Pete was one of more than 23 million aged over 50 in the UK but certainly did not put himself in the same category as a Werther's-quaffing pensioner wrapped in a blanket waiting for a knock at the door from the grim reaper. He made a mental note to stop eating Werther's.

They spent the next couple of hours ferrying stuff from the car, putting it away and doing little jobs to get the house back to feeling like home. Pete looked through the patio doors that had been the site of such a heart-stopping incident less than 18 months ago and thought how much had happened since then. He nodded admiringly at the garden, realising that his £20 a week investment in a local gardener had been money well spent. The rhododendron bushes were looking a little straggly and the patio could do with a god jet-wash but he'd get onto that at the weekend.

Marcie came up behind him, wrapped her arms around his chest and nuzzled into his neck. 'As you said Pete, it's nice to be home but it hasn't made me feel that we made the wrong decision with the move to France. I thought being back might make me question it but no. How about you?'

'No. I do miss certain things of course, but it's been an incredible few months. I feel it's given us the new lease of life we both needed. And, I'm relieved to see how well mum has settled. Sometimes you just have to make the jump and see how things turn out.'

'I agree love. It was a scary leap to take but I think we've landed on our feet. Now, do you want something to eat? There's a pizza in the freezer.'

'No thanks love. I'm absolutely knackered. Doing that journey in one go without an overnighter doesn't get any easier. I'm going to bed.'

Joyce, suitably rested from her slumbers in the car, decided that she was staying up to watch a bit of TV. Marcie put a meat feast pizza in the oven and said she would join her. As Pete trudged up the stairs, he couldn't help thinking that maybe the marketers were right after all.

## Chapter 90

Pete turned on the radio. His default listening was Virgin and while he knew he could it get it as a digital station in France, somehow he had got out of the habit. About 20 minutes into plugging back into the lively chat that he'd missed on the Chris Evans breakfast show, Pete did a doubletake. Surely he'd misheard. He listened intently to the next 3 minutes of music before Chris opened his mic to say 'That's Strawberry Split from Chunky Funky Monkey. Vasos, you love them, don't you? I think we'll be hearing more from those young men.'

Pete almost spat out his coffee. He wondered if Pipes knew that his nemesis had not only released a single but that it was getting airplay on national radio. He couldn't resist it so reached for his phone and clicked on Pipes.

'Harsy, so you're back then?'

'Yes – last night.'

'What's that in the background?'

'It's the radio – you won't believe what I've just heard'

'Not that irritating twat from the talentless bunch Chunky Funky Monkey by any chance?'

'Yes, how did you know?

'I know you and knew you wouldn't be able to resist if you heard it. I caught it myself last week on CWR but couldn't bring myself to say anything. Why, where did you hear it? Don't tell me it's gone beyond local radio.'

'Only the Chris Evans Breakfast Show on Virgin.'

'Bollocks – you are kidding. What the fuck.'

The conversation continued in a similar vein for another five minutes, Pipes incredulous and full of expletives and Pete stoking the fire whenever it threatened to die down. Eventually, though, even Pipes could not keep up that level of vitriol, nor Pete that level of bating. 'So, enough about talentless foetuses. When are we going to get together to play some proper music?' asked Pipes.

'Well, I spoke to Pudding last week and he said it was about time for another of his stomach bugs so was planning to come up one night in the week. How are you fixed for Wednesday?'

'I'm supposed to be on a late shift but I should be able to swap that no problem so count me in.'

'What about Mark?'

'Well, I've seen him a few times since you swanned off on your French Odyssey so I'll give him a call.'

With the call ended, Pete clicked on 'Aggie'.

'Pete, how are you? Presumably you got home safely?'

'Yes thanks, a long drive but no real hold-ups and we got back late afternoon. I'm still knackered though – can you get jetlag travelling from France to the UK?'

Aggie let out a throaty laugh. 'You Brits, you're never happier than when you're moaning. Remind me to tell you about the time me and Princess Margaret went on a bender in Mustique which started on the private jet and lasted for three days.'

Pete made a mental note to do just that.

'Anyway, if you're phoning to check up on progress, then you'll be pleased to know that Bill arrived early this morning. We went through the list and he estimates there's about five weeks work. The only potential issue he saw was with your plan to extend the outhouse to accommodate the logs and to provide some undercover parking. He suspects it might need planning permission. But, if it does, don't worry, I'll have a word with the mayor. It won't be an issue - I know where all his skeletons are buried.'

'Thanks Aggie. You are a godsend.'

'You're too kind Mr Harriman. Oh, and you know I suggested a neutral fawn colour for the boot room, I woke up in a different mood this morning and thought a nice bright lemon might work better?'

'OK, let me have a word with the boss and I'll get back to you. Thanks again for doing this, we both really appreciate it.'

'No problem. It's just like the good old days, although I think I'd have had trouble convincing Jack Nicholson that lemon was a suitable shade for his den.'

## Chapter 91

'I'll have another thanks Mark and see if they've got any pickled eggs would you?' Pipes put down his empty glass and grinned at Pudding who had grimaced at the pickled egg reference.

As Mark gathered the four empty glasses, Pete said 'So, gents what are we going to do about getting some gigs?'

It was Wednesday evening and they had all met in The Swan. Pete had picked up Pudding from the train station and they had gone back to his house to drop off his bag before catching a cab into Leamington.

'Well, as it happens, I have some news on that front' announced Pudding, 'but let's wait until Mark gets back with the beers.'

Mark returned a couple of minutes later – considerably quicker than if he'd been served by Chas thought Pete, with a rueful smile. With the drinks distributed around the table, Pete said, 'Come on then Pudding, what's the news?'

'Well, I have a mate...when I say mate, the bloke is actually a bit of a knob. But for the purposes of this, let's say he's a mate. Giles is head of the Music Technology Department at the College and he's been organising a small music festival. I got a couple of the eejits on my course to design a poster for him – absolute shit of course but that's by the by. Anyway, I was chatting to him the other day and mentioned that you were back for a couple of months Harsy. I hadn't said anything before because I didn't think it was an option with you being out in France, but I asked if there might be a slot for us. He said yes - one of the bands that he'd booked had pulled out because the lead singer had thrown his toys out of the pram and 'gone solo'. By that he apparently meant that he's now singing to backing tracks in pubs by all accounts. The festival is the last weekend in October. He can't pay us but he'd give us a free pitch for camping and stand us some beers behind the bar. So, what do you reckon?'

Pipes said 'I think it would be great. I know none of us have played together for ages but that would give us at least a couple of weeks to get our chops back.'

Pete and Pudding exchanged a swift guilty glance at the reference to not having played together.

'I agree' said Pete quickly. 'It sounds perfect. Any chance to play would be brilliant but to play at a festival.'

'I don't know what it's going to be like' admitted Pudding. 'It's the first year he's done it so it might be a load of old bollocks.'

'And you reckon it's always me that is the miserable, pessimistic sod' quipped Pipes. 'It might be fantastic and, let's be honest, we haven't got people beating a path to our door with offers.'

'OK, OK. So, Mark, what about you then?' said Pudding.

'Will I need to take any time off work? It's just that I've used a lot of my annual leave already and I've promised Marjorie that I'll keep a week back for a trip to North Wales at the end of November.'

'Wales in November? Rather you than me mate but no, you won't necessarily have to take time off. The festival opens on the Friday morning but we wouldn't be playing until the Saturday afternoon.'

They spent the next hour discussing the festival, with Pudding filling them in on the little he knew. It was to take place on a farm in Sussex and there would be two stages. If confirmed, Old School would be on the 'Up & Coming' rather than the Main Stage, which led Pipes to quip that presumably they weren't having a 'Been & Gone' stage. The headline act for the weekend had been announced as Dr & the Medics which gave another in for Pipes. 'Bloody hell, are they still going? Once they've played Spirit in the Sky, what are they going to do for the next 55 minutes?'

When Pipes started to ask about camping arrangements, Pudding said 'Hang on a minute. I haven't even firmed it up with Giles yet.'

Eager to strike while the iron was hot and spurred on by several beers, Pete said 'well call him now then.'

After a bit of cajoling from Pipes, Pudding said 'OK, OK. But I'm not doing it with you two herberts grinning and making inane comments and anyway, it's hard to hear in here.'

Five minutes later and Pudding was back. 'Right, we're on. 3 o'clock on Saturday afternoon with a 30-minute set. I agreed that I'd talk to him more about it next week when we're both in college.'

'Great' said Pete. 'Do you know what the festival is called?'

'Yes – BillieFest. He's named it after his wife. I told you he was a bit of a dick.'

'Well, daft name or not, here's to BillieFest' said Pete, raising his glass.

'To BillieFest' came the resounding reply.

## Chapter 92

Pete was on the viewing balcony of the local sports hall watching Jack and his mates playing in a five-a-side football tournament. It had taken some cajoling to get Jack to agree to him coming along. After an initial flat 'no', Pete had played the nostalgia card. 'Come on son, it'll be like old times. I haven't seen you play in ages.'

Jack had gradually softened, helped by the offer of a post-match trip to the pub with the beers on Pete, followed by a Chinese. He concluded the discussion with 'Oh, OK. If you must but please don't do anything embarrassing.'

There were about 30 spectators in all but Pete was the only one supporting Morrisey's Marauders (Jack, and presumably his mates, showed no sign of growing out of a love for the balladeer of teenage angst). This was the Marauders' fourth game on the back of two wins and a draw. There were only two minutes left of the second half, with the Marauders 8-2 up against a very average side. Team spirit was obviously not a platform on which their opponents' strategy was built; a bloke with a ginger crew cut had christened his goalkeeper a useless wanker when a weak effort from Jack had squirmed under his bulging belly.

30 seconds later and said Ginger unceremoniously upended Jack with a swift kick to the calf. Pete just managed to stop himself from shouting out, remembering his commitment to not embarrassing his son. The carrot-topped hatchet man's remonstrations with the ref, complete with diving action, were to no avail as the man in black produced a yellow card and a stern warning. This did nothing to lighten his mood and he was even more vociferous with cries of you fuckin' twat when, just seconds before the final whistle, a ninth goal went in off the keeper's left knee.

Pete was glad to see that Jack had developed a strong sense of sportsmanship, shaking hands with the Ginger Warrior as the game ended. GW took his hand with a surly nod before looking over his shoulder to berate his keeper with more abuse that was unlikely to have come from The Complete Guide to Sport Motivation.

Next up was a young Asian team against an outfit with a mish-mash of ages kitted out in an ill-advised lilac strip. Pete had no real interest in the outcome of this match so his mind started to drift as he watched the game unfold. He picked out an older guy, probably in his early forties, who had obviously played a bit. Unlike many of the others, he was not charging around like a headless chicken but rather playing quick and often incisive passes while strolling casually around the centre circle.

Pete decided that this was Dave, an ex-West Brom professional, whose promising career had been prematurely ended in his mid-twenties by a snapped achilles tendon. He had run a pub in Gornal for a while, trading on his minor celebrity status, but after a couple of years he was doing more drinking than serving. Following a few years in the wilderness, including several months living rough, he had joined AA and got himself clean. He had become a born-again Christian, marrying a former junkie from Halesowen. They had produced two sons, neither of whom were showing any inclination to take-up football. This had made Dave realise just how much he missed the game, so he had joined a five-a-side team earlier in the year and was enjoying reliving his youth, without taking it too seriously.

Dave stretched to reach the ball and pulled up sharply, raising his arm at the referee. Pete wondered at the potential authenticity of his musings as he limped from the pitch. The little interest that Pete had in the match was now gone with the bursting of the ex-pro bubble. He wandered to the end of the spectator gallery, put a pound coin in the vending machine and spent the next couple of minutes wondering just how Mars Bars could have shrunk quite so dramatically.

Ten minutes later and Morrisey's Marauders were back on the pitch. Their three wins and a draw had got them a place in the semi-finals. Jack was the team's top goal scorer with eleven and Pete felt a sense of pride at how well he was playing. He was also somewhat taken aback, the goal-hungry 19-year-old seeming so far removed from the shy and retiring 9-year-old left-back that had refused to take on Sasquatch.

Despite another sweet volley hitting the back of the net from Jack, at half-time, the Marauders were 3-2 down after a frenetic first half. Less than a minute into the second and Jack drilled a low right foot shot into the bottom corner, making it all square. The opposition was starting to flag, with the Marauder's youth beginning to tell against a team with an average age some ten years older. A clumsy challenge from a clearly tired defender saw Jack's mate Ollie tumble to the ground.

The ref blew his whistle. Ollie didn't get up, prompting Jack and Phil, the goalkeeper, to stride over to see how he was. After a minute or so Ollie was helped to his feet and gingerly put his right foot on the ground. Pete could not hear from his vantage point but a shake of Ollie's head showed that his game was clearly over. Jack and Phil helped him from the pitch, with the referee walking alongside.

All of the Marauders were now at the side of the pitch. There were heated discussions going on, with Jack furiously shaking his head. The referee pointed to his watch and held up five fingers.

After another minute of deliberations and several glances in his direction, Jack turned and with a body language that needed no sound to communicate a heavy sigh beckoned his dad to come down.

As Pete walked into the changing room, he waited to be told he had been designated to drive Ollie to the hospital. Kurt, one of Jack's friends who Pete had met on a couple of occasions, stepped forward. 'Mr Harriman, you might have noticed that Ollie here is injured.'

'Yes, it's no problem. I'm happy to take him to the hospital to get his leg checked out.'

With a quizzical look Kurt said 'no, he's pretty sure it's just a pulled calf muscle but the problem is we don't have any subs. I know that you played a bit in your day, so I asked Jack if you'd be prepared to take his place. He seemed to think you'd say no but we are desperate and another body is better than nobody at all.'

Too shocked to take offence Pete bumbled 'I'd love to but I haven't played for years and anyway I don't have any kit.'

'That's OK, those trainers you've got on will do and you can have Ollie's kit.'

'Err, OK. But what about my glasses. I haven't got my contacts with me and I wouldn't see a thing without them.'

'I'm sure we can sort something. But sorry to push, we need to decide quickly. The ref has agreed but said we only had 5 minutes to get it sorted.'

3 minutes later and Pete walked onto the pitch. He had thought himself in relatively decent shape for a man of his advancing years but while the kit looked great on the teenage team, it did not travel well. Ollie's shorts threatened to ensure that if any more children had been planned, then that door had just been squeezed tightly shut. As for the shirt, Pete thought

back to Pipes in his 'Chas Special' and wondered if anybody present remembered Andy Bell in skin-tight lyrca during his portlier days in Erasure. Looking down he realised that not taking up Ollie's offer of his football socks had been a mistake; even more of his pasty legs were on show above his calf-length black Calvin Kleins. His look was completed by his glasses secured around the back of his head with a lace from Ollie's trainers.

## Chapter 93

'How did you get on love?'

Marcie looked up from watching 'Grey's Anatomy' to pose the question to Jack as he came in through the front door.

'Ask Nobby Stiles here' said Jack, dropping his bag and marching into the kitchen.

'Pete, are you OK?'

With a quick shake of his head and an exaggerated raising of his eyebrows in response to Marcie Pete said 'Jack, come on. It wasn't my fault that Ollie got injured.'

Armed with a glass of water and, pointedly, not one for his dad, Jack came back into the living room.

'You could have said no.'

'Hang on, that's not fair. It was you that told me to come down.'

'It was the boys who kept on at me to ask you, but I didn't think you'd actually agree.'

'Well, what could I do? It was me or nothing.'

Pete thought he detected a muttered 'nothing would have been better' but he wasn't sure so let it slide.

There then followed about 20 minutes of debate about Pete's brief but eventful resurrection from retirement.

It had started OK. Well, his first touch of the ball had at least gone to Kurt rather than the opposition. But that was really the highlight – he had peaked too early. He spent the next 90 seconds tearing around trying to get the ball. As he stopped, hands on knees and gasping for breath, an image of

Boris Johnson charging like a randy rhino at Robby William's Soccer Aid charity match came unwelcomingly into his head.

30 seconds later and he'd badly mis-timed a tackle and scythed down the opposition centre forward. They scored from the resulting penalty to take a 4-3 lead. He lasted around another minute before another impromptu pit-stop, heaving in great lungfuls of air in an attempt to prevent himself from passing out. Jack, with a mixture of worry and irritation said, Dad, you'd better go in goal.

A quick change of jersey, with Pete self-consciously trying to cover up his torso during the process, and he swapped places with Phil. A couple of minutes and two goals later, the ref blew to confirm that the Marauders had been dumped unceremoniously out of the competition. The final goal had been Pete's particular nadir. An innocuous and speculative shot from just beyond the halfway line had hit the post, bounced back and hit his right foot before dribbling over the line. The first thought that came into Pete's head was that he was glad he was not playing for the Ginger Warrior's team.

As they walked dejectedly from the pitch, Jack scuttled off, clearly scarred by the whole experience.

'Thanks for stepping in Mr H' said Kurt with a consoling pat on Pete's sweat-soaked back.

'I'm just sorry that I couldn't make more of a contribution. Sorry about that last goal.'

'No worries. I hope I'm still breathing when I'm your age, let alone playing.'

There was obviously no malice intended by Kurt; just the sometimes clumsy and non-thinking comments of a teenager, thought Pete.

As they walked into the changing room, Pete had started to feel decidedly light-headed. He took a quick left turn towards the toilets and with a loud bang, barged his way into the nearest cubicle. He just about made it to the bowl, retching violently and noisily, amazed that the Mars Bar now seemed to have taken on epic proportions.

The tale over, Marcie was clearly gritting her teeth in an attempt not to laugh. 'Pete, I thought you said you were getting a Chinese.'

'No chance. Jack lost his appetite and I'm going on a diet.'

## Chapter 94

'You'll need to knock it in further than that mate. One of us is going to go arse over tit.'

Pudding had a rubber mallet raised above a tent peg as Pipes took on the role of chief tent architect. They had arrived at the festival site about an hour ago and were now wrestling with the intricacies of a tent erection that Pete was convinced should be nowhere near as difficult as they were making it.

'Are you sure that's right?' said Pipes, quaffing from a bottle of Peroni. 'Should that bit be flapping about?'

Holding out the mallet, Pudding replied testily 'Look smart arse. If you think you can do any better, be my guest.'

'No, no, you carry on. After all it was you that said you'd been in the scouts.'

'Look let's take five minutes and have another squint at the instructions' said Pete, recognising the potential for escalation.

As Pudding scrabbled in the tent bag, Pete looked out over their surroundings. It was a beautiful late October morning and he shielded his eyes to gaze across the rolling West Sussex countryside. In the far distance he could see what he knew to be Cowdray Park. He had been invited there once on a corporate hospitality day to watch the British Open polo Gold Cup. While the polo itself had not been much of a spectacle, the free-flowing Bollinger and the opportunity to see how the other half lived had made for an interesting day out.

The reason for such spectacular views was the location of the festival camp site on a plateau at the top of a hill. At the bottom, to his right, was the Main Stage; to the left the Up & Coming Stage where they would be performing tomorrow afternoon. Pete had been impressed at the thinking that had gone into the location. The hill provided a natural sound buffer between the two stages, as well as a beautiful spot to take in the views. There were already about a hundred tents pitched which seemed to bode well for a decent turn-out.

On arrival, Pudding had introduced them to Giles. 'Ah, Charlton, great to see you. I thought you said there were four of you?'

'There are. I mean there will be. Our bass player is arriving tomorrow morning.'

With that Giles proudly handed over four laminated lanyards, explaining that they were backstage passes for the Up & Coming Stage. He then directed them to the camping area with the parting shot of 'I'm looking forward to seeing you guys play.'

They had trundled through a rutted field in Pipes' Volvo estate. Most of the gear had fitted in, including what was admittedly a limited amount of camping equipment. Mark would be bringing the rest with him tomorrow. Pete's proposal of getting a stove had been met with scorn from Pipes. 'If you think I'm sitting around for half an hour waiting for a paltry tin of beans to heat up over a candle, then you can forget it Harsy. There's bound to be catering vans there and I intend to try them all.'

He had been right. They spotted a number of caterers as they made their way to the camp site, including a burger van, a tent selling Chinese food, an inflatable pub and a yurt offering a range of vegan meals and snacks. The latter had prompted an outburst from Pipes – 'they all look good apart from that vegan nonsense. If the hippies want to eat grass and sawdust, then more burgers left for me.'

There were also some other attractions dotted around. Several bouncy castles and a rather scary woman offering face painting suggested that it was going to be a family-oriented festival. A small dodgems enclosure confirmed this, making Pete think back to his musings on roadies being seemingly direct descendants of the 'carnies' who travelled around in the dodgy fairs of his youth. Right on cue a heavily bearded guy with gravity-defying hair appeared from round the back, with his trousers halfway down his arse, languidly zipping up his fly

They had finally arrived at the camp site, given special dispensation to park the car next to their pitch as it contained the instruments.

This was all the precursor to Pudding now poking around in the bag to find the instructions on how to pitch the tent. He found them and lay them flat on the Volvo's bonnet.

'Look, that's how I've done it. We only have the pictures to go on unless you've taken a crash course in Chinese?'

Pete, keen to maintain harmony, replied 'Pudding, you've done a good job and I realise that neither me nor Pipes have been much help. Just looking at this though, I think there's supposed to be a divider inside that creates some sort of sleeping area. It looks like that's the panel that is sticking out from the back there?'

Pudding scrutinised the drawing. 'Mmmm, you might be right. The last time I pitched a tent they hadn't even thought of a sleeping area. It was one big space and the last one in got to sleep next to the door.'

With Pete glad that his gentle interjection seemed to have taken some of the heat out of the situation, he looked to press home his advantage. 'Pipes, grab those tent pegs, the guy ropes and the mallet. Pudding and me will redo this section and you secure them in place.'

Fifteen minutes later and the Old School tent was complete. Or so Pete thought. 'And now for the crowning glory' said Pudding, reaching into the back of the Volvo. He brought out a long thin bag and tipped the contents onto the ground. He started to assemble a lengthy stick. He then undid a cellophane wrapping to reveal a 3 metre by 2 metre flag with the Old School logo front and centre, under-scored with the word BillieFest picked out in yellow. 'Ta-da. What do you reckon?'

'It's great' enthused Pete.

'Nice' added Pipes.

'I ran it off on the college's large format graphics printer when nobody was around. Here. Help me stick it into the ground next to the tent door.'

They stood back, all smiling broadly, as the flag fluttered gently against an azure blue sky.

'Right' said 'Pudding. 'Let's get our sleeping bags out of the car and put them down. Mark will have to sleep on that big bump. There has to be some forfeit for turning up late when all the work has been done.'

'Agreed' said Pipes, reaching for the Volvo's rear door. 'Then let's go and get something to eat. I'm starving.'

## Chapter 95

'Shit' cried Pipes, laughing as he tripped over a guy rope.

'Keep it down' came an angry voice from a nearby tent.

Pete, Pipes and Pudding were making their way back to their tent. The cloud cover blocking out the moon was not helping but of more significance was the couple of hours they had spent in the inflatable pub followed by another hour in a surprisingly convivial beer tent.

'Ssshhhh' said Pete at a volume that was pretty ironic. 'I'm sure it's over to the right.'

'Harsy you muppet,' cried Pipes triumphantly. Still lying on the grass he pointed to the left where the Old School flag was fluttering in a stiffening breeze.

'Will you shut the fuck up' rang out in the chilly evening air.

Giggling like schoolboys, the trio negotiated the 50 metres or so to reach their own accommodation for the night.

Squatting unsteadily on his haunches Pete reached for the tent's zipped door and made an exaggerated gesture of placing his finger on his lips. This was rendered completely futile with a loud clunk from the Volvo door as Pudding retrieved a torch from the front seat. He switched it on and started sweeping it slowly across the tents with an accompanying deep-throated, 'This…is the voice…of the Mysterons.'

Pete, holding his hand over his mouth to try and stifle his laughter, climbed in, losing his balance and rolling onto the groundsheet to realise that it was not particularly warm and a little damp. He was followed, not particularly swiftly or elegantly, by Pipes and then Pudding.

'I'm sleeping in my clothes' said Pipes, trying to step into his sleeping bag and failing miserably. After another couple of attempts and a 'fuck this' he dragged it outside where he could stand up fully. This time he managed to get in, jumping repeatedly as he pulled it up to his chin. He wriggled cocoon-like back into the tent. Pete had a vision of the cover of one of Charlie's favourite bedtime reads, 'The Hungry Caterpillar', though from the bulging fabric he mused that no caterpillar could be quite that hungry.

Meanwhile Pudding was down to his boxers and had donned the Rolling Stones t-shirt that Pete had last seen after their drunken night out in Leamington. Pete stood as high as the tent roof would allow, which still saw him pretty much bent double, and started to remove his Levi 501s. With one leg half extricated he started hopping. A couple of seconds later gravity won and he crashed into the side of the tent. The opposite side wrenched the pegs from the ground with a loud ripping sound.

'Harsy, for fucks sake!' cried Pudding, grasping for a half-empty beer bottle but not quickly enough to stop it spilling its contents all over his sleeping bag.

As Pete lay in a heap, laughing uncontrollably, Pipes took out his phone and the tent interior was momentarily illuminated. 'One for the album' said Pipes, grinning.

Ten minutes later and they were all finally wrapped in their respective sleeping bags. A gentle rain was falling and the rhythmic sound, coupled with the soporific effects of the evening's entertainment, meant that they were soon asleep.

Pete woke with a start. He picked out the luminous hands on his Breitling to see that it was just after 3.30. He reckoned he'd been asleep for about 3 hours. He soon recognised that he was unlikely to be asleep for another 3 as he realised why he had woken so suddenly. Pipes was snoring at a volume that beggared belief. Pete half-expected to hear another 'shut the fuck up'. It took him back to his stint in hospital following Terry Fletcher's party. This snoring was up there with the levels of Krakatoa-Bert.

There was also a reminder of the reasons behind his hospitalisation. The steady pattering of rain on canvas that had helped lull him to sleep was now an incessant and driving thrum. If earlier had been reminiscent of Pipes using brushes during their failed attempt at playing The Cure classic Love Cats, it was now more like his energetic thrashing around the kit at the end of I Predict a Riot.

Pete turned over, wriggling to do so as his sleeping bag enveloped him in what felt like a half-nelson. He tried to ignore the rasping lead vocal of Pipes as the rain's backing track morphed into Slipknot drummer Joey Jordison on Wait and Bleed. But, inevitability, the more he tried, the more of a torture it became. After about fifteen minutes, which saw a couple of accompanying flourishes on the arse trombone from Pudding, Pete gave up. He extricated himself from the clutches of Big Daddy Sleeping Bag as quietly as he could, picked up Pipes' car keys and unzipped the tent door.

He immediately stepped into a puddle. It was lashing down. He needed a pee but a trudge across the field to the portaloos in the driving rain was never going to happen. As he hastily zipped his fly and decided that he'd done Pipes a favour in cleaning his rear wheel, he clicked the fob and popped open the doors. The whole of the estate section, including the folded down rear seats, were taken up with the band's gear. He flirted briefly with the idea of taking out Pipes' drum kit – surely that's what the protective cases were for? But he couldn't bring himself to do it and instead headed round to the front passenger door.

He popped the keys in the ignition and started fiddling with the seat controls. He got it reclined as far as it would go, turned up the heating, and settled down to try and get some sleep.

## Chapter 96

Pete's nostrils flared involuntarily. He came round slowly, a dull ache in his back. As the fog started to clear he realised he was in the Volvo. He slowly sat upright, rubbing his lower back, and saw the source of the awakening of his smell receptors. Outside the tent immediately behind their own were two young women clad in matching striped onesies and wellies. They were smoking, sitting in camping chairs and watching a pan of sizzling bacon. Pete suddenly wished he'd been more forceful in his argument for the camping stove.

As he stretched out his cramped legs, he realised that it was not just his olfactory organ that was awake. He glanced down at the bulge in his boxer shorts and wondered if the inspiration for the seminal Oasis album (What's The Story) Morning Glory? had been Noel waking up with a stiffy. One of the two young women caught his eye and waved. He waved back. She then got up and started walking towards the car. 'Shit', mouthed Pete thinking what the hell he could do to prevent her thinking he was some sort of old pervert who had a fetish for watching women cooking while reclined in a Volvo. His saving grace was the state of Pipe's car. He grabbed an old newspaper that was sitting in the footwell and draped it across his lap as if he had been halfway through reading it.

He wound down the window and the girl reached into the car. 'Hi, I'm Imogen' she said, shaking him warmly by the hand.

'Pete. Nice to meet you' he said, careful not to dislodge the paper as he returned the shake.

'Forgive me for being nosey but me and my girlfriend Camilla over there were just admiring your flagpole. What's it all about?'

Pete briefly panicked that this was a euphemism but then saw she actually was looking at the Old School flag which was listing at 45 degrees from the tent. 'Oh, that's the name of our band – Old School. My friend Charlton thought it would be a good idea, so we knew which tent was ours. It has obviously suffered a bit in last night's wind and rain.'

'Oooh, a band. Are you playing here then?'

'Yes – we're on the smaller stage later today.'

'That's exciting. What sort of stuff do you play?'

'A bit of everything – all covers. From the 60s up until the early noughties – at our ripe old age we don't do anything current so I'm not sure it's what you're looking for.'

'No, I love the old stuff. I blame my dad. What time are you playing?'

'3 o clock, for about half an hour.'

'Great – we'll see you there. Come over and say hello to Camilla, I don't think she's ever met a rock star.'

'I think she'd be sorely disappointed. Err, I'll pop over a little later, if that's OK.'

'No problem, I'll leave you reading your paper then.'

Imogen walked back to her tent and after a brief chat Camilla animatedly waved at Pete. As he returned the greeting, he was grateful that Little Pete seemed to be subsiding and that he'd soon be able to get out of the car without bringing a whole new meaning to having to tamp down a tent peg.

## Chapter 97

Pete, Pudding and Pipes were seated around a rickety white plastic table, having breakfast at Bobby's Burgers. Pete had gone for a sausage baguette, Pudding opted for a bacon sandwich and Pipes was halfway through a mountain of pancakes oozing with maple syrup. The seating area in front of the burger van was full. It was already beginning to cut up, the grass turning a nice shade of 'festival brown' as the impact of the night's downpour started to take effect. Pete and Pudding were both in wellies, but Pipes had not been quite so forward-thinking on the packing front. He was sporting a pair of dirty old trainers that were caked in mud. Pete suspected they were the same ones he'd seen about 18 months previously, when Pipes was trying to maintain a low profile after an alcohol-fuelled New Year's Eve at the hotel.

'How about this lot on the main stage at 1.00pm? Wicker Man. It says here they are "…a blend of country and new wave who are taking their hometown of Stevenage by storm." Might be worth a watch' suggested Pudding.

'What does it say about us?' said Pipes, picking up a programme from the table which outlined the festival itinerary. 'Bloody hell, nothing. It's still got Tinted Specs down for 3.00pm.'

'I know. Giles had already had the programme printed before they pulled out. I tried to get him to reprint it, but he said he was on a tight budget. If you look at the website, at least he's updated that' replied Pipes defensively, taking out his phone to prove the point.

The muffled but still spine-tingling guitar solo from Hey Joe sounded from Pete's pocket. He'd decided that Old School's inaugural festival performance warranted a change of ringtone and what better than the encore that Jimi Hendrix had played, probably with his teeth, to close Woodstock back in 1969.

'Hi Mark. How are you getting on?'

'I'm here Pete. I'm at the entrance outside a portacabin office.'

'Great, we've got your lanyard so if you just pop in, ask for Giles and he'll point you in the direction of the camp site. He should be fine to let you drive your car up here but take it easy as it will be slippy after last night's downpour. If he needs confirmation of who you are just ask him to phone Pudding.'

'Oh, OK, but I presume he'll have him down as Charlton Davies?'

'Yes, good point – I don't think you'll get very far if you say you're here with Pudding. You should be able to pick out our tent. It's the one with the great big bloody Old School flag flying above it. We'll meet you there.'

Ten minutes later and they all rendezvoused at the tent. 'Where shall I put my sleeping bag?' asked Mark.

'Well, you've got two choices: here by the door or over by the side there where the big hole is. Ask Harsy to explain that one to you' said Pipes with a grin.

'Here by the door looks fine, said Mark, attempting to stamp down a large lump in the groundsheet with his foot. Have you seen any bands yet?'

'Yes,' replied Pudding. 'We saw a couple of decent ones yesterday afternoon. And then we watched another three last night. One was excellent, the second lot we didn't think much of and, to be honest, I can't remember much about the last one as let's just say that the effects of the beer tent had well and truly kicked in by then. Here you go, here's the programme for today. Giles has asked us to be at the Up & Coming Stage by 2.30pm so we've got a few hours to watch some music. Shout if there is anything that particularly takes your fancy.'

Mark said he liked the sound of Calorific, a three piece from Chesterfield who promised "...a jazz-funk influenced sound which will take you back to the clubs of the early 80s." So it was that the three of them found themselves near the front of the main stage watching a bearded and grizzled old white guy on lead guitar, a young good-looking black guy on bass and a tall and athletic young black woman with a shaved head and a look of Grace Jones about her. She could certainly hold a tune and Calorific were going down well with an audience of about 800 people. Pete was enjoying the set. It was great that they were being treated to an impressive performance, but it brought with it an undercurrent of trepidation that, in just a couple of hours' time, it would be Old School that had to impress. Mark's viewing had been interrupted on several occasions by disappearances to the portaloos and he was starting to take on the ghostly pallor that seemed to be his standard pre-, during- and post-performance face.

As the band finished with a cover of Isaac Hayes' Theme from Shaft, during which the lead singer had strutted her stuff with some impressive bongo playing, the crowd gave them a hearty response.

'Let's go and congratulate them,' suggested Pipes. 'We need to make use of these backstage passes.'

They all walked round to the side of the stage to be met by a squat pensioner in a high-vis vest with the word 'Security' stretched across his ample stomach. He was wearing a peaked cap, with 'Security' also emblazoned across the front, below which poked a few wispy ginger/grey hairs.

Taking a stance with his legs spread to create a barrier, he held up his hand and said 'Stop there please gentlemen. Artists and VIPs only I'm afraid.'

'Yes, that's us' said Pipes.

'What do you mean?'

'We're artists' replied Pipes, theatrically brandishing the lanyard looped around his neck.

Taking it in his hand and putting on his half-moon spectacles, the security guard carefully studied the lanyard, only centimetres from Pipes' face as he leant in.

After an age, he said 'Ah, sorry sir. But this is clearly for the Up & Coming Stage. This is the Main Stage so I'm afraid it's invalid for this restricted area.'

'Restricted area? You mean a few tents at the back there. This is not Glastonbury mate. You're not protecting David Bowie as he bathes in asses milk surrounded by nubile young groupies.'

With a sharp pull on his high-vis vest clearly designed to draw attention to his Security status, the man reached for his walkie talkie. 'Security 2, this is Security 1. If I could have some backup; potential security breach in zone 3……over.' Puffing out his chest and turning to Pipes he said – 'rules are there for a reason sir. I am afraid you are not allowed in here and it is my job to make sure that access is granted only to those who have the necessary permissions.'

Glancing at his watch, Pete said 'Come on Pipes. Look at the time. We better start making our way over to the Up & Coming Stage.'

## Chapter 98

Mark's timid 'How many do you think will be watching us?' was just about audible above the excited screams of a young girl as she and her mum were shunted into a group of stationary dodgems that looked like a traffic jam in some dystopian Knotty Ash.

'Oh, nothing like the crowd we've just been in at the Main Stage' said Pete, telling himself that he was just trying to calm Mark's nerves when, in truth, he knew it was just as much for his own benefit.

'It's a good job you stepped in there Harsy' joked Pipes. 'I reckon Jean Claude Van Grandad was just about to take up a Jiu Jitsu stance and he might have put his hip out.'

'Pipes, did you really have to make a scene? Remember I've got to work with Giles back at the college on Monday. I thought you'd have learned your lesson from your night in the cells after the last time.' There was a definite edge to Pudding's voice.

Pete intervened. 'Look, you two, let's not start now shall we. Let's enjoy the experience. We might never get to play a festival again.'

Peace, or at least a temporary truce, settled back over the group as they made their way past a clown entertaining a gaggle of bored looking children. One of them even had his phone out, completely ignoring the efforts of Chico and his never-ending hankie in preference to a game that appeared to involve shooting rabbits between the eyes.

A couple of minutes later and they had reached the Up & Coming Stage. It was a flatbed trailer and with a steady drizzle starting up, Pete was glad to see that it not only had a roof but also three curtain-sides to protect the performers from the elements.

'Charlton' cried Giles, waving at them from a small gazebo at the rear of the stage. He turned to a harassed looking woman with a clipboard. 'This is Old School. They are on at 3pm – they've taken the place of Tinted Specs. If you can get Tom to check out that generator as it was making a bit of a weird noise earlier.' He came bouncing over. 'How are you guys enjoying the festival?' he asked expectantly, clearly hoping for some encouraging words.

'It's brilliant Giles. Really well organised, a great spot to have it and we've seen some good bands. It's bigger than we expected so you must be delighted with the results, particularly as it's your first year' Pudding responded.

With an almost audible sigh of relief, he replied 'Yes. We've had a few inevitable hiccups, but if it carries on like it has so far then I'm hoping for even bigger and better next year. I've got a real treat for you guys. You've got the lady herself introducing you.'

With a quizzical look Pudding said 'sorry Giles, the lady?'

'Yes. My beautiful wife Billie who all this is for.'

'Oh right. That will be great won't it gents?' said Pudding looking around.

Enthusiastic nodding, 'yeses' and 'greats' resounded around the group.

'Also, I have a favour to ask. Can I pinch a few minutes in the middle of your set? I have a tribute to Billie that I want to do.'

Pudding replied 'Yes, of course, no problem.'

'Great. OK, let's get you set up. I've got a couple of the lads from the Music Technology course here helping out as roadies/gofers so if you need any fetching and carrying, just ask them. I'll send them over.'

As they walked across to a locked shipping container where they'd dropped off their instruments earlier, Pipes hissed 'You what? We've only got half an hour as it is and now he wants to nick half of it for a tribute to his fucking wife?'

'Look, what could I say' whispered Pudding. 'It's his festival. I'm hardly in a position to say no, fuck off and do your lame tribute some other time, am I?'

'He's right Pipes and anyway, it's hardly half of the set, is it? It'll be a few minutes. Put your toys back in the pram and open that lock.' Pete handed Pipes his phone in which he'd made a note of the container's combination.

As they started to move their equipment two teenage lads appeared. Both had on what had obviously been white trainers at some point, the lure of fashion seemingly overcoming the practicality of wellies. 'I'm Christian' offered one, 'do you need help with anything?'

Pete wondered for a moment if this was his name or his religious persuasion. He was small and quite rotund, sporting the sort of jumper Pete associated with his dad and a pair of what could only be described as 'slacks'. Though their light green hue was somewhat darker at the bottom due to the wet having seeped up, they had a sharply ironed crease down the front and were topped off with a neat tan belt. He also had florid acne, with several particularly angry white pustules that looked like they were about to explode at any minute.

His mate was tall and languid, wearing a pair of ripped jeans that had more air than denim. Despite the chill, he had on a Velvet Underground t-shirt, though his head was evidently feeling the slightly inclement weather as he was sporting a grey beanie from which flowed blonde, unkempt locks.

As Pete and Pudding carried their guitar cases to the stage Pete nodded in the direction of the two lads who were lugging Pipes' floor tom and cymbals. Pipes walked nonchalantly behind them, puffing on his e-cigarette and clearly enjoying having his own roadies.

'I know what you're thinking,' said Pudding. 'You tend to get two distinct types on the Music Technology course. I'm betting that Christian is into his classical music and hopes to be micing up the woodwind section of the London Philharmonic while old Ripped Jeans thinks he's going to be the next Alex Turner.'

There had been a collective pat on the back for Pipes as he took his kick drum from its case. Bright and shining on the front skin was the Old School logo. Pete still loved it. The 80s beer bottle, with its white label and 'Old School' picked out in a red Brush Script font. It summed them up perfectly. The frothy beer flowing down the bottle and pooling around the metal cap seemed to leak from the drum onto the stage floor. When the designer in Pudding had asked how he'd got it produced, Pipes replied 'It's a self-adhesive decal so if I get fed up with you lot and go and play with somebody decent, then I can just peel it off.'

In what was record time, with the help of Christian and what turned out to be Ryan, Old School were set up. Pete took the first real opportunity to take note of the crowd. There were a good 400, including Camilla and Imogen who were waving at him with the Old School flag planted between them. His stomach did a flip as he waved back. He looked across at Mark who was clearly using his ritual tuning routine to block out the audience. His hands were shaking as he turned the pegs on his bass.

'Right' said Pipes, tightening his crash cymbal. 'Let's do this.' He gave the thumbs-up to a guy wandering around in front of the stage with an iPad in his hands. 'That's Stewart – he's the sound engineer. Let's just play the intro to You Really Got Me, as it's not in the set, so he can get the levels.'

He counted them in with a 4-count on his sticks and they started playing. Well, all apart from Mark. He was still fiddling with his bass.

'Sorry everybody. I wasn't ready.'

'With a look skywards, Pipes started another 4-count. They all came in on time. About 30 seconds in and a thumbs-up, this time from Stewart, brought them to a halt. Back to Pipes and it was a third thumbs-up, this one directed to the side of the stage.

It prompted the entrance of a woman that screamed femme fatale. Tottering on six inch stilettos that she could only have put on at the side of the stage, she sashayed on. Her impeccably coiffured auburn hair swayed slightly in the breeze, with a skin-tight red dress prompting a couple of wolf-whistles from the crowd.

'Hello BillieFest' said the eponymous Billie in a deep, throaty drawl that had a hint of a southern American accent. 'It's great to see you all here and it looks like the sun might poke through any second.'

'I've got something else about to poke through' said Pipes, drawing a steely stare from Pudding.

Billie continued – "It is my pleasure now to introduce Old School. They have joined us all the way from The Midlands and, according to this, received a lot of press coverage last year following their appearance in the national Battle of the Bands competition.'

The copywriter in Pete had to applaud how the salient points behind that press coverage had been edited from the piece of paper she was clutching.

'So, can you all put your hands together and make some noise for……Old School.'

Another 4-count on the sticks as Billie strutted to exit stage-left and the opening of 'She Loves You' burst from the impressive speaker stack.

## Chapter 99

'Thank you – you're all very kind. Now I'd like to welcome on stage the reason we're all here. Ladies & Gentlemen, Mr Giles Forsyth, the man behind BillieFest.' Pete started applauding as Giles strode on, waving to the crowd.

'Thank you, Pete. That was fantastic – I'm sure we are all looking forward to the rest of your set hey guys?'

Enthusiastic applause from the crowd suggested that the first three songs had gone down well. Pete was not happy with his own guitar playing in Brown Sugar but, given how little time they'd had to practice, it had all seemed to come together surprisingly well.

Giles pulled up a stool that Pete had not noticed at the side of the speakers and grabbed an acoustic guitar from its stand. 'Some of you may have gathered from the name of the festival that I have named it after my beautiful wife.' He ignored another wolf whistle and ploughed on. 'She is my very reason for being and, with that in mind, I'd like to pay tribute to her on this, the first of what I hope will be many more BillieFests.'

He started gently strumming and then came in with his vocal – 'Thanks for the times that you've given me…'. The volume increased slightly as Pete spied Stewart with his iPad.

Pete was standing with Pudding and Mark at the side of the stage while Pipes remained steadfastly seated at his drum kit, presumably in an attempt to remind Giles that he needed to get off and let them continue as soon as possible. 'Christ' whispered Pudding 'Three Times a Lady?' As Giles warbled 'There's something I must say out loud', Pudding glanced down and muttered 'Do you really have to?'

As Giles reached the chorus and confirmed Pudding's suspicions, he shifted into a weird falsetto – 'you're once, twice, three times a laydeeeee.'

'Jesus, it's like Barry Gibb on helium' whispered Pete. 'As a Music Technology lecturer, I thought he'd be pretty good.'

'I've never heard him sing but those courses often attract frustrated musicians. You know the old saying – 'Those who can, do; those who can't, teach'. I just didn't know he was quite that frustrated.'

Pete elected not to ask if the same applied to lecturers in Media Studies.

As Giles continued to strangle Lionel Richie's vocal, he reached the second chorus and as he went back into a voice that sounded like he'd been grabbed by the bollocks, Billie walked onto the stage, blowing kisses. Pete could see that her mascara was running. He glanced across at Pipes who was staring resolutely at his base pedal, but his shoulders were visibly shaking. Pete just hoped that the crowd were at sufficient distance not to notice.

After another couple of excruciating minutes in which Giles and Billie gazed into each other's eyes, seemingly completely oblivious to the fact that another 800 were fixed on them, Giles strummed his final chord. The end came just in time as his voice had been breaking in the last couple of bars. They wrapped their arms around each other rather clumsily given that Giles' guitar was swinging between them before waving to the crowd in perfect synchronicity and walking off the stage, hand-in-hand.

Pete looked at Pudding who shrugged his shoulders. He made his way back to the microphone, Pudding and Mark following to resume their positions. 'Ladies and gentlemen, let's hear it for Giles and the lovely Billie.' There was a smattering of embarrassed applause accompanied by a cry of 'Get a room'. 'OK, a slight change of pace' continued Pete. 'Hopefully most of you are familiar with I Predict a Riot.'

## Chapter 100

A watery sun appeared from behind the clouds, bringing an extra cheer from the crowd as they bounced along to the Kaiser Chiefs' anthem. Pipes brought it to a finish with his customary thrash around the kit and they responded in kind with enthusiastic whoops and applause.

'Thank you. You've been amazing. This is our last one. Enjoy the rest of the festival. We've been Old School.' Pete turned to Pudding who struck up the intro to Mr Brightside which was immediately recognised by the crowd. As soon as Pete started in with 'Coming out of my cage', almost en-masse he was accompanied by 400 voices. 'Now, this is what it's all about' he thought, taking the volume up a notch with 'it started out with a kiss'.

They were really rocking now. Mark had even wrenched himself from his statue-like posture, walking over to Pipes to feel the energy as the drums and the bass ramped up to drive them on.

It was then that Pete noticed a bit of what David Walliams might have termed 'a kerfuffle' at the side of the stage. He tried to maintain his focus, picking out The Old School flag waving in big arcs as Imogen looked as if she was atop the barricades in Les Miserables. The next minute his view was blocked. Blocked by a woman dancing wildly directly in front of him in what appeared to be a mud-spattered, flesh-coloured body-stocking. It was only when he glanced down that he realised that there was no stocking involved. This was a rather hirsute middle-aged lady who had decided it was time to roll back the years and recreate the Summer of Love in a Sussex field in October.

The crowd was now cheering wildly as the woman leapt across the stage to gyrate wildly in front of Mark who looked like his face had been injected with a litre of botox as he tried valiantly to completely ignore what was happening. She then careered to the front of the stage, flinging her arms wide to let it all hang out for the crowd and the cheering went off the scale. Pete stepped back smartly as a security guard came skidding in front of him. He was of a similar age to the one they'd encountered at the Main Stage so the fact that he'd run on at all was impressive. He had, however, lost his footing as his mud-caked boots failed him and he was now lying spread-eagled, his right foot jammed up against Pete's stage monitor. He got up much quicker than Pete imagined he might, evidently a sprightly old bugger, to then run across the stage in the direction of the naked interloper, wrestling to take-off his hi-vis vest. She spotted him coming and began to run herself. Pete could almost hear the clapping of her pendulous breasts and wondered if it was in time with what they were playing. He was amazed that they were still playing at all. It would have been more apt to break into the Benny Hill theme tune as the bizarre chase continued to unfold all around them.

The security guard made a lunge, trying to protect the modesty of who Pete's mind had now christened Stacia after Hawkwind's legendary dancer. He marvelled at the human brain's capacity to cope with so much input and still maintain an output as he belted out 'Open up my eager eyes, 'Cause I'm Mr Brightside'. Pipes was now standing to get a better view but continued to play, his drumming operating on auto-pilot as his own eager eyes darted around to follow the on-stage pantomime.

Pudding was grinning like a maniac, hopping from foot to foot as he somehow continued to maintain a rhythm guitar part that had the right rhythm. They reached the song's climax, with the three crashes on the drums in perfect unison with the final chords. Almost as if it had been choreographed, on the last crash the security guard managed to bundle Stacia to the stage, throwing his hi-vis vest over her as she collapsed like the dying swan in Tchaikovsky's seminal ballet.

## Chapter 101

'Well, that's something you don't see every day.'

Pete's comment was addressed to nobody in particular as the four of them made their way back towards the tent.

'You can say that again' replied Pudding. 'Did you get to see much Pipes stuck at the back there?'

'The problem is that I now can't unsee it. It looked like Terry Waites' allotment down there.'

They burst into uproarious laughter, apart from Mark who just appeared non-plussed and said, 'I really didn't know where to look'.

Pete took up the theme. 'You're too young to remember Mark but in the 70s and 80s you couldn't watch a sporting event without some woman flashing her tits or a bloke getting his knob out. Streaking was all the rage. Erika Roe was the really famous one when she got her kit off at Twickenham but there was that idiot who almost caught his bollocks on the bails hurdling the wicket at a Lords test. I really can't see the appeal. I know people want their five minutes of fame but getting your gonads out on live TV to do it? Really? Though now you see those people who are supposedly painfully shy about having a bollock the size of a space hopper and they whip it out on Embarrassing Bodies. And you lot must have seen that Naked Attraction. What the fuck is that all about?'

'I reckon in our case she must have been on something and off her tits, forgive the expression,' laughed Pudding. 'Either that or she'd caught a whiff of Pipes' pheromones and couldn't help herself.'

'Yes, I heard the security guard talking to Giles about phoning the police. From what I saw, he wasn't keen, probably not wanting to draw attention to any drug use which might affect his chances of getting a licence for next year' Pete said.

They were still laughing as they made their way into the inflatable pub for a celebratory drink.

The performance had left them all on a high, which was now being fuelled by beer. Pete went to the bar for their fourth refuelling. They had found a table outside the pub from which there was a view of the Up & Coming stage. Pete flashed his artists' pass and ordered three pints of lager and a snakebite and black. Pudding's drink of choice for the afternoon took him back to the night when, awash with several pints of the stuff, Pete had attempted some DIY. Rather unsurprisingly it had not ended well.

Sitting back down he placed the four plastic pint glasses on the table.

'Cheers, Harsy, this is the life, eh?' said Pudding waving an expansive arm across the scene in front of them. The sun was out, just about to dip behind a small wooded copse at the back of the festival site as the afternoon morphed gently into early evening. Its warmth was still sufficient for them all to be in shirt sleeves. A new band had just taken to the stage and were into their first number – a decent cover of the Black Crowes' 'Hard to Handle', although Pete had some vague recollection that theirs itself was a cover. He thought the original was by Otis Redding but made a mental note to Google it later to check. To their left Chico the clown had been replaced by a magician in the 'Children's' Entertainment Arena'. There was a decent number of kids in his audience, with many of their parents having taken the opportunity for some free baby-sitting while they had a drink.

Immediately to the right of the Old School table was a case in point. A large woman with a spider web tattoo escaping from her massive cleavage, picked up what appeared to be a pint of cider and pretty much downed it in one. Wiping her mouth with a bingo-winged arm that spelt out Tracy in red gothic-style lettering, she shouted to what was presumably one of her brood. 'Tyrone, stop fucking about with that straw and watch the magic man will ya!' A lad of about eight in a dirty vest, raggedy shorts and a pair of cut-off wellies turned around and threw a handful of straw he'd plucked from the bale seating onto the floor.

Pete spotted another young boy who was poking around at the back of the small gazebo immediately behind 'The Great Gonzales'. There was a trestle table with the magician's various props neatly laid out. Intent on his audience, the magician had not seen the interloper and was busily making his magic wand float between his out-stretched hands. Pete had never been into magicians, loving the TV series The Masked Magician who had supposedly incurred the wrath of the Magic Circle by revealing the secrets behind some of their best loved tricks.

The lad picked up a box and promptly dropped it to the floor as a couple of white doves flew out. The child's scream prompted the magician to turn around. Seeing his next spectacular illusion in tatters, he shouted, 'Oi, you little shit'. Spiderwoman immediately jumped to her feet, her fat still wobbling, as she shouted, 'Who are you calling a shit, you motherfucker.' She strode over to the gazebo, grabbing what was presumably another son by the back of his tatty hoody, and kicked over the magician's table. Gonzales, now not quite so Great, performed another magic trick, seemingly frozen in time as he contemplated an appropriate response. After a few seconds he decided on a high-pitched 'Guards, guards', seemingly channelling the spirit of Kenneth Williams in Carry on Cleo. The same security guard that had intervened and eventually apprehended the lovely Stacia made his way over from the stage.

As he drew himself up to his full height of five foot two, Spiderwoman screeched 'And what the fuck do you think you're doing you fascist gnome.'

'I'm sorry madam, but I have just seen you attack Mr…err…Gonzales' equipment. The management of BillieFest has a strict zero tolerance approach to violence.'

'Violence. I'll show you fucking violence.'

Just as High Noon threatened to imminently unfold, Pete heard the 'Are You Gonna Go My Way' ringtone that he reserved for texts from Marcie. He took his phone from his pocket, clicked on 'Messages' and was greeted by a photo of himself, mouth wide open, next to the naked Stacia with her arms aloft. Typed below was the message 'ENJOYING YOURSELF?!'

He quickly rose from the table with a 'gents, I just need to make a call.'

## Chapter 102

'I really thought you were pissed off with me.'

'Don't be daft, Pete. I didn't think you'd be humping a woman live on stage. You might think your rock n roll mate but come on,' chortled Marcie.

Slightly miffed at her response, Pete replied 'Mick Jagger is nearly bloody 80. He's still rocking it. He had his eighth kid in his 70s, he's a great-grandad and when we saw them at the Ricoh Arena a couple of years ago you said you still would.'

A raise of the eyebrows accompanied by 'Please tell me you're not comparing yourself with Mick Jagger' had Pete deciding that returning to making the bed was probably a sensible move.

He tried to stuff the pillow into a pillowcase that seemed intent on staying empty as Marcie wrestled to thread the duvet into the corners of the green and white striped cover. It was the day after he'd got back from BillieFest and Pete was still feeling decidedly jaded.

'But the capital letters and no kiss?'

'I thought that might get you going.'

'Bloody mobile phones. They can really leg you up.'

'Yes, you might want to remember that the next time you have a naked female draped all over you. I think Gillian was hoping I'd go apeshit when she sent it to me. She's always been a bit of a shit-stirrer.'

'I know. I didn't even realise she was there. Anyway, changing the subject, is everything ready for going back to the chalet?'

'Yes, I got all the new bedding last week, the towels are being delivered tomorrow, your mum has finally chosen some wallpaper for her bedroom and that log-splitter you wanted should be here next week. You still haven't called Aggie to get an update on the building work have you?'

'I know, I know, I'll do it tomorrow. Promise.'

## Chapter 103

'Hello Aggie. Sorry are you in the middle of something?'

Pete tried to make sense of the image on his screen, something flesh-coloured with a hole in the middle. The hole began to move around as he heard the cultured voice of Aggie – 'I'm fine Pete, how are you?'

'I'm err, fine thanks. Aggie, I'm on FaceTime.'

A quick blur and then Aggie's surprisingly youthful face appeared, though the angle did little to accentuate it as Pete gazed up her nostrils. 'Oh, sorry, I assumed that you'd call like you usually do. Peter, you know what I'm like staring at a screen. I hate seeing an old lady looking back at me. In my head I'm still a teenager; well, perhaps early twenties.'

'Sorry, do you want me to call back and, by the way, you don't look like any old ladies that I know.'

'Ooh, you are such a smooth talker Mr Harriman. No, let's carry on now that you're here.'

'OK, I just thought I'd call for a catch-up. How are things coming along?'

Aggie took Pete through the progress on the building work. She was in the chalet and held up her phone in an attempt to show him the work that had been done in replacing the log-burner in the bar/lounge.

'Aggie, can you flip the screen?'

'Remind me, how do I do that?'

A minute or so and some even more interesting angles of Aggie's face later and she finally managed to get the log-burner into view.

'That looks fantastic. I presume Bill has got the rustic oak beam to go above it that you managed to get from that reclamation yard?'

'Yes. He's cursing me. Apparently, it weighs a ton. He thought he'd get away with a new slim modern option that he could just glue above the fireplace but now he's got to get some seriously heavy-duty bolts. Still, I told him it's a small price to pay for a bit of authenticity.'

'We can't wait to see all the changes. Marcie and my mum will be back in a couple of weeks as they are flying. I'm driving a van over with all the bits and pieces we've bought this end so I should be back on the 24th. We really can't thank you enough for all you've done.'

'Nonsense Pete, you have done me a favour. It's been just like the old days, choosing colours, chatting with suppliers and ordering builders about. In fact, there's also been the odd perk.'

'What do you mean Aggie?'

Aggie poked the 'flip' icon, this time getting it right first time. As she panned across the room, Pete saw a young builder in a pair of tight jeans and a black vest. He grinned at Aggie and gave her a sly wink.

Her face came back into view, a glint in her eye that belied her years.

'You haven't?'

'A lady never tells Peter', she replied before the screen went blank.

## Chapter 104

Pete was barrelling along the M40 having dropped Marcie and his mum at Birmingham Airport. The Foo Fighters were blasting from the Volvo's stereo, and he was considering the correlation between loud rock music and speed. Not the stuff that many musicians were known for hoovering up their hooters but how a good track had you pressing down on the accelerator just that little bit harder. He contemplated what the response from a traffic cop might be if the defence was 'sorry, officer, but I was listening to Motley Crew. You know how it is.'

He started moving across the carriageway, gliding into the inside lane and reducing his speed as he approached the sign for Warwick Services. It was still another 15 miles to Banbury and he realised his bladder wouldn't hold out. He groaned slightly as he climbed from the car, arching and rubbing the bottom of his back. As he walked across the car park he was struck by the difference between the British and French approach to motorway pit stops. While the 'Aires de Services' focused on providing a welcoming respite from your journey, with green open spaces to encourage a picnic, fresh baguettes and areas to walk le chien, the British take was much more utilitarian. Stepping through the glass doors he wondered if 'Welcome Break' had ever been sued under the Trades Descriptions Act.

In the entrance a toddler was sitting in a plastic elephant, rocking violently back and forth as if he was approaching the finishing line in the Grand National. A bored dad leaned against the wall, checking his phone but making full use of both hands with his left reaching into the back of his grey tracksuit bottoms to scratch his arse. Pete swerved to his right to avoid a teenage girl, head bowed in submission as she forlornly pushed a mop and bucket on wheels. The repetitive squeak seemed to sum-up the never-ending drudgery that was mapped out before her, like Sisyphus but in a lime green blouse and voluminous black slacks.

He walked past a mountain of books piled high on a table with the promise of '3 for £5', turning left to follow the sign for the toilets. The beeps and flashing lights from the small amusement arcade briefly grabbed his attention, at least fulfilling their remit. A teenage lad who certainly did not meet the 'No Under 18s' stood transfixed, feeding coins into a fruit machine. His blank expression remained eerily constant, despite a clattering noise indicating that he had got a return on his investment. He scooped up his winnings, immediately reinvesting them via the coin slot, a hungry mouth with an insatiable appetite that the feeder seemed intent on overcoming. It was difficult to identify which one of them was the machine.

Pete arrived at his destination, slightly wrong-footed by the old man who veered to his left just in time to stop himself from ending up in the Ladies. He shook his head with a rueful smile, mumbling to Pete in a thick Yorkshire accent 'why do theys have to have these bloody confusing drawings. What's wrong with word 'Gents'? Is it going to upset some bloke who thinks he's a lass?' Pete gave him a quick shake of the head, deciding not to engage in a conversation about cross-lingual icons, illiteracy, or gender politics.

Pete stood at the urinal trying to ignore the old man who was now standing right next to him, despite there being a row of about 15 unoccupied porcelain piss-pots to welcome the needy traveller. He was still mumbling something about 'blokes is blokes, lasses is lasses', Pete assumed to himself rather than to Pete, as he fumbled with his flies. The man kept glancing disconcertingly down at Pete's knob, presumably verifying that he was indeed a bloke and therefore at his rightful station. Ablutions completed, Pete dried his hands at the third attempt in a Dyson Airblade that was actually working, before meandering back into the main public space.

It was pretty busy for a late Tuesday morning, with all of human life on display. Spotting the yellow & green 'Subway' sign Pete's stomach rumbled. The reason for his trip to Banbury was to pick up a coffee table that he'd bought on e-bay. He had seen it during a late-night browsing session and decided that it was perfect for the seating area where they served tea and cakes to the hungry skiers returning from the slopes. He looked at his Breitling, realising that it was a good hour and a half until he needed to be at his destination. So, what was it to be, Subway, KFC or Burger King? He immediately discounted the latter being more of a Big Mac man. And, while Subway was tempting, an opportunity to sample the Colonel's secret recipe was drawing him in. Marcie hated fried chicken, often saying that the benefit of a Bargain Bucket was that at least it gave you a receptacle to throw up in. So, with the words of his wife currently 25,000 feet above the English Channel, KFC it was.

He joined the queue. Despite being only three-deep it took a good 10 minutes to be served, the spotty youth behind the counter putting old Chas to shame in the speed stakes. Pete spent the time musing over the fact that he was now an avid consumer of fast-food, with a focus on immediacy and a lack of patience that seemed to be the underscore to life in general. He wondered how he'd been sucked in. One of the factors behind him considering early retirement was the expectation of clients. When he'd first joined the world of advertising, there was a process to be followed: a brief from the client, some time for creative thinking, ideas pitched, tweaks made, approvals sought, and artwork developed. Over time these lines had been blurred almost to the point of non-existence. The advent of Apple Macs made it increasingly common for clients to give a woolly brief, with the expectation of seeing finished artwork in a matter of days, even the same day if it was from Clarissa Dowerty, the Marketing Director of Cosmeticon, who had proved the final straw to break what increasingly felt like a donkey's back.

Both Pete and Pudding had felt the creativity was being leached from their jobs, the desire and expectation of an immediate response superseding any opportunity for the all-important time to reflect and think. You needed space to come up with ideas and then to allow them to truly develop properly. He knew it was just another indicator of the 'I want it now' society, fuelled by an internet which gave instant answers (even if they were often wrong). He was keenly aware that he was also a fully paid-up member of that same society in which disposability was king. While his dad would painstakingly glue bits back onto their aging transistor radio to allow Terry Wogan to welcome his mum into the kitchen each morning, only last week Pete had thrown away a perfectly good kettle just because he could not be bothered to reaffix the lid handle. Five minutes on Amazon and admittedly £30 poorer, it was job done – delivery the following day without even having left the kitchen.

Pete was dragged from his reveries by a mumbled 'What can I get you?' Though the temptation was strong to retort 'somebody who moves quicker than a friggin' sloth on Prozac' he opted for the less confrontational 'a 3-piece original recipe meal please.'

Pete sat at a table which gave him a full view of the other KFC connoisseurs. He fixed on a family to his left: a mum, dad, three boys and a girl. He was particularly drawn to the youngest, a lad of about eight. He had a serenity about him. While his brothers and sister argued and fidgeted, their harassed mother valiantly trying to keep a lid on proceedings while her husband buried himself in the sports pages, he quietly munched on his popcorn chicken. He was almost zen-like in the way he focused on each piece, ignoring the tumult around him, carefully studying, chewing and finishing each individual sphere before moving onto the next. For most people this would be a boy whose obsessive relationship with food was already evident and who was well on his way to joining the ranks of obese kids that would ultimately be the death-knell of the NHS. But not for Pete.

This boy was destined for great things. In a year's time his head-teacher would be calling in his parents to discuss how best to meet the needs of their clearly gifted child. It was decided that 'Onyx', for that was his name, was to be sent to a school which specialised in nurturing exceptional children. Here he blossomed, always popular with others, despite continuing to eclipse his gifted brethren. Securing a place at Cambridge to read religious studies, he seemed at last to fail, quitting after less than a year. But it was clear that theological doctrine was not for Onyx. He was on a different and less trodden spiritual plane, travelling to Tibet where he joined a monastery at the tender age of nineteen. He would ultimately become the youngest ever Dalai Lama, going down in Glastonbury folklore for his 30 minute set in which he espoused peace and compassion against a backdrop of heavy drum and bass.

'Come on Carl, bring your bloody chicken with you. We're going.' As Carl was pulled to his feet by his mother who knew not what she did, Pete gave a nod of serene acknowledgement to Dalai Lama Carl.

## Chapter 105

'Bring us another beer will you Harsy.'

Pipes was fully reclined on the sofa, his feet resting on the coffee table. To his left was Pudding, who was checking his WhatsApp messages while Mark was in the armchair, studiously examining the Money section from last Sunday's Times.

Old School had all convened at Pete's house to watch a video of their performance at BillieFest. It had been professionally produced by a company that Giles had engaged to capture the spirit of the festival for the marketing of next year's event. The sound had been edited from the recording captured through the desk, so it really was the best material they were ever going to get. At least without having to shell out any money.

Having furnished everybody with a beer, Pete had slotted the data-stick into the back of his Panasonic 65-inch smart 4K TV and had waited for Old School to appear in Ultra HD. The heady mixture of excitement and trepidation was palpable. Though they were all looking forward to seeing themselves, there was the inevitable concern that the image they each held in their own heads might be spectacularly blown out of the water. It took Pete back to the time when he'd invested in some golf lessons. Part of the process had been a video analysis of his golf swing. As Pete and the golf pro watched it back, Pete's image in his head of being like the imposing Aussie Greg Norman was replaced with a bloke that looked more like Norman Wisdom.

Pete inwardly cringed at the sound of his voice as he launched into She Loves You. All he could hear was the nervous tremor and fully expected to have some choice comments lobbed in his direction. But there were none,

Pudding and Pipes presumably too concerned at the potential for retribution at their own shortcomings to volunteer comment this early on. By the time they had got into Brown Sugar, Pete could see a difference. The nervous pitchiness in his voice had largely gone, reflected in his face which was much more relaxed.

The tension in the room was also dissipating, with Pipes volunteering 'a few bum notes in there hey Harsy' accompanied by a big grin as they reached the point where Pete knew he'd made some errors.

They continued watching, all but Mark throwing in the odd barb when an opportunity presented itself. Pipes had held his hands up to pre-empt the comments when his crash cymbal came too early and drowned out Pete's vocals in Call Me. He got his own back only minutes later, with a simple but highly effective 'what the fuck' when the camera zoomed in on Pudding as he adopted a power stance during Crazy Little Thing Called Love.

As they reached a decidedly raucous ending of Call Me, the screen faded to black, with the words 'Copyright, Castella Video Productions' scrolling across the bottom.

'Hang on a minute' said Pipes, removing his feet from the table and sitting upright, 'what about Mr Brightside?'

Pudding, looking a little sheepish, replied 'Aah yes. When Giles gave me the data stick he did mention that. He said he'd asked them to edit it as he couldn't have that footage out in the public domain for obvious reasons.'

'So, no Stacia then?' said Pete.

'Stacia, was that her name?' queried Pipes.

'No. You know, the dancer with Hawkwind?'

Quizzical looks all round brought an 'oh, never mind' from Pete.

'But I think that was one of our best songs of the set' said Mark, his first contribution of the last half an hour.

'I know. It would have been a nice to have but what could I say?' replied Pudding defensively.

Pipes was straight in with 'well, you could have said that if you're asking for editing, why the fuck did you keep in that abomination of a rendition of Three Times a Lady. I could feel my toes curling at the time but watching it back was torture. If we ever get to use this as a bit of self-promotion, please tell me we'll take out Sonny & Cher necking on stage.'

'Necking – are you from the 1920s? But yes, don't get your mutton chops in a twist, I've got some editing software on my Mac, so I'll create a version with just us.'

## Chapter 106

Pete was in the Spiced Chi coffee shop, sipping his caramel macchiato and eating a small piece of carrot cake. He looked around, marvelling at how cafés had morphed from the greasy spoons of his youth. The bright, colourful interior and the gleaming, hissing contraption from which oozed the brown gold could not have been further from Kath's Kaff and her stained ancient tea urn that he'd frequented in his teens. The same could also be said not only for the prices but also for the clientele. This morning it was largely a mixture of hipsters, their clacking keyboards signifying another tough day at the coalface, and yummy mummies, stopping off for a quick caffeine fix after the school run. Pete wondered what Cauli Colin, christened because he always gave off a faint stench of cauliflower, would have made of this had he time-travelled, leaving behind his mega-breakfast with extra beans and a builder's tea with four sugars that was his daily constitutional at Kath's.

Pete opened the Notes function on his phone and went straight to 'France stuff'. It was two days until he was due to drive the van back to Chalet Le Nid and he wanted to make sure that everything was in order. As he scrolled down, mentally checking off each item, he came to the bottom – 'linen basket (large)' and 'toasters x 4'. They were his mission for the day, after which he would load everything into the van ready for the journey.

A sultry 'hello Pete' had him turning to his left. 'Ah hello Sammy, how are you?'

'I'm fine thanks sugar. Can I sit?'

'Yes, of course.'

It had been over a year since Pete had seen Sammy Fletcher and his mind automatically raced back to the fateful night of her husband Terry's birthday party. The intervening months had done nothing to soften Sammy's approach to fashion, with a rack that was almost bursting out of a cropped white blouse set off by a pair of black leather trousers so tight that Pete wondered if hot spoons had been involved in getting them on.

'So, how is life in France then Pete?'

'Oh, early days yet but we're getting there.'

'Are you still with Marcie?' A slight pout had Pete remembering her man-eater reputation, bringing a swift and somewhat high-pitched 'yes'.

They spent the next ten minutes catching up on life in general before Pete asked 'So, how's Terry?'

'Dunno – I haven't seen him for about three months. We're getting divorced. His constant questioning and jealousy just got too much.'

'Oh, that's a shame.'

'Well, you, like everybody else, probably thought he was too old for me but were just too polite to say anything. And, in reality, he was. I'm looking for a younger model and am between boyfriends at the moment.'

The same tell-tale pout and a lean forward to reveal what was an impressive cleavage had Pete blushing and quickly reaching for an alternative topic of conversation. 'And Calum, how is he doing?'

'He's fine. He's living with me. He's almost seventeen now and has just started at the Technical college doing fashion design.'

Pete was shocked, thinking back to the geeky ginger son that he had last seen at Terry's party. He couldn't think of anybody more at odds with the seemingly effortless elegance of a Giorgio Armani or the peacock flamboyance of a Marc Jacobs.

Just as Pete was about to make small talk on Calum's choice of course, Jimi Hendrix burst forth from his trouser pocket. Taking out his phone Pete saw the grinning photo of Marcie that he'd captured at her birthday party.

'Excuse me a second Sammy. Sorry but I need to take this.' Normally Pete would have stayed in his seat, but he felt almost as if he'd been caught in the act and reflexively wanted to put some distance between himself and his voluptuous neighbour. He opened the door and took a few paces up the road to stand outside the tanning salon.

'Hi Love. How's things?'

'Pete, I'm sorry but there's no easy way to say this. It's your mum.'

## Chapter 107

'Would you like a drink sir?'

Pete smiled politely at the grinning air stewardess, who he realised in the new gender-neutral times he should now be thinking of as a flight attendant. 'No thank you, I'm fine.'

He looked at his watch. Two minutes had passed since he last looked. He was willing the hands to speed round to let him get to his mum.

Marcie had been calling from the hospital. She had little information at the time other than that Joyce had collapsed at the chalet, been taken to the hospital by ambulance and was now being assessed. Pete had jumped in his car, shot back to the house, thrown together a bag and driven straight to the airport. Having phoned on the way to book a flight to Geneva, he realised that he'd not even said goodbye to Sammy, just leaving her at the coffee shop. He had contemplated phoning to apologise but hadn't wanted to get into talking about his mum. He knew he was on the edge already. He'd phone once he'd seen her and explain.

The flight landed just five minutes late but to Pete it felt like five hours. He rushed through passport control and thankfully jumped straight into a taxi. A quick 'Hôpital De Chamonix, si'l vous plait' and they were on their way.

Pete pressed a wad of Euros into the hands of the taxi driver. He burst through the glass entrance doors and immediately spied the reception desk. 'Bonjour Madame. Je suis looking…err chercher…for my mum…ma maman. Sorry but do you speak English?'

The haughty-looking receptionist peered over her glasses and with a tone that immediately questioned why Pete had the audacity to assume otherwise said 'Yes, of course.'

'That's great. My mother. She was brought in earlier today. Sorry, I'm not sure what time. She came by ambulance… with my wife. She's 80.' He realised he was gabbling so took a deep breath in an attempt to get a grip and impart more relevant information rather than just a stream of consciousness. 'Her name is Joyce Harriman.'

'Let me see sir.' False nails on immaculately manicured fingers clacked on a keyboard. 'Yes, she is in Soins Intensifs - Intensive Care.'

The phrase hit him like he imagined a Mike Tyson blow might feel, with an accompanying tightening in his chest and a sensation in his stomach that felt like his intestines had been tied into a bowline. He tried to concentrate on the instructions being given by Madame Le-Haughty. All he heard was left at the elevators, so he mumbled a thanks and headed in the general direction.

Thankfully some part of his brain had managed to assimilate the phrase Soins Intensifs and it was well signposted so five minutes later and he came to a seated area outside a set of forbidding double doors.

'Pete!' Marcie appeared from around a corner and flung her arms around him.

He hugged tightly, not wanting to let go and to have to embrace instead the reality of the situation. Marcie put her hands tenderly on each side of his face and stared into his watering eyes. 'Come and sit down and I'll tell you what I know.'

'I've not been able to see her yet, but I spoke to a doctor about an hour ago. She has had a stroke. They are still assessing how severe it is but that is pretty much all he could tell me.'

Pete had a multitude of questions bubbling in his head and as they tumbled out, the calm and practical element of Marcie kicked in and she answered them as best she could.

Just as she was explaining that the ambulance had arrived only 10 minutes after she had called, a man in dark blue scrubs pushed his way through the door. 'Ah, Mrs 'arriman. I am sorry for your waiting.'

'No doctor, please don't apologise. I understand how busy you must be. This is my husband, Pete. It's his mother that you are looking after.'

'Mr 'arriman, I am pleased to meet you. Kindly sit and I will give you, how do you say, an update.'

'I am Doctor Arnaud and I look after your mother. Maybe your wife explains. She has a stroke. When she first get here she was very confused. We assess her and it was clear that it was stroke. I'm sorry but it looks like it is quite a bad one. At the moment she cannot see from her right eye, cannot move her right arm or leg and you can see that her face is drooped. This may change over time, but it is too early to say right now.'

Taking a deep breath and digging his nails into his palms to keep the panic at bay, Pete said 'Can I see her?'

'She is sleeping right now, and it is good that she get rest. We take good care of her, and I will tell you once she awakes. Do you have questions for me?'

'Is she going to be OK doctor?'

'That I cannot tell yet. But she is in good hands.'

Doctor Arnaud stood, smiling gently and clasping Pete's shoulder. 'I will be back once I have more news.'

As he presented a card to a reader and disappeared through the Gates of Hell, Pete slumped in his seat. 'I should have come back with you. I should have been with her.'

Marcie took his hand and said quietly 'Pete, there's no way you could have known this would happen. Don't torture yourself. Let me get you a cup of tea. I'll add a couple of sugars to help with the shock.'

Pete said nothing, just letting Marcie take control of the situation and was grateful for it.

As Marcie disappeared around the corner, his mind wandered back to a holiday they'd taken in Majorca. It was their first foreign holiday as a family. He had been about five so Judith would have been eight. He'd had some sort of reaction to something he'd eaten, coming out in large and itchy red wheals all over his body. Following a quick trip to the local hospital where his dad had tried out his strangled Spanish before a nurse had put him out of his misery with her fluent English, they had returned to the hotel with the instruction for him to stay out of the sun. His mum had spent the next three days constantly at his side, shooing his dad and sister out of the door every morning with 'go on, enjoy yourselves. Have a lovely day and tell us all about it when you get back.'

She had regularly slathered him in calamine lotion, stroking his hair as he dozed fitfully on the room's cheap plastic sofa. What was he going to do now if he had a similar reaction? Who was going to place a cool flannel on his forehead and tell him in a voice so soothing yet so convincing that everything was going to be alright?

Marcie returned, a polystyrene cup of tepid coffee in her hands. 'Sorry no tea but I've heaped some sugar in it.'

They sat in silence, Marcie instinctively knowing that trying to cheer Pete up was not the right approach. Eventually, in a tremulous voice, he said 'Do you think she'll be alright?'

Marcie took his hands in hers and stared tenderly into his eyes. 'You know that I want to be able to say yes but in all honesty love, I don't know. What I would say is that she is made of strong stuff and, from what I've seen of Dr Arnaud, he knows what he's doing. Let's just wait and see.'

'Even if she is OK, what will we do?'

'Try not to think too far ahead. One step at a time, eh?'

They drifted back into an uneasy silence.

Pete tried to focus his mind on something other than his mum. He spotted an elderly gent sitting around the corner from them and attempted to engage his backstory-creation gene as a distraction. But it just wouldn't materialise. All he could muster was that he was waiting to see his dying wife, who could well be in the bed next to his mum.

After an interminable hour and a half, the doors of Soins Intensifs opened to reveal Dr Arnaud. 'OK, Mr 'arriman, your mother awakes. Do you want to come and see her?'

## Chapter 108

Pete stood at the door, not sure if he could actually go in. On this side of the threshold he could convince himself that she was fine, his image of her intact with a smiling face and the slightly raised left eyebrow that made her look as if she was constantly pondering a question. He thought about the time at his sister's wedding when she'd sported a swanky new hair-do and professionally-applied make-up, as well as trying out contact lenses; how somehow she'd briefly stepped out of her normal skin to become not exactly a stranger but someone who required a double-take for him to recognise. How he longed for such a small transformation now. Opening the door meant that it could perhaps never be closed, the Pandora's Box of stark reality taking hold with such a simple action.

A nurse appeared at his elbow and gently gestured for him to enter. He took a deep breath, pressed down on the handle, and pushed.

The first thing he noticed was how slight she looked. The bedclothes were pulled up to her chin, but he could see the outline of her body, topped by a head that he felt sure was smaller than he remembered. He fixed a smile and walked slowly over to the bed. He bent towards her, trying not to linger on the palsy that was clear on the right-hand side of her face, planting a kiss on a cheek that looked and felt like parchment.

A 'hello mum. What have you been doing with yourself?' was delivered in as positive a tone as he was able to muster.

She appeared to be attempting a reply but there was just a harsh rasping sound coming from the side of her mouth that still worked.

'No, mum. Don't try to talk. I'm here now. Everything's going to be OK.' Again, the memory of the calamine lotion floated to the top of a sea of memories in which she'd said the same to him. The words caught in his mouth as he realised that when his mum had said it, he'd believed her.

He pulled up a chair and sat down at the side of the bed. He took her hand in his, and, like the rest of her, it seemed to have shrivelled and shrunk, taking on the appearance of a scrunched-up white paper bag whose toffees had long been finished. Had it really been less than a week since he'd last seen her?

He felt a tear run down his cheek. He took off his glasses on the pretext of cleaning them, allowing him to turn his face away to concentrate on the polishing process. As he looked back up, he saw that she had already fallen back to sleep.

He sat for an hour or so, gently cradling her hand and trying desperately to not let emotion overwhelm him in case she woke. He realised that he must have started nodding off himself as the noise of the door opening brought him back to full consciousness. It was Dr Arnaud.

He smiled gently. 'Mr 'arriman. We need to do some testing of your mother. Perhaps you could go back to our wait area and I will come to see you when they done.'

Pete stood, numb and glad for the instructions from someone who knew what they were doing. He kissed his mum on the cheek and whispered 'Sleep tight mum. I'll see you soon.'

Marcie was waiting for him back at the seating area. She hugged him tightly and then sat down, giving him time to compose himself and say what he wanted to say.

'She looked so frail. She was only awake for a couple of minutes. It just wasn't her Marce, it wasn't mum.'

As he broke into quiet sobs, she put her arms around him again. 'Oh, love. Let's just hope and pray she'll be alright. She is a tough old devil, you know that.'

She let Pete pour out his emotions for another 20 minutes or so before he seemed able to plug the dam.

She smiled and said 'OK then. What do you want to do now?'

'I don't know, what do you think we should do?'

Marcie's sense of the practical kicked in, its constant presence just below the surface in any crisis taking on even greater significance as she realised just how lost her husband currently was.

'Well, if you feel able, I think you should maybe stay here while I go back to the chalet and sort out what needs doing there. I'll pack a bag with some of your mum's things and bring them back with me later. How does that sound?'

Pete gave an almost imperceptible nod.

A couple of hours later saw a nurse approach. 'Mr Harriman?'

'Yes.'

'Dr Arnaud told me that it is OK for you to come and see your mother.'

Pete stood, ignoring the cramp in his back given how inconsequential it seemed. He stood outside the same door but this time there was no stalling and he went straight in, determined to be strong for his mum, even though he actually felt like an 8-year-old-boy.

This time she was propped up on pillows and turned towards him as he entered. Just the act of her being more upright brought a surge of joy, buoyed even further by the fact that she somehow looked like his mum again. Her face was still clearly drooping but somebody had run a comb through her hair and she did not have the ghostly pallor that had much greater potential repercussions than Mark's performance-face.

He hugged her gently, afraid of breaking her. 'Mum, you look so much better.'

She tried to speak but, realising that it was perhaps a step too far, resorted to nodding.

He drew up the chair and sat alongside the bed, taking her hand in his once again. She gave a gentle squeeze and he felt as if his heart might burst.

After a few minutes just sitting in silence, she tried to say something. Pete thought he detected the word 'love' but the rest was unintelligible. Clearly frustrated, Joyce pointed to a pad and pen on the bedside unit. Pete placed them on her lap and she picked up the pen in her left hand. A couple of minutes later and she passed the pad to him. In child-like scrawl, Pete read 'I love you son x'. In a faltering voice, with his heart breaking, he said 'I love you too mum.'

A polite cough announced the presence of Dr Arnaud. 'Mrs 'arriman. It is good to see you sit but I think you must rest.' She nodded and Pete thought he detected an attempt at a smile.

'Of course, doctor' said Pete rising. He kissed a cheek that had miraculously transformed from parchment back into skin in a matter of hours. 'You get some sleep now mum and I'll see you a little later.'

Once outside the room, Pete could not contain his excitement. 'Doctor, she looks so much better. Surely that's a good sign that she is going to be alright?'

With a gentle smile Dr Arnaud said 'Yes, it encouraging but it still early. We must not get ahead.'

Pete sat back down on the same seat in the waiting area that he'd occupied pretty much since he'd arrived. Somehow, it seemed more comfortable. The old man had gone, Pete deciding that his wife had been given the all-clear and they were now in their Citroen C3 on the way home to feed their two miniature poodles waiting in a small cottage at the foot of Mont Blanc. It was the most positive he'd felt since that fateful call from Marcie. Unbidden came a recollection of a programme on the Milky Way in which a cosmologist had spoken of stars being at their brightest just before they die. He pushed it from his mind, just grateful that his mum had not only survived but was on the mend.

## Chapter 109

Pete woke with a start to see the face of Dr Arnaud staring down at him.

No words were necessary.

# ACKNOWLEDGEMENTS

There are many people to thank for their help in getting this book over the finishing line. Thanks, as always, to my family and friends for their patience and support. I might not always say it so I'm taking the opportunity here to make up for all the times that I didn't.

A big thanks to author and Arsenal aficionado Dave Seager for his input – it was great to catch up just the 33 years after sharing a few footballing exploits at Essex University. I look forward to more of your published musings on The Gunners. Also, my thanks go out to another Dave, renowned sports journalist and author Dave Armitage, for his invaluable advice on that tricky first chapter.

Thanks to Grace McGrath for being my Irish Catholicism expert (and to her husband Chris Purvis who continues to be a source of witty, if sometimes toe-curling, repartee). To Simon Trott for his encouragement to write a second book (and for allowing me to purloin his 'Eric Clapton' anecdote).

To Michelle Pearson, the perfect sister-in-law and the inspiration for the quote about Mick Jagger still being a 'you would, wouldn't you' at the ripe old age of 78.

Thank you to Helen Corbet of Collett's Chalet Angelo in the beautiful Italian Dolomites' ski resort of Corvara for her time in guiding me through a typical day (if there is such a thing) in the life of a chalet manager. I spoke to Helen just as Covid was starting to hit Europe and I can't help but think how much has changed since then and how the spirit of friendship that hopefully runs through this book has taken on an even greater significance. At the time of writing this we can't come to Italy (without quarantining for 2 weeks – some enforced time to write book 3?) but we'll be back in the Dolomites Helen, as soon as we can – keep those Aperol Spritz on ice.

Thanks again to my fellow band members in The Forty Thieves and Stoneage Mushrooms. You continue (albeit unintentionally) to provide the stimulus for many of the escapades of Old School.

For his creative interpretation of my thoughts for a cover, thanks to Richard Logan.

And finally, a big thanks to all of you who bought the first book – if you're reading this, then you've also been kind enough to spend your hard-earned on the second. I hope you feel it's been a worthwhile investment. If you haven't yet sampled the first and want to know how Pete and his mates fared pre 'the morning after', then head to Amazon, type in 'Chris Twigger' and you'll find 'Thank you Leamington & Goodnight'. If you are reading the Kindle version, then you can simply click on the following link:

https://www.amazon.co.uk/dp/B07YZNVJ7R

## Praise for Thank you Leamington & Goodnight

"Superb story of mid-life-changing romp of rock n roll revisited and responsible parenting with a dash of empty-nesting. The real craft is the realism of each and every character who are all likeable without ever being sentimental or perfect people. The humour and banter that bounces off this cast of characters is the real joy of the story which delivers a laugh and a smile on every page."

"Talking from personal experiences and with humour throughout this is undoubtedly an excellent read by an author who doesn't take himself too seriously. It truly is a brilliant debut novel."

"A book for those of us at the age where we wonder if, or in fact how much of, life has passed us by. This is a very funny book in which I can see shades of myself - as I'm sure just about any mid-50s British male who reads it will. If you like Nick Hornby, Tony Parsons and even Tim Lott then you'll very likely enjoy this as much as I did."

"A brilliant literary offering from a very talented author. Once I started reading, I couldn't put it down."

"Think Nick Hornby but without the commitment-phobia. An engaging and recognisable tale of mid-life crisis. At times laugh out loud, at others quietly comforting. Beautifully written and thoroughly enjoyable. At times impossible to put down."

"Reading this book is like dusting off and listening to one of your old beloved vinyls. You instantly remember the scratches and pops before the music starts - but that's how you made it your own. TYLAG brings back those happy memories and everyone will find something to identify with and laugh out loud at."

"Whoever you are, whatever you do, wherever you live you will recognise some of the characters and situations wonderfully portrayed in this lovely feel-good story. But if you play live music of any kind in any type of band you will empathise completely with the trials and tribulations of Pete and his band. And more importantly you will understand that the author has beautifully captured the raw thrill of playing live music, while your friends and family dance drunkenly in front of you, bringing that joy to life on the page with vivid authenticity."

"Fantastic read.....a must read for middle aged wannabees. Beware of people looking at you strangely whilst you chuckle away on the train at the experiences of Pete and his merry men."

"A funny & compelling page turner! Anyone who is into music or loves a good laugh will enjoy this story."

"Well observed, absorbing, affectionate and downright funny."

"If you are a middle-aged man (or married to one actually) you will relate and enjoy this hilarious, honest and uplifting tale of midlife crisis. The author combines his obvious love of music, friendship and family into a heart-warming story that will have you turning the pages, nodding, grinning and reading lines out loud to your wife (in my case)."

"For any chap 'of a certain age' who has dreamed of, or actually been 'in a band', this is a hilarious page-turner. Many of us have day-dreamed about 'packing it all in' and following a long-held dream, well Pete, the protagonist in this novel, does just that.
Punctuated by 'Blokey' nicknames, jokes and japes, this a true-to-life portrayal of one man and his pals 'living the dream' and realising what true friendship is all about."

"This was a great holiday read. Easy to pick up and put down, fun, nostalgic and most importantly great characters and storyline."

"Its real life feel, packed with amusing observations & anecdotes keeps you turning the pages."

"A great romp of a book. If you've ever been in a band, you'll love this. If you've ever wanted to be in a band, you'll love this. If you've ever endured living with someone in a band.... you get the picture. Fast-paced, well observed - the author sounds like he's talking from personal experience - and funny from start to finish."

"Excellent read. Easy to just pick up, sit in the sunshine with a cold beer and let the afternoon slip by in the company of the affable Pete and his mates."

"Very enjoyable feelgood romp."

"Chapter 24, about the 'rehydrating' former 'It' girl, or 'Chelsea-gate' is a laugh-out-load episode where the reader gets to the punch line ahead of time - but nonetheless enjoys the reveal.' Thank you Leamington & Goodnight' is a journey, one that anyone can relate to. It's insightful, great fun and a cracking good read."

"For anyone who remembers Chorlton and the Wheelies and loves music, this is the perfect read. Pete Harriman's story will strike a chord with anyone who ever wanted to be in a band."

"Chris has a fabulous eye for detail and a great turn of phrase, not to mention a terrific sense of humour. His characters ring true and it is a perfect nostalgia fest."